Chaos erupted behind them, but all I could concentrate on was keeping the darkness at bay. The golem strained at the cracks and pushed hard against the wall of my skull. The stars flashing in my eyes grew to one big sheet of light. Noise whooshed out of existence like all the oxygen had been sucked away. *Breathe in. Breathe out. Breathe in. Breathe out.*

The last time this happened I killed my father. Though I wanted nothing more than to punish Gabby, Olivia, Destiny, and the dude who clocked me, there were innocent people here, and I didn't want to hurt them. I didn't want to accidentally hurt Layne.

I found focus imagining his brilliant blue eyes. They were almost the same shade as my father's. And I couldn't handle more lifeless blue eyes waking me at night. *Breathe in. Breathe out. One. Two. Three. Four. Five.*

Wicked Wish

by

Alex Gordon

Wicked Wish

Contact Information: info@thewildrosepress.com

Cover Art by *Kristian Norris*

The Wild Rose Press, Inc.
PO Box 708
Adams Basin, NY 14410-0708
Visit us at www.thewildrosepress.com

Publishing History
First Edition, 2023
Trade Paperback ISBN 978-1-5092-4946-6
Digital ISBN 978-1-5092-4947-3

Published in the United States of America

Dedication

To Dave–because without you, this story wouldn't exist.

Chapter 1

Glitter and Glass

I hate you was the last thing I said to my father before I killed him.

"So, Regan," my dad tugged on the fishtail braid hanging down my back, "this is your last scheduled appointment. How ya feel about that, kiddo?" He linked my elbow with his as we strolled down the city sidewalk.

Though it was supposed to be spring in Anchorage, Alaska, his breath puffed into a white cloud. Break-up—the local slang for when winter finally surrendered to spring—was my least favorite time of year. It was gray and dismal, and the overwhelming stench of dust and dog poop hovered in the air from mid-April to mid-May. Honestly, I was just happy it wasn't snowing.

Today the steady drizzle of rain helped drown the smell and the dust. Rushing water flowed, a torrent down the city street into the nearest storm drain. Car tires swished through the overflowing ruts; the water splashed those oblivious enough to walk near the edge of the curb.

We stopped at the intersection and waited for the walk light to appear.

"Yeah, good," I mumbled even if it weren't the truth. I was sick and tired of talking about my feelings, mostly my anger issues. Those that landed me a weekly date with my therapist—court-ordered. And boxing lessons to help with my aggression—Dad's idea. And a guided class in meditation—Mom's idea. They all helped. But when my mind was quiet and I was all alone, I could feel something waiting, crouching in the shadows, biding its time. Like I'd shoved whatever feeling it was—anger, sorrow, guilt— into a glass box, closed the lid, and locked it shut. Yet sometimes, without my permission, the darkness leaked from the cracks, curling its fingers around my brain, then twisting its tentacles around my mind. My unstable emotions created a golem sculpted from smoke instead of clay. Its intangible form poked holes in my armor and escaped no matter how tight I held on. Blowing my top or losing my cool was the only way I kept my grip on reality. Unfortunately, my sanity only got better with my bouts of anger. Like a pressure cooker releasing steam. Otherwise, I became paranoid and suspicious like someone was following me or someone was out to get me. Hence the therapy sessions.

A horn honked, and both of us jumped before we scurried across the road so the car could turn the corner. My dad held up a hand to the irritated driver, a sorry of sorts.

"That's my girl. Tough as nails," he said with pride in his voice.

My heart swelled with love. I was a daddy's girl and proud of it.

"So, you ready to slay some halibut and salmon this summer, my little fish whisperer?" He bumped my shoulder with his own. He's called me that ever since our first fishing trip together. For some reason, fish liked me. It never took me long to catch my limit.

"I already have our annual trip planned. An off-thegrid cabin in Seldovia with its own outhouse." He wiggled his eyebrows up and down.

A laugh burst from my nose. To most people, including my mom and my brothers, our fishing trips were a nightmare. But a cabin with an outhouse—score—that was an upgrade.

I leaned my head into his bicep. He snaked his arm around my shoulder. His cologne, the fancy one mom bought him, tickled my nose.

"Ah, kid, I love you." He squeezed me hard.

"You, too, Dad."

He took a deep breath and sighed. "But there's something I've been meaning to tell you." He pulled me in closer, tighter, as we kept walking. In the windows of a trendy pizzeria, patrons sat with their micro brews and breadsticks. My stomach growled as the scent of fresh-baked pizza dough and garlic wafted in the breeze.

"Kid, I hate to do this to you." He shook his head and ran his hand across his smooth chin. "Especially right now, but something has come up. The military, they uh. . . they denied my retirement. We're moving again."

I stopped abruptly. "What?" I turned my whole body toward my dad and looked up. I wasn't sure I'd heard him right. I finally had a place to call home.

A crease marred the usually smooth skin between his eyes. "I know. I know. But we're going overseas," he said like that would help. He held his hands up in surrender.

Under his fingernails ran a fine line of grease. No matter what Mom tried, the line never went away. Even though he'd been promoted and no longer flew jets for the Air Force, he still owned and maintained a tiny prop plane we used every summer for fishing.

"I know I promised we'd stay in Alaska. I'd retire here, but sometimes things don't work out like we want. And with your last episode at school, your mom and I thought a fresh start couldn't hurt." He rubbed his hands together, trying to get them warm. The friction sound scraped against my eardrums like nails on a chalkboard—only much, much worse.

I shivered from the fury crawling up my spine. A knot tightened in my throat, and my stomach clenched. From my therapist, I learned to visualize my feelings and separate them into different containers inside my brain. This allowed me to deal with them one at a time. But for everyone's safety, anger was secured in a glass box so I could keep tabs on it. And that box began to fracture like ice on a lake. Tiny lines fanned jerkily over the thin, glossy surface.

"With this whole world crisis, they aren't letting many of us go—especially those of us who are difficult to replace." He stuck his hands inside his pockets and shifted his weight from one foot to the other, acting as if this conversation were no big deal. A minor hiccup in our lives.

But I'd made a home here. I was not leaving Alaska. I had friends, and I wanted to keep them instead of leaving them behind with promises to stay in touch that inevitably faded away with the miles. At one point, I'd even had a boyfriend. He broke up with me after I assaulted my art teacher.

It'd been a rough week already. My brothers, Kennedy and Lincoln, after they graduated from the University of Alaska, unexpectedly joined the armed forces. Our family dog, Buttons, had to be put down. And then, to top it all off, my art teacher messed with my near perfect GPA. She said I earned a B because I lacked talent. I lost my temper, pushed her up against a wall, and threatened to do her bodily harm if she didn't change my final grade. In my defense, I'd received an A on every project and written assignment. Though, looking back now, I may have overreacted. She pressed charges. Hence the court-mandated counseling—so much for therapy. Here I was again, about to lose my temper.

A red-hot ball of fire pulsed in my chest. Bright white light flared from the corners of my vision. I squeezed my eyes shut and tried to contain my irrational emotions. But the golem won. Inside my brain, the glass box I kept so tightly closed burst into tiny fragments. It showered glitter and glass behind my closed eyes. The noise from the city street vanished.

I blinked slowly. My dad's lips moved, but nothing echoed in my ears. Concern and a hint of panic wrinkled the skin around his eyes. He reached out to grab my shoulder. I sidestepped and rolled my arm away to avoid his touch. He had promised. *Promised.* My dad always said his word was his bond, and he'd broken it. To me, of all people. His baby girl, his fish whisperer. My dad was my rock and my best friend. In my mind, he'd hung the moon and the stars, and now he let them crash to the ground. Bright sunlight stabbed through a break in the clouds and reflected off the running water. It shimmered like broken pieces of stars that had fallen at my feet.

A city bus, plastered with advertisements, zoomed down the street, and all I could think through my rage was—*I wish. I wish you would die.* A tingling spread from my chest to the ends of my fingers and the tips of my toes.

Walk out in front of that bus and die . . .

"I hate you," I hissed between clenched teeth.

His hand dropped to his side, and his blue eyes glazed over. The muscles in his face relaxed to the point where his mouth drooped open and any expression vanished. Almost as if the bones in his face had melted, leaving behind shapeless flesh. Then he turned and stepped off the curb into the path of the speeding bus.

Chapter 2

Normal as a Setting on the Washing Machine

Fluorescent lights buzzed loudly and flickered over the concrete walls. Ancient cigarette smoke lingered under the harsher smell of cleaning chemicals. I set my elbows on the metal table and rested my chin on the palms of my hands. My mom sat next to me wearing a pink sweatshirt with matching nail polish. She stared at her lap and picked at her mangled cuticles.

We'd been waiting in the room for at least half an hour. A woman in a starched Air Force uniform had taken our phones away as soon as we'd entered the building, promising we'd get them back as soon as we were done. My mom, Sara, managed a small protest. I think being in a room alone with me terrified her. We'd barely spoken since I'd gotten released from API, the Alaska Psychiatric Institute, a month ago. Today was the two-month anniversary of the day my dad died.

The crappy cup of coffee sitting in front of me was cold. A weird oil slick of something floated in the liquid, making me glad I hadn't taken more than one sip. My mom's cup, stained with lip-gloss, sat empty next to mine. I had to give her credit—she'd showered today and put on some make-up. Though she looked tired with the dark circles and red-rimmed eyes. Funny how she could look that bad and still be the most beautiful woman around.

The doorknob twisted and a man and a woman carrying briefcases walked in.

The hairs on the back of my neck prickled. They did not look like they were in the military. They were dressed like Federal Agents—black suits, starched white shirts, and polished shoes.

One was around my dad's age with a full head of tightly buzzed silver hair. The woman, I estimated to be in her twenties, was taller than her partner by a few inches and wore her dark hair pulled back in a severe bun.

The man reached out a hand and said "Regan, I'm John Smith and this is my partner, Willa Zehn."

I stayed seated but gave him a firm handshake exactly as my father had taught me. His cologne drifted under my nose forcing me to hold back a sneeze.

"Mrs. Braaten," Smith said, reaching toward my mom. She held her hand out like she was a princess receiving a kiss on her royal ring. He shook it awkwardly.

They simultaneously set their briefcases on the table with a thud. Smith laid his flat and opened it. He pulled out a stack of papers and tapped them on the table making sure the edges were straight. His flat brown eyes met mine. "We have a few questions."

They pulled their chairs over the old, but shiny, linoleum floor and sat down.

I began to think maybe they were attorneys or insurance agents who'd collaborated on matching outfits this morning. The thought made the corner of my lip quirk.

Smith pointed towards the door. "Mrs. Braaten, if you'd like to wait outside," he said like she didn't have a choice.

She blinked a few times before saying, "No, thank you. Regan is a minor and unless you'd like me to call our lawyer, I think I'll stay."

He smiled tightly and sent a side glance to Zehn. "Suit yourself."

Zehn focused her hazel eyes on my mom. Her stare was intense and I found myself wanting to wave my hand in front of her face in order to break her eye contact away from my mom.

Smith turned his attention back to me, "Regan, can you please tell us what happened the day your father, Captain Braaten, died."

A hint of wariness settled in my chest. My lips parted. "What? You mean the police report wasn't enough? Or the trial transcripts?" After I was released from API, the military held a private court hearing to determine my dad's mental competency.

Sara had heard the story a hundred times but not once had she asked me what happened herself. She flexed her fingers into tiny fists and straightened them back out again. She shifted sideways and started bouncing her leg under the table. I glanced over to see if she was okay.

The legs of the chair screeched over the floor as she abruptly stood up. "If you'll please excuse me," she said. "I must use the lavatory."

She bolted from the room.

My eyes darted between Smith and Zehn.

Smith cleared his throat. "Regan, please go on. We'd like to hear the account of that day from you."

"Shouldn't we wait for my mom to get back?" I hesitated.

"Do you really think she needs to hear the story again?" Smith stared at me with narrowed eyes.

He was probably right. I huffed out a deep breath and relayed the gist of the story, minus the fact that I'd killed my dad. With a simple wish, *I wish you would walk in front of that bus and die*, I'd made my dad walk in front of that bus.

He quickly scanned a document with his finger. "It says here in the EMT's report that you were screaming that you were the one who killed your father."

I landed a hard gaze on him. "I did. I just told him I hated him."

"They said you were very insistent." He tapped his pen on the stack of papers.

I didn't answer since he hadn't asked a question. And I had been very insistent, screaming that I'd killed him, until the paramedics stuck me with some kind of sedative.

"I recently watched the video footage. Have you seen it?" He pulled a laptop out of his case.

The question set my teeth on edge. Of course, I'd seen it. Though as far as I knew, my mom had not seen the recording. She refused to watch it, insisting she wasn't strong enough. I'd watched it over and over again punishing myself. Then I'd replay it every night in my sleep.

I nodded and inhaled deeply through my nose. It was as if he was trying to bait me—trying to make me mad. Despite the cold air pouring from the vent, sweat pooled in the small of my back and dampened underneath my side-swept bangs. I tucked them behind my ear.

Zehn sat quietly with her hands folded on the table staring at me giving me a full-on predator vibe. I wouldn't want to meet that chick in a dark alley. But the golem that I'd locked away in the little glass box inside my brain, shivered with excitement at the prospect.

"Yeah. I've seen it," I said like I thought he was stupid.

Smith cocked his head slightly and studied my face. "And what do you make of it? Your dad's face? Your eyes? It's kind of weird right?"

"So? Someone took it on their crappy cell phone." I pushed my chair back from the table and crossed my arms and legs.

"Actually, it was filmed on the latest model."

"Well, then they're just a bad photographer and they shouldn't quit their day job." I threw them attitude. I needed them to think I was your typical, run of the mill, teenage punk-hole.

"I'd like you to watch it with me so we can go through it frame by frame." He opened the computer.

Anxiety flitted behind my ribs.

"Ahh, no," I said, glancing at the door. *What was taking her so long?* "I'm waiting for my mom to get back. We were told this was a routine debriefing on the closure of my dad's death so my mom could receive the life insurance benefits."

Smith's thin lips pressed into a flat line and he, again, side glanced at his partner.

Zehn placed her hands on the table with her fingers spread loosely. She focused on my face. After a few moments, she gave a slight shake of her head.

"Interesting," Smith said. "Well, while we wait, tell me about your dad. Did you ever notice anything unusual about him?"

I wrinkled my eyebrows. "No."

"You know he lied to you about the military granting his retirement. I have the paperwork right here." He slid a sheet of paper in front of me with a fancy government seal at the top.

I twisted my tongue behind my teeth.

I slid it back aggressively without reading it. I didn't care. What difference did it make? My dad was dead.

"Doesn't it make you angry that he lied?" He tapped the paper hard with his index finger.

I shrugged.

"It would make me angry. My father lying to me about something like that. Though he was probably using it as an excuse to get you out of Anchorage, well, with everything surrounding your suspension and all. Am I to understand this wasn't your first offense?"

I sniffed and scratched my temple. I concentrated on keeping my breathing even, in through my nose, out through my mouth. I'd learned a lot about controlling my anger at API. And the skills came in handy on a daily basis. If Smith was trying to make me mad, he was going to have to do much better.

When he figured out I was ignoring his questions, he switched gears. "What about your brothers?" He looked down at his stack of papers. His fingers followed sentences until he found what he was searching for. "Lincoln and Kennedy. Have you ever noticed anything unusual about them?"

"They're mirror twins, one's right-handed, the other left. They also have situs inversus. Their guts are on the opposite sides. I suppose that's unusual," I said. Lincoln was quite proud of having his heart on the wrong side of his body. He often teased that it made him superior to the rest of us peasants.

He smiled but it didn't reach his eyes. "No, I'm wondering more about their behaviors."

"I don't know," I said, scrunching my face. "Lincoln is a dumb ass; Kennedy is a smart ass. Or it might be the other way around. Apple doesn't fall far from the tree." I threw him a sarcastic smile. "Are we done yet?" I flicked my hands into the air with my fingers spread. "Where's my mom?" I got up from the chair and looked out the tiny window. I couldn't see much through the closed blinds.

I grabbed the doorknob and turned it. It was locked. A jolt of fear quickened my pulse and my palms clamed up. I closed my eyes and reigned in my panic swirling inside before I relaxed my shoulders and turned around. I shoved my hands into the pocket of my hoodie.

"Look, I don't know what you are getting at. My family is boring. Normal." *Except for me*. I was anything but normal. But I had an eerie gut feeling they already knew that.

"Who did you say you worked for again?" I asked.

"I didn't. That information is classified," Smith said, gathering up the papers and laptop and placing them in his briefcase.

"Who you work for is classified? There's no such thing."

Zehn spoke for the first time. Her voice was smooth with a hint of grit. "If we told you we'd have to kill you," she said with a wink.

My mouth parted. I held up my palm. "Whatever." I gestured to the door. "Are we done here?"

Smith pursed his lips but got up and unlocked the

door. He pushed it open and let me go first. I scanned the room for my mom.

I spotted her pink sweatshirt. She was holding a cup of coffee and laughing with the lady who'd absconded our phones.

I stomped over to her. "Where were you?" I accused.

"Excuse me?" she said in her dangerous mom tone. "Where were you?"

My mouth hung open. "In there waiting for you to get back."

"Well, I looked all over for you and you were nowhere to be found," she snapped.

What was she talking about?

"Captain Blackmore was kind enough to get me some coffee and keep me company while I waited on you to find your way back."

I looked at Captain Blackmore. "Those guys in there," I pointed towards the room I'd just left. "Who are they?"

"What guys?" she said.

"The dude and the chick dressed for a job interview with the Feds," I said.

A frown arched her lips but there was a sparkle of knowing in her eyes. "I'm sorry, there's no one here who fits that description."

I cocked my head and then slowly shook it. She was lying.

I decided to wait to push the issue until my mom and I were alone in the car. Something strange was afoot.

I slammed the vehicle door and clicked my seatbelt into place.

"What's going on?" I asked.

Sara stuck the key in the ignition of her white SUV.

"I don't know what you're talking about. While I was signing the paperwork, you disappeared."

"That's not what happened. We were in a room with two people who, after you left me," I paused, "they quizzed me about dad and the twins."

Sara gripped the steering wheel, her knuckles turning white under her pale skin. "Regan, I don't know what you are talking about." She turned her head to look at me. "We were in a room to sign the paperwork and you said you had to pee, then you took off and didn't come back."

WTF. Did they rufie my mom? I was thankful I hadn't drunk the coffee.

"Did someone ask you questions about our family?" she said.

I narrowed my eyes. "Yes."

"What did they want to know?"

"If Dad, Kennedy, or Lincoln were unusual in any way."

Her shoulders tensed and her voice rose almost an octave. "And what did you say?"

"I said they were as normal as a setting on the washing machine," I quoted one of her favorite sayings. "Why? Is there something you're not telling me?"

"Of course not," she said. She pulled out onto the street and dogged crater-sized potholes in the road.

That evening, she started packing our belongings into boxes. By July we were on the road.

Chapter 3

Millionaires and Billionaires

The rooster's crow woke me long before my alarm went off. I didn't sleep well anymore, nightmares kept me restless. I stayed under the warm covers and counted my breaths—a little meditation technique my therapist taught me—trying to fall back asleep. My mind refused. Images of blood, broken glass, vacant blue eyes, and whispered prayers haunted my subconscious. I tossed off my down quilt and threw my legs over the side of my bed. The old springs creaked with every move. I slid my feet into fleece slippers placed strategically so I didn't have to touch the chilly wood floor.

After the strange incident at the military base, my mom insisted we move back to the place she called home: a small ranch in Wyoming. Right before we left, I questioned her again as to why Smith and Zehn interrogated me about my dad and brothers.

I needed to be cautious how the subject was approached because I didn't want her to think I was crazy—*ha, ha*—and send me back to API. "Is there something you're not telling me about dad and the twins?" I asked her after she insisted for the four-hundredth time that I pack my suitcase before the movers arrived. I'd been dragging my feet. I wasn't ready to leave. Alaska wasn't just my home, it was my identity. The place where wearing rubber fishing boots and hanging with your dad made you normal. Cool, even, especially when you had a float plane to go with it.

"No," she snapped. "Now go do what I asked."

I stopped in front of my bedroom door. "Then why do we have to leave?" I whined.

"Because I said so."

I hated that excuse. My eyes narrowed and I crossed my arms. "I don't want to go," I said snidely.

"Not everything is about you, Regan."

I clenched my fists and brought them to the sides of my face. Her arrogant, condescending tone rankled my nerves like nothing else. "It never is! Now tell me what is going on! Why was I questioned at the base? What are they looking for?"

"You were NOT questioned at the base. You are a liar and as far as I'm concerned, you've proven you can't be trusted. Now go pack your," she pressed her lips together biting down on whatever swear word was going through her head, "things," she yelled, pointing at me, her neon orange polish flashing in the sunlight.

I stomped my foot. "As far as I'm concerned, this isn't over. Because you're the liar, not me." I turned my back on her and slammed my bedroom door in her face.

And that's why we had to move. Because, according to her last comment, screamed through the closed door, without my dad and brothers—how was she going to raise a delinquent like me alone?

So, here we were stuck between BFE and nowhere Wyoming.

For the last two months, we'd lived next door to my grandparents in the old foreman's cottage. After Gramps downsized the ranch a few years ago, it sat empty. It hadn't been updated since, like, probably the 1940s. It was retro, but not the cool-trendy type of retro. Cracks graced the ceilings and walls, letting in almost as much cold air as the ancient windows. The kitchen cupboard doors hung catawampus, and the drawers, more often than not, crashed to the floor when opened.

My great-grandparents, fresh off the boat from Norway, had found this little piece of paradise, and the rest is history. My family has been here ever since.

The floorboards groaned as I shuffled to the window and folded back the curtains. A breeze rolled over my arms, and I hugged them close to my chest. It was the first week of September and already small crystals of ice gathered in the corners of the single-pane glass. I scratched a fingernail over the frost. It curled away and melted at my touch.

Soon this cold would be a thing of the past. My mom planned on remodeling our little cottage with her winnings from the Servicemembers' Group Life Insurance sweepstakes. Compliments of me.

Tears stung the corners of my eyes and threatened to fall. I gulped in a few deep, shaky breaths and clenched my fists. I ground my teeth and quickly shoved my feelings back into the boxes where they belonged.

I liked to compartmentalize my life. It was the only way I was able to keep the darkness, the golem, under control. When I let feelings mingle—when pain and sorrow bled into anger and hurt, and then swirled with guilt and self-loathing—it created a recipe for disaster. The only safe solution was to keep all the feelings separate. My coping mechanism. I refused to allow my emotions to control me. I knew I was a monster and what

I was capable of.

A hazy glow separated the jagged mountains from the dark morning sky. A heavenly mist of gold spread slowly behind the peaks and backlit the gray, hovering clouds.

No wonder my mom wanted to come home. It was beautiful here. A lonely light twinkled from my grandparents' kitchen window. My grandma's shadow passed in front of the yellow curtains. While Gramps fed the livestock, Grams cooked breakfast—bacon, eggs, toast, and coffee with fresh cream. It was the same routine every morning except for the weekends when I helped with the chores. Then she added French toast to the menu. My favorite.

I yanked a clean towel out of the cupboard and took a long, hot shower. Steam filled the tiny bathroom so I blow-dried my pixie hair in my room. I swiped on some lip balm and dressed in jeans, a tank top, a gray sweatshirt, and a pair of flip-flops.

Today was the first day of school for everyone. Technically, my last first day since it was my senior year. And I wanted to be incognito—as much as the new girl in a small school could be.

I flipped on the porch light and walked out the front door. Mom could turn it off when she got up—whenever that would be. I sucked in the smell of fresh mountain air and manure. Cows mooed, roosters crowed, and the pigs snorted and snuffled through their slop. The joys of ranch life. Otherwise, the valley was silent.

Until I started my ancient 1985 pickup. It hesitated for a few seconds before the engine roared to life. Heavy black smoke belched from the tailpipe. I wanted to get into the habit of starting my vehicle every morning before the snow flew. My grandparents had recently replaced the farm truck with a shiny new version, so I inherited their old one. No complaints here; wheels were wheels.

I ducked into Gram's kitchen and tried swiping a piece of bacon before she caught me. A gray cat curled in a figure-eight pattern around my legs. Its purr was audible.

"Oh, here, sweetie. Have some breakfast." She opened an oak cabinet door, grabbed a plate, and set it on the brown tile countertops. The brass light fixtures completed the early eighties ensemble. Her accent was heavier than my grandpa's. He'd been born here, but occasionally you could hear his parents' influence in his speech. My grandma was born in Norway, the old country, and came over with her parents to visit friends. She never left. Both of them claimed they fell in love with each other at first sight.

She'd been quite the beauty when she was younger. Still was really. High forehead framed with thick silver hair. She had perfectly sculpted cheekbones, full lips, and startling ice blue eyes. My mom was her spitting image. But Grams had more grit. More substance.

"And this is for you." She handed me a package wrapped in Christmas paper even though it was only the first week of September. I cocked my head and started to protest but she stopped me with a wave of her hand.

"I know you asked us not to make a big deal about your birthday." Her brows furrowed as if she didn't agree with my request. "I had to do something sweetie. It's not much, I promise."

Birthdays were a big deal in our family. But the thought of celebrating without my dad was more than I could bear. I'd asked everyone if we could skip it this year.

I carefully picked the tape, pulled it away, and unwrapped the squishy package. Inside was an infinity scarf in a steel blue—the same color as my dad's eyes. I hugged it to my chest and swallowed back the tears. She'd knitted it herself. "Thanks, Grams. I love it." I put it over my head and stroked the silky material.

"Are you sure you don't want a cake?"

I shook my head.

"Well, then I'll make a pie. But it won't be a birthday pie," she said quickly.

I had a feeling I wasn't going to win the argument, so I let it go with a shrug of my shoulders.

She motioned to the table for me to sit down.

"Thanks, Grams, but I don't have time." I shifted my backpack higher on my shoulder and reached for the bacon.

"Did your mother pack you a lunch?"

I stuffed the salty meat in my mouth and shook my head.

She pursed her lips into a thin line, deepening the wrinkles around her mouth, but she didn't say anything. "Well, here." She opened the antiquated fridge and handed me a paper sack. "Just in case you want to eat in your truck today instead of the cafeteria."

My heart squeezed. I'd probably take her up on that advice.

"And this too." She gave me a travel mug with hot coffee and fresh cream.

"You're too good to me, Grams." And I meant it.

"Nothing is too good for my granddaughter."

I wanted to correct her. I bet she wouldn't say that if

she knew what kind of person I really was.

She laid the back of her cold, weathered hand on my cheek. "Try and have a good day. We will see you tonight."

I tilted my chin up, smiled, and waved. My mouth was full.

Without any side steps on my truck, I hauled myself up by what my dad called the "oh shit handle." The joys of being vertically challenged. I flipped on the lights and drove through the gate. My teeth vibrated over the cattle guard and down the dirt road until I turned onto the highway. Hi-ho. Hi-ho. Off to school, I go.

I pulled into the almost deserted parking lot and enjoyed my coffee as the sun rose over the Grand Teton mountains. The domed brick school building was ugly and depressing against the glorious backdrop. You'd think somebody amongst all these rich people could have come up with a better design. Soon cars of all kinds began to fill the empty spaces. Old beaters like mine equaled the shiny European sports cars and SUV's, American muscle cars, and new limited-edition pickup trucks. This area was once just a quaint farming town. Then some rich dude *discovered* it, and apparently invited all his rich buddies. Now the local joke was: a town where the billionaires drove out the millionaires. Quite the cultural clash.

With my head down, I shuffled over the newly sealed pavement into the school. I stayed invisible amongst the other students until homeroom.

I darted to a desk in the back corner and slunk down into the cold chair. A young woman—not much older than her class—with sleek blonde hair, a black pencil skirt, and a tight-fitting sweater showing off her curves wrote her name on the dry erase board: Mrs. Glasgow.

Students jockeyed for position trying to sit next to their friends as they laughed and joked, glad to be back in school at least for today. Copious amounts of cheap body spray, high-end perfume, and fruity shampoo wafted through the classroom. After everyone found their seats and settled down, Mrs. Glasgow passed around a wicker basket and demanded our phones. We'd get them back after class.

In a southern accent, she said, "Now, I need everyone to welcome Regan Braaten." I cringed. She pronounced it like brat—which I was. But the correct pronunciation was bra, as in my favorite item of clothing to ditch at the end of the day.

I instantly disliked her. I'd done so well sneaking in—not being noticed. She'd blown my cover.

Everyone turned and stared. Amongst the sea of white were only a few students of different ethnicities. After years of military schools, I was used to a classroom full of all colors and flavors. Mind you, this homeroom class wasn't very big. Twenty kids at the most.

One guy looked to be Native American, which wasn't unusual, considering the part of the country we were in. The casual way he sat in his chair, with his arms folded and legs pushed out under his desk, did nothing to disguise the tension in his shoulders or the tightness in his jaw. His deep-set black eyes glared from under his thick, sharp brows and messy dark hair. He cocked his head, almost like he was trying to find a better angle to study me. He was gorgeous if you liked pretty boys with chiseled edges and perfect lips. Not to mention the huge chip he carried around on his shoulders.

Students shifted in their seats, adjusted their clothes,

played with their hair, whispered, and snickered. It was like their fingers didn't know what to do without a phone in their hands. Everyone moved as if they couldn't contain their restlessness. Everyone except for him. Though energy radiated around him, an almost visible disturbance in the air, he didn't move. Not one twitch of a muscle. Not one blink of an eye. I wasn't sure if he was even breathing. His eyes found mine like a wolf locking on its prey. Goosebumps rose on my forearms, and a chill slid down my spine. I shivered. Then I brushed the feeling of fear away. I leaned forward, crossed my arms on my desk, and narrowed my eyes at him—*I am the wolf.*

His features settled into the same scowl that all the girls wore. I knew why they were throwing me dirty looks . . . I was fresh meat, possibly competition in this narrow dating pool. Okay, perhaps I was being naïve. Maybe he liked dudes too. I shrugged and glanced away.

The blonde sitting in the second row took her scathing look to a new level. She sized me up and down deliberately, slightly rolled her eyes, and then turned away, not bothering to glance in my direction again. Her hair was stylishly tossed into beachy waves; her makeup was just enough but not too much, and her French manicure screamed money. No detail had been overlooked. Including her ability to exude arrogance and indifference. It took many hours of practice to achieve that level of perfection.

The nerds in the front row, with trendy glasses and bad haircuts, allotted me only a moment's notice before they dismissed me. I wasn't worth their time. Don't judge a book by its cover, people . . . I was smart, and my grades were my ticket out of here. With a scholarship, I could afford college on my own.

The farm kids, in their wrangler jeans and dusty boots, didn't glare but didn't smile either. One of them, with a five o'clock shadow and a hat ring indented in his hair, tipped his head. It was the warmest welcome I'd received thus far.

"Regan, would you please stand and tell us a little bit about yourself?" Mrs. Glasgow clasped her hands behind her, drawing more attention to her already prominent chest.

I pushed myself up from the desk and buried my hands in my pockets trying to appear casual and carefree. In reality, a nervous sweat broke out under my hoodie. I smiled tightly at her.

"I moved here from Alaska. My dad . . ." I paused and swallowed, even saying the word hurt. "He was military, so I've lived a lot of places." I flopped back down and pulled my hood up over my head.

"Well, Regan," Mrs. Glasgow said in her nasally southern accent. She sat on the edge of her desk and folded her hands over the front of her skirt. "That's all good, but what do you like to do, darlin'?"

I controlled the urge to roll my eyes and took a deep breath, concentrating on my dislike for this nosy woman. A small shot of endorphins spread through my body. It tingled from my chest to the ends of my fingers and to the tips of my toes.

I wish. I wish you would get up.

She stood up, whether she wanted to or not.

Turn around.

She did an about-face.

Go back to your desk.

Her high heels clicked over the linoleum floor.

Forget about me.

I looked from one side of the classroom to the other, then focused back on her. "I like to be left alone." Before she could register my words and irritate me further, her brown eyes glazed over, and she sat rigidly down at her desk before staring vacantly out into the room. It took her a while to recover.

Most of the students seemed horrified by my disrespectful answer. Except for the dark-haired dude that was glaring at me only moments before. A grin curled on his beautiful lips. Interesting. But it wasn't a nice smile; it was more of an *I-got-your-number* kind of smile.

I didn't have to worry about damage control with Mrs. Glasgow. She'd already forgotten about my rudeness. I'd made sure of it. But the others, they would remember. I didn't want anyone to like me. I didn't deserve to have friends.

The rest of the day proved to be uneventful. Everyone just watched and whispered amongst themselves. Girls sized me up—some even said hi—and so did the guys. I caught a few admiring glances out of the corner of my eyes. But I kept my head down and did my best not to interact with anyone.

By the seventh period, I was almost home free. Art class. My hardest subject. Though I loved art, it didn't always love me. I'd been told I lacked talent. Hard facts and numbers—no problem. But before registering for this class, I double-checked the requirements for an A. He graded on effort, not talent. *That* I could handle.

Fluorescent bulbs buzzed from above, shining their obnoxious light on the long stainless-steel tables. Permanent splashes of paint coated the concrete floor like an abstract painting. The instructor, Mr. Clark, in his brown corduroy pants and dated sweater vest, said to sit wherever.

I found a spot in the back corner of the room and hunkered down with crossed arms. I'd made it through my first day unscathed.

Then in walked the dark-haired pretty boy, who, for some reason, didn't seem to like me. Which was fine with me.

He pulled a plastic bag out of the pocket of his unbuttoned, gray and black flannel shirt and tossed it on Mr. Clark's desk. He smiled and said something in a deep, quiet voice, but I didn't catch it.

The teacher's worn face lit up.

Pretty boy stopped and surveyed all the empty spaces. He inhaled, his nostrils flaring, and exhaled for a long time before he strolled nonchalantly over to me. He swung the plastic chair around, its metal legs grating the floor, then straddled it. He stared at my profile, his gaze traveling slowly over me. It was as if I could physically feel his eyes caress my skin. The desire to reach up and brush the foreign feeling from my cheeks was strong. Instead, I concentrated on the paintings hanging above Mr. Clark's desk. Abstracts. My favorite. I liked the way they invoked emotion without telling what it should be. After a full minute of this discomfort, I tilted my head toward him and said, "What?"

The overpowering lights matted his bronze skin, but it wasn't unflattering. He looked like he'd been carved from stone. His eyelashes were so thick and dark I couldn't tell if he was wearing eyeliner to go with his black nail polish or not. Tiny silver hoop earrings hung from both his earlobes.

His silence made me twitchy. I turned my chair so it was facing him. I crossed my legs and folded my hands on my lap, mimicking my previous therapist. "And Johnny? What do you think about this new girl? The one that seems to irritate you?" I blinked my long eyelashes rapidly.

He fiddled with a polished arrowhead that hung from a braided leather rope around his neck. "It's Jude actually," he said in a deep, smoky voice.

I already knew that having had four classes out of seven with him. All advanced placement classes and art.

Jude's eyes were so black that, even in this bright light, I couldn't differentiate his pupils from his irises. He swiveled his head, trying to see what was behind me, which was weird because the only thing there was a wall. "And I think there's something wrong with the new girl."

A laugh caught in my throat and I pursed my lips to one side. *If he only knew*. "Really, you don't say," I said in my best impression of an old-time sportscaster. I switched back to my counselor's voice, "And what exactly do you think is wrong with her?" I was curious to hear his answer.

A few more kids strayed in after the tardy bell. The stoners, wearing retro grunge T-shirts and leather biker jackets, stumbled in smelling like cigarettes and weed. Thankfully, they sat well away from us. Their sluggish laughter echoed on the painted brick walls.

He ran his fingers over his messy dark hair. "I can't quite put my finger on it." He squinted his eyes and cocked his head, but he didn't look angry, more puzzled.

"Well, when you figure it out, let me know, will ya?" I snapped. I started to turn my chair around.

"Sure thing. Oh, here's your phone by the way." He

held out a black phone and wiggled it in front of my face. I shoved my fingers in my pockets and rifled around in my bag only to come up empty-handed.

"Yup." I shrugged my shoulders. "Why didn't you give it to me earlier? We've only had, like, four other classes together."

He smiled for real this time. His teeth were white and perfectly straight. *Of course, they are.*

"Glad you noticed. Really, I just wanted to see how long it would take ya to figure out it was missing. Impressive. You went all day without it," he chuckled.

I was infamous in my family for misplacing my phone. "Yeah, well, there's nothing on it I need." All I used it for was music, books, and checking the weather and the time. I noticed it was missing at lunch as I sat in my truck, eating my sandwich, but figured it was in my locker. After that, it was forgotten about again.

"I wouldn't know. I couldn't figure out your code." He twitched a dark eyebrow.

My eyes widened. "Seriously? You tried?"

"Hell, yeah. I like to know people's darkest secrets. And so many idiots keep them on their phones." He winked at me.

"Here ya go. Knock yourself out." I typed in my code and thrust my phone at him. "It's 6666 should you ever need it again."

"No, it's not. I tried *that* one first." He flipped his chair around and crossed his black work boots under the table.

My mouth dangled open not knowing whether to be flattered or insulted.

Mr. Clark stood up from his desk and wrote out our weekly schedule on the old-fashioned chalkboard.

Sketchbooks due every Friday. Otherwise, we were free to work on a project of our choice. He'd check our progress at the end of the week and discuss our goals individually.

Jude held my phone under the table and scrolled through my pictures first. Mostly scenes from Alaska—mountains, whales, salmon, and halibut fishing. No friends, but a few pictures of my family. Mom, Dad, Kennedy, Lincoln, and me. Yes, we were named after presidents.

"Can you say *Sieg Heil*?" he muttered in a fake German accent.

His humor caught me off guard. I choke-coughed and laughed at the same time. "We're Norwegian, not German," I clarified.

My brothers had white-blond hair and light blue eyes like my mom, but they were tall like my dad. Me, well, I looked like my dad—light brown hair and stormy blue eyes, but I was short like my mom.

"And that fish . . . wow." He could only be talking about the giant lingcod I caught in Seward, Alaska.

He glanced up from my phone and stared at me for a few seconds. "You like to fish?"

I shrugged. I used to.

His eyes kept darting above my head and around my shoulders. I peeked at my arms, then back at him. I couldn't figure out what he was looking at.

He gestured to the top of my head. "You have glitter in your hair."

I messed up my long bangs trying to remove it.

He shook his head.

I tried again.

"Nope. Do you mind?" He pointed a finger.

"Knock yourself out."

He reached up and brushed his fingers through my hair. A current of electricity jolted from his fingers to my forehead. Then an invisible force blanketed my skin in a tingly glow. As if a set of gentle hands skimmed my body.

"Sorry," he apologized for the shock before he continued to scroll through the rest of the pictures quickly.

"So, glitter girl—no friends? Boyfriends?" His eyebrow flicked upward. His eyes darted down my frame, and a dark and dangerous smile curled on his lips.

I could feel the heat rising to my face. I snatched the phone back. I'd deleted those photos and all of my social media accounts before we moved here. I didn't want a constant reminder of what I'd left behind. Besides, I didn't deserve friends.

He chuckled. It wasn't a friendly sound. He turned his chair forward and ignored me for the rest of class.

Chapter 4

From a Nine to a Firm Fifteen

After school, I drove to work. Storefronts with wooden boardwalks, set up to look like the Old West, surrounded part of the town square. Across the road, the buildings looked like old-money ski lodges with huge raw logs and open beams. Both sides of the street housed multiple high-end art galleries, jewelry stores, and fancy clothing and home boutiques. Amongst the new—made to look old—buildings were a bank, a hardware store, and some restaurants and bars. I parked behind the restaurant and tied my black apron around my waist before going in. Though I didn't need a job, it kept me away from the house. My mom and her depression were more than I could deal with. Especially knowing I caused it. And being around her only reminded me of the horrible person that I was.

The smell of fried food slammed into my face upon opening the back door. A corkboard full of notices and advertisements lined one side of the wood-paneled hallway. A flyer with border collie puppies for sale had half of the tabs torn off. The bathrooms, with hanging plaques designating Fillies and Colts, were on the other side of the corridor.

I dumped my phone into my designated staff locker

and clocked in.

"Regan." Miss Molly's wide blue eyes beamed down at me. Honey-blonde bangs framed her youthful face. I asked her once how old she was. Thirty-two. She then proceeded to give me the *don't get knocked up as a teenager* lecture. Good advice.

She bent way down because she was almost six foot tall and hugged me. She smelled like greasy French fries and sweet perfume. She was the only friend I had. Not that I wanted one, but some people just don't give you the option.

"You have to come meet my son." She clapped her hands rapidly in front of her face. She took me by the elbow and tugged me to a corner booth.

Over the summer, I'd gotten to know Layne, though I'd never actually met him. I'd even been to his house a few times, but he was always away at one football camp or another. Miss Molly talked about him constantly. And, if half of what she said were true, he was amazing. *Impossibly* amazing.

He sat relaxed in the 1970s high-back leather booth—complete with studded nail heads and swanky porn lighting. Overhead the speakers played a country western duet. The music enhanced the atmosphere. Welcome to Wyoming.

I preferred music that wasn't in English. Usually opera. I didn't want to know what they were saying. I wanted to feel what they were feeling: the shivers on the high notes and the twisting of my heart on the lows. The moments when I forgot to breathe.

"Regan." Layne stood up, almost knocking over his soda. He caught it quickly before it spilled and dried his hands off on his faded jeans. A blue knit thermal shirt stretched tight over his wide muscled chest and if I stared hard enough—which I was trying *not* to do—I could make out the ridges of his hard stomach. He grabbed my tiny hand in his massive one and shook it while he said, "Mom's told me so much about you." He spoke quickly, which seemed at odds with the deepness of his voice.

I tilted my chin up, way up, to meet the bright blue of his eyes. I wondered how Miss Molly even knew anything about me. I was pretty close-lipped. She was not, however. She was a single mom with three jobs in order to make ends meet in this expensive little town. All to make sure her son didn't have to work, so he could concentrate on school and, most importantly, football. Apparently, according to the whole town, he was destined to be the next Heisman trophy winner, whatever that was.

So, to say the least, I was skeptical of her assessment of her only child.

I laughed nervously. "Oh, okay. She's told me a lot about you, too."

"Oh, God." He rubbed his forehead. "It's never-ending. Will the woman ever stop?" He held his hands out, palms facing upwards, and shook his head slowly. "Sit down?"

Though the restaurant was deserted, I needed to start my prep work. "Sorry, can't. I already clocked in."

"Oh, no," Miss Molly interrupted and physically pushed me down into the oversized booth. She set a soda in front of me. "I'll take care of that. You two visit for a while." She pulled the lighter out of her apron and lit the candle in the middle of our table. Warm light slithered over the heavily varnished ebony surface. She winked at me before she hurried to the next booth.

My eyebrows came together. What was that all about?

I propped my legs up under me to be taller. As he watched his mom walk away, true admiration sparkled behind his eyes. "Let me tell ya, that woman's something else."

I nodded in agreement. She was.

"Most amazing person I know." He focused his blue, blue eyes back on me. He ran his fingers through his thick hair. Under the dated yellow lights, it shone like gold. I'd seen pictures of him almost daily. She was a very proud momma. But the photos hadn't done him justice. They captured his looks—tall, wide shoulders; eyes framed with thick lashes, blonde at the base but dark at the ends; a tiny cleft in his chin—but they didn't capture his boyish charm.

"She works so hard for us. Mostly me. Someday I'm going to repay everything she's done for me."

On a hotness scale from one to ten, he skyrocketed from a nine to a firm fifteen.

"So, what about you? Miss Molly says you moved from Alaska? What's it like there?" He pushed up the sleeves of his shirt. Soft blondish-red hair covered his thick forearms.

"Lot like here, I guess. Only more mosquitos. We have an ocean though." He was uncomfortably good-looking, and he seemed so genuine that he was making me nervous.

"I hate mosquitos. Momma says I have sweet blood," he said in a fake southern accent.

I bet you do, I almost said aloud. A flush spread up my neck and burned over my face. I leaned down and put my elbows on the table and my hands over my cheeks so he wouldn't notice.

He waved at somebody behind me. I turned my head and saw the blonde from homeroom, dressed in her black-and-red cheerleading outfit, walking toward us. Her ponytail swung gently behind her, almost reaching the middle of her back. Her face glowed with delight until she saw me. Her eyes widened in surprise; then they contracted.

"Regan, this is my girlfriend, Gabriella. Gabby, Regan."

"Yes, we're acquainted." She wrinkled her pert nose, looking like she'd just eaten moldy foot cheese. She wasn't beautiful, and she was too tall to be considered cute, but she wasn't ugly either. And she knew how to make the most of what she had: pretty eyes and a fantastic body.

She heaved her very expensive brown leather purse off her shoulder and scooted down next to him. She cozied herself up next to his large bicep that was straining against the material of his shirt.

"Oh, sure, you girls probably have some classes together." He passed his soda to her. She took a drink, then puckered her face. "Uh, it's not diet." She snottily pushed it back in front of him. Stacked diamond rings and platinum bands sparkled on her fingers.

"Sorry, baby." He kissed the side of her hair.

"Bob," Gabby said as she stared at the bartender, her voice sharp like a gunshot. "I want a diet, now." She tapped the table hard.

Bob pushed the beer tap off and set down the half-full glass. He muttered an apology to his current customers before he wiped his hands off on a bar towel. He filled a glass with ice and poured Gabby a diet soda.

He shuffled over and set the drink on the table along with a straw. "So, so, sorry, Miss Gabriella," he stuttered. A tight unfriendly smile unfolded on her face before she turned her attention back to me.

"What's your name again?" she said rudely.

"Regan," both Layne and I said at the same time.

"Oh, yeah. We have homeroom together," she said. She studied my face, then my attire, her clear green eyes taking note of all my flaws. A small air snort escaped from her nose. I didn't pass inspection.

"No others?" He looked confused. "I didn't see you all day," he said to me.

"Yeah, well, I have mostly AP classes," I said. I opened my straw, dropped it in my drink, and took a swallow.

Respect tinged his voice. "Dang, girl. Good for you."

I clasped my hands together on the table. "I have a lot of free time." I didn't like to point out that academics came easy to me.

"You're a senior too, right?" I confirmed. His mom had mentioned it a million times, but for some reason, she forgot to point out he had a girlfriend. Not that I cared, but nobody like to be blindsided.

"Yeah, but I'm not in any of *those* classes," he said with a good dose of humor and sarcasm. He wadded up the paper from his straw and tossed it at my face. I dodged it. "I struggle with the normal ones. Not really. Just math," he teased. "Hey, maybe I could get you to help me out one of these days? Help me study?" He nodded enthusiastically as if I'd already said yes.

Before I could answer, he continued. "You're the one who said you had plenty of time on your hands." He shrugged his impressively wide shoulders. A huge grin bloomed across his face, crinkling his eyes to almost nonexistence. I'd been cornered.

Gabby stiffened. She blinked rapidly, and her mouth fell open. She recovered quickly. "You don't need *her* help," she said the word *her* like it was a filthy substance. "I'll help you." Though her tone left no room for argument, Layne didn't seem to notice.

He nudged her playfully with his arm. "No offense, beautiful, but math ain't your strong suit."

Her face froze—she looked surprised by his insult—then her jaw clenched, and tiny lines formed between her eyebrows. I recognized that look. Controlled rage. Being an expert in the subject, I stayed silent. I was *so* not getting in between this.

"Come on, I need help." He turned his attention back to me. "If you won't do it for me, do it for my momma. Someday I want her to live like a queen," he pleaded. He fluttered his lashes like that would help. He placed a hand over his heart. "You're my only hope."

How could I deny him? I really, really liked his momma. I threw my hands up in the air. "Okay, fine. You win." I stood up and faced the table.

Gabriella slid her tongue over her front teeth but said nothing. Though not having passed her earlier inspection, I now had the impression that I was a blip on her radar.

"You figure out a time that works. Your mom knows my schedule. I gotta get back to work. Later." I pointed a finger at him like it were a gun. Could I be any more of an idiot?

"She looks like a boy," Gabby said as I walked across the aged wood floor.

"I don't think so," Layne said. Then he recovered, "But she isn't near as pretty as you are."

I smiled and kept walking. A familiar feeling blanketed my skin. The endorphins. A tingle spread from my chest to my head and worked its way down to the tips of my fingers and toes. I concentrated and pictured how I wanted it to happen.

I wish. Pick up your glass. Hold it over your lap. Tilt the glass—farther—I felt only a small amount of resistance—*now farther.*

Then she squealed before she said, "What the heck!"

I turned. She danced all around, wiping the sticky soda off her bare legs with Layne's letterman jacket. She didn't have that glazed look in her eyes because I wanted her to remember.

"Layne, you clumsy oaf. Take me home now." She threw his wet coat at him.

Funny, I was pretty certain she'd poured the contents of that glass on her own lap.

"Okay, okay. Give me fifteen minutes. I have to wait for Mom."

"I said now!" Every word was punctuated with a foot stomp. Her ponytail bobbed with every step.

Layne rubbed his hand over his mouth but escorted her out anyway.

I walked over to the bar and thumped my fingers on the polished wooden surface. Rows and rows of alcohol lined the mirrored back wall.

"Is she always that rude?" I asked the bartender, referring to Gabby.

Bob and I'd worked together for a few months now, and though he was polite, he was a man of few words. He pushed the bridge of his glasses up with a finger.

"You do know that's the boss's daughter, right?" He chuckled at the look of confusion and horror on my face before he turned around to polish the hard water spots off the glasses.

I shook my head in disbelief. I'd never met the boss. And I'd only seen him and his wife once. They owned the place, but they didn't run the place. Though by the looks of it, some of the staff were afraid of their daughter.

"So, what was that all about?" I asked Miss Molly as she passed by.

I dimmed the lights of the wagon wheel fixtures to accommodate the dinner crowd before following her.

"I believe she spilled soda on her lap. Though didn't it look like she did it on purpose?" she asked.

I shrugged. There was no way I was confessing.

She filled a glass from the bar tap and set it on the serving platter.

"You know what I mean. The girlfriend. I believe you forgot to mention her."

She widened her big blue eyes innocently. "What girlfriend? I don't like her. I like you." She spun away and picked up the order waiting in the kitchen window.

"Don't get any silly ideas in your head." I pointed to her as she carried stacked meals in her buff arms. "Your kid's way too good for me."

I meant that with all my heart. He was a gem. And I wasn't.

Chapter 5

Wicked Wishes: Five Months ago

Five months ago, I'd woken up secured with padded straps to a bed in a room I'd never seen.

A faint buzzing emitted from the overhead lights. Its stark brightness reflected on the sterile white walls, illuminating even the corners. The absence of windows, the low ceiling, and the checkered linoleum floor added to the creepy ambiance. The caustic smell of hospital chemicals and ammonia floated in the air along with the sour musk of fear sweat wafting from me. A dull fogginess clouded my head. Some kind of concoction dripped slowly into the IV hooked up to my left arm. Where was I? And why?

"Hello?" I whispered. I winced. My throat was sore. Then I said it again louder.

"Miss Braaten." A voice came from the corner of the room.

A dark-haired woman, somewhere in her early forties, came to me with a clipboard in her hands. A white doctor's coat was draped over her black skirt and pinstriped shirt. Sharp, intelligent eyes shone from behind a set of frameless glasses.

"Welcome back. How are you feeling?" she asked in a soft voice.

"I don't know." I tried reaching up to brush my long

hair out of my eyes, but my wrists were tied down.

She gathered the thick weight of hair and pushed it off to the side. She pulled a few stray pieces out of my mouth and said, “Do you know where you are?”

I shook my head. “No.” I ran my tongue over my fuzzy teeth. Gross.

“You’re in the hospital. The Alaska Psychiatric Institution. You’ve been in a coma for three days.” She paused. “Do you know why you’re here?”

I gazed through squinted eyes at the noisy lights and listened to the ticking clock and quiet beeping coming from the machine next to me.

“What is the last thing you remember?” She placed a cold hand on my arm.

“My dad and I . . . Oh, God, no,” I said. Small whimpering sounds escaped between my cracked lips. I clenched my gritty eyes shut remembering those final moments. Flashes of blood, broken glass and strangers standing around me as I screamed. When the EMT’s arrived, they injected me with a sedative.

And then I woke up here.

Most of the staff were friendly, and my personal doctor, Dr. River, was a brilliant woman full of compassion. But even she couldn’t cure my condition. My insanity and insistence that I killed my father was diagnosed as an altered mental status: psychosis unspecified. A brief psychotic disorder—sudden, short-term display of psychotic behavior triggered by extreme stress—versus an acute stress reaction—a psychological response to a terrifying or traumatic experience. Though I checked all of the boxes, both of her diagnosis’s were wrong.

She did, however, help me deal with my all-consuming guilt.

As Dr. River slowly weaned me off the medication, I discovered that with the right amount of controlled anger and concentration, I could get people to do things. With a simple wish, humans obeyed my every command. *I wish I may, I wish I might, have the wish I wish tonight* . . .

By this point, I realized I'd be safer and get released faster if I kept my abilities secret.

At first, my attempts were awkward. People's posture mimicked marionette dolls: heads tilted, shoulders shrugged, arms dangled loosely. Puppets on my strings. But after practicing, it became easier, like second nature. Though the more substance and grit they had, the harder it was to control them. Unless I was in a rage. Then no one could fight my will. I could make people remember—or I could make them forget. And with every mischief I created and every chaos I caused, I became more grounded. My bouts of anger faded to almost nothing. The glass box I'd created to contain my emotions was still full of darkness, but the golem wasn't straining to escape.

If I denied myself access to my powers, my grip on reality wavered. Black smoke seeped from the edges of its glass prison; my rage returned, and the golem slowly seized the upper hand.

Even though I didn't like controlling people, the euphoria that came with my abilities was intoxicating. It was as if my powers were a drug pulsing through my blood, numbing my emotions, making me forget. It inflated my self-esteem with power, arrogance, and invincibility—I was a God.

Until it ran its course. Then came the crash. Reality

burned like a brand on my soul—a mark I could never erase. I was born evil.

I learned I could do good things also. Once I made this guy turn just in time to see the wallet he'd lost from his coat pocket. I highly encouraged one of the nurses to ask out another nurse on a date; otherwise, left to their own devices, it was never going to happen. Once I made an older woman slam on her brakes before she hit a child who had darted out into traffic . . . But with any amount of kindness, I didn't get my usual high. Quite the opposite really. Instead, I got severe chest and stomach pains, a face full of zits, and itchy welts—only to name a few of my mysterious ailments. The worst was when my beautiful, long, thick hair started falling out. There were wads on my pillow and handfuls in the shower that wrapped around my fingers. While it wasn't painful in the conventional sense, it hurt on a deeper level. I loved my hair—pale brown with silvery-blonde strands. I always envisioned that, instead of being highlighted by the gold of the sun, it was kissed by the light of the moon. Eventually, it had to be cut off.

I am not going to lie—suicide crossed my mind. But that was the easy way out, and I deserved the punishment of living. I deserved to whither in misery and to watch the anguish I'd caused. I believe Dr. River suspected, but I never gave my thoughts a voice.

I confused every physician I saw. For a long time, I confused myself. And then I figured out how to cheat the system. Become a modern-day Robin Hood of sorts. Steal from the rich and give to the poor. Only in my case, I did bad things to bad people—those who did bad things to good people. A vigilante wielding wicked wishes. This way I could atone for my sins because I was right

I'd killed my father. I wished for him to die. And my whole family paid the price.

Chapter 6

The Musketcheers

By the end of the first week of school, I'd mastered the art of blending in. I did it so well most of the students forgot I even existed. My presence was a regular addition to the student body. Perhaps not welcome—but tolerated. The only group who had bothered being nice were the stoners. They invited me to hang out with them after class. They heard I was from Alaska where pot had always been legal, and they wanted to know all about it. I politely declined. They were barking up the wrong tree. I had a much more powerful drug at my disposal.

By the end of the school day, I was surprised to hear my name called from behind as I made my way down the dim hallway past the black lockers.

"Regan, wait up," Layne yelled over the noisy crowd.

All the students, previously content with ignoring me, now stared, ranging from shock to alarm, as the crowned prince of football jogged up behind me. The whispers began.

I backed up against the nearest locker, trying to hide, I suppose. As if the locker could save me.

He propped a hand well above my head and leaned in. I shrunk down. Tide laundry detergent and a nice cologne trickled to my nose. “Hey, so I have a game tonight, but if you are willing, can you come over tomorrow and help me with geometry? I’m lost already. I don’t want to fall behind,” he said in one quick breath. His eyes bugged out.

I froze. He reached out with his free hand and waved it in front of my face. I lifted my head from its upright and locked position.

“Please.” He grinned. The dimple in his chin, normally subtle, became more pronounced with his bigger smile.

“Ahh, yeah. Sure. Text me a time?” My gaze darted nervously from him to the students slowly walking by. Some were shaking their heads; others rolled their eyes.

“Great!” He popped his hand on the locker, clanging it loudly, startling me. Then he took off in the other direction. Halfway down the hall, he turned back and hollered for all to hear: “Hey, come to the game tonight. Miss Molly will be there.”

I didn’t answer. No way was I committing to that with everyone watching. The cheerleaders who I secretly nicknamed The Three Musketcheers—Gabby and her two skirted henchwomen, Olivia and Destiny—stood down the hallway. Students walking by gave them a wide berth.

The girl gang glared at me with their hands propped on their bare midriffs. They were allowed to wear their cheerleading uniforms all day on game days. Something about school spirit. Between classes, they walked the hallways and chanted, “We got spirit. Yes, we do! We got spirit! How ‘bout you?”

“What was that all about?” Jude’s head tilted toward Layne. He stepped in front of me, shielding me from the angry Three Musketcheers.

"Umm, he needs help with his homework . . ." I said as if it were a question.

"No, the whole inviting you to the game with his girlfriend right there. She's gonna be pissed."

I shrugged my shoulders and walked into the art room.

He followed. "She's not somebody you want to mess with," he said over my shoulder. His warm breath tickled the bare skin of my neck.

I snorted a laugh through my nose. Neither was I.

"That girl's all sorts of crazy. Like a certifiable psychopath."

I almost choked and started coughing.

He patted me on the back. "You okay?"

I nodded.

We both pulled our sketchbooks out of our bags and dropped them in the wire basket holder on Mr. Clark's desk. Jude snatched two clean aprons hanging from the wooden dowels on the brick wall. He held one out for me.

"Thanks." I scowled. He hadn't said a word to me since the first day. Which, of course, was only four days ago. Mostly, he'd watched me from afar. He seemed to vacillate between suspicion and confusion—both looked tinged with annoyance. At least that's how I interpreted his broody expressions. He didn't even bother to hide it when I caught him staring. He would simply smile like the cat that caught the canary. And I was the canary. All he was missing was the toothpick to pluck the feathers from between his perfect white teeth.

"I assume you're going to the other room to work on your painting?"

"I guess." I didn't have anything else to do.

I followed him to the expansive back room. Colorful easels sat stacked against the wall next to the cabinets full of art supplies. Old plywood doors hanging on rusty hinges creaked as I opened them. The football players had new uniforms, and the gymnasium had been remodeled in the last ten years, but the art room looked like it hadn't been touched since the sixties. Some things never change.

Paint thinner fumes burned my nose hairs. I fished out what was needed and set up a spot next to Jude.

We were the only two in the room. Apparently, we were the only ones who'd finished our homework.

He rolled up the long sleeves of his black-and-green checkered shirt over tightly-muscled forearms. He seemed very fond of wearing the same style every day: jeans and a tight-fitted T-shirt molded to his fit frame under a flannel and a pair of heavy dark boots.

"So, ya going to the game tonight?" He dipped his paintbrush into red paint, then orange, then a dab of black, and he mixed them all together, creating a deep vermilion. Bold strokes of color slashed over the canvas as he filled in the bare white background. He added a dash of black to his brush, then he layered depth on top of the brilliant red.

I stood back and stared at my mediocre painting. Snow-capped mountains beyond the ocean's edge. My skills were not equipped to capture Alaska's beauty.

An evil chuckle rumbled deep down in my throat. "I think I'll stay home. I don't really like football."

"Me either. Not anymore. But if you want to go, I'd go with you."

I turned my head slowly toward him with a look of

confusion and horror written on my face. "Why? So we can both be miserable?"

He didn't stop what he was doing. Only a slight twitch on his sculpted cheek let me know he'd even heard me.

A bundle of nerves worked their way to my stomach. I was puzzled. Did he just ask me out? Or was he simply being nice? Most of the time, he watched me like I was a thorn in his side. Though I couldn't figure out for the life of me why.

For forty-five minutes, we worked side by side without another word. He brushed the canvas with his right hand and used a pallet knife in his left. His strong dark fingers were so confident in their strokes. He pushed thick glops of paint one way, then pulled them the other. Instead of working on my project, I kept glancing at him out of the corner of my eye. I noticed his every move—how he shifted his hips when he stopped to think about the direction of his art, the narrow focus in his eyes, and then the slight nod of his head when he'd found what he'd been searching for.

Mr. Clark poked his head into the room and said, "Time to clean up. You have about ten minutes before the bell rings."

Wow. I hadn't accomplished anything other than staring at my painting. *Whatever.* So, what if I were staring mostly at Jude?

I walked over to the washbasin with the only brush I'd managed to use and placed it in a mason jar full of solvent.

"You got a lot done today," Jude said, heavy on the sarcasm. He slid up next to me, and his broad shoulders touched mine. A surge of pleasant electricity shot all the way to my feet. I wanted to move away, but I froze. The fine hairs on my face and neck reached toward him, like when you rub a balloon on your head and your hairs follow the static as you pull it away. The feeling pulsing through my body was almost as exhilarating as the one I got when I made people do bad things. *That* feeling was mostly under my control. *This . . . this* feeling was not.

And I didn't like things I couldn't control.

He tossed his brushes into the solvent and squirted a dash of soap in his hands. I finally leaned away. The tingle lessened but didn't completely stop. His energy buzzed around me even though I wasn't touching him.

"What? No black nail polish today?" I asked. His fingernails were bare.

"Eh, well, I saw ya looking earlier. I didn't want you to get the wrong impression."

"And what impression would that be?"

He laughed and flicked his head slightly. "That I might be gay."

"Oh, so that's what that means," I faked astonishment.

"And I'm not, by the way. Not that I care one way or another. But . . . well . . . just so you know."

I wasn't positive, but I thought I could see pink color his cheeks. It was kind of cute when he rambled. I was pretty sure those were the most words I'd heard him say in a row.

"So that's not eyeliner you are wearing either?"

"No," he said like I insulted him. He ran a wet finger over his lashes to prove he wasn't lying.

"Screw me," I muttered under my breath. Only guys ended up with eyelashes that thick.

He spread his hands out, and a fake wide-eyed

innocence unfolded on his face. “Well, if you’re offering.”

I glared at him. “Don’t be a smartass.”

He clamped down his grin, but it didn’t stop his chest from shaking with laughter.

I finished washing my brush, then dried my hands off on the towel hanging over the side of the industrial sink.

“Hey,” Jude said as I turned to go. He grabbed my hand before I could get far. The tingling increased, and my breathing became shallow. His hand was warm despite the cold water he’d used to clean the brushes.

“I meant it. I’ll pick you up at your house at six.” It wasn’t a question.

I snatched my hand away. Surprise and then hurt flashed across his face.

“Or not.” He turned his head slightly sideways and dropped his arm to his side.

“No. No.” I shook my head and stuttered. “Yes . . . I mean, yeah, whatever. That’s fine.” I shrugged.

“Okay? Sooo?” He drew out the short word. “Is that a yes or a no?” He was smiling. He already knew the answer.

“I’ll meet you there.” I walked out as confidently as I could with my shaking legs.

I kept my head down and dodged in and out of the people traffic to my locker. My insides rattled and jittered.

What just happened? I was trying to keep to myself. And in a single week, I’d been coerced into tutoring and going to a football game. A part of me wanted to be excited. But I didn’t deserve to be. I pulled my phone out of my pocket to text Jude but realized I didn’t have his number. Oh, well, he would eventually figure out he was going solo.

I stuffed my books into my backpack and slammed my locker shut. I rested my head on the cold metal and took a couple of deep breaths.

Someone rammed into my side and knocked me off my feet. My ankle buckled; pain shot up my leg, and I fell to the floor. At first, I assumed someone ran into me accidentally. A cacophony of giggles quickly changed my mind.

"Walk much?" one of the Musketcheers, Destiny, asked, sneering down at me. Her curly dark hair, piled in a messy bun on top of her head, wobbled precariously as she talked. "You." She pointed a sharpened white nail at me. "Stay away from Layne." Heavy black liner and thick, clumpy mascara marred the oily skin under her eyes.

The other one, Olivia—with brown hair, darker at the roots but white-blonde at the ends—stood silently with her arms crossed.

Other students completely ignored what was happening. They skated around us and looked the other way. Cowards.

I clenched my teeth and glared at her. I could easily make her do something humiliating. A coiling black smoke of ideas floated in my head. But I wouldn't. I tried not to use my gift to avenge myself, especially if I was angry. It wasn't worth it. I swore only to protect people who didn't deserve to be tormented. Though, occasionally I did use my powers when people irritated me. But only harmless pranks—nothing catastrophic. Otherwise I had trouble controlling the golem. Sometimes the monster needed a snack.

I wiped the nasty expression from my face, pushed myself up from the dirty floor, and dusted off my jeans. I ignored her threats and walked away.

Only to find, in the parking lot, my truck with a note scratched on the side of the red paint. *Slut*.

Great.

I used my car key and scratched over the word *Slut* so now it read *Stop*. That would have to do until I could get it fixed.

Chapter 7

Confessions

On the narrow dirt road leading home, I had to pull over and wait for a black SUV to drive past. I waved at the two men in the front seat both wearing dark sunglasses. They didn't wave back. That was strange; in Wyoming, everyone waved. I watched them in my rear-view mirror as they sped down the wash boarded road. Dust billowed in the air behind them. *Rude*.

A few minutes later, I pulled into the driveway and gave the haze a minute to settle before getting out. I opened the front door to find my mom nestled in a mound of blankets in front of the TV. Glassy round eyes, greasy blonde hair plastered to her scalp, and a tiny red nose made her look like an ugly baby bird—naked and vulnerable. She held a glass of water in her hand, though I suspected it was Vodka based on the empty bottle sitting on the kitchen counter. A pile of used tissues sat scattered on the coffee table and in her lap. Sitting on the couch next to her, in its see-through bag, was my dad's military flag.

I swallowed the knot forming in my throat as I stood there and stared at her. Today was their twenty-sixth wedding anniversary. I knew the exact number because last year was their silver anniversary, a big deal and rightly so. Being married for that long is an accomplishment for sure.

I closed my eyes and remember my dad getting down on one knee and handing her a small box wrapped in glittery paper with a matching bow. When she opened it, her chin began to tremble. Inside, was a huge Yogo sapphire the exact color of her eyes. It was set in platinum but my dad insisted it looked silver, so it counted.

My dad said, "Sara, love of my life, I'd do it all over again." The adoration shining in his eyes was something straight out of a fairytale.

Her trembling chin grew into one of her famous smiles—the kind that lights up the universe—and she handed my dad a tequila bottle, a salt shaker, and a lime. He wore a goofy smile and cocked his head like he wasn't sure what was going on. Then, with flourish, she pulled two plane tickets from her back pocket. They both busted out laughing. Me, Linc, and Kennedy exchanged exasperated glances. Sometimes our parents behaved like teenagers. Finally, my mom handed Kennedy a wad of cash, because he was the responsible one, and told us to go get lost for a few hours.

Only a short time ago, she'd been a beautiful and vivacious woman. But, if I were being honest, she was never strong. That's where my dad came in. He was the brawn; she was the beauty. She needed him, and he needed to be needed. Now she'd been reduced to this. And it was my fault.

A bout of sympathy flooded over me. "Hi, Momma," I said softly. She tried to smile, but her lips quivered then fell. Red inflamed tracks from acidic tears lined down her tight, shiny skin.

"Was someone here?" I asked.

She nodded without looking at me.

"Who?"

"The cable people. They hooked up our new high-speed internet." She pointed towards the new router next to the television.

Though getting a high-speed connection was exciting, dial-up was archaic, I hadn't noticed a logo on the vehicle that had passed me. "Huh. Did they leave a company card?"

"On the counter," she said.

"Have you eaten today?" I said, noticing an untouched sandwich next to the business card.

"Grandma brought me food." She stared at the TV. Some reality show rerun.

"Yeah, but you didn't eat it?" I petted her hair.

She flinched. I pulled my hand away as if I'd been burned. Our relationship was rocky before my dad died, but it was never like this. Before we just argued, rolled our eyes at one another, and occasionally slammed doors. The usual Mom-and-daughter rigmarole. Now she could hardly look at me. It was painful.

I pleaded with her. "Momma, you gotta eat."

I barely caught her answer. "Why?" she squeaked.

My head drooped. I tossed my jacket on the coat rack next to the front door. I didn't know how to fix her. I couldn't even fix myself. It wasn't that I didn't feel the guilt. It ate away at my stomach constantly. It burned like fire. The doctors said it was acid reflux from stress. That I shouldn't eat certain foods: caffeine, chocolate, and citrus. I did it anyway.

I opened the fridge and sliced some cheese, then grabbed an apple and a soda. Dinner. I should've sat on the couch and at least tried visiting with her, but after my day, I couldn't do it. I slunk to my room.

I tossed my bra haphazardly on my dresser, and then I slid a tank top over my head and stepped into fuzzy fleece pajama bottoms with dancing penguins on them. I pulled on my *Go Army* sweatshirt, a gift from Lincoln. My dad and Kennedy hated it because they were both in the Air Force. I was surprised when Linc joined the Army and not the Air Force with Kennedy. They were unusually close even for twins. They always bragged they were ordinary on their own but invincible together.

Now, after everything I'd been through, I wondered if they really meant that. But they returned to the service the day after I'd been released from the mental institute, and I never had a chance to ask. Besides, how was one supposed to approach the subject? Would they even believe me? Or would they think I was actually crazy? Trying my powers on them occurred to me, but the last time I'd done that on a family member. . .

I shook my head, trying to erase that horrifying memory. I sat down on my bed and opened my laptop to commence with my wild Friday night ritual. I liked to watch hair and makeup tutorials—not that I utilized what I learned. When that got boring, I switched to a television series—usually something about murder—or a good book. Anything to keep my mind occupied.

A quick knock rattled my door. "Yeah? Come in." I expected my mom.

Tall, dark, and handsome leaned against the frame of my bedroom door. Not in a million years did I expect Jude.

"What are *you* doing here?" I slapped my screen shut.

"I figured you'd stand me up. Looks like I was right." His eyes traveled from my hoodie to my penguin bottoms. Then to my lacy red bra on my dresser. He raised a sharp eyebrow and tried to hide the smirk. He was wearing dark jeans, a black coat, combat boots, and a black beanie. While he was steaming hot, he looked like he was here to rob the place. He tucked his hands in his pockets.

"I was going to text you, but I didn't have your number." I laid my palms flat over the smooth surface of my computer.

"Yes, you do," he said.

"What?"

He stepped in, shut the door behind him, and grabbed my phone off the quilted bedspread. His presence dominated my cozy little room; he filled the space with a vibration of sorts. It hummed low and warmed my exposed skin. His energy felt strong, though I wasn't sure if it was negative or positive; all I knew was it intimidated me, even if I didn't want to admit it. I got the eerie feeling he could see the real me—the darkness I locked away in my glass box. I didn't appreciate it.

He typed in my passcode, the one I didn't give him, and he brought up his number. "I programmed it under 'Hottest Guy in School.'"

I kept my expression neutral. "Oh, sorry, I thought that was Layne's number." Ha, ha. I didn't even know it was there.

"Ouch." He clasped his heart. "Well, get dressed anyway. I'll wait." He reached for the doorknob.

"Stop," I said shortly. "Stay in here. Just don't turn around."

"O—kay?" He drew out the two syllables.

I didn't want to go to the game. But I didn't want him out there with my mom. The state she was in embarrassed me. I shimmied out of my tank top and contorted myself into my bra while still wearing my sweatshirt. I slipped on the same jeans I wore to school.

"All right," I said.

Jude turned back around. His eyes moved from my shoes to my baggy sweatshirt. "No need to dress up for me."

I snarled and motioned for him to go out.

When he smiled, it softened the hard edges of his face. Made him most approachable.

"Mrs. Braaten, what time should I have Regan home?" He stopped next to our couch: his eyes darted to the American flag sitting beside her.

She lifted her bony shoulder wrapped in a tattered wool blanket, Air Force issued, without looking up from the TV.

"Come on." I clasped him by the arm with one hand and yanked him outside.

He opened the door of his older pickup, and I scrambled in. The inside was in pristine condition and smelled sexy: masculine, like coming in from the outdoors on a cold winter night into a warm library with leather furniture and a roaring fire.

With those dark, mysterious eyes, high cheekbones, and shapely lips, he could easily be a model. I could see him standing next to a horse with an old saddle hanging from his hand, advertising whatever cologne he was wearing.

A chilly breeze swept inside the cab after he climbed in, giving me another whiff of his yumminess. He shifted the manual transmission into reverse, looked over his shoulder, and backed out of the driveway. Impressive. Not many of us can drive a stick shift. My dad insisted that my brothers and I learn on one. Initially, I'd been cranky about it. Now, not so much. I cherished every memory of him, even though I seldom let them roam free in my mind.

I stared out the window as he drove down our long dirt road. The evening sun, setting behind the mountains, surrounded the jagged peaks in an amber glow. Sometime during the week, a small amount of snow accumulated at the higher elevations.

"Your mom all right?" he asked.

"Eh," I said without further explanation. I didn't want to get into it for fear that I would get emotional. We rode in a comfortable, uncomfortable silence the rest of the way. He seemed comfortable. I was nervous, trying to pretend I wasn't.

He maneuvered his truck into the school parking lot between a sports car and a fancy jacked-up off-road vehicle that looked as if it had never seen a real dirt road.

He rushed to the passenger side of the truck and opened my door before I had time to unlock my seat belt. I muttered, "Thanks," but didn't really mean it.

He picked up on my sarcasm and pushed my head away good-naturedly with his hand. We crunched over the gravel toward the blinding lights of the football field.

When Miss Molly saw us walking up the metal bleachers, she waved madly. The fluffy top nob on her aqua hat bobbed frantically. A hand-knitted scarf fading from one pastel to the next hung over her black puffer jacket.

I scooted in next to her.

The smell of hot dogs, nachos, and popcorn mixed

with freshly cut grass and decaying autumn leaves.

"Jude." She smiled tightly, leaning forward to look around me. "It's nice to see you out," she said.

His jaw clenched, hollowing out his already prominent cheekbones. "Thanks, Molly."

My eyes darted between the two. What was that all about?

"I'm so excited to see you here." She squeezed my arm. "Layne said you were coming, but I wasn't sure. I distinctly remember you saying you didn't like football."

"I don't."

"So, you came to root for Layne then." She pulled me in for a side hug.

"I don't know why I'm here." I tossed Jude a dirty look, which he ignored, though I knew he heard me.

The loudspeakers blared from above, introducing the starting lineup. First—Layne Prescott: 6'5", senior, quarterback. The crowd roared. The cheerleaders shook their pompoms and kicked their legs high over their heads. Miss Molly hollered. Jude and I clapped politely, my mittens making no noise whatsoever.

Layne ran to the center of the field, holding his black helmet in his hand. The bright stadium lights shone on his gold hair making it appear as if he was wearing a halo. Subsequently, the rest of his teammates joined him, fist-bumping each other on their way.

Jude scooted closer to me, his arm touching mine, as more and more people crowded into the stands. I was grateful for his added heat, even though his proximity made me feel like tiny bubbles of carbonation were shivering in my blood.

Right before halftime, Jude asked, "Ya wanna get some hot chocolate? You're cold."

I nodded. I was cold and utterly bored. It was more entertaining watching Miss Molly. "Go, go, go, go," she would yell in rapid succession, rising halfway out of her stadium chair. She clapped and jumped up and down when Layne threw a pass. Even though Layne was a talented quarterback, it hadn't stopped them from falling behind. It was 14-7 so far.

I shook her, trying to get her attention. "Hey, we're going to get some cocoa. Do you want any?"

"No, thanks. I'd just spill it anyway." Her cheeks and the tip of her nose were pink.

Good point. As much as she was jostling around, she was bound to spill it on someone, probably me.

Jude held out his gloved hand. I hesitated before taking it. When we got to the bottom of the stairs, I dropped his hand.

The line in front of the concessions was already long. I ordered coffee and a package of hot chocolate—punishment for enjoying myself. I was sure to get a bout of heartburn from the combination. And I was kind of enjoying myself, even if I didn't want to admit it. Being with Jude made me feel like a normal high school girl at a normal high school football game.

People, all familiar with one another, visited together, laughing and slapping backs until they noticed us. The women pursed their lips and looked away. Some of the men puffed up like fighting cocks. They tightened their shoulders and inflated their chests before they cast Jude hard, unforgiving looks.

"You ready to go back up?" he asked. Sorrow or something similar flashed behind his eyes.

"Not really." I clutched my coffee in my freezing hands.

"Come on. We'll sit in my truck for a minute." He hit the auto-start button on his key ring. "Maybe get you warm." He didn't hold out a hand, and I wasn't sure if I was relieved or disappointed.

I crawled into his pickup after he kindly opened the door for me again. The heater blew on my face and brought the circulation back to my extremities.

"So, what's the deal between you and Miss Molly? That greeting was kind of tense." I didn't mention the scathing reception from the rest of the crowd.

He gripped his steering wheel and tapped it with his thumbs. A glittering black arrowhead, different than the one he wore around his neck, hung on a silver chain from his rearview mirror. It swayed gently. "It's nothing between the two of us. But you don't know, do you?"

"Know what?"

He exhaled heavily. "I guess I better tell you before someone else does." He waited a long minute before he started. "When Gabby moved here, we dated. Then I broke up with her. Let's just say that didn't go over well. She spread some pretty harsh rumors about my family."

My hackles rose. I turned toward him. "What did she say?"

"That my father made advances toward her. Nothing serious. Just comments that creeped her out and made her uncomfortable."

"Were they true?" I laid my mittens and my hat over the defrost vent to warm them up.

He shrugged a shoulder but didn't deny it. "She was convincing enough that my mom kicked him out and filed for divorce. I think she'd been waiting for a reason for a long time."

"Wow. That's awful. I am so sorry."

His hands tightened on the wheel, his knuckles whitening under the glowing street lights. “Gabby said I broke up with her because she wouldn’t sleep with me. Then she accused me of sexual assault.” His voice cracked. He stared out the front windshield between the chips in the glass.

I sat forward. “Seriously?” At first, my nerve endings flared with fear. Here I was alone with a guy twice my size who showed up at my house uninvited. Then silently, I scoffed. The only dangerous person in this truck was me.

“Yup.” He pressed his lips together and nodded. “I was hauled to the police station and questioned for hours. Thankfully, her story was so specific she got caught up in her own lies. The dates she gave coincided with her summer trip to Europe.” He paused, then whispered agitatedly, “She wasn’t even in the country. She didn’t press charges, but the damage was done.” He folded his fingers together and rested his chin in his thumbs.

“So, her accusations are bogus?” I needed to hear him say it a loud so I could see the truth on his face.

He turned his head slowly. A heavy burden sat behind those black eyes. I knew what that was like. The sorrow inside them broke my already mangled heart. I pinched my lips together. His pain was almost palpable, like a thick fog settling inside the cab of the truck.

“I would never, *never* do that. She was mad because I’d broken up with her. She said I’d be sorry. She said I would pay.”

“So, everyone believed her?” I didn’t understand the students’ fascination with Gabby. So what if her parents were rich? Half of the families here were dripping in wealth. She wasn’t the smartest girl or the nicest. And she certainly wasn't the most beautiful girl in school. She made the most of what she had and what money could buy, but her two minions were prettier.

"Not everyone believed her accusations, but enough did. And those that didn't are too scared to say anything," Jude said.

The unfairness of it all needled me. Who did Gabby think she was? The golem perked up inside its box as if it were raising a tiny eyebrow in interest.

"So, if you don't want me to drive you home because you don't feel comfortable with me, I'm sure Molly would give you a lift. Honestly, I assumed you knew already."

I shook my head.

"I thought that's why you stood me up. But I wanted to be able to explain my side to you in person. Sorry about that by the way. Just showing up at your house unannounced. I didn't want to go the whole weekend without telling you." He twisted open the cap on his water bottle and took a swig. The plastic crinkled under his grip.

"First of all, I believe you. It surprises me how everyone else thinks she is such a do-gooder."

He set his water bottle in the console and shrugged. "She's pretty. She has money. She's nice to the right people. Her posse does her dirty work in the spotlight, conveniently keeping her hands clean. She works behind the scenes. Gossip and lies are powerful weapons." He cracked his knuckles one at a time.

"Plus, as if that wasn't enough, her parents own a lot of businesses in town. People are afraid if they're nice to my family, or they step out of line they'll lose their jobs. My mom did. They waited a couple of months before they canned her so it didn't look like they were firing her because of what happened."

"Well, they don't scare me." I slapped him lightly on the arm; his coat thumped under my hand. I didn't need my job. But what about all the other people in town? Not everyone who lived here was wealthy.

"Well, they should. They scare everyone else. Her mom is the President of the PTA, her dad is on the school board, and I'm pretty sure a couple of the judges are firmly in the LaCroix's pocket. The only reason I wasn't brought up on charges was because our Sherriff is a fifth generation local and his department's not for sale. At least not yet."

I hadn't realized how much power the LaCroix's wielded over this small town. But my dad always said, "Perception is reality." And Gabby thought she was royalty. I could tell by the way she walked in a room with her head held high and her nose turned down on her subjects. It was like she wore an invisible crown. Only now was I finally beginning to understand—her crown was built on a mountain of money, fueled by lies, and bought with people's fear.

But I could fight back without ever being caught. "Don't worry, I'm far more dangerous than Gabby is."

He chuckled under his breath and ran his fingers through his shiny dark hair. "I don't doubt it. But why do ya say that?" The look on his face said he was just humoring me.

I shook my head fiercely and clenched my teeth.

A sad smile lifted the corner of his lips.

"Because I killed my father."

It spilled off my tongue without my permission. It burst forth like a dam breaking apart under pressure. I think I'd held on to my sin so tightly it sprang free the moment it felt a crack in my shell.

Shock, curiosity, and then sympathy fleeted in his eyes. "How?"

I cupped my face in my hands. "You wouldn't believe me if I told you."

He laid a hot finger under my ice-cold chin and swiveled my head toward him. He brushed my bangs away from my forehead. "Try me."

I crawled up on my knees and held on to the console, and concentrated on what I wanted him to do. Even though I would pay for it dearly later. It'd been so long since anyone had touched me. Really touched me. My mother avoided me; my brothers were gone; my dad was dead. And my grandparents, while they loved me, were conservative with their affection.

I swallowed. Although his actions wouldn't be his, I allowed myself this moment of make-believe. Tingles spread from my chest to my fingers to the tips of my toes.

I wish. I wish for you to lean in and kiss me. Thread your beautiful fingers behind my head. Pull me to you. Kiss me. I wish for you to kiss me like you mean it.

And he did.

His fingers molded to the back of my head and he drew me in tight. His mouth burned on my chilly lips. He tasted of hot chocolate and mint. Heat pulsed inside my body, and all of my wishes came true. The ever-present humming and buzzing in the cab of the truck increased. I gave up and stopped trying to control its hold on me. I let the feeling wash over like waves caressing the shore. Deep vibrations touched the innermost parts of my body and soul. The endorphins, which accompanied my normal wishes, didn't come close to the high traveling through my every nerve.

Too soon, he stopped.

Before he sat back completely, he brushed my long bangs from my eyes. His fingers left a residue of the twinkling sensation.

I plopped down in the bucket seat. "See?" My voice quivered.

"See what?" He sounded confused and out of breath.

"I made you do that," I whispered.

"Made. Me. Do. What?" Every word was a sentence of its own.

I twisted my head sideways, not losing contact with the headrest. I was pretty sure it was the only thing keeping my head on my shoulders. "Seriously? I made you kiss me."

He laughed. His whole face flushed with humor. His eyes crinkled and all but disappeared.

I put my hand on the door handle.

"No, no. Please. Wait." He caught his breath and pinched the sleeve of my down coat between his fingers.

I bit the side of my cheek, waiting.

He grabbed my arm and hauled me closer like I weighed nothing. Then he gently cupped my cheek with his warm hand and forced me to look at him. "You didn't make me kiss you." His deep voice was still shaking with laughter. "I've wanted to do that since the first time I talked to you. Ya know? When you left your phone with Mrs. Glasgow all day. What kind of girl does that? And not one selfie to be had. Then, to top it off, you like to fish." All the humor vanished from his voice. "Against my better judgement, I've wanted to kiss you since day one."

"Oh." My face caught flame as embarrassment

heated me from the inside out. I wasn't sure what he meant by *against his better judgement* but I brushed the comment aside and said, "Well, let me try something different. You aren't going to like it though."

He tilted his head, like I was lying.

I concentrated, waiting for the invisible blanket of pleasure to coat my skin. It calmed me; it made me feel as if I were floating on a cloud. All my worries and guilt vanished as my powers leached into my veins. I used to compare it to a lover's touch. I was mistaken. Jude's touch made me feel awake, alive, and reckless. There was nothing calm or safe about it.

I gazed out the window at the darkened sky. My fingers and toes were already tingling.

I wish. I wish for you to slap me. Raise your hand with an open palm and smack my face. Make it hurt.

I turned. Nothing happened. I tried harder until the blanket of pleasure turned into the pain of tiny needles poking at my skin.

He held his hand up and shook his head. The glow of the overhead street lights was mirrored in his black eyes.

"Huh," I said. I chewed on my lower lip. It didn't work. My face morphed from concentration to confusion. Even the normal euphoria from my wicked wishes didn't come.

"I can take you home now if you want me to?"

"Absolutely not. Come on." I opened the door and jumped down. He didn't move. "I'm going to show you I'm not lying."

"I believe you. You don't have to prove anything to me."

"Yes, I do," I insisted. "You're the only person I've told. I need someone to know."

Chapter 8

Trippin'

We headed back to the game and scooted in next to Miss Molly. She'd saved our seats. "You were gone an awful long time," she said like it was an accusation.

"I was cold. Jude was so kind as to warm up his truck before I froze to death."

"You're from Alaska. You're not supposed to get cold." Her words verged on snotty.

"Sure, that's how it works," I said dryly as I sat down. Sometimes it was colder here.

Jude wrapped his arm around my shoulder and pulled me close.

Her nostrils flared. "Does your mother know you're here?" What she really meant was: Does your mother know who he is? What he has done?

"Of course, she does. Jude picked me up. Introduced himself and everything."

Miss Molly stiffened.

I stood up not needing a lecture about who I chose to hang out with.

"Where are you going now? You've missed half the game already."

"I have to pee," I snapped.

She huffed.

"Come on." I held my hand out this time. People mumbled and grumbled as we passed by again.

Jude waited outside the restroom. I zipped up my pants and flushed the toilet with my foot.

The squeaking of tennis shoes over the bathroom floor halted before someone hissed, "What were you thinking?" I recognized the voice coming from outside the stall. Olivia. One of Gabby's goons. A sharp smack of a hand slapping a face echoed on the tiled walls.

A cry pierced the air. "I'm sorry. I'm so sorry," a high-pitched, hysterical voice answered. Feet scuttled backward.

"You little freshman skank. Think you're hot shit because you made varsity? Well, let me tell you what, little girl: You're nothing. If you ever pull a stunt like that again, you'll pay. I'll make sure you never cheer again. Got it?"

"Yes . . . yes . . . Tell Gabby I'm sorry."

"Her name is Gabriella. And don't bother coming back out on the field. Go home."

"But . . . but . . . Coach Carlson will bench me," the muffled voice quaked.

A slamming stall door made me jump.

"Take your pick. It's her or me." Another slam. More sobs.

I waited a minute and peeked my head out of the stall. A tiny blonde girl crouched in the corner. She buried her face in her hands, and her chest shook.

"Hey."

Her head popped up. Fear then relief flashed in her eyes. I wasn't the person she was scared of.

"You okay?" I quickly washed my hands.

She cried harder.

I leaned down in front of her. "Hey, really, are you okay?" I pried her fingers from her face.

Doe brown eyes met mine. Red tear streaks, an imprint of a hand and black mascara stained her fake-tanned skin.

She nodded. "Come on, stand up." I tucked a chunk of hair behind a slightly protruding ear.

I ran some paper towels under the faucet and handed them to her.

"What the heck did you do to make her so mad?"

Her chest heaved a few times before she spoke. "I did more backflips than I was supposed to." She pressed the cold cloth over her eyes. When she pulled it away, tiny impressions of black eyelashes stayed behind. That—paired with her rosy cheeks, large eyes, and Cupid's bow lips—made her look like a sad, broken doll.

"What do you mean?"

"Gabby only wants me to do one since she can't do any." She rolled her shoulders forward as if she were trying to make herself smaller than she already was. She shivered from cold or fear, I wasn't sure.

"They're that mad at you because you did an extra flip on the field at half-time?" I said.

"Uh-huh." She sniffed and wiped her nose with the wet paper towel.

"Wow." I emphasized the word by puckering my lips. "The Three Musketcheers are real bitches."

The corners of her lips quivered. "I have to go home before they get done."

The perfect plan formed inside my brain. "You know what? I think you should stay for a while."

Her skin paled.

"No, really. Go get a coat and then stay hidden under

the bleachers, out of sight. I'm telling you. You're gonna want to see this," I said as I tossed the wadded-up paper towel in the garbage on my way out. I had work to do.

"What took you so long? I was about ready to come get you." Jude held out an elbow for me to hook my arm through.

Visions of mayhem warmed my blackened soul. A sly smile curled on my lips. "You'll see."

Back on the bleachers, the team called a time-out, and the cheerleaders took a break. Tingles flowed from my chest to my fingers to the tips of my toes.

I wish.

I concentrated on Olivia.

I wish for you to pick up the sports drink bottle. Unscrew the cap. Set it aside. Get Gabby's attention. I wish you would call her a whore. A bitch. A slut. Now throw the drink in her face.

I sat back and let the audience enjoy the show while I enjoyed my high.

The crowd gasped. Then conversations buzzed. (As did I.) Gabby stood dumbfounded, red liquid dripping down her face onto her white uniform. A real horror movie sort of moment. I was quite proud.

Jude turned to me. I smiled my most wicked grin. It helped that my canine teeth were more pointed than straight. Amazement and something darker, heavier—something that made my pulse race even harder—intensified behind his eyes. The kiss from earlier played in my mind like an old-fashioned movie reel. I had to look away.

Once Gabby regained composure, she stomped over to her friend and shoved her down onto the green turf.

Rage contorted Olivia's face. She sprung from the

ground faster than a cat. She balled up her fist, and then she slammed it into Gabby's nose. Soon they were rolling on the ground, pulling hair, and throwing punches. Grass, dirt, a red sports drink, and blood stained their uniforms.

He lifted the corner of my hat and whispered in my ear, "So, you did that?"

I squeezed my fists to keep from visibly shivering. The texture of his breath on my skin was like bathing in water a few degrees too hot. At first you think it hurts, but the more you immerse yourself, the better it feels. "Yup."

"Awesome! Can you do something else?" The darkness behind his eyes faded, replaced by a level of excitement that made my toes curl.

"Sure, but I have to do something bad. Otherwise, I'll get sick."

"Really?" He sounded concerned.

"I'll tell you about it later," I dismissed with a wave of my hand. "Pick someone from the other team that's a real jerk."

"The quarterback. Number 7. He's a piece of work. Uses women and throws them away. They're just a notch on his belt."

"How do you know?"

"Because I used to play football. Boys brag. Remember?"

A plan began to hatch.

"Okay. Now, on our team, who deserves a break?" So long as I created chaos, mischief, and mayhem, no harm would come to me, even if something positive were the end result.

"Kaden, number 26. He could use a break."

Oh, he was going to make me work for this. Kaden was on the bench, and as far as I knew, he hadn't played once.

I finished forming my three-part plan. I lifted the corner of my glass box. Tingles spread from my chest to my fingers to the tips of my toes.

Step one.

I wish. Coach Glasgow, take a time out. Do it now. Replace 24 with 26.

He resisted. Interesting. I concentrated harder. Coach surrendered. They always did.

Kaden strapped on his helmet and then all 5'5" of him ran onto the field. The crowd hushed. Layne looked to the coach, nodded once, welcomed Kaden into the fold, and patted him on the back.

Step two.

Once the ball was snapped to the opposing quarterback, number 7, I focused.

I wish. Throw the ball to Kaden, number 26. Yes, I want you to throw the ball to the wrong team. Send the pass. Straight and sure.

The football left his hand in slow motion and spiraled into the sky.

Now I concentrated quickly on Kaden.

Step three.

I wish.

He stopped running and turned just in time for the ball to smack him in his tiny chest. It almost knocked him flat on his skinny behind.

I wish. Grab it. Catch it. Hold it.

I wished in a panicked, rapid succession. He caught it—interception.

The crowd exploded and rose from their seats. The

stands quaked under their stomping and clapping. Whooping and hollering rang in my ears.

I wish. Run. Run. Run.

"Run!" Jude yelled next to me sounding half-serious, half-joking.

Kaden's scrawny chicken legs, even smaller because of all the padding he wore, pumped like firing pistons. Huge angry players bore down on him. But he was going to have to do the rest of the work on his own. I was trippin'.

His teammates from the sidelines followed him down the field, pumping their fists. The cheerleaders, minus Gabby and Olivia and the girl hiding under the bleachers, shook their pompoms.

My head swam in euphoria. Lights twinkled and formed kaleidoscopes on the outer edges of my vision. A drunken smile lifted my lips. My fingertips and toes tingled. All my worries disappeared only to be replaced by the vast emptiness of a guilt-free existence. That was the most dangerous part of my gift. It allowed me to escape the horror of being me. A whole new persona formed. One who thought she was a god. One who, for a moment in time, knew she was a step up on the evolutionary chain.

"Wow," Jude said. A whole new level of respect dawned on his face. At least I think it did. I was busy studying his lovely mouth. The one that kissed me soundly earlier. My eyelids drooped and blinked slowly. I wanted him to do it again. I pulled off my gloves and ran my finger over the sensuous curve of his bottom lip. A shock sparked up my arm. I trembled and stopped breathing.

Jude's eyes narrowed then opened wider in

amusement. “I think we better get you home,” Jude said.

I laughed. My body was numb, but it tingled at the same time. We scooted out of the wild crowd. He pretty much supported my weight.

I winked at the petite cheerleader watching from under the stands. Her hand hid a giant grin.

In the parking lot, Jude picked me up and twirled me around. My legs free floated behind me. I threw my head back and opened my eyes. The cold air stung my cheeks, and tears pooled in my lower lids. The stars above me flashed by, a years’ rotation in a short moment of time. It seemed longer. My weightless body rode the wind until the spinning stopped.

He put me down, and I stumbled. High and dizzy didn’t mix. He caught me and scooped me into his strong arms and carried me the rest of the way. He opened the door and, one-handed, set me on the seat of his pickup. I snaked my arm around him before he could escape. Our eyes connected. My walls were down. The intensity in his gaze charged the air, creating almost a haze, a blurry fog.

I’d kissed boys before. But this frenzy of electricity between us was new to me. A kicker to my already intense high. I wondered if it were because I couldn’t control him. Like my powers didn’t dampen his will or his wants. And I couldn’t change them.

He pushed the cap off my head and tangled his fingers through the back of my short hair. His hand easily palmed my skull. He firmly pulled me in. His lips seared. His tongue twisted around mine. He unknotted my scarf and slid it off my neck. The hairs on the back of my head rose. I wrapped my legs around his body and brought him closer to me. He groaned in the back of his throat.

His lips dipped down to my chin and then went over my neck to the opening of my coat. I tilted my head back for better access. I gripped his shoulders. Blood pounded in my head and between my legs. I reached up and started to unzip my coat.

"No, no, no," he said as he laid a hand over mine. He inhaled deeply and pulled away from me. "We are not going there tonight."

I threw my head back and laughed and laughed. The sound of joy raced over the wind. If I could have controlled him, I might have made him finish what he'd started. Okay, not tonight then.

"That was awesome." Jude pounded on the steering wheel after he hopped back into the truck. "So, you really did that?"

"Yep. Me and my wicked wishes."

He turned on the headlights and rolled out of the parking lot. "It looks like you may have broken up the G.O.D. squad. Gabby will never forgive Olivia."

"Seriously, they call themselves 'the G.O.D. squad'?" I giggled. *Yes. Giggled.*

"Yup. Gabriella, Olivia and Destiny."

"Puke. We could call them the dog squad, but I like dogs." My words were slow but animated.

"And Kaden made the winning touchdown. I know you did that one. He sometimes gets to play on the JV squad but never varsity. He gets to sit with them because of who his father is. But his dad's a dick. Treats his kid like garbage. Kaden takes after his mom. Small and dainty. Not anything like his father."

My phone dinged.

"That your mom?"

"No, don't be silly. My mom doesn't concern

herself with me. It's Miss Molly reminding me I have to help Layne with his math homework in the morning."

I could have sworn he rolled his eyes before he said, "So, what did you mean earlier when you said you had to do something bad or you would get sick?"

I told him things I'd never spoken out loud. Perhaps I confessed because my guard was down or perhaps because I needed to tell someone.

"This spring I accidentally killed my father with my powers. I . . . I didn't know at the time," I stuttered, "that I even had powers." I swallowed hard. "I got mad. Told him I hated him. Then wished he would walk in front of the oncoming bus and die." My voice cracked and I whispered, "I didn't mean it. Every day I wish I could take it back. Every day I wish it had been me."

Jude reached over and squeezed my hand. His lack of repulsion gave me the courage to continue. "Right after the accident, I was admitted to a psych ward. That's where I learned what I was capable of. And what my limitations were. If I use my powers for bad, I get—well, there's no other way I can describe it—but it's like I get high. But it's more than that. I feel invincible. Untouchable. It's amazing. But if I use my powers for good, I get sick. Sometimes really sick. I'm afraid that if I do something really good, I'll die. And if I don't use them, I start to go crazy. Coo, coo," I said like the bird inside the clock. I was trying to make a joke, probably bad timing.

He didn't say anything so I continued. "So, I kind of found a loophole. I use my powers on people who are bad. That way they get what they deserve and I don't get sick or go crazy."

He let go of my hand and cupped my cheek. "Regan

Braaten, you're a good person."

My heart swelled. I wanted to believe him. He knew everything, and he didn't look at me like I was a monster. Quite the opposite really. I allowed myself to believe, maybe, if I tried really hard, I could be the hero, not the villain.

Chapter 9

Advice

I parked next to the curb in front of Miss Molly's cottage. Layne's ancient beater of a car sat in the cracked driveway next to an empty spot pockmarked with old oil stains. Crunchy brown leaves tumbled over the tired-looking cement.

Even a house as dated and tiny as this went for well over half a million dollars in this remote little town.

Plant boxes filled with dead, wilted flowers were lined under the peeling white window frames. Slate blue siding, faded to gray where the sun hit the hardest, matched the dismal sky above.

I made my way cautiously over the walkway leading to the house, careful not to trip over the tree roots pushing through the cement. I hopped up the crumbling steps and opened the screen door. I knocked three times on the hollow wood.

Layne answered the door wearing nothing but slippers and sweats hanging low on his hips. His smooth, wide chest led to an impressive six-pack. Hard v-shaped muscles dipped below the elastic waistband of his pants. His phone, pressed against his ear, did nothing to stop Gabby's shrill voice from echoing through the small living room. He nodded for me to come in. His hair stood up in weird cowlicks all over his head. He covered the mouthpiece. "I'll be done in a minute."

A cream candle with black smoke twirling from the wick embraced the house in its warm vanilla scent. I set my purse on the coffee table, sat down on the sagging red couch, and waited. A line of pictures, youngest Layne to oldest, hung crooked on the living room walls. I got up and straightened them. From bad haircuts to missing front teeth, he'd always managed to be cute. But the last one, probably from last summer, stopped my breath. He stood in front of the mountains, shirtless, holding a football high over his head. The warm afternoon rays gilded his hair and glistened off his golden skin. The sun, though soft and bright, was nowhere near as blinding as his smile or his impossibly blue, blue eyes. Happiness oozed from the photo.

"So, we going to do this or what?" I asked Layne after about fifteen minutes. I made myself at home on the kitchen table amongst the scattered papers and textbooks.

He held up a finger and covered the mouthpiece. "Give me a minute. Gabby's really upset."

"Oh, poor baby," I muttered under my breath.

Layne threw me a dirty look and whispered, "Be nice."

I didn't mean for him to hear me. But I thought, *Seriously? You're dating the ultimate mean girl, and you tell* me *to be nice?*

He finally hung up the phone and grabbed a couple of energy drinks out of the fridge and set one on the table in front of me. He yanked the T-shirt hanging on the back of the kitchen chair and slipped it over his head before he sat down. "She's not as bad as she seems. And she certainly didn't deserve what happened to her last night. She and Olivia have been friends for a long time."

I mentally rolled my eyes. "Ready?" I tapped the math book.

His phone dinged. He read the text and then typed something furiously with his long, broad fingers.

I bit my tongue. I grabbed his geometry textbook and fished my calculator out of my purse.

"Okay, so here's the deal. First . . ."

His phone dinged multiple times. He snatched it up and went back to ignoring me.

I slid the textbook away and threw my hands into the air. "Whatever." I pushed out from the table, chair legs scraping angrily on the battered wood floor, and stood up.

He followed. The 1970s popcorn ceiling wasn't very far from the top of his head. "Wait. Don't leave." The panic in his eyes made me pause. "Just give me a few minutes to calm Gabby down. Please. I have to pass this test, or I won't be able to play in next week's game. Coach is strict."

I glared. "Fine." I wasn't staying on his account. His poor mom didn't have a lot of extra time working three jobs, so I made myself useful while waiting on Layne.

He dialed Gabby's number.

I filled the kitchen sink with soap and water and washed the dishes piled up on the peeling laminate counter. Besides working at the restaurant with me, she cleaned houses and did some light bookkeeping on the side. To top it off, she always made it to her son's games. Yeah, I wasn't staying on Layne's account.

I tied up the garbage and caught Layne's attention. I pointed to the hefty bag. He motioned to the door leading to the one-car garage.

Once I finished, I snapped my fingers in front of his face. "Okay, Layne. Wrap this up. Otherwise, I'm leaving."

He held up a finger. My fists balled up. I closed my eyes and counted to ten.

I focused.

I wish. Shut off your phone. Forget about it for the next hour. He complied immediately. No resistance.

I'd pay for this later. I was doing it for his own good . . .

"You ready now?" His glazed eyes blinked a couple of times before he nodded and a crooked grin rose on his lips.

It took him awhile to catch on, but once he had it, he had it. I put a lot of the context into football terms. It seemed to work.

"My mom said you went to the game with Jude last night." He paused between problems. His knee bounced frantically under the table, making everything vibrate.

"Yeah, so?" I snapped defensively.

He pushed his chair back and clasped his hands behind his head, his T-shirt clinging to every ridge and valley of his sculpted stomach. "You need to be careful. He's dangerous."

I tried focusing on his eyes. "Or maybe your girlfriend is a liar?"

"I don't think so. She was really a mess when it happened."

I reached over and set my hand on his hyperactive leg. The skin underneath his sweats was warm against my palm. When his leg stopped shaking the bejesus out of us, I let go. "Did you ever take a minute to think of how she ruined not only Jude's family, but his life as well?"

"Of course, I have. But I know him better than you do. We played football and basketball together until Sophomore year. He has quite a temper." He leaned forward and rested his elbows on his knees with his hands nestled together. His face was only inches from mine. A fine, dark gray line circled the outer rim of his corneas. Inside, a ring of icy blue fanned around his iris.

"So do I, but I have never forced . . ." My words dropped off. What was I trying to say? That I'd never forced anyone to do things they didn't want to do? I did that all the time. I sat back and crossed my arms. "Just because he has a temper, it doesn't mean he hurt Gabby."

His shoulder twitched. "Sure, but look at the facts. Most of the school has sided with her. They know what kind of guy he is. He's a loner. He has no friends. Plus, he's strange."

And you just told me to be nice. I crossed my legs. "Or, perhaps, everyone is scared of her. From what I've heard, her family doesn't fight fair. What if the rumors aren't true? She ruined Jude's life. What would stop her from ruining theirs?"

"Really, she's not like that. When you get her away from everyone, she's sweet and kind."

My eyes opened wider in an *are you for real?* look. "Seriously, don't you see how she treats other people? I heard her screaming at you over the phone. She called you stupid. She called you a coward."

He folded his arms, sat back, and frowned. "She's just a little strong-willed. She doesn't mean anything by it."

"We have a name for boys like you. It begins with a

P and ends with a whipped." He opened his mouth a couple of times to say something, a fish gulping for air, then changed his mind. He slipped his foot over to mine and kicked it gently.

"Okay, let me ask you this: What would she do if you broke up with her?"

His face paled.

"That's what I thought." I sat forward. "Can I be honest with you?"

He unclenched his jaw and wrinkled his forehead. I took that as a yes.

"First, your mom told me what your dad was like. He left when you were what? Seven?"

He fiddled with the corner of his notebook. "What? Are you a therapist now too?"

I snorted out my nose—not my most attractive habit. "No, but I guarantee I have spent more time in therapy than you have at football practice this year."

The loud buzzing of the ancient fridge and the ticking of the clock were the only sounds in the room. He furrowed his brows. But the expression behind those flaming blue eyes held sympathy, rather than confusion. Most people knew that my dad had died earlier this year. I wasn't above letting him think that was the reason I had a therapist.

"Really, I'm not messing with you. But you're the only one I've told. So please don't tell anyone."

He surprised me by reaching up to tuck my hair behind my ear. "No. Never," he whispered.

"So, you can take my advice or leave it. Your choice. But I ask you to do this. Remember the way your dad used to treat your mom. How he told her she was stupid and could never make it on her own. How she was a useless human being and she was lucky to have him."

He started to interrupt me. I held up a hand.

"At first, Miss Molly made excuses for why he acted the way he did. How he didn't really mean all the awful things he said."

"But . . ." Layne interrupted again.

I put my finger up to my lips to shush him. "Now compare the two. Not right now. Later when you have some time to think. But when you do, I want you to know—you aren't stupid. And you're not a coward. My dad always used to tell me . . ." I swallowed hard. "'The opposite of courage in our society is not cowardice, it is conformity.' Some psychologist said it."

"Now, will you take some advice from me?" he asked while frowning.

"Hit me." I bit the insides of my cheek.

"I know Jude better than you. I've grown up with him, remember? He's dangerous. I mean it. Maybe not in a physical sense. Apparently, that's still up for debate." He pursed his lips to the side. "But he's manipulative. He pushes people's buttons, then stands on the sidelines and watches the mess he's created."

Manic laughter bubbled from my chest but I swallowed it down. My bangs tumbled back into my face. I kept them there to hide the guilt in my eyes. If he only knew—he was describing me to a T.

"And I bet he hasn't told you that this wasn't the first time his father has been accused of sexual harassment. The apple usually doesn't fall far from the tree."

I started to make a snide comment that you can't judge a kid by the sins of the father, but instead, I clutched my stomach. All my air rushed out between my lips from the pain. A sharp stabbing under my ribs twisted like a knife into my side. I pressed my hands over the spot and mumbled, "I gotta go."

"You okay?" Layne said.

"Yeah," I said between my teeth. I faked a smile. My cheeks quivered. "I'll be okay. I need some fresh air."

"Maybe I should drive you home?" He put a firm hand on my shoulder.

"No, I got this. You go finish your homework. I'll see you tomorrow."

I could tell he didn't believe me. An internal war with the chivalrous male battled on his face. I slipped out of his grip and shut the door behind me.

Chapter 10

Modern Day Vigilante

I rushed to my truck and sped away.

I gripped the steering wheel with white knuckles. The pain hit me in waves, making it hard to breathe. I opened my window. I would have rolled down the passenger side too, but the old truck didn't have automatic buttons. The cold air burned my cheeks and tossed my short hair wildly around my head. I counted my breaths. Inhale for three seconds; exhale for three seconds. In through the nose, out through the mouth. About two miles from my house, little stars danced above my head. They always showed up right before I passed out. I pulled over to the side of the road.

I stumbled out onto the swaying yellow grass and bent to the ground, holding on to my rusted bumper. I whimpered in agony. My muscles quaked from exhaustion. Every time the pain hit, my body tensed and contracted until the surge passed. Then started again. Sweat pooled between my breasts and ran down my back, soaking into the waistband of my jeans. *Please just don't let my hair fall out . . . Please just don't let my hair fall out . . .*

Blue lights flashed behind my truck. A car door thumped shut. "Miss, are you okay? Do I need to call an ambulance?"

I shook my head from my bent-over position.

"Are you sure?"

I held up my hand and took as deep of a breath as I could manage. I straightened up as much as the pain allowed me. "Can you just give me a ride home? I'm afraid to go any further."

"Miss, I'm calling an ambulance," he said in an authoritative tone.

"No!" I yelled. "I . . . I have kidney stones," I lied. It was all I could think of on short notice. "I need to get home to get my medication."

"Okay, okay. Aren't you kind of young for kidney stones?" He patted my back and helped me to his squad car. He placed his hand on my head to make sure I didn't hit it on my way in.

"Runs in the family." My dad had one once, and we all thought he was going to die.

"Where should I take you?"

"Teigen Ranch," I whispered through my clenched teeth.

"Oh, is your mom Sara? Sara Teigen . . . I mean Braaten?" He glanced at me in his rearview mirror.

"Uh-huh."

"I graduated with her. She was the prettiest girl in school."

I grinned. Or I tried to. It came off as more of a grimace. Thankfully, it didn't take even a couple more minutes to get home. We passed over the cattle guard and under the hanging sign: Teigen Ranch Simmental Cattle. It was a strange choice of livestock for these parts. Most ranchers had Herefords or Black Angus.

My grandparents came running out to the cop car

with my mom following behind. She'd showered today and put on clothes. Real ones, not yoga pants. Her blonde hair shone in a river of gold even under the cloudy sky. Flecks of copper and platinum intertwined with the molten metal. Her eyes lit up when she saw the cop, and she smiled for the first time in months. I'm not sure she even saw me.

"Barry—I mean Officer Baylock, is everything all right?" My mom bent over in front of his rolled-down window. She glanced into the back seat and tossed me an angry look as if the delinquent had struck again.

Gramps helped me out of the car. He smelled like hay, coffee, and bacon. "You okay, kid?" He supported my weight with a steady, strong arm.

"Regan, are you okay?" Grams smoothed my hair, then laid the palm of her rough calloused hand on my forehead. It burned against my clammy skin.

"I need to go to bed." I doubled my arms around my stomach.

"Here, I'll help you to the house." She traded places with Gramps and put her arm around my waist.

Officer Baylock got out of his squad car. "Sara, you look exactly the same. I'm so sorry about your husband." His voice was slightly higher than it had been.

"Thank you," I heard her say quietly. I knew exactly how this would play out. Her eyes would lower, and she would bat her long eyelashes, tipped at the ends in the same gold as her hair. Her perfect lips, with their deep Cupid's bow pucker, would turn down in a sad smile. The smile would be genuine; she loved my dad. But still, she wouldn't be able to help herself. She was a flirt and she was beautiful. That's what she was. Her identity and self-worth were built around her looks.

We shuffled to the house and Grams sat me on the corner of my bed and slid my feet and arms into some pajamas.

"Your mom said this happens sometimes. You getting sick. And the doctors can never find anything wrong." She pulled back the covers to my messily made bed.

I popped a couple of prescription muscle relaxers (pain killers didn't help) and swallowed them down with the rest of last night's soda. "Yeah," I snapped.

My mom chose to believe that I made up my sickness for attention. But I knew better. I'd wished for Layne to put his phone away and forget about the drama at hand. I did it so he could study and pass his upcoming test—not for his own good but so Miss Molly didn't have to work three jobs for the rest of her life. It didn't matter if that I didn't like Gabby or that Layne was being rude—it only mattered that both Layne and his mom would benefit from my actions.

"I'm fine. Thanks for your help, Grams." I curled up in the fetal position and gritted my teeth as another wave of pain twisted through my guts.

She tucked my blankets around me and kissed my hair before she left.

Tears ran down my face into my down pillow. Soon the medication would lull me to sleep.

My mother's laughter carried through the single pane windows. On one hand, I was glad she'd found a reason to laugh. Even if it was because of a man. On the other hand, my heart weighed heavy—she hadn't even bothered to ask if I was okay.

My dad had been the head of the family. He was the leader; we were the followers. Lincoln was in the Army and Kennedy was at Officer Candidate School. They both had a purpose. My mom floundered. She was a note in a bottle on the vast open ocean with no direction and no purpose.

At least I had a purpose. Atone for my sin and become a modern-day vigilante. Punish the bad; reward the good. Easy peasy—one would think.

Chapter 11

Human Nature at its Finest

Monday morning, Jude waited casually next to my locker. He leaned back against it with one foot holding him steady and the other propped against the metal door. Instead of being absorbed in his phone, he was reading a real book—something about building furniture. A thrill snaked in my stomach even if it shouldn't have. I didn't know if I could trust him. I struggled with that question after my time with Layne.

He slapped the hardback book shut. His eyes gleamed like polished obsidian. "You didn't answer my calls." Accusation rolled heavily off his tongue.

I took a step back. "Sorry, I was sick." It wasn't a complete lie. I was sick. By Sunday, I felt better. I had spent most of the day helping Gramps mend fences and left my phone in the house. I did as Layne had asked and thought about what he had to say; he did know Jude better. What if I were wrong? What if Jude were a bad person? I had no way to control him. That made him dangerous. I needed time to think.

"So sick you couldn't pick up your phone and tell me you were okay? What? Did you break all your fingers?" His eyes flickered to my hands.

Irritation flared, but I refused to take the bait. "Do

you mind?" I motioned for him to get out of my way so I could get into my locker.

He straightened up. His shoulders tensed, and the tendons in his neck tightened. He shook his head like he couldn't believe it. "Oh, I see how it is," he growled. "One day with the golden boy, huh? Now you believe all the lies about me. I should've known you'd be just like the rest of them." He leaned down into my face, his dark eyes angry and hurt. "Baa," he said before he stalked away.

I pressed my forehead into the cold metal of my locker. I didn't want to believe Layne.

I banged my head onto the door; the metal clanged loudly. The thumping knocked some sense into me. Layne didn't get to make my decisions for me. Besides, Jude could have taken advantage of me Friday night. It's not like I was in any condition to stop him. And I practically threw myself at him. But he didn't. 'Actions speak louder than words,' my dad always said.

"Jude, wait," I hollered right before Gabby blocked my way. Her long blonde hair flowed over her shoulders. The smell of sweet cotton candy drifted all around her. She looked down at me from her four-inch, thigh-high leather boots. Sometimes I really despised tall people.

She stabbed a flesh-toned nail into my chest. "Stay away from my boyfriend. This is your final warning." Her breath smelled of spearmint gum.

I quirked an eyebrow and skewed my lips curious why she was so angry with me. I was just tutoring Layne. It's not like I was trying to steal him from her evil clutches. Never one to back down from a bully, I snapped, "Or what?" She might scare others, but she couldn't scare me.

“Or I’ll make your life a living hell.” She tapped my sternum with every word. Large almond-shaped eyes with long lashes extensions held my stare. But even her professionally-waxed brows and flawless skin couldn’t make her attractive. Because she was downright mean.

My nostrils flared. Then I smiled. She was funny, too. Make my life a living hell? *Good luck with that.* There wasn’t anything she could do to me that I didn’t deserve. “Layne’s a big boy. He can make his own choices.”

Her thin lips scrunched into a tight ball, and her grassy-green eyes swelled then narrowed with anger. Redness crept from under her turtleneck and stained her cheeks pink. “Who do you think owns the bank, therefore the loan on your family’s pathetic farm? I’m sure my daddy would be happy to call in their debt,” she hissed. Her clenched teeth didn’t part.

Rage scratched along the edges of the glass box in my brain, its talons squealed over the surface trying to cut its way free. White lights sparkled along my peripheral vision. Everything inside of me screamed "Kill. Kill her now”. And God how I wanted to. But that would make me a worse person than she was. I concentrated on breathing. One, two, three. Breath in. One, two, three. Breath out. The squealing in my head subsided.

“Gab—bee . . .” a boy’s voice echoed from down the hall. She spun her head sideways. A large diamond earring sparkled in the yellow overhead light.

She chuckled at my trembling hands. “You’ve been warned,” she said before she tilted her chin up and sauntered away with one long leg in front of the other, making the checkered floor into her personal catwalk.

People dodged out of her way, all the while worshiping her even though they feared her. “Car—son,” she hollered in two distinct syllables, a false cheer coating her voice in a dripping honey. She flipped her long hair over her shoulder; it cascaded like a wavy waterfall over her back. “Boy, aren’t you looking fine today.” She eyed him from head to toe. His remotely handsome face beamed. That’s how she worked the popular boys. She complimented them, giving them just enough hope that one day, they too, could have a chance. A chance to belong to the elite inner circle. Compliment them, act interested, build their egos, and hold them at arm’s length. Everyone wants what they can’t have. Human nature at its finest.

Wow, I hadn’t even made it to first period, and already I owed Jude an apology and contemplated killing Gabby. Eventful morning.

I would catch Jude in art class this afternoon. As for Gabby, I was going to have to think about that later. Because if I did it now, I was liable to throw caution to the wind and follow her. It’s one thing to threaten me personally, it’s a whole other thing to threaten my family.

The rest of the morning blurred by. I kept my head down and made no more enemies—at least none that I knew about anyway.

I chose to eat lunch in my truck. Alone. Just because.

A tap on my passenger side window made me jump. I spilled a drop of yogurt on my pants. *Son of a gun.* I lifted it off with my finger and licked it clean.

Layne, on the other side of the glass, looked slightly dazed with his eyes locked firmly on my lips. He shook his head slightly, then a wide grin with straight pearly whites broke out on his face.

He tried the locked door. “Let me in,” he said, but the sound was muffled. His cheeks and the end of his nose were pink from the cold air.

I sighed, reached over, and pulled up the lock lever.

A gust of wind blew in with him. A promise of snow smell hung in the air; its icy crystals stung my nostrils. “Hey, I just wanted you to know that I’m pretty sure I passed my test. I’ll know tomorrow, but I felt good when I was done.” Excitement poured off of him. It was contagious.

My face lit up. It was the first feeling of joy I’d had today. “Awesome! Good job.”

“Hey, so can we do it again this weekend? Saturday morning-ish? It will make my life so much easier,” he said.

“Uh, yeah, about that. Your girlfriend cornered me this morning and told me to stay away from you.”

Crowds of people getting back from lunch stared into my truck as they made their way from their cars to the school. They elbowed one another and jutted their chins toward my truck. A few kids dressed in designer jeans and expensive jackets snapped pictures. In a matter of minutes, the rumor mill would be buzzing.

“Oh, Gabby.” He scrubbed a hand over his head. The muted afternoon light covered his blond hair, turning the messy spikes into a crown of gold. “Don’t worry about her. I’ll take care of it.”

“Layne, I think she’s serious. Aren’t you worried she’ll do something to hurt you?” *Ruin your future career? Get your mom fired? Accuse you of rape? Take away your home?*

“She would never take things that far.” He said it so

sincerely that I think he really believed it. I hoped he was right.

I agreed to help him again Saturday, but only with a promise that he would keep his girlfriend on a leash. He hopped out of my truck, smiled, and waved before he bounded through the parking lot to where his group of guy friends, all dressed in identical black and red letterman jackets, waited in front of the school.

By art class that afternoon, I'd been shoulder-bumped aggressively multiple times. My books were now firmly in my backpack since I'd gotten tired of picking them up off the floor as students kicked them out of my reach. They all seemed to be in on a humiliating game of keep away. Rich kids. Ranch kids. Nerds. And the jocks, which surprised me. I would have thought Layne would have told the jocks to back off. Only the stoners left me alone. I could tell by the look of pity on their faces that they wanted to help me, but the consequences weren't worth the risk. Upon arrival at this school, I wondered how Gabby kept *all* of them under control. But slowly I was learning.

Jude sat alone in the back corner under the burnt-out fluorescent lighting, reading the same book from earlier.

"Hey, can we talk?" I tucked my hands into my hoodie.

The planes of his face were hard and unyielding. My fingers tingled. I balled them into a fist.

He pushed his chair away from the stainless-steel table. My heart squeezed. But he didn't get up like I thought he was going to. He tilted his chair back on two legs, crossed his arms and legs, and continued to watch me without emotion.

"I owe you an apology. I should've returned your

call. I was sick Saturday. But on Sunday, I should have at least texted you."

He ran his tongue over his teeth without opening his mouth. Then nodded, only once.

"So, am I forgiven?"

He shrugged. "Sure." Then he got up. He stretched his arms high in the air, his gray T-shirt lifting over his smooth, rippled stomach. His jeans hung low on his hips. "We're cool," he said before he switched tables, leaving me sitting alone in the corner under the burnt-out light.

Chapter 12

At Least Someone Liked Me

The next month or so of my life blurred by. During class, most students avoided me. Layne straightened out the football team. He told them if he didn't pass, he didn't play, and they wouldn't win. Once they backed off, all the other students capitulated. It didn't bother me that everyone else ignored me, it bothered me when Jude did it. All I could coax out of him was the occasional nod. He made it clear that he wanted nothing to do with me.

Every time I saw him, my heart twisted into a tight knot of sorrow, and a lump of regret clogged my throat. I'd been so close to having a friend or possibly something more. He knew my worst and didn't hate me for it. But then I betrayed his trust.

I didn't worry about him giving away my secret. He didn't have any more friends than I did. Besides, I knew that deep down, he would never do that to me. The connection between us felt as if it were at a cellular level. Something I couldn't yet describe accurately. Being around him left jitters in my stomach and made my heart pitter patter like a school girl. And I couldn't deny that there was something alluring about the fact that I couldn't control him. He was like riding a motorcycle;

fun, exciting and a bit dangerous. Just thinking about it sent a thrill down the back of my neck.

Work was okay. The best part was being with Miss Molly. She was always a good distraction in my life. She treated me like a human being. My lack of popularity didn't matter to her. In fact, she seemed to like it. She was ecstatic that Layne and I had a 'weekly date.' That's what she called it. I had to remind her several times that he had a girlfriend and she needed to stop pestering me. My purpose was to make sure his math grade stayed firmly in the average category. An accomplishment both he and his mom claimed was a miracle. I hadn't known this, but I wasn't the first person to help Layne, but I was apparently the only one able to get through to him. She did mention the others weren't nearly as pretty. I believe '*smokin' hot, smart and not easily intimidated'* were her exact words. I wasn't sure if that's what made Gabby jealous or kept Layne interested in our sessions.

Saturday mornings, except when Layne had a game, were tutor days. I don't know what he said to Gabby, but whatever it was, I let him believe it worked. It hadn't. Every week, there was a gift in my locker: dead mice, used tampons, and a doll that looked like a Voodoo curse, stick pins and all.

On one random Friday, I opened my locker expecting the next level of gross only to find a plastic see-through bag full of pills sitting on the top shelf of my locker.

"Miss Braaten," said a stern voice from behind.

I stepped back and shut the metal door with a soft clank, then turned around. My heart beat rapidly.

"I have a report that you've been selling drugs. I'm going to need you to step aside." The principal, Mrs.

Potter-Davis, held a tiny key in her hand.

Shit! I gritted my teeth but stepped away. All the students in the hallway slowed down.

"The rest of you get to class," she snapped.

They shuffled along, rubbernecking slowly like they were witnessing the aftermath of an automobile accident.

I wanted to stop her from getting inside my locker but there were too many witnesses around. It would look strange if she suddenly forgot what she was doing. My goal was to stay *under* the radar.

I crossed my hands behind my back—the picture perfect of co-operation—and furiously mapped out a plan inside my head. The golem perked up. If it had hands it would have rubbed them together like a cartoon villain.

She clicked open my locker and grabbed the bag from the shelf. Pastel-colored pills ranging from triangles to hearts shapes dangled between her fingers. Her lips pursed. "I'd heard you were trouble." She pulled her phone from her blazer pocket and started dialing a number.

I wish. Electricity shot from my chest to my fingers and toes. *Drop your phone.*

It clattered to the floor.

Lean over—pick it up. Trip. Step on it.

She faltered forward, her stilettoes crunching her phone. The screen spiderwebbed.

I couldn't let her call the cops. Trying to control one person was hard enough. I didn't need them getting involved.

"Blast," she said, scooping up the remnants. "Come with me," she snapped, stuffing it's remains back into the pocket of her plaid jacket.

I followed her down the hallway to her office, whispers clinging to us like shadows.

Once she closed the door, I let out the breath I'd been holding.

"Sit down." She pointed to the chair across from hers as she sat. "You have some explaining to do." She shook the confetti of pills before she placed them on the organized desk.

I laughed. Her face flushed red.

She picked up the phone receiver.

Tingled flared from my chest to my fingers and toes. *Put it down. And forget.*

Her brown eyes glazed over and her lips hung open.

I got up and wandered into her private bathroom. I opened the medicine cabinet and found an industrial sized bottle of ibuprofen. I bit my bottom lip and smiled.

A knock on the office door startled me. "Mrs. Potter-Davis," the secretary said, "Officer Baylock is here at your request."

My nerve endings flared with panic. She must have called the police before she even opened my locker.

"Just a moment." I made her say.

I selected a pill, a pink heart, out of the bag and made her swallow it dry. It was ecstasy and it couldn't hurt for me to have a backup plan. Besides, she deserved it for thinking I was guilty before she even searched my locker.

I dumped the rest down the toilet and flushed. They swirled in a rainbow of colors, then disappeared. I poured half of the bottle of ibuprofen into the plastic baggie and hurried back to the desk.

I set the pills in the same spot, sat back down, and released my control over her. Her eyes blinked rapidly, then she pressed her eyelids with the pads of her fingers.

"Mrs. Potter-Davis?" the secretary said again.

"Yes?"

"Ahhhh, Officer Baylock is here to see you."

"Send him in." She stood up and smoothed out her skirt. The nervous look in her eyes said she was wondering what had just happened. *Mystery minutes.*

The door opened. The same cop that had escorted me home stood towering above me.

"You requested our presence?"

"Yes, thank you. Ms. Braaten was caught with drugs in her locker. Ecstasy, I believe. She needs to be arrested." She smiled like she was pleased that one of her students was caught with drugs.

"It's over the counter pain killers," I said calmly.

Her angry brown eyes meet mine. "Young lady, I've been a principal for over ten years and I know a bag of Ecstasy when I see it." She crossed her arms.

I looked up at Officer Baylock and shrugged my shoulders.

"Mrs. Potter-Davis, I, ahh, believe Ms. Braaten is correct."

He picked up the bag and inspected its contents. It was hard to deny what the pills were, they had the brand name right on them.

She snatched it out of his hand. Her nostrils flared and the muscles of her jaw rolled. I made her forget what had happened in the room, but I didn't make her forget what she'd found in my locker. But if she denied what was in the bag now, she was going to look crazier than she already did. Crazier than I was.

Satisfaction curled my lips into a twisted smile.

"Get out!" She thrust a finger towards the door.

And I didn't even get sick later.

What? I had to do something bad so I didn't get sick or die. And making her take Ecstasy was quite entertaining. Ms. Potter-Davis was high for the rest of the day. High. As. A. Kite. She kept grabbing people in the hallways between class periods and telling them she loved them. When she saw me, her nostrils flared and she quickly turned away. But by the end of the day, she looked to be sweating and shivering all at the same time. Her usually neat hair was frazzled and dark circles marred the skin under her eyes. I doubted she'd be back in the morning. As far as I was concerned, the miserable night she was about to have, served her right.

Gabby looked furious and kept staring at me. I assumed she was trying to figure out how I escaped punishment.

Jude sent me a text. *—Diabolical.—* With a devil emoji.

I tried to engage but he didn't text me again.

Gabby laid low after that. I mean, who walks into the principal's office with a bag of actual drugs and walks out a free person. I didn't tell Layne any of this because I didn't want him confronting her, for fear that she would retaliate and lie. Just like she did with Jude. Though her accusations weren't true, she'd destroyed Jude's reputation. Not only could she destroy Layne's reputation, she could destroy his future. And there was no doubt I could protect myself. So long as Gabby left him alone and didn't threaten my family's farm, I could manage.

****

For a while, my life proceeded comfortably. When Layne had a game on Saturdays, he would beg me to come by Sunday mornings to attend church with them and help him with homework after. I declined, pretty sure I would burn upon entering any place of worship.

Besides, every Sunday I got up early—like painfully early—and helped with the ranch. I loved spending time with Gramps. He was a comforting presence in my life. My self-deprecating thoughts were fewer around him for some reason. Probably because working so hard didn't leave me time to think.

He didn't speak much, but he taught me how to do so many things. Drive a tractor. Mend barb wire. Run a chainsaw. There wasn't anything that man couldn't do. It made me wonder where my mom came from.

By mid-October, I was a fair ranch hand, and it seemed as if Gramps actually enjoyed my company. It made me feel good. At least someone liked me.

Chapter 13

Halloween

The Saturday morning before Halloween, I pulled my pickup along the sidewalk in front of Miss Molly's house and let myself in the door. Candy corn wafted in the air. She had a candle for every occasion. Purple and orange lights twinkled around the fireplace. Synthetic webs hung from the corners of the ceiling; fake spiders dangled from the silk. Colorful sugar skulls sat on the coffee table, and a witch's hat hung next to a black velvet cape on the coat rack. Miss Molly was dressing up as a witch for work tonight, even though it wasn't Halloween until Tuesday. The restaurant liked us to participate. I was working tonight and going as a Viking, a nod to my ancestors. I'd ordered a wig, bought myself a fake sword, and customized my serving platter to resemble a shield. Grams made my costume: brown leather pants, a linen shirt, and fake chainmail. The entire get-up looked authentic.

I set my purse on the table and poured myself a cup of coffee, added some creamer, and rolled up my sleeves. I did the dishes and waited for Layne to rumble out of bed.

Barefoot, wearing a ratty school sweatshirt and pajama bottoms, he rolled in a few minutes after I loudly put away the pots and pans. This was our ritual. Now he would drink an energy drink all at once as he stood in front of the living room window.

Instead of sitting down at the table, Layne disappeared and came back five minutes later. He pulled out a chair for me. I quirked an eyebrow and plunked on the seat. He smelled good. Like he'd put on some cologne. And he'd wet down his messy hair.

He seemed nervous. He straightened the math book and lined up two pencils and an extra eraser. He flipped the chair around and straddled it before he sat.

I reached down to grab my calculator.

"Wait," he said.

He took a small package out of his pajama pocket. It was wrapped in gold paper with a fancy silver ribbon tied in a bow. "Here." He thrust the gift right in my face. "This is for you."

I grabbed it with two fingers and cocked my head sideways. "What's this for?"

He folded his arms over the back of the chair and rested his head on his wrists. "It's . . . it's a thank you for helping me."

"You didn't have to do that. I'm happy to help you."

He laughed through his nose. "No, you're not. You're doing this for my mom. Don't get me wrong, I appreciate it. We both have the same end goal—to make her life easier. I like that about you." His blue eyes held mine.

I held the package but didn't open it. Was I doing this for Miss Molly? At first, yes. But now? I really liked Layne too. He was one of the best of us. What all humans should aspire to be. He was kind. Gentle. Humorous. Generous. Hardworking. Patient. And a natural leader.

I'd been to plenty of his games with her—she didn't give me much of a choice. I watched as his teammates followed his lead. They trusted him.

He half-smiled, his eyes crinkling at the corners. "Come on, open it." His hyperactive leg bounced wildly. He needed to stop with the energy drinks. He had more than enough of his own.

I tugged at the ribbon. It dropped on my lap, and I carefully pulled the tape at the corners.

"Oh, come on," he ribbed me, shaking my shoulder. "I should have known you were *that* kind of present opener," he said as if he were accusing me of a much greater offense.

I gave up and tore the gold paper away. Inside was a handmade wooden box inlaid with mother of pearl. I lifted the lid. Sitting on a navy velvet cushion was a bracelet. Dainty silver strands, braided together into the thickness of a licorice rope, shone against its dark bedding. Two cuffs, sculpted dragons' heads, held together each end.

"Wow. Really? For me?" I glanced at him. He nodded.

"It's perfect. I love it." I ran my finger over the cold metal. I lifted it out of the box and secured it around my wrist.

Relief flooded his face. He swung his chair around and sat back heavily with a deep breath. "Oh, good. I picked it out myself so I wasn't sure. Mom said you were going to be a Viking for Halloween, and I thought this would work."

"Absolutely. I'm going to wear it tonight for sure. I love it. Thank you." I held out my arm and admired the piece.

"I'm glad you like it." He reached out and picked up the discarded ribbon from my lap. His fingers lingered on my leg. Tingles shot from my thigh straight to my—yup, there.

He stared down at me. For weeks, I'd come here. Helped him with his homework. Not once did I get the feeling he wanted to be anything more than friends. But the way he was looking at me made me question my ability to assess such things.

His gaze studied my eyes, the curve of my cheek, and then lingered on my lips. I licked the spot he was staring at. His hand moved from my leg and brushed my fallen bangs out of my eyes. Then he tucked them behind my ear. I stopped breathing. He cupped my face and tilted my chin up toward him. My mouth parted. My heart beat loudly inside my ears. My body trembled with nerves.

A rock song, often played at high school ball games blared from his phone. We both were startled. Caller ID said Gabby Babby—spelled with double b's. *How stupid.*

"I-I got to get this," he stuttered and stood up. The silver ribbon dropped from his hand in slow motion and coiled lifelessly on the wood floor.

This was the first time I'd forgotten to ask him to turn off his phone. Good thing too. I shouldn't have let things escalate. I certainly didn't deserve someone as good as Layne. I didn't deserve anyone. But even though my mind agreed, my heart continued to argue.

First, my dad would want me happy—deep inside I knew this to be true. Second, I didn't ask for my abilities—I realized this. Third, I was trying to atone for my sin—didn't that count for something?

I squeezed the bracelet tighter around my wrist and put the beautiful box in my purse. When he finally returned, we went about business as usual. Except for the awkward tension hanging in the air like a bad smell. When our hands touched, we both jumped as if we burned each other. When we spoke at the same time, we stuttered weird apologies.

Relief swept through me when we finished. Before I left, I thanked him again.

"Anytime. It looks good on you." He smiled sweetly, but he stayed well out of reach.

****

It took me the rest of the day to assemble my costume. Grams helped and, surprisingly, so did Mom. I had to give her credit; she has mad makeup skills. She lined my eyes in jet-black, glued on a set of fake eyelashes, blushed my cheeks, and stained my lips. After I wiggled into my getup, I stood back from the mirror.

"You are gorgeous, sweetheart," my mom said.

My long blonde wig was ratted and braided into warrior hair, and my eyes glowed a glacial blue. I looked pretty badass.

"You should wear makeup more often." She touched my cheek. It was the first time in months she'd laid a hand on me. I think, for her, looking at me was painful. I was my father's doppelgänger with the same cool, brown hair with silvery highlights and long black eyelashes. I also had the same lips—the bottom fuller than the top— and same straight nose. Not a hint of my mother's sculpted cheekbones or the exotic tilt of her eyes. I wanted to hug her. I wanted to tell her I loved her. But I was chicken. How could she love me? How could anyone love someone like me?

Appropriately costumed for Halloween, I drove to work. Halfway there, it began to snow. Big, fluffy flakes pelted my windshield and reflected as bright as stars in the yellow headlights. It was hypnotizing. The roads were getting slicker by the moment. The truck had studded tires, but I didn't want to stop to manually put it in four-wheel drive. With clenched teeth and shaking hands, I made it to work. The rusted green dumpster was already covered in a three-inch blanket of powder. I wouldn't think about the drive home until later.

Saturday nights were always busy, and I could tell from the already full parking lot that Halloween weekend was going to be worse. The snow didn't slow down these tough—slightly crazy—Wyoming folks.

Once I got out of my truck, I lifted the windshield washer blades so they wouldn't freeze to the glass and ran carefully to the employee entrance. Laughter echoed outside the wood building and got much louder once I stepped inside.

I threw my things in my locker and clocked in for my shift.

The saloon doors to the kitchen thumped repeatedly as the wait staff carried orders out on their overflowing trays. Meat sizzled on the grill; the deep fryer hissed with every batch of fries and onion rings. An occasional dish crashed to the floor as the dishwashers hurried to keep up.

Customers—some in costumes, some not—sat at tables, holding onto their beers or fruity drinks with umbrellas. Even through all the chaos, I noticed a few admiring glances. Maybe Mom was right. Why hide behind baggy clothes and no makeup?

Sometime around eight o'clock, Miss Molly waved

at me from across the room to catch my attention. "Hey," she hollered over the noisy crowd. With her green-painted face, crimped blonde hair, black pointy hat, blood-red lips, and heavily coaled eyes, she was still the most beautiful woman in here. "Can you get table twelve? I have a ten top that just sat down."

"Sure thing," I said and nodded in case she couldn't hear me through her hat and the noise.

A lovely woman with shiny dark hair sat in the back-corner booth. She wore a long fur coat and a scarf. Melted snow clung to the expensive cashmere. "Hi! Name's Regan. Can I start you off with something to drink?"

I glanced at her, then at the person sitting across from her.

For a moment, the perimeters of time ceased to exist. The air became heavy. I forgot to breathe. Sound and movement skipped a beat before they continued.

Jude. Dark. Disinterested.

When he finally looked up and our eyes met, my heart lurched with a kind of joy I've rarely experienced—something like coming home after a long absence. It retreated after I properly chastised it. Who did it think it was, reacting without my say-so? "Oh, Jude. Hi," I said in a stilted, robotic voice as I took a small step back. "Do you want me to get you another server?"

He screwed up his face. "No. Why would I want that?" He pulled off his hat and rubbed his hands over his hair, messing it into place.

I shrugged my shoulders. *Perhaps because of the annoyed look on your face when you saw it was me?*

"I didn't recognize you." He started to say more, then stopped and pointed at me instead. His finger twitched a couple times.

I hesitantly touched my wig. “I don’t think anyone has. It’s kind of a relief.”

“Wow. Maybe I should wear a costume. Would be nice to walk around as someone else for a change.”

I grinned. He grinned back. That was the first time in a month that he’d done more than simply nod. It transformed his serious face into one that made my stomach butterflies flitter. I needed to beat the life out of them. Capture them in a net and smother them to death.

“This is my mom, Jacy,” he said. I strained forward to hear his gritty voice amongst the noise. It was music to my ears. It had been a while since I’d heard it.

“Hi.” I held out my hand. Hers was cold from the outside. “Nice to meet you.”

“You too.” A genuine smile bloomed like a flower finding light on her face. “You and Jude know each other? You go to school together?” Deep lines creased between her sharp brows.

“Yeah, we have four classes together.”

Her mouth formed an O shape. “Oh, good.” The lines softened.

“My mom thinks I don’t have any friends,” Jude growled. He leaned back in the booth and crossed his arms.

“You don’t,” escaped out of me before I could catch it. I slapped my mouth shut with the palm of my hand.

Jacy’s eyes widened. Jude busted out laughing. “You don’t either.”

“Uhhh, I got Miss Molly,” I said, faking testiness. I didn’t want to mention Layne, my feelings about him were confused at the moment. “If you weren’t such a douche, we could be friends too.”

His normally hard face softened. “I’ll work on that.”

“You do that.” Behind me, I heard more people stumble in from the cold.

“Sorry to cut this short, but . . .” I tilted my head to the side, motioning at the arriving guests. “What can I get you?”

I didn’t have much more opportunity to speak with Jude and his mom, but a weight had lifted from my shoulders. Perhaps he would finally accept my apology. I really did believe him over Gabby. I wondered how anyone in their right mind had sided with her. She was evil.

I made my way to a high-top table with two gentlemen dressed in identical black suits with white shirts and black ties. My feet stopped short and my heart tripped. The golem cocked its proverbial head like a dog listening for a snack. I studied their faces but I didn’t recognize them. They weren’t from here. What if they were from the same organization Smith and Zehn worked for? I thought about those two from time to time trying to figure out their gig. Then I realized I was being paranoid again. It was Halloween. Relief loosened the tension between my shoulder blades, and I swear the golem let out a disappointed sigh.

“Who are you supposed to be?” I said as my eyes darted between the two dudes.

“Pardon me?” The guy with the buzzed haircut said.

“Oh, so you’re just going to deny you’re dressed up for Halloween? Or did you guys just call each other this morning so you could coordinate outfits?” I teased, tapping my pen on the pad of paper I was holding.

The other guy smiled; big dimples creased his cheeks.

"Excuse me?" Buzz cut guy seemed genuinely irritated.

I glanced down at their outfits and raised an eyebrow.

Dimples put his hand up next to his lips and fake whispered, "We're spies. If we told you which Government agency we worked for we'd have to kill you." He winked.

I glanced down at my own costume, shrugged, and patted my fake sword—though I wouldn't need it. "Well, you can try."

He threw his head back and laughed.

The sound was contagious, and a grin tugged at my lips. "What can I get you guys?"

"Well, since we're on the job, two sodas please."

"On the job! Ha. Ha." I jotted down their orders and whisked away.

I didn't get much time to joke with them further since the restaurant was only getting busier. At nine o'clock, the dinner crowd thinned out, making room for the drunk crowd. Technically, my manager didn't want me working past nine, but since we were so busy, she'd asked me to stay later. I didn't mind. The inebriated tipped better. And they were an easy target.

I used the drunks to relieve the pressure building up in my little glass box to help ease my earlier paranoia.

If a patron was rude to any of the staff, they might *accidentally* trip over an untied shoelace, forget a zipper after a restroom stop, smash broccoli between their teeth, spill drinks on their laps, or snort soda out of their nose, spraying everyone around them with bubbly snot. I tried to keep my impulses under control and only let in a little of the familiar tingling buzz. It was difficult. The more I used it, the more the golem and I craved both the high and the power. Sometimes I wondered what would happen if I opened the lock and let all the crazy out at once.

As Jude left, I caught his eye and sort of waved. He pointed to the rude guy at the bar who just spilled a drink down the front of his pants. I smiled and blinked innocently. He laughed and shook his head.

A large figure stepped in front of me, blocking my view of Jude. Layne bent down to my level. “Hey, is that you?” He took off his letterman’s jacket, heavy with athletic pins, and shook the snow out of his hair. Droplets of water landed on my face. “Wow. You look . . . wow.”

“I look what?” I snapped, in need of food. I teetered on the edge of hangry.

“Hot.” He stopped stuttering. His eyes traveled from my head to my toes, stopping for a fraction of a second on my cleavage. My chest warmed under the weight of his gaze.

“And your bracelet looks good with that getup.”

“Yeah, it does. Thank you again. I really do like it.” I clasped my wrist in my hand. “You want something to eat?”

“Yup, the usual.” Which was like half of the menu. The boy could pack it away.

“Hey, Mom says you should stay with us tonight. It’s dangerous out there. You can drive home in the morning when it’s light.”

“Um . . . I’ll think about it,” I said. I rushed away and typed in his massive order. Miss Molly needed this job just so Layne could eat for half-price.

I set his dinner and a soda on our break table in the back and left him there to eat while I finished my closing work.

Before clocking off for the night, I stepped out the back door with a bag of garbage. Huge snowflakes smacked on my cheeks. A ten-inch mountain of powder covered the dumpster lid. I set down the shiny black bag and glanced up at the industrial light pole. The flurries pelted to the ground.

"You need to stay."

A scream popped out of my mouth like a violent burst of air with a mind of its own.

"Jumpy much?" Layne chuckled. I hadn't heard him sneak up on me. The snow muffled all sound. "Here. Call your mom." He handed me my phone.

I threw him a dirty look. How did he get my phone out of my work locker?

"Don't get all pissy," he said with a smirk on his lips. "I figured out your combo. Wasn't hard. You didn't change it after the last person . . . which was my mother."

I yanked off my rainbow mittens and punched in Mom's number.

"Hey, Mom. Sorry to wake you." I probably should have called my grandparents.

"You didn't," she said.

"Oh, I didn't?" I heard a dude's voice in the background. "Who's there?" I don't know why I bothered asking.

"Barry."

Anger flared. Officer Barry Baylock was at my house. "Oh. Well, I'm going to stay at Miss Molly's tonight. The roads are bad."

"Not a problem." Sara sounded irritatingly chipper.

"Oh, I'm sure it isn't," I said with a full-blown attitude. I'm sure me not being home wasn't a problem.

That way Officer Baylock didn't have to sneak out in the morning before I woke up.

I puffed a white cloud of breath and hung up the phone while she was still talking. Then I powered it off.

"So, if you're staying, can I catch a ride home?" Layne said.

"Yeah, but only if you scrape off my truck." I tossed him the keys, hard. My anger at my mother fueled my throw. He snatched them out of the air.

"Of course. I'll start it too." He winked.

I went back inside and clocked out.

"You kids be good," Miss Molly hollered over the loud bar crowd. She blew me a kiss with one hand, then the other. "One of those is for Layne. Don't forget to give it to him." Someone in the crowd hooted. I shook my head. How come I had the feeling that she would be happy if we were the opposite of good? The thought *had* crossed my mind.

For the whole day, I'd been going through the reasons why it was okay for me to be happy. I debated with myself. Weighed the pros. Weighed the cons. I decided so long as I stayed the course—punish only those people who deserved it—I justified a small measure of happiness for myself. I could stay on the right side of good, even if I were born evil. I killed my father, but I didn't mean to. Besides, when happy, it was easier to stay on the right path. When mad, ugliness tended to consume my every thought. Sliding down into the depths of hell was much simpler than climbing toward the light.

I waded through the deep snow and jumped into the cab of my truck. Not able to stand one more minute with this bulky itchy wig on my head, I pulled it off and set it on the seat between us. I scratched my fingers through my matted hair and put on my stocking cap to cover the ugly mess.

"Better?" Layne asked, looking up from his phone.

I nodded.

"I agree."

"What? You didn't like my long blonde hair?" I placed my hand on my chest, smashing down my puffy purple coat, and opened my mouth in false offense.

"Yeah, it looked great, but I like your hair better. The color's pretty." He shrugged nonchalantly.

I wanted clarification but didn't know how to ask without feeling like I was fishing for a compliment.

I snuck a look at him as I drove out of the parking lot. The top of his head almost brushed the roof. His dark blond hair dried in spikes from the melted snow. A warmth of fondness curled in my chest. I had a protectiveness that couldn't be explained. I decided someone like Layne would encourage me to be good. Keep me on the straight and narrow. Hold me and my actions to a higher standard. He never needed to know what I was. When around him, I wanted to be a better person.

"Dang. The plows can't even keep up," Layne said as I created a path down the side street to his house. Thankfully, it was only on the other side of town.

When we got inside, he took my coat and led me down the hall to his mom's room. A pink flowery comforter draped half on her queen-sized bed and half on the red-rose-shaped area rug. Bottles of perfume lined the rickety dresser. Bras and T-shirts hung from the haphazardly pushed in drawers. Layne opened her closet, which was more of the same, and grabbed me a long nightgown covered in pink kittens.

"Here. It's clean." He tossed it to me.

"Thanks." This was a big change from sweats and old T-shirts.

He flipped on the light to the bathroom. White towels were draped over the rack. One was spread out over the floor as a makeshift bathmat. Single strands of long, highlighted hair curled over the countertop, and green paint stained the powder blue sink.

"Here are makeup remover cloths and a new toothbrush. In the top drawer, there is toothpaste. Can I get you anything else?" His size, from his height to the athletic width of his chest, dwarfed the door frame.

"No, thanks." He'd thought of everything.

I shut the door behind him and breathed in deeply. It smelled of his cologne. My hands were shaky even though I'd eaten earlier. Last week, a sleepover would have been fine. Fun even. Not so much after the awkward interlude we had this morning. I was positive he was about to kiss me before his phone rang. Now nerves buzzed inside my chest. I wetted my crazy hair and slicked it back from my face. I wiped off the heavy makeup and brushed my teeth. Better.

I kept on my socks and my bra and pulled the ridiculous-looking nightgown over my head. I shuffled out into the living room. He was already in pajamas and covered in a blanket. He held a huge bowl of popcorn on his lap. He patted the spot next to him.

"You have to sit close if you want some." He pointed to the snack. "It's the only clean bowl."

Plates and bowls were stacked precariously high in the sink—one good jolt and they would come a tumbling down.

"How do you do that? Does it ever occur to you to

do the dishes?" I rolled my eyes and sat down next to him even though I wasn't really hungry. He threw the blue-knitted blanket over my legs.

"Hey." He pushed my arm playfully. "Mom does the dishes. I do the laundry."

"You do?" I gave him a look that said I didn't believe him.

"Yeah. I do try and help." He pouted. "I got us a movie. You want to watch it?"

"Sure." I grabbed a handful of popcorn. He hit the buttons on the remote. *Great.* He'd picked a movie about superheroes and villains with unusual powers. My clan. The knowledge that they didn't actually exist often disappointed me. Though I still wondered about my brothers and my dad, but my mom refused to talk about them.

The charged tension between us made it impossible for me to relax completely. I wasn't uncomfortable around him, just simply aware of his every move. By the end of the movie, I had my legs curled up under me, and his thigh was touching my knee. "Wouldn't that be awesome," he said. "Having one of those gifts. Who would you be?"

I choked on a kernel. He patted my back and handed me his energy drink. I motioned for my water.

"You okay?"

I nodded after taking a few big swallows.

Did it ever occur to him to drink water? How did he sleep all hyped up on caffeine?

He picked the bad guy. "Think about it," he said. "The core of this planet is made of molten metal. The earth has a gigantic magnetic field and everything we build and use in our day-to-day lives are made of metal."

He'd put a lot of thought into this. He continued, but I faded into my own head.

If the villain was his favorite character, then maybe someday I could come clean with him. Maybe he wouldn't hate me.

"So, you would be?" He set the empty bowl on the coffee table.

"The dude in the wheelchair?"

"Bor—ing." He extended the word into its own sentence. "But if anyone could pull off the bald head and still look good, it would be you." He laced his hands behind his neck. The credits finished rolling on the TV, and the screen turned bright blue, throwing a green cast on his hair.

My face warmed from the compliment. "Uhh," I huffed. "Then who would I be?" I wiggled my head at him.

He leaned in closer, smiled slyly, and whispered his answer in my ear. A shiver ran down the back of my neck.

"Well, the attitude hits the mark." I teetered my head back and forth.

"She's had a rough life. The same as you lately." He trailed a fingertip over the side of my cheek, searing my skin. "You really don't have any idea how beautiful you are, do you?" His bright eyes held mine, and then he dipped his mouth towards my lips.

My pulse raced. His hand slid out of his hair and wrapped around the back of my head. He pulled me to him slowly. His breath tickled my cheek. His lips were warm and soft. His five o'clock shadow prickled around my mouth. He kissed like he played football. He called the play and carried it out—and all he did was ask me to follow his lead. His hands caressed the tender skin on the back of my neck and played with the short strands of my hair. The kiss ended too soon.

He sat back and stared at me for a long twenty seconds before he spoke. His gaze wandered from my face to my body curled up beside him. He wanted to kiss me again. The desire in his eyes couldn't lie.

I could make him do it if I wanted to. But where was the challenge?

"I'm sorry. I shouldn't have done that." He didn't look apologetic.

Not the words I needed to hear. "Seriously?" I snapped.

"No, no," he stuttered. "I mean, I wanted to do that."

Okay, better.

"I wanted to kiss you for a while now, but . . . Oh, man, here I go making a mess of things."

I reached over and took his hand. "Whatever you want to say, say it. It's just me."

His shoulders sagged. "I really like you."

"Me too," I said, even though I hadn't fully realized it until this morning.

"But I should break up with Gabby." His eyes said it all. That girl would ruin him, just like she'd ruined Jude. He was afraid of her, I could tell. Even though he sided with Gabby, he believed Jude.

"How about we wait until after you win State? Then decide what to do." I rubbed the back of his strong hand with my thumb.

He gave me a smile of relief. A huge amount of stress erased with a few words. "Really?" He brightened.

"Yeah, right now you need to focus on your future. After the season is over, then we'll figure out what to do—together. But until then, I think we need to play it safe and stay friends. She's got spies everywhere." I pulled my hand away from his.

"Okay, on one condition." He quirked an eyebrow.

"What's that?" I furrowed my forehead.

"You let me kiss you one more time." His eyes skimmed over my face and down the rest of my kitten nightgown.

I knew I should say no, but I didn't want to. "Please." I bit my lip.

One kiss turned into many. And by the time the front door lock jingled, my lips were swollen and tender.

"You kids still up?" Miss Molly asked. It was well past two o'clock.

"Yup, just been talking," Layne said easily.

"Uh-huh," Molly said like, *yeah sure.* She bit back a smile.

Layne stood up and got some extra blankets out of the closet and a pillow. "Good night, Regan. Night, Mom."

"Looks like it was," she muttered under her breath. She kissed the top of my head before she headed to her room.

Chapter 14

Props to you Barry

I rose early, early, the next morning thanks to my trusty phone alarm, folded the blankets, and wrote a thank-you note on the bottom of Miss Molly's grocery list. *Wow, food alone must cost her a fortune*.

I wanted to make it home to help Gramps with the chores. It wasn't completely light out yet, but the roads had been cleared and sanded. The plows worked through the night.

The sun's rosy morning glow spilled its magical light on the jagged peaks. It crested slowly over the billowy white mountainsides, spreading a blanket of pearlescent pink. A foot of unmolested powder covered the rolling pastures. The evergreen trees sagged under the weight of snow. I stopped in the middle of the road and snapped a picture with my phone.

A bald eagle soared high above my head, catching the thermal currents in the air. Its wings glinted bronze as the sunlight glanced off the feathers.

I pulled into our driveway just as Gramps was starting the tractor.

"Hey." I hopped out of my truck. "Let me go change. I'll plow the road. Go get some coffee." I shooed him away. "I'll be in for some when I finish."

Officer Baylock's squad car was still in the driveway. I steeled my core for what I was about to encounter when entering my house. I clamped down tighter on my glass box of darkness.

Both he and my mom were at the table drinking coffee, too. His ears and nose were tinged pink. He was good-looking enough if you were into the whole cop thing; he had a crew cut and thick neck. Too much time in the gym and not enough time spent working out his brain.

"Oh, good. You're home. Barry helped Grandpa feed the cattle this morning." Sara's tiny hands clasped around the hot surface of her favorite mug. On its white ceramic face was a picture of her kids. I was five; I still had light blonde hair and a button nose. The twins were 10; they were skinny with extra-long arms and legs.

"Your name is *Barry*," I said like it tasted bad on my tongue. "What? Your parents didn't like you, or they ran out of names?" I had heard that he had like eight or nine siblings. It wasn't that I really had a problem with his name. I had a problem with him.

"Regan!" My mom stopped with her cup in mid-air. "Be nice."

"Oh, look at you," I said with fake sincerity. "You found a reason to get out of bed and stop drinking. Perhaps take a shower occasionally? Good for you." Shock, then shame filled her pale blue eyes. Her lips thinned into a hard line, probably to keep from crying.

"Hey," Barry said like I had hurt his feelings. "There's no need to disrespect your mother."

I flipped them the bird before slamming my bedroom door. I threw on some ratty clothes and stormed outside. I shoved sunglasses on my face. It had only been seven months. *Seven months* since my father died. Anger pressed against my chest like a boulder.

I set my butt on the cold metal tractor seat. What if Barry thought he could replace my dad? What if he wanted the money from the life insurance policy? Fury and paranoia tapped their blackened talons on my brain. The golem's sharp claws scratched the surface until I was raw. I needed to release some steam before it built up and I ended up back in the nut house.

I shifted the tractor into low gear, lowered the plow blade, and meticulously cleared the long driveway. I seriously contemplated piling snow around the cop car.

Instead, after I finished plowing, I sat in front of Grams's kitchen window, drinking cocoa, and waited for Barry to leave. By the time he meandered out of my house, I'd drank four cups of coffee on top of the cocoa. But the tingle growing from my chest to my fingers to the tips of my toes was not the caffeine. The growing concern on Grams's face didn't faze me.

I wish.

Hmmm. Barry struggled; he didn't like my idea. An evil laugh echoed inside my head. I concentrated harder. He fought back. The high was much stronger when they put up a good fight. *Props to you, Barry*. Then I pushed. He shifted the car into reverse, and his studded tires propelled his car into the sharp edge of the steel plow blade. His rear bumper didn't stand a chance, and it crumpled under the stronger metal.

I sat back and relaxed into the high.

Chapter 15

Lion's Den

Later that night, I flipped aimlessly through the satellite dish channels. Sara unloaded the dishwasher, putting the pots and pans away like she was intent on breaking them. She stomped over the floor, slammed cupboard doors, and huffed intermittently. We successfully ignored each other all day. Usually, I'd go to my room to avoid her silent treatment, but that would be letting her off the hook too easily.

I wanted to make her uncomfortable. Squirm. She needed to think about her betrayal to my father's memory. I know what I did might seem worse. I killed him; but it was an accident. Sara was making a conscious choice to date so soon after my father's death. But, as unpleasant as this was for me, it had to be worse for her because my face, which looked just like his, was a constant reminder.

My phone began to buzz in my pajama pocket, startling me out of my angry haze.

Miss Molly, the caller ID read.

"Hey, what's up?" I answered.

"Oh . . . I hate to do this. I know it's kind of late."

I looked at the time: nine p.m. "No worries. What do you need?"

"It's Layne."

I sat forward in my seat. "Is he okay?"

"Yes, for now. But I hear he's at the Clearwater's. Apparently, the football team is having a small get-together. If they are drinking, and Layne gets caught . . ." The rest of her sentence slipped away into the background of a cacophony of voices and drunken laughter.

"I'll go get him."

"Oh, Regan, I'm so sorry. I tried getting out of work, but we have our hands full here." Her voice was filled with exhaustion. "And I really could use the money."

"Enough said. I got this. Text me the address." I hung up. I flipped the cozy, warm blanket off my lap and hightailed it to my room. I googled the directions.

I threw on the necessities: bra, T-shirt, leggings, sweatshirt, and snow boots. I grabbed my coat, hat, and mittens as I walked out of the house.

"Where are you going?" my mom yelled. Her voice was cut off by the slamming of the door.

"Like you care!" I yelled back.

The door swung open and hit the side of the house with a crack. "Get back here right now!" she screamed.

So much for the silent treatment. I kept walking. Really, what was she going to do? Tackle me? Ground me? Punish me?

I threw my truck in drive and turned up my stereo. Angry opera blared from the speakers. Out of my rearview window, I watched as my mom ran after me in untied snow boots and a billowing pink bathrobe. I cackled. She was screaming in sync with the music, but I couldn't hear her over the powerful aria.

Soon my phone began to buzz. I shut it off.

This was the first time I was thankful I'd been reduced to using a CD instead of my phone. My truck was antiquated so it lacked Bluetooth connectivity, and the internet was sketchy here in the country at the best of times anyway.

I drove around and only got lost three times. By the time I found the correct road, I was steaming mad. This whole day had piled one heap of dung on top of another, and I was having a hard time controlling my temper. Little wisps of smoke began to escape from the glass box. The golem's darkness wove its way through and around, curling and weaving, finding the cracks in my armor. Every place it touched, its inky stain spread like blood through a bandage. With a white-knuckle grip and clenched teeth, I eased slowly into the crowded driveway and parked next to a shiny black SUV.

I concentrated on the madness and angry thoughts seeping into my brain. My mom and her new boyfriend were erasing my father's memory. He was everything to her, and so quickly she was willing to forget. Her selfishness made me want to hurt her. I pumped my fists and focused on my breathing. In through the nose, count to three. Out through the mouth, count to three. And again. I sat there for ten minutes, reigning in my temper. My crazy needed to be on lockdown before entering the lion's den.

And what a lion's den it was. A modern fortress cloaked in powdery white snow. Hard concrete edges morphed into endless walls of glass. Flat lines of the roof slashed harshly across the backdrop of the jagged mountains.

I plodded up the three flights of heated cement stairs to the front door. Softened light shone through the slated wood and frosted glass door. I knocked gently, waited, and then rang the bell.

No one answered so I tried the door.

It opened.

For as cold and hard as all the materials used to create this house were, the lighting and décor was soft and warm: cherry floors, suede couches, a silent fireplace, and a large mirror above the hearth that reflected the windows and muted scenery outside. Floral paintings, grand landscapes, and a large canvas of a family photo lined the hallway to my right.

"Hello," I said. It echoed down the corridor, bouncing off the tall ceiling.

I stopped in front of the family portrait. Two parents. Ten kids. Some obviously adopted. Others not. But they all appeared happy. Now at least I knew I was at the correct house. Brad Clearwater. I didn't know his last name until now.

He was one of the few that left me alone.

"Hello," I said again louder this time. But where was everyone?

"Hey," I heard from down the hall. Brad appeared around a corner. He was dressed in jeans, a striped button-up shirt, blue sweater, and the ever-present letterman jacket.

He stopped when he saw me. His rosy cheeks, wide brown eyes, and soft, fine hair tapered tight on the sides that was longer on the top made him look perpetually young.

"Well, you're about the last person I expected to show up here," he said with a very slight southern accent. Thankfully, his voice had matured, even if his face hadn't caught up.

"Sorry. I know I wasn't invited, but I'm here to give Layne a ride home." I held my hands out in front of me.

His eyes crinkled, and a one-sided smile lifted his lip. "No, don't be sorry. You're fine. I just didn't take you for a masochistic type of person."

"So, the G.O.D. squad is here?"

He nodded and tucked his hands into his jacket. "Yeah, to be honest, I'm not much of a fan, but you know . . ." He lifted a shoulder. "Come in here. Can I get you anything to drink? We have beer, wine, or whiskey if you prefer."

I followed him to the kitchen. Sleek white cabinets and silver-flecked granite countertops hovered above marble floors. Professional stainless-steel appliances and minimal upper-shelving completed the modern design. Pops of color and a vase of fresh flowers broke up the sterility. He pulled open the fridge door.

"Water?" I asked. I was shaky from the energy I had expended shoving the golem back in its place.

He pulled out a green bottle of bubbly water and handed it to me. I did my best not to roll my eyes.

He leaned against the huge island and opened himself a bottle of some fancy microbrew. His flushed cheeks and glassy eyes made me think it wasn't his first beer of the night.

"Thanks," I said.

"Yeah, no problem. It's the least I can do."

I cocked my head. "So, is Layne here?"

"Yup, down at the barn with the rest of 'em. But it's nice to get away for a few minutes."

"How did you know I was here?"

He held up his phone and tapped an app on the screen. "Lets me know when the door has been breached.

Nifty little piece of technology. My dad got it from Gabby's dad. He owns a big security company. Black ops kind of shit. Does dirty deeds for the government. He's a dangerous mo fo." He tucked his chin and looked me hard in the eyes. "You know that, right?"

"I suppose I heard it somewhere." I sipped the fizzy water.

"It's how she gets her dirt on everyone." He stuffed his free hand into his coat pocket.

"What are you talking about?"

"You've never been curious as to how Gabby keeps all of us under control?" He laughed jadedly.

I splayed my fingers by my head. "I figured she did it the old-fashioned way: brass knuckles, baseball bats, and cement boots." Along with her parents owning half the town and having judges on the payroll. But still?

This time, he laughed for real. "Well, yeah, something like that for the locals. But the rich people who live here? Most of us think she has an inside man at her dad's corporation. Someone who can access the things people want to hide. And if that doesn't work, she lies. Kind of like she did with Jude."

"You don't believe her accusations?" I said.

He scrubbed his hand over his smooth, hairless face. "Nah, no one does really."

"Then why does everyone bow down to her?" I scowled.

"You know Jude wasn't the first person she took out. She trampled over a few to get to the top. Most notably Brenda, a local girl and a cheerleader, popular enough and pretty enough to give Gabby a run for her money. They both wanted to be captain of the squad. Then rumor had it that Brenda got knocked up and didn't tell her parents." He took a deep swallow of his drink and wiped his mouth with the back of his hand. "None of us knew any of this until after it all happened. Brenda went and 'stayed with a friend for the summer'," he gestured with air quotes. "And when she came back, she wasn't prego no more. Her parents are devout Catholics . . . seriously pro-life." He tapped the side of his beer bottle with his neatly manicured fingers.

"When her parents found out, they disowned her. They kicked her out of the house. She disappeared. Nobody knows where Brenda went. Gabby was elected captain of the squad. She pretended she had nothing to do with the mysterious paperwork from the doctors' clinic delivered to Brenda's dad certified mail so he had to sign for it. Soon everyone got out of Gabby's way. Better to be safe than sorry." He finished his beer, then threw it in the trash. Then he held his hand out for my water.

"Why are you telling me this? Aren't you scared of her, too?" I gulped the final swig, carbonation burning my nostrils, and handed him the empty bottle.

"Hell yeah, but this is my house and there are no witnesses here. As soon as I take you to the party, I'll revert back to the douchebag you think I am."

I almost spit out the bubbly water.

"Truthfully, I feel sorry for you. You walked into this without a clue. First, you agree to help her boyfriend, then you catch her ex's eye. Yeah, you're screwed. You might've been safe tutoring Layne. It's no secret mathing isn't his strongest suit. And now that he's passing, well, she might have been able to overlook that. But with the way Jude stares at you . . . She can't stand it. Drives the little green monster inside of her crazy." He checked the text message on his watch.

"Seriously? He barely talks to me." I crossed my arms and pursed my lips to one side.

"Wow, you can't see it? I thought you were supposed to be smart." He glanced at his watch again.

"Ah, that's not very nice. Besides, she hates Jude. I mean, she basically accused him of rape."

He tried raising one eyebrow, but the other one followed. "Yeah, but no one believes it."

"So, if no one believes her, then why—"

He cut me off. "You're just not getting it. Because she has dirt on everyone."

I wanted to ask what she had on him, but everyone is entitled to their secrets.

His eyes narrowed as if he were reading my mind. "Besides, she doesn't have to have dirt on you personally. What would *you* do to keep your family safe?"

I thought about my mom. Even if I were mad at her, I would go to the ends of the earth to keep her out of harm's way. And my grandparents with the ranch, my brothers, Jude—even if he wasn't talking to me—and Layne. I was starting to understand the influence Gabby's family had on this town.

I couldn't imagine Layne having any skeletons in his closet. But it's easy to control people when you threaten their loved ones. Gabby had the means to uncover their secrets. Her ability was almost as maniacal as mine.

"Come on, we better go before someone comes to find me." He led me into a mudroom neatly packed with rubber boots and thick jackets, then outside to a curving cement sidewalk.

"I really wish you wouldn't have gotten off on the wrong foot with Gabby. You're nice. Easy to talk to. In another life, I think we could've been friends."

I believed perhaps it was the beer that made me easy to talk to, but I didn't correct him.

Tall lamp posts with flickering yellow lights lit the path to a huge white barn that looked like an old fashion carriage house. A peaked black tin roof, gabled dormers, and black shutters clashed with the enormous modern mansion.

"The house was my father's choice. The barn was my mother's. You can take the girl out of the south, but you can't take the south out of the girl."

Long-legged horses corralled in a separate white fence didn't even lift their heads from their hay as we walked by.

Brad opened a side door and shut it behind us.

Domed steel lights hung from the post and beam ceiling. Horse stalls with crisscrossed wooden gates and rod iron uppers ran the length of the brick cobblestone floor. Only a faint scent of manure hovered in the air.

It was overpowered by wood smoke. On the other side of the open barn doors, a bonfire roared inside a stone firepit in the middle of a vast concrete pad. Students congregated into groups, most with alcohol in their hands. Some with joints. Others danced to the loud country music.

"You want me to go get Layne so you don't have to?" he said loudly.

"No, I'll be fine. Curiosity and that cat thing, ya know?"

Brad pressed his lips together. "Okay, well, sorry, you're on your own now."

I nodded. "Thanks." My voice was like a double-edged sword. Both sincere and sarcastic.

I stuck close to the stall doors. My floppy boots clunked on the patterned floor.

A silver stock tank full of ice and beer sat next to a wooden table covered in snacks and half-consumed bottles of wine. I swiped some cheese and chips and nibbled while I rested against the doorway.

A student with headphones propped above his ears spun music from a makeshift DJ station under a covered tent just outside the barn. He played a mixture of rap and country, sometimes both together. I kind of liked it.

The flames swayed with the beat of the music and were actually doing a better job than most of the drunk girls. Except for the G.O.D. squad. Gabby and Olivia officially mended fences. The G.O.D. squad was back together. 2.0. *Puke.*

They moved like professional strippers. Every guy in the place was mesmerized by their slinking bodies in tight clothes and four-inch heels. Even Layne. He stood with a group of his friends, holding on to a beer and laughing. At the end of the song, Gabby scooted up behind him and wrapped her arms around his waist. She slid her hands into his front pockets. His body went rigid, and his jaw knotted under clenched teeth. He took a deep breath and then smiled tightly.

Jealousy reared its ugly head. I closed my eyes for a second reigning in my emotions. If it and the golem were to meet, I could only imagine the disastrous outcome.

Then apparently another great song began to play because she, Olivia, and Destiny ran back to the dance floor.

A small amount of hope jolted my heart when

Layne's shoulders dropped with what appeared to be relief.

Now seemed to be the perfect opportunity to make my move.

I strolled across the cement.

I stepped up next to Layne and tugged on his jacket. He looked down, as did all his friends. Sometimes I forgot how little I actually was. It irritated me but often worked to my advantage. People underestimated small things. Every year, bears kill less than ten people. Sharks the same. Yet we're all terrified of them. No one gives two thoughts about a mosquito. More than 600,000 lives lost per year. The numbers don't lie.

A real smile lit up his face. "Regan." Then it faded to concern. His eyes darted to the makeshift dance floor. His friends glared at me and crossed their muscled arms. Except for Brad.

I pulled Layne down and whispered in his ear, "Your mom asked me to come get you. She said people in town are talking about this party, and she doesn't want you to get busted."

He shook his head like I was ridiculous. "I'm fine. Really. You need to go." His eyes flickered toward the flames.

I caught the tail end of Gabby swiping her hand across her neck toward the DJ. The music stopped. The cracking and popping of the fire and the faint mooing of distant cows were the only sounds. Gabby stood stiffly, glaring at me with one hand on the curve over her hip. Perspiration on her forehead glinted in the light. She ran her fingers through her long golden hair and tossed it over her shoulder. Everyone's focus shifted from her to me, then back to her. Her tongue rolled behind her cheeks and then a scary smile spread on her face.

She cocked an eyebrow at Olivia and Destiny, and they followed her as Gabby cat-walked her way over to Layne's side.

She clasped her elbow around his. "Who invited this trash?" She peered down at me.

"Gabby," Layne admonished. "There's no need to be rude. My mom sent her to pick me up. She's worried the party's going to be busted."

"Oh, you poor people are so naïve."

I wasn't sure if she meant *poor* as in she felt sorry for us or *poor* as in finances. I was betting on the latter.

"*Our* parties don't get busted. Seriously. You can go now." She dismissed me with a wave of her hand. Her diamonds sparkled in the firelight.

I didn't move.

"Brad," she demanded. She tapped her foot.

Brad tilted his head toward the door. I could tell by the look on his face he felt bad. Seeing as he'd been so nice to me earlier, I decided not to make a scene.

"Are you coming?" I asked Layne as I took a step backward. Olivia and Destiny took three steps forward.

I inhaled sharply. *Breathe. Breathe.* I had just gotten the golem calm, but it wanted nothing more than to escape captivity. Ideas of malice danced through my mind. The smoke darkened from gray to black in anticipation, slithering along the seams, testing the security of the glass box.

Layne's head fell. "Gabby, I'm going to go. It'll make my mom happy."

Her eyes widened, then narrowed. She hissed, "Don't you dare go with her. I'm warning you."

Horror struck his face. Deep lines creased between

his brows. "You don't own me." He yanked his arm away from her.

Challenge accepted, her expression said. But her concerned voice contradicted her face. "Of course, I don't." She batted her fake eyelashes.

Everyone else's eyes rose in surprise. They were *all* owned by her. She was the puppeteer.

A slight nod of her head was all the warning I received before something slammed into the side of my cheek, then bashed my stomach. Pain radiated over my eye socket, my cheekbone, my nose and my guts. Bells tolled between my ears. I fell to the ground. My breath refused to cooperate as I tried to inhale. Rocky grit from the cement bit through the thin material of my leggings and blood ran hot in my mouth. Finally, I gasped for air and filled my lungs. I opened my jaw wide and blinked my eyes, trying to get rid of the flashing stars in my vision. Three sets of feet stood around me, two sneakers and a pair of shit-kickers.

Chaos erupted behind them, but all I could concentrate on was keeping the darkness at bay. The golem strained at the cracks and pushed hard against the wall of my skull. The stars flashing in my eyes grew to one big sheet of light. Noise whooshed out of existence like all the oxygen had been sucked away. *Breathe in. Breathe out. Breathe in. Breathe out.*

The last time this happened I killed my father. Though I wanted nothing more than to punish Gabby, Olivia, Destiny, and the dude who clocked me, there were innocent people here, and I didn't want to hurt them. I didn't want to accidentally hurt Layne.

I found focus imagining his brilliant blue eyes. They were almost the same shade as my father's. And I couldn't handle more lifeless blue eyes waking me at night. *Breathe in. Breathe out. One. Two. Three. Four. Five.*

Muffled sound came back first as if I were listening to the mayhem from underwater. Then the white light dimmed, leaving me almost in total darkness. I squeezed my eyes shut and opened them, allowing my shot pupils time to adjust.

Once I had most of my anger under control, I got up and dusted the gravel from my hands and knees. Three football players held on to Layne. He was struggling to get to the guy who hit me.

Brad was having some serious words with the dude and was pointing for him to leave. Gabby was huddled with her squad, their arms locked together like a doll chain. She caught my eye. The fake fear plastered on her face morphed into a sly smile.

I spit blood onto the ground, its red color black on the gray concrete, and walked away.

I'd made a promise to myself not to exact revenge on my account, at least on this kind of scale. And tonight, I was having a hard time keeping my promises.

"Regan!" Layne hollered from behind. I stopped with my hand on the barn door. "Wait!" Heavy footsteps smacked the stone floor, slowing down right before they got to me.

He turned me around by the shoulders. "Oh, my God! Your face." He reached up but hesitated. His jaw twisted tight. His hand shook. Beer and his cologne wafted over the smell of hay, oats, and campfire.

"Let's get you home so I can clean you up." He placed his hand on my midback and guided me out the door.

We made our way out of the fancy house to my pickup.

"Are you okay to drive?" Layne asked. "I would but I had a couple of beers. And while the cops might ignore that, they certainly wouldn't overlook drinking and driving."

"I'm fine." It wasn't far to his house.

"Regan, I'm so sorry. I don't even know what happened back there. One minute I was arguing with Gabby, and the next minute you were on the ground with Carson standing above you. I can't believe he hit you. What the hell? And why?" He tapped a closed fist to his forehead.

"Gabby."

"What do you mean?"

"She made him do it. She must have some dirt on him," I said.

He let out a deep breath. "I'm starting to think the rumors are true. Carson must really be scared of her. I still can't believe he hit a girl."

"She threatened you, too."

"Yeah, I caught that. She thinks she owns me." He scrubbed his hands over his hair. Frustration and fear bled into his words. "Perhaps she does," he whispered, staring out the passenger side window into the blackness.

We drove in silence. I focused on the road, trying to be extra careful now that my depth perception was altered. My puffy eye made it difficult to see.

I pulled up into Layne's driveway, parking in his mom's spot.

He stumbled out and opened my door. He helped me down from the truck seat and swept me immediately into his house and into the kitchen.

He wet a washcloth, then found a bag of frozen peas. He wrapped the two together and then set it against my eye. I twitched from the sting, but the cold soothed the pressure building behind the socket.

He squatted down in front of me and used my knees as balance. His warm hands instantly penetrated my thin leggings.

"You know I don't usually drink. I had to . . . just to make it through the night. I didn't want to go to the party with her. Not after last night with you."

He cupped my good cheek and swiped his thumb over my bottom lip. It quivered and parted at his touch.

His blue eyes dilated, and his nostrils flared as he took a deep breath. "I know we agreed to just be friends for the time being, but I want more. Seeing you thrown to the ground like that . . ." He looked away. "I've never been so scared and angry. I can't let anything happen to you." His free hand squeezed hard on my thigh.

I wanted to tell him not to worry about me. I could take care of myself. But how could I convince him without showing him? He would know I was as much of a monster as Gabby. Given my abilities—worse.

"I don't know what to do. I want to break up with her, but I am afraid. I'm afraid for you, and if I'm being honest, I'm afraid for me too. She could jeopardize my career. It's the only shot I have at a better life for my mom. I ain't no rocket scientist."

"You're smarter than you give yourself credit for." I set my hand against his hard chest. His heart beat under my palm. "But we're not going to worry about it right now. You have football to focus on. Let that be your excuse not to hang out with her as much." I put my fingers in his hair and petted it down. "Your mom said you've already received multiple offers. Full ride scholarships. Let's do this one step at a time. I'm not going anywhere. I'll still be here after the season is over. Then we'll figure it out. Okay?"

He smiled. "But what do I do about Gabby until then? I'm a terrible actor."

"Drink more beer?" I offered.

"Not helping." He tapped gently on the end of my nose.

I flinched. "You'll figure it out." I closed my eyes, trying to ward off the impending headache.

He groaned.

"But I have to go before my mom sends the posse after me. So, I'll see you Monday?" I said.

He pursed his lips and nodded.

I hopped in my truck and turned on my phone. An obscene number of messages awaited me. I deleted the voicemails from my mom without listening to them. Most of the texts were from Jude. I hated how I my heart stuttered seeing his name.

—R U OK?—

—I heard what happened.—

—Why didn't U kick her ass?—

—RU still ignoring me?—

What? He's the one who's been avoiding me.

I responded.

—I'm fine. I look like crap but otherwise ok.—

I got back a quick thumbs-up symbol.

Nothing more. That was it.

So, I drove home to the nonexistent welcome of my very angry mother who was already in bed. Good.

Chapter 16

Satan

Football season came and went. They were state champions thanks to Layne. His golden boy status skyrocketed to platinum. Baylor, Penn State, Syracuse, Florida, and Washington (go Huskies) were all on the list of full-offer scholarships. Most schools had made their intents known by the end of his sophomore year, but he was going to have to commit to one in the next few weeks. Gabby wore his success as a badge of honor. You would have thought she was the Queen the way she strutted around. *The Queen of Denial,* I thought. Everyone could tell Layne wanted to break up with her. He really wasn't that good of an actor.

Layne and I had kept our growing *friendship* on the down low. The only times we truly interacted were at his house on tutor days. We had decided, together, after the season was finished, he would break up with Gabby. It was December 20, almost a month later, and he hadn't severed the cord. So maybe it was me who was in denial.

He promised to do it after he got back from Christmas break. He was spending it with his dad (the first time ever). Fancy that . . . *Now* his father was interested in him. He was going to visit the Florida State campus when he was down there.

Besides, the timing wasn't good for me either. I'd taken the holiday off work so I could pull my weight on the ranch. Gramps hadn't been feeling well lately.

I set my alarm for 4 a.m. and awoke to two feet of powder and it was still snowing. Dressed in an obscene amount of clothing, I stood on the edge my front porch and stared into my grandparents' kitchen window. Rainbow Christmas lights lined the roof of their house. The trees in the middle of the yard with corkscrewing, blue-and-white string lights made the ranch look like a winter wonderland. Barry had hung them. Then Mom had invited him to Christmas dinner. He couldn't make it. He was working that day. Something about being the low man on the totem pole after he wrecked his squad car. I couldn't control my maniacal grin.

I checked the temperature gage: a balmy two degrees. I trudged a path to my grandparents' front door.

The lights were on, but Grams was nowhere to be seen. No coffee brewing. No breakfast on the table. A terrible wet hacking noise came from the back of the house. For the first time, I noticed it smelled like old people. But riding over the smell of roses, powder, cats, and grandpa's dog was the stench of sickness. Raw and damp. Dusty and brittle.

"Hey, Grams? Is everything okay?" I hollered in the empty house.

She stepped out of the bedroom door and shut it behind her. Her long silver hair hung over her shoulder in a thick ropy braid. The creases in her face and the dark circles under her watery-blue eyes startled me. She looked frail. Tired. "Baby, Grandpa isn't feeling so well. He's determined to do chores."

"Tell him to stop being ridiculous. I got this. It's not

like I haven't helped him like a thousand times." I lifted my chin.

"But there is so much snow . . ." She looked helpless and lost.

"What difference does that make? I'll put chains on the truck." I shrugged my shoulders like it was no big deal. My stomach heaved, twisted, and then tied itself in a tight, little stress knot.

"I'll text you after every chore is done. Okay. I'll take pictures and send them to you so Gramps can check my work." I winked.

I snatched the keys off the wall and hit the automatic start button for the fancy farm truck. Thankfully, it was already in the barn. I would let it warm up before I took off. I made it outside past one of the decorated trees before the panic set in. It was one thing to help; it was a whole new adventure doing everything on my own.

I pulled the chains from the slatted wood wall. I knelt down on the dirt floor, and, one by one, wrapped them around the tires. They had studs, but today, with the snow being so deep, I wasn't sure it would be enough.

I dragged a seventy-pound hay bale off the pile and propped one end against the open tailgate. I heaved the other side and lifted and pushed. I did it three more times, then climbed into the back of the truck. I grabbed the twine and wrestled the hay bale on top of the first layer. Once I finished the pyramid stacking system, I took a picture and sent it. I filled four five-gallon buckets with cow cake—a fortified food for the cows that was pressed into cylindrical cubes—and opened the barn doors. Snow, accompanied by a fierce wind, screamed in. It whirled around like an angry swarm of bees before it settled to the ground.

Hopping into the cab of the pickup, I drove out and then shut the barn doors behind me. This was so much nicer than my truck. It had automatic everything and heated seats. I didn't turn them on. I was already sweating. No need to feel like I peed my pants.

Heavy gray clouds hung low in the dark sky. I turned on my headlights. I wasn't sure they were helping.

The rutted dirt road was missing; it was buried two feet under the snow. I created my own path to the first gate. I didn't have far to go. But I couldn't feed the small herd without the truck.

The cows didn't bother me, I actually liked them, however, the prize bull, Gaston, who I secretly referred to as Satan, scared the bejesus out of me. He was butterscotch and white with bulging shoulder muscles and a meaty hump on the back of his neck that sat higher than his blocky head. He had a bronze ring through his nose and balls that nearly dragged the ground. He and I were *not* friends. He loved everyone but me. My grandparents claimed he was a gentle giant. He seemed to think I was a danger to his harem. A predator. A wolf in sheep's clothing. Ultimately, he was right. *Smart bovine, that one.* Didn't mean I liked him, though.

I opened the gate and used all my strength to squeeze it shut once inside. I drove through the pasture in four-wheel drive and made it to the next gate with no issues.

My phone dinged.

—Grandpa said to make sure you have the hot shot with you.—

I checked the back seat. Hot shot, cattle prod—nope. *Son of a B.* Oh, well, I was too far to turn back now.

I checked my surroundings before opening the final

gate. All clear. No Gaston.

I drove a bit farther and pulled to a halt in front of the wooden windbreaker used to keep snow from drifting. It prevented me from getting very close to the stock tank. I left the truck running and hopped out. When I got around the slatted wood, I saw the automatic watering system had frozen, and the tank was almost empty. The electric heater was dangling in mid-air by its cord.

In the distance, the cows mooed. They knew their breakfast was here. I left the water pump running. I would come back for it after they were fed. I awkwardly clambered into the cab, shifted the truck to low gear, and jumped out while it was still moving slowly forward. It was an easy way to spread out the hay so all the less pushy cows could eat without getting bullied by the others. Waiting until the tailgate was within reach, I grabbed it on its way by and scurried into the hay-filled pick- up bed seconds before Gaston figured out it was me and not Gramps. He pawed the ground and lowered his head like he was going to take on the truck if need be.

My shaking hand dug the knife from my pocket and slit the twine. I kicked the hay bale off the moving vehicle. The cows immediately started eating. Gaston not so much. I emptied a bucket of cake in one of the snow ruts, hoping that would distract him. It worked. Thankfully, they were cold and hungry. I switched between hay and cake. Now I had to jump out and make it to the cab before it ran into the barbwire fence. It was somewhere in the near distance, even though I couldn't see it through the storm.

I flew over the side and ran fast, lifting my legs high, trying to traverse the deepening snow. I slipped and fell, but managed to jump in the cab and stop the truck in time before it hit the fence.

Turning the steering wheel wide, I drove away snapping a picture of my work along the way.

Cows fed. Check.

I maneuvered the truck next to the wind break approximately twenty feet from the water tank. The cows were eating peacefully, but I couldn't spot Gaston through the blizzard. Better safe than sorry, I tucked the shovel under my arm—just in case.

I shut the water spicate off and turned around. My cocky pride crashed quickly. Gaston stopped between me and the wooden windbreak. White steam puffed from his nostrils like a cartoon character. Two feet of snow buried his burly legs but did nothing to diminish his massive size. His ears twitched under the large flakes. He snorted and shook his white head. The ring in his nose bounced. He lowered his face and dug into the snow with a cloven hoof.

I threw the shovel at him like a spear and bolted around to the other side of the water tank. My aim was true. I heard the shovel's metal blade clink off his thick skull even if I didn't see it. But all it did was piss him off. He stared at me from the other side of the tank, a mere eight feet away. *How did he get there that quickly?*

I moved to one side; he followed. My heart raced. Fear cramped my stomach. I tried to control him with my mind.

I wish. Go back to your food.

Nothing. Not even tingles. I tried harder. I opened the box and let out a small measure of darkness.

I wish. Go away.

His nose rose into the wind searching the air. A long

pink tongue snaked out the side of his mouth to his nose. He snorted. Snot flew across the tank and hit me in the face.

Nothing.

My toes were numb, my fingers not far behind. And my phone was sitting on the passenger seat.

I couldn't even call for help. Fear trickled inside my brain. Sweat ran down my spine, soaking into the elastic waistband of my long johns.

Outsmarting him was my only move. I took off my jacket and waved it in the air. He followed the movement with his whole head. I balled it up and threw it hard to my right, and then ducked down behind the variegated metal. My ski pants rasped through the snow as I crawled around to the other side. I was now closer to the fence and the truck. I peeked over the edge of the water tank. He'd taken the bait. He rammed my jacket and tossed it in the air.

I scrambled towards the fence, but he didn't notice. I ran to safety and opened the pickup door. I rested my head on the wheel and gave myself a minute before putting the truck in gear. I flipped on the heated seat and drove home—short a shovel and a jacket.

I finished with the chores. Fed the horses. Fed the pigs. Fed the goats. Milked the cows and gathered the eggs.

By the end, I knew what I *didn't* want to be when I grew up.

Chapter 17

Help

I dragged my tired bones to Grams's house to see how Gramps was doing. No change. She had called the doctor even after he threw a tizzy fit. He had pneumonia and was going to be bedridden for the next few weeks so I asked if they would mind if I called a friend to help.

They seemed relieved by my suggestion.

"Good job, kid," Gramps said before he broke down coughing. It rattled thick in his chest. It wasn't easy to see him like this. I loved him. I didn't want to lose him too. I would do the chores until he was fully recovered.

Later that day, after I took a nap and ate what amounted to a small feast, I tapped *Hottest Guy in School* on my phone. For some reason, I couldn't bring myself to change it. My first instinct had been to call Layne. He would have happily helped me, but he was in Florida.

Jude didn't say anything when he picked up.

"Hello? Are you there?" I said when it stopped ringing.

"Yeah." His voice was deeper over the phone.

"You know what? Never mind. This was a mistake. Sorry," I said before hanging up. The last time I'd talked to him was on Halloween. I thought perhaps we'd made some headway that night since he sent me the barrage of texts after Carson punched me in the face. Now all I got was a nod here and there. A brooding stare occasionally. That was the extent of our recent interaction. Brad was wrong. Jude didn't have a thing for me.

I would simply take the cattle prod with me. Wouldn't leave home without it. Perhaps I could take it to school with me and use it there. The thought made me laugh.

The phone buzzed in my pocket. Jude.

"Regan, why did you call? Seriously? I heard your grandpa's sick. You okay?" Concern tinged his voice.

"Are you for real? How did you hear that already?"

"Small town, sweetheart." He chuckled.

"Oh."

"Whatcha need?"

I almost told him again to forget it. Instead, I packaged up my pride and tucked it safely inside my tiny glass box. I was going to need a bigger container soon. "Your help." I explained my morning to him.

"Yeah, no problem," he said like we were still friends. "Let me tell my mom. She won't mind."

"My mom said you can stay the night if you don't want to drive. We have an extra room. This whole ranch business comes way too early in the morning."

"I get it. I'll be out later. Text if ya need anything."

I rubbed my forehead, confused. How did he go from cold to "we're cool" again that quickly?

I told my mom and Grams who was coming to help, and I expected them to treat him well despite the rumors in town.

Both women stuck up for Jude. Apparently, Officer Baylock told them the whole story. *Score one, Barry.*

Jude arrived in time for dinner. Mom actually

cooked real food: mashed potatoes, steak, and salad. Too bad the steak wasn't named Gaston.

He put a basket of fresh baked Indian fry bread on the counter. His mom made it for us.

I took his bag and pillow to the extra room. I pressed my face in it and inhaled before I threw it on the twin bed. It smelled so nice. Glutton for punishment here.

Mom, Barry, Jude, and I sat down for dinner. It was the first time the table had been used for anything other than vodka bottles, tissues, and empty retail boxes.

Mom and Barry discussed the remodel plans. I gritted my teeth and pushed my potatoes around on my plate.

Jude placed a hand on my knee and squeezed in sympathy. Heat flared up my leg. I tried to ignore the sensation, but my mind and body were at odds.

They lured Jude into the conversation. I learned a lot about him in a short time. I wish I'd known some of the stuff earlier, but he wasn't talking to me until today.

He enjoyed hands-on projects. He wanted to be a carpenter when he finished high school. He spent his summers with his grandparents on the reservation learning how to track, hunt and build things. Sure, he would love to help this summer. Mom offered to pay him. After next year, he planned to attend a trade school rather than a traditional college. He had goals.

I was surprised how easily he held a conversation. In school, he offered answers, but beyond that, he didn't talk much.

My mom was completely smitten. It was hard not to be.

After we finished dessert—vanilla ice cream and homemade fudge sauce (my dad's favorite)—I showed

Jude to his room. I didn't want to hang out with my father's replacement any longer.

Grams had the *come to Jesus* conversation with me last week about judging my mom.

"Honey," she had said, "your mom isn't like you. She isn't strong. She never has been. But she is a good person. She loved your dad with all her heart. But she struggles if she doesn't have someone around."

"You mean someone to put her up on a pedestal and pretend she's a princess?" I growled.

"*That's* what I am talking about, young lady." That was the first time she had ever used a sharp tone with me. I didn't want to hear it again. The weight of a thousand guilts were laid to rest upon my weary shoulders.

"Every person has a purpose and your mom's is—"

"Is what, Grams? Can we be honest?" I interrupted.

She dusted her flour-covered hands off on her apron and then rested them on her hips. "Your mom loves to take care of her man. And if that's the only way she will function in this world with a measure of happiness, then you need to back off."

There was that tone again. Tears escaped down my face. She was right.

"I understand you're angry. Your daddy is gone. But we will never forget him. He took such good care with our little girl. From the moment he met her, he promised to look after her. We worried so much about her. She was so easily led astray. Evil picks up on those characteristics. But your daddy poured sunlight upon her. Let her shine. I see the same honesty and kindness in Officer Baylock. Give him a chance."

I left the conversation with my tail tucked firmly between my legs.

I eased up on Barry—was even sort of nice on occasions.

"Man, your mom's a good cook. I'm stuffed." Jude patted his belly as I opened the door to the spare room.

Yeah, when she has men to cook for, I thought sourly. Then I instantly regretted it. I needed to be nice.

"She is," I grudgingly admitted.

He unbuttoned his shirt, took it off, and threw it on the foot of the bed. Then he pulled his T-shirt off over his head. His broad shoulders narrowed to the waist of his jeans. I had to close my mouth. His chest and stomach were nicely etched and so smooth. A thick silver chain and black arrowhead hanging around his neck contrasted with the bronze of his skin. He sat down and dug into his duffel bag.

"The only thing my mom makes is the bread," he said as he laughed. He slipped a cartoon T-shirt over his head and laid matching bottoms on the bed. I had to bite my lip to keep from laughing. His bad-boy reputation was instantly destroyed by a pair of pajamas. "That's what she brings to every dinner party. Every holiday."

"At least it's good." I plopped down in the bean bag chair on the floor.

"I'm sorry about your dad being gone. I know that must be hard on you." He tilted his head towards the living room.

I raised my brows and rolled my eyes.

"But Baylock is one hell of a guy. He advocated for me through the whole . . . you know, ordeal." He leaned forward and propped his elbows on his knees.

"Where was your dad during the whole thing?" I curled my legs under me.

"In Europe on business."

"He didn't even come home?" I was astonished. What kind of parent wouldn't come home for something that serious?

"Nope."

"Were you scared?"

"Terrified. I didn't assault her. Honestly, if anything, it was the other way around."

I held up my hands and covered my ears. "No, no, no, no, no. I don't want to hear this part." The idea of Jude and Gabby together caused the golem to twitch with anger. Funny, it didn't react that way when I thought of Layne with her. Sure, it bothered me, but the golem had no issues with it.

The smirk on Jude's face said he liked my discomfort, but he didn't comment. "Anyway, afterward, Barry checked in with me at least once a week. I think my mom was afraid I'd do something stupid. When I went back to school, I expected everything would go back to normal. I was innocent. I hadn't even been arrested, just questioned. But it didn't matter. All the students are terrified of her. From that moment on I was branded a pariah. Or worse." He paused as if he didn't want to say more. He pressed his lips together and continued. "Do you know what it's like to have people who you've been friends your whole life hate you for something you didn't do? To side with a girl they know is lying? To have adults whisper things like rapist, half-breed, and savage," his voiced cracked, "behind your back?"

I pressed my hand to my lips and shook my head. I chewed on the inside of my lip to keep the tears in check.

"Sometimes it's debilitating. At first, I fought back. But it just made my mom worry more." He shrugged.

"Eventually, I stopped caring. It was the only way I could survive. Until you came along." He glanced at his lap, like even saying he cared what I thought was difficult.

"Jude, I'm so sorry." I got up and walked over to him and wrapped my arms around him. His shoulders relaxed under my touch. "First, for or all those dick-wads treating you like crap, but mostly for doubting you for even a second. Will you ever actually forgive me?" I stepped back, afraid that if I hugged him longer, I would never let go.

"I'll think about it." The softness around his eyes said he already had. But once bitten twice shy. I had to win back his trust.

Chapter 18

Smoke and Mirrors

Jude knocked before he opened the door to my room and thrust a thermos of coffee mixed with cocoa and cream in my hand. Delight fluttered in my stomach. He remembered how I liked my coffee. He leaned against my dresser and picked up the box Layne had given me on Halloween. A tiny smirk tugged his lip. "Where did you get this?"

"A friend gave it to me." I really didn't want to tell him who.

"A friend gave you a box?" he said sardonically.

"No," I grabbed it out of his hand and set it back down on the dresser. "My friend gave me a gift inside the box but I liked the box too, so I kept it."

The corners of his bottom lip dipped downward in a frown, but the rest of his face said he was amused as he nodded his head. I zombie-walked past him out of my room, rubbing my eyes and yawning.

We dressed in a ridiculous number of layers. It was twenty below, not counting the wind chill.

The dry, powdery snow blew sideways, stinging my eyes as we trudged to the barn. The tiny hairs inside my nose instantly froze together, making it harder to breathe. Puffs of fog clouded my vision.

I texted Grams to let her know we were on our way.

Loading bales of hay was much easier with his royal hotness. *What? I did help.* I stacked the hay on the bed of the truck in the pyramid formation.

He didn't even complain when I drove. Then he opened the gates and shut them. No wonder Gramps enjoyed my help. I did all the work.

Once we got to the field, Jude made me stay in the truck and drive. He threw hay and cake. Gaston didn't seem to mind him. Then, at the water hole, he rescued my shovel and my jacket.

He held the coat up by the collar. Frozen solid and covered in cow shit, it didn't change shape. He used the shovel to bust the ice with a few hard hits and filled the tank. The dang cows kept unplugging the electric heater. Jude solved the problem with some baling twine—the rancher's version of duct tape.

I turned on his heated seat and waited for him. I felt useless and lazy.

"Done!" he said when he fell into the passenger seat. Ice crystals clung to his thick, dark lashes, framing his eyes in a white frost and making his brown eyes seem black. His nose ran. I handed him a tissue from the middle console.

When we got back to the barn, I insisted he go inside. I could do the rest. He refused.

Together we finished the chores in record time.

That afternoon, we returned to muck the horse stalls. It was negative three degrees. Downright toasty compared to this morning.

The horses nickered in welcome, sticking their heads over the gates. I clipped a lead rope on their halters one at a time and transferred them to the outside pens.

"So, am I forgiven yet?" I asked with a scoopful of horse dung in my poop fork. I flipped the last of it into the wheelbarrow and sprinkled fresh sawdust down.

"Sure," he said but he lacked sincerity.

"Could've fooled me," I muttered under my breath, but he heard me.

He didn't say anything until we finished bringing the horses back inside the barn. He sat down on a straw bale and took a deep swig of water. I sat across from him.

It was cold, but without the wind blowing on us, it was tolerable.

He shucked his gloves and rubbed his hands together. Then he said, "I trusted you. You told me your secret. Then the next day you disappeared and ignored my phone calls. What was I supposed to think? Besides, I was right, wasn't I? After spending a few hours with Layne, you questioned my guilt."

"No . . . Okay . . . So, a little. I came to my senses quickly. Doesn't that count for anything?" I took off my hat and scratched the itch on my head. The cold burned my ears.

He leaned forward on spread legs and propped his elbows on his knees, his hands casually crossing.

"I suppose. But as much as I hate to admit this, and if you told anyone I would deny it, you hurt my feelings. And I try to keep those bastards tightly locked away. You were the first person at school to treat me normally in a long time. You even seemed to *like* me."

"I do like you."

"Yeah, but do you still?" He tapped the back of my hand. The tiny hairs on my arms prickled.

"Of course, I still like you. I was the one being an idiot."

He smiled and sat back up. “Do you remember the first day we met?”

I nodded.

“Remember when I said you were different? I meant that. You have a gift, but so do I.”

My eyes grew, and then I scowled. I stuffed my rainbow hat back on.

“Nothing nearly as cool as yours. I see people’s colors. Their ‘auras’ for lack of a better term. The purer the person, the brighter the color. People with issues, their colors are deeper, not more pigmented per se, but matted. Dull. Drab. These can change as our lives change. Take your mother, for instance. Her color is pink. Right now, like an old person’s bedspread, it’s tired and worn. But, then again, so is her life. I believe, given time, it will brighten. Baylock’s is a nearly blinding leaf-green. That’s how I know he is a *good,* good man. Both of your grandparents are a bright but deep yellow, like God’s haloed them in a blanket of gold.”

His eyes didn’t leave my face. His gaze was strong and steady.

My chin trembled, not from the cold. My aura was probably as black as my soul. I swallowed, but I refused to ask.

“You want to know what yours is?”

I looked away.

Despite the frigid air, a fine sheen of sweat broke out under my layers. I shook my head and got up. He seized my hand to stop me. He stood up and drew me close. The heat from his body warmed my cheeks.

I didn’t want my worst fear confirmed. I stared at the small pocket of skin peeking out from the gap between his coat and scarf.

"Yours is black. The dingiest, darkest color of soot."

A sob caught in my chest. My bottom lip quivered. I knew it.

"But." He lifted my chin. His hands were warm, even in this temperature. He gazed steadily into my eyes, past their bright blue color straight into my spirit, the essence of my very being. "Amongst the smog, little particles of light shift and sparkle. Tiny stars in the darkened sky. Snowflakes glittering under the moonlight. Diamonds tossed into a stormy sea. Smoke and shattered mirrors. And it is the most beautiful aura I have ever witnessed." His fingers brushed over my cheek. A small flutter rolled in my chest like my heart was trying to gulp air. Frost escaped my opened mouth as I finally remembered to breathe.

"Why do you think I touch your hair? I'm dusting off your glitter. It clings to you."

He leaned down and kissed me. Every star, every snowflake, and every diamond swirled around my soul. A current sparkling just under my skin. Fire. Ice. I was hot. I was cold. My toes curled; my knees weakened. My heart raced. My heart stopped. Flashes of intense, white light burst behind my eyes. I felt like tiny shards of tingling fairy dust floated inside my body.

From the moment I saw him, my body had reacted as if it were electrified. Unseen static had always zapped between the two of us. Then I had to go mess it all up. Then he had to finish the job I started.

A loud *but what if* traveled through my head. Always with the what ifs. I sighed.

But I'd made a promise to someone else. Someone that could keep me on the straight and narrow. Someone who didn't ignore me for months at a time because his feelings were hurt. I realized I didn't like Layne until he showed an interest in me. But I'd made a promise. And unlike my father, my word was my bond. And I wasn't about to break it. Together Layne and I agreed. After Christmas, we would officially be a couple.

I pulled away from the sweetest kiss I'd ever tasted. My spirit screamed like it was being torn in half, skin flayed from my body.

"I can't." My voice cracked with pain. I pressed a hand to his chest. Even through his coat, flannel shirt, and thermal underwear, his heart beat strongly under my palm.

"Can't you feel that between us?" Furrows creased between his eyebrows, and he compressed his lips. He laid his hand on mine and pressed it tighter to his chest.

I nodded.

"So, you don't deny we have something?"

I shook my head.

"Then what?" He lifted his shoulders. His perfect lips parted as if he were about to say something else.

"I made a promise to someone else," I whispered quickly.

"Layne." Jude's hand dropped to his side. Disappointment read plainly on his features. "I heard whispers, but I didn't believe them. I didn't think you'd be that reckless. I understand you have a gift, but don't underestimate Gabby." His nostrils flared, and the hollows under his cheeks deepened. He cupped my chin in his hand and rubbed his thumb over my bottom lip. Sparks raced to the furthest parts of my body, every nerve ending prickled with pins and needles. I almost caved.

"Just remember, I like you. All of you. The shattered

mirrors of light and the darkness that holds it all together. Come on my glitter girl, let's get you inside and warmed up." He held out an elbow.

While I liked Layne, our chemistry wasn't combustible. He wasn't the fuel that stoked the fire. Instead, he was the light to my dark. And I needed his kindness to guide me. And I'd made a promise to myself to protect him, even if he didn't know about it.

Jude, on the other hand, I could lose my heart to. My very soul. Probably already had. But he liked *all* of me. And parts of me were dangerous. Parts that shouldn't be liked.

Chapter 19

One Wicked Wish Will Control Them All

On Christmas morning, Jude left right after we finished the chores. We'd been invited to dinner at his house. Jude said his mom was going to need his help.

I sat down on the living room floor, dusted fallen pine needles off the presents, and separated them into two piles. Mom's and mine. The aroma of the fresh tree diminished over time, but sitting this close, it still smelled outdoorsy.

Gramps still wasn't feeling tip-top, so we agreed to celebrate Christmas with them on New Year's Eve. And it was a bummer that neither Lincoln nor Kennedy was able to make it home for the holidays. Disappointment lingered in my chest, I missed them. Mom and I had assembled a care package for each one of them: homemade cookies, candy, and pajamas—a family tradition. Every year, we all got a matching set from Santa.

She scooted down next to me on the cold wooden floor. Her long hair was pulled back into a ponytail. Naturally pink lips and rosy cheeks set off her wide blue eyes. Sitting there with her hands folded in the lap of her buffalo plaid pajamas, she didn't look old enough to be my mom.

I found a Holiday station on my phone and hit play. It helped with the painful silence. This was our first Christmas without him.

Last year all of us sat around the tree. Mom—dressed in her fuzzy pink robe and red-and-white striped socks—passed out presents. One at a time, we opened them while the rest of us watched and waited anxiously for our turns. Kennedy always guessed what he was getting for Christmas. He was never wrong. I accused him of opening his presents early, then re-wrapping them. He said I'd never know. But now, knowing what I did about myself made me question if he was physic or something. But if he was, wouldn't have he warned me about killing dad?

Ken and Linc always sat closest to the tree, cross-legged like little kids, even as teenagers. Blinking Christmas lights flashed green, blue, yellow, red, and orange in their platinum blonde hair. They competed for attention, the stars of the show, tossing bows and torn paper at my face while I neatly undid the corners of my gifts. Dad egged them on. My family was loud, obnoxious, funny, and did I mention loud? Our laughter echoed in my head. The memory was an ice pick to my skull and another crack in my heart.

Mom and I, in this worn-down house, were a diluted, sad image of the past. On a million occasions, I thought about bringing up my suspicions again. But the last time I tried, she really hurt my feeling by calling me a liar and telling me I couldn't be trusted. Then she drove the knife deeper by saying she didn't know how she was going to raise me, the juvenile delinquent, alone.

So, to keep the peace on this fine Christmas morning, I kept my mouth shut and opened my pajamas, socks, an entire collection of makeup, new jeans, a couple of nice sweaters, and a gift card from my favorite shoe store.

Mom had about the same and a beautiful single-solitaire diamond necklace (thanks, Barry). I told her it looked nice on her. *See? I can be good.*

Barry picked us up in his sporty truck at promptly three o'clock. I guess someone forgot to tell him she was *always* fashionably late.

We pulled onto the heated cobblestone driveway thirty minutes later. A grand log house with a green tin roof jutted over the mountainside. It had a prow front, massive stone chimney, wraparound deck, and a four-car garage. Not what I expected.

"Come in, come in," Jacy welcomed us. A small black Scottish terrier wagged its tail and danced in circles. I scratched the back of his ears.

My mouth began to water; the scent of turkey and bread floated in the air. Jude stood behind the kitchen island in black jeans and a tight black shirt that set off the color of his glorious skin. He also wore an apron that said, "Vegetarian is an old Indian word for bad hunter." *Of course, he cooks, too.* He picked up a long knife and scraped it across the sharpening block, never taking his dark eyes off me. Tension squeezed in my chest. He winked before he turned to the turkey and began to carve, the juicy meat folding under the sharp knife.

I set the pumpkin pies on the counter in front of the window and put the ice cream in the professional-sized fridge-freezer combo.

The doorbell rang, and in walked Miss Molly, carrying green bean casserole. She was alone for dinner, so I'd asked Jude if it was okay to invite her. Jacy said the more the merrier.

An elk head mounted above the stone fireplace wore a Santa hat and green garland around its neck. Real wood crackled and popped in the hearth under the dancing flames. A zig-zag, diamond-patterned rug in primary colors sat under the pine coffee table, which was surrounded by brown leather couches. In the corner was a beautiful Christmas tree. It was ten feet high and decorated in twinkling white lights and crystals. Late afternoon sunbeams shot through the faceted decorations, spreading tiny rainbows all over the walls and the floor.

We gathered around the dining room table, two long slabs of solid wood with raw edges held together in the middle by a wave of gold and silver acrylic. Miss Molly was on one side of me and Jude was on the other. Christmas music played overhead on the built-in stereo system.

Heaps of real mashed potatoes, stuffing, cranberry sauce, fresh rolls, and other tidbits surrounded the turkey. First, Jude had helped me with the ranch work, and then he'd come home and done most of the cooking. *If only,* I thought to myself. A stab of sorrow tightened my throat. He was a ship that had passed in the night. And now that it had sailed, I would never be in a position to catch it again.

Jacy dimmed the chandelier, then poured a rich red wine into crystal goblets for the adults before she sat down. Silverware clinked against the fine white china as we loaded our plates and then dug in. Conversation buzzed in the air. While my mom didn't talk to me much, she was downright chatty with other people. At the end of the delicious dinner, Jude asked me to follow him.

Miss Molly's eyes narrowed slightly, but she caught herself and then gave me a smile. During the meal, she'd mentioned Layne was excited to get home and see me. Jude had clenched his teeth.

The solid cherry floors continued through the house and up the stairs. We passed by a workout room with professional weight machines, an elliptical, a treadmill, and a large, mounted TV with a stereo system.

Jude's room was in a wing by itself. Black-and-white photos hung from the navy-blue walls. The space was so large that the dark color worked. A gray down comforter and fluffy pillows graced the queen-size bed. The headboard was similar to the dining room table downstairs. I ran my fingers over the smooth wood.

"This headboard? Where did you get it?" I asked.

He hesitated and rubbed the back of his neck. The tension in the air was uncomfortable after yesterday. "I made it," he said.

"You did?" I sounded surprised.

He shook his head at my disbelief. "Yes."

"Wow. It's beautiful. And the dining room table?"

"That too. I have a workshop in the garage."

I knew he was artistic, but this was new to me. "I'd love to see it."

A tinge of pink darkened his cheeks. "Someday, maybe. But first I have something for you."

"You do? Ah, come on." I tilted my head to my shoulder. "You shouldn't have done that! I didn't get you anything."

"Yeah, well, you've been pretty occupied the last few days. Besides, I got this for you a long time ago."

I followed him into his closet which was the size of my bedroom. Half of the space stored his clothes. Leaned against the wall, taking up the rest of the closet, were stacks of finished paintings. Color exploded from the canvases, defying the lack of color in his wardrobe. I stepped in and picked up the top one. The one he'd been working on earlier this year in class. Live flames roared over the canopy and burned deep into the forest floor. Black trees embraced by a beautiful monster. Mesmerizing, dangerous, tempting, and deadly. Orange, yellow, and red-hot fire were reflected into the meandering river of blood. The painting was a mirror of life. The gentle river flowed directly through the destruction, changing momentarily, but still managed to survive.

"You weren't supposed to come in here." Jude crossed his arms. "It's a mess."

"Sorry, it's not every day a girl gets to see a closet the size of her bedroom. And this painting. It's spectacular. Why are these not hanging on your walls?" I admonished.

He shrugged. He pulled a small package from the top shelf.

His eyes shifted away from my face. He fiddled with one of the tiny silver hoop earrings hanging from his ear. "This is the first time I've had a chance to give it to you."

He shut the closet door behind us. We climbed up on his bed, and he handed me a gift wrapped in paper covered with stars. I lifted the corners of the paper gently. I liked to take my time. Savor the moment. Inside was a polished wooden box stained black with a light dusting of mica somehow suspended in the finish. It sparkled under the lights.

My eyes narrowed. The box seemed familiar. Sitting at home on my dresser was a similar one. "It's beautiful.

You made this didn't you?" I said.

"Yeah, yeah, now open it," he waved impatiently.

Inside was a bottle of perfume. I opened it and sniffed the contents. "Oh, this smells good." It was spicy vanilla with an undertone of cedar wood and citrus. I should have known he would have good taste. His cologne was my favorite.

"Put it on."

I sprayed my wrists and dabbed them behind my ears.

He leaned in close and inhaled deeply. His breath scorched my neck. I tucked my hands underneath me. *Stay*, I ordered them.

"Yeah," he said huskily, "that's perfect. Sweet yet dark."

The hairs on my arms rose. My chest compressed. "Thank you," I said. I loved the perfume, but the box, I'd never part with. My heart pummeled my chest walls. I shifted my gaze away.

Dozens of books lined the solid wood bookcase: myths, legends, and horror. "No way." I scooted off the bed and grabbed one off the shelf. I reverently held it in my hand and ran my fingers down its worn spine. This trilogy was mine and my dad's favorite series. I swear he taught me to read with these books.

"Yeah, my grandpa gave 'em to me. Said they had some important lessons. You know us Native Americans, big on lessons," he mocked himself.

"Well, obviously you haven't read them." I propped my fists on my hips.

"How did ya know?" He leaned back against his headboard and crossed his arms.

"Because if you'd learned the lesson, you wouldn't

be hanging out with me." I gestured gracefully to my chest like the Queen, then I bowed slightly.

"Why do you say that?"

"One wicked wish will control them all." I held up my index finger and wiggled it a tiny bit.

"What?"

"Haven't you watched the movies either?" I stared at him suspiciously.

"No."

I held up my hands and feigned disgust. "Dude, I'm not sure we can be friends anymore."

"Don't worry; I'll read them just for you."

"Ah, aren't you sweet." I stole a pillow from under him and hit him with it. I jumped back on the bed and set it on my lap, shoving my elbows into its downy feathers.

"You know, I've been thinking about this whole thing you got going on." He waved his hand in the air around me.

I shrugged.

"In Native American folklore, we have the legend of the trickster. Mostly he shows up as a coyote. In some stories as a raven. He bucks society, breaks rules, and tricks both humans and gods. Sometimes he's the villain; sometimes he's the hero. Seeing any similarities?"

I cocked my head and stared at him from under my eyelashes. "So, are you saying I might be Native American?" I looked down at my arm, then threw him a look that said he was crazy.

He laughed and shook his head. "That got me to thinking further. Your grandparents still have Norwegian accents. They're only one step off the boat. Here look at this." He slid down from the bed and snatched a book from the shelf. He opened it and tapped the dogeared page. As I skimmed the text, he kicked off his shoes and sat back against his headboard.

Loki—the Norse God of mischief and fire. Shapeshifter, trickster, adulterer, creator of chaos and mayhem, and an all-around pain in the butt. *Awesome.* But not really. Regan Braaten, long-lost descendant of the God Loki. A god that didn't exist.

"You can take this home and finish reading it if ya want to." He laced his fingers behind his head, the fabric of his T-shirt stretching over his muscular pecs. He wasn't nearly as tall as Layne, but he was every bit as in shape thanks to the state-of-the-art workout room in his house.

I didn't want to take it, but I stuffed it into my bag anyway.

"So, you think there is truth to these stories?" I said.

"Who's to say? Stranger things, right? Either way, your gift is pretty badass."

"Speaking of gifts, how or when did you discover yours?"

He shrugged. "I always knew there was something different about me and my grandpa did too. A couple of years ago he sent me on a vision quest. When I came back, well, let's say, I saw life in a new light."

I wanted him to elaborate further but there was a question burning inside of me. And if I didn't address it now, I might not be able to work up the nerve again. "I've been wondering about something . . ."

"Yes?" A half-smirk pulled one corner of his lip.

"If you can read auras, why in the world did you date Gabby?" The thought of him and her together awakened the golem.

His hands, still clasped behind his head, lifted when

he shrugged his shoulders. “Well, it’s not an exact science. Gabby’s aura is purple, but deep like an old bruise. Usually, that’s a warning.” He huffed out a big sigh. “But she’d just moved here, and I figured she was probably scared and, with time, her aura would brighten. I was wrong. It’s easy to confuse pain, sadness, fear, anger, and hate . . . They all look similar. As soon as I realized who she really was, I broke it off. Auras can be misleading. Take yours, for example . . .”

No, please don’t, I thought. But he continued.

“Your first week here, I watched you.” He smiled apologetically. “I waited for you to do something horrible, something awful. But you didn’t. Even when people were mean to you. You didn’t retaliate. You confused the shit out of me. By the end of the week, I couldn’t help myself; I needed to know more. And once I got to know you, I understood.” His midnight-colored eyes drilled into mine.

The heat radiating from his gaze excited me in a very uncomfortable way. I quickly changed the subject. I didn’t care what he understood. “This house?” I took in the view from his window. It overlooked more snow-covered mountains. “Not what I expected.”

“What do you mean?” He kicked me with his black-stockinged foot. Even that small gesture made my skin tingle.

“Dude, you’re rich,” I said.

“Yeah, so?”

“I just didn’t expect it; that is all. You seem so normal.”

Irritation flashed across his face. “I am normal.”

“Okay, that came out wrong.” *Surprise. Surprise.* “Your truck. Your clothes. You’re one heck of a farm hand. I guess I just didn't suspect." If I had known he lived like this, I would have had the decency to be embarrassed when he stayed at my house.

"I don't live like this all the time. The summers I spend mostly on the reservation with my grandparents. My mom was raised there. It can be rough place. The only reason we have all of this," he pointed to the wood-planked ceiling with pot lights, "is because of my dad. He's an art broker specializing in Western and Indigenous art.

"He claims to be part Native American, though he never had proof, and is obsessed with the old west and anything Native. You can imagine what he thought when he met my mom. She was eighteen. He was thirty. He took one look at her and swept her off her feet. It didn't end well. She got this house; he got the house in New York."

"What about you? You visit him, or does he come here?"

"Not if I can help it. Mom got full custody. And those rumors you have heard about my dad . . . probably true. He's a real piece of work. I don't know if he harassed Gabby or not, but he has quite the reputation. He's rich and handsome. Seems to be a dangerous combination."

"Well, then you're screwed." I snorted out my nose.

A sweet half-smile tugged on his lips. "You think so? I'm good-looking?" He sounded sincere. But he couldn't be.

"Oh, please," I dismissed him. He had to be fishing for compliments.

"No, really?"

I threw him a worm. "You're so far beyond good-looking. Don't you own a mirror?"

A big smile crinkled the corners of his eyes and dimpled his cheeks.

He crawled over to me and stopped—his face inches from mine. The fine hairs on my arms and neck reached toward him, beckoning me to do the same. I held my breath and willed every part of my body to stay put. *Don't move. Don't reach out and caress the smooth bronze skin of his face. Don't run your fingers over his perfect lips. Don't. You. Dare.*

He raised a dark eyebrow up in a challenge, as if he could see on my face exactly what I'd been thinking. "Better looking than Layne?"

I jumped off the bed. I needed to get out of his room. Was he better looking than Layne? Just depends on your taste. Both were hot. One was dark. One was light.

And I needed to stay far, far away from the dark side.

Chapter 20

Cat Got Your Tongue

Winter break ended on a high note. Gramps was better, and Jude went home.

Jude was dangerous. My whole family adored him. Before Jude left, Gramps said he was welcome here any time and was looking forward to working with him this summer on Mom's house. Also, my mom, having fallen in love with Jacy's dining room table commissioned him to build her one. He had a thriving business on the side. His ambition made me like him even more, if that were possible.

Layne got back late Sunday night, so I didn't get to see him until Monday morning at school. His hair was lighter, and his skin had a healthy sun-kissed tan, making his eyes the color of the Caribbean Ocean.

He winked as he passed by my locker with his arm around Gabby. Her hand was tucked in his back pocket.

Following directly behind Gabby was a kid with startling green eyes and messy brown hair. His face seemed familiar, though I knew he wasn't a student here, but I didn't have time to dwell on it. I had to concentrate on my breathing before I lost my temper. I counted through the anger as the golem searched for signs of weakness in the glass box.

Layne, whose hand was resting on the small of Gabby's back, hadn't kept in contact with me much over the holiday. My phone and I aren't really friends. Layne knows this. His phone is like an extra appendage to him. Probably the second most important one.

We had plans for Saturday. I gritted my teeth. It couldn't come soon enough.

Finally, tutor day rolled around. Now we had to work around basketball. Though Layne wasn't the star player, he was good.

Rumor had it that Jude was their best point guard, but the team refused to play with him on Gabby's account. The Musketcheers cheered for the basketball team as well.

The minute I entered Miss Molly's house, Layne picked me up in a big hug and squeezed me hard. His massive frame engulfed mine. He buried his head in the nape of my neck and kissed up to my jaw.

"You smell good," he said, his lips murmuring over my skin. Quivers skated down my body.

"Thanks." I shivered.

"You get this for Christmas?"

I nodded. I wasn't going to tell him from whom.

"I missed you," he growled into my ear.

"I missed you, too." I gripped a handful of his hair.

"I wish I would've been here to help you. Miss Molly told me about your grandpa. He's feeling better now, right?" He set me down on the couch and sat on the coffee table in front of me.

"Yeah, much."

He leaned forward on one knee and raised a sun-bleached eyebrow. "And?"

"And what?"

“Are you gonna tell me who helped you?” He twined his fingers together and cracked them backward.

“Yeah, Jude did. He saved my butt.”

Serious irritation crossed Layne’s face, and he shook his head, but he didn’t say anything else about it. “Here.” He handed me a present.

A small set of silver starfish hung from a delicate pair of earrings. “Thank you,” I said as I took them from the box.

“Here, let me.” Layne picked up the tiny earrings in his long fingers and gently threaded them through my ears. My skin tingled under his touch. But it was missing the hot, the cold, the fire, and the ice. The heart pounding and the blood pumping. His touch was nice. Warm. Comfortable. Safe.

I pulled a package out of my purse. I had gotten him a present.

He ripped the paper like a kid on Christmas. He petted the soft cashmere. “How did you find this? It’s awesome.”

He wrapped the white scarf, with England’s cross of St. George in red, around his neck.

While he loved football, he also loved *football*—soccer.

“How was time spent with your dad?” I reached up and brushed an eyelash off his sun-kissed cheek.

His face darkened. “Let’s call him Dean, shall we?”

“Oh—kay.” I drew the one word out.

“Florida is great. Dean…let’s just say he’s not going to win the father of the year award anytime soon.” He rubbed his hand over his thick stubble. His scruff made him look more mature than all the other guys at school.

I stood up and hugged him, hiding my smile in his

new scarf. Even when I stood in front of him while he was sitting on the coffee table, I wasn't much taller.

"And tomorrow, I'm going to Gabby's, and I'm going to break up with her. I can't do this any longer. She badgered me the whole time I was away. She panics when I get too far away from her. Like her control of me lessens. I get it now, what she's doing. I don't want to be a pawn in her game anymore."

My heart actually sank. I had planned to tell him if he wasn't ready, he wasn't ready. I wouldn't force him to break up with her. We could just stay friends.

I plopped back down on the couch; its old, broken frame sagged under my weight. "Okay, do you want me to come with you?"

"No, I'm a big boy. I got this."

He leaned forward and kissed the tip of my nose. He hesitated and then moved to my lips. His large hands squeezed my knees tight, then crawled slowly up my thighs. His thumbs rested inches away. The pounding between my legs steadily got stronger. His thumbs brushed back and forth, never touching, but coming oh-so close. He moved his hands, wrapped them around my bottom, and lifted me easily onto his lap. The longing deep in my belly thumped to the beat of my pulse.

A cough came from behind us. "So, I guess you've broken up with Gabby then? Good," Miss Molly said.

I scuttled off his lap like a crab crawling backward. My face burned fifty shades of red. Layne's too.

"Tomorrow, Mom. Tomorrow."

"Take Regan with you. You're going to want a witness. I mean it." She leveled him with the mom look. "I need to get to work now." She opened the door, but before she stepped out, she said, "You kids be good. Or don't. There are condoms in the top drawer of my dresser."

And I didn't think my face could get any redder.

"Mom!" Layne snapped at her as she shut the door.

"Sorry about that." He raked a hand over his messy blonde hair. "You want to watch a movie?"

"I can't. I have to go home. I promised I'd help Gramps load hay on the truck tonight so we don't have to do it in the morning." *And I keep my promises* I reminded myself.

We said a long goodbye and then I drove home. I tried everything imaginable to keep images of Jude out of my head. Gramps didn't help. Though he was usually quiet, Gramps went on and on about Jude. What a nice *man* he was. How polite and such a hard worker. And how well he'd handled himself in a nasty situation. Blah, blah, blah . . .

The next morning, Layne picked me up around noon. I invited him in to meet everyone since all of them were gathered around Gram's kitchen table. He shook Gramps's hand and Barry's. He thanked my grandma and mom for the sandwich and cookies. Then he waited while I finished eating. He'd scarfed his lunch down in two seconds flat. They talked football; I tuned them out.

Getting to Gabby's house was an event all on its own. First, we had to stop at a gate manned by an actual human carrying a pistol on his hip and a small microphone in his ear. Surrounding the perimeter of the property was a ten-foot stone fence equipped with cameras. And heaven knows what else. The guard waved us through after he examined my driver's license. Then we wove down a long, paved driveway. As the wall of trees thinned out a mansion—a castle, a compound—

materialized. I thought I understood Gabby's family was rich. This wasn't rich, this was insane. This was 'buy yourself a country' insane.

A feeling of dread coated my skin. "Seriously?" I looked at Layne. He threw me an apologetic smile and half shrugged. At least he wasn't dating me for my money.

He knocked on the mansion door; the expensive wood muted the sound. Then he rang the doorbell.

My heart began to pound. Gabby didn't scare me, but I didn't like confrontation. My dirty work was done from the sidelines. I was an invisible sort of monster. Like the one in the closet. You knew it was there, even if you couldn't see it.

The house had rounded turrets and gray stone walls. It was nothing less than twenty thousand square feet of a modern-day castle. And that was just the house. I could only imagine how the snow-covered lawn was perfectly manicured in the summer. How the shrubs and bushes were sculpted to perfection. How the water in the marble fountains created hazy rainbows as light filter through. It was more than what I expected. My mouth went dry.

"What is *she* doing here?" Gabby surprised me by answering her own door. She wore a pair of black leggings and a flowy white shirt with a very low neckline. A black sports bra shone through the gauzy white material.

"Gabby, can we come in?" Layne cleared his throat.

She opened the double doors wider, daggers forming in her eyes, as I followed him in. A huge crystal chandelier spread a cool glow over the veined marble flooring of the entryway.

"Regan, can you give us a minute?" Layne said.

I smiled tightly.

"Wait in there." She pointed me to a formal sitting room. "Don't touch anything," she said before she grabbed his hand and pulled him away.

I wandered around the curved room. Over the blue-and-white French wallpaper hung gold-framed pictures of pink-cheeked damsels. And when I say pink-cheeked, I mean both sets of cheeks. Some maidens had downy white wings; others were draped in luxurious material covering everything but the important parts.

Six tiny teacups and a pot sat on an occasional table under the leaded glass window. A crochet doily protected the shiny wood. Lace curtains, pulled back from windows frames, pooled on the herringbone wood floor. Floor lamps with gold shades and hanging tassels lit the area in a soft glowing light. A rose-colored fainting chair and a tufted Victorian couch completed the fussy room.

"Well, Regan, you're the last person I expected to be here," a soft southern drawl startled me. Leaning against the door frame was the green-eyed guy who followed Gabby into school last week. I'd forgotten all about him. But instantly, the feeling that I knew him from somewhere nagged at me.

"You and me both," I said. I studied his face, probably a bit rudely but I needed to remember where I'd seen him before. He wasn't *slapped in your face* handsome like Layne or Jude, but the more I stared, the better looking he became. It was his eyes framed in dark thick lashes that pushed him over the edge. They were captivating, deep set and intense. The color bright and haunting in a way I'd never witnessed. As if emerald green was an emotion instead of a hue, all bottled up and kept inside his irises.

"And you are?" I squinted. It was driving me crazy. Where had I seen him before? It was like an itch I couldn't scratch.

He stepped forward and held out a hand like a polite southern gentleman. "Pardon me, I'm Gabriella's cousin, Christian. Most people call me Gin."

His grip was warm and firm. And little bolts of electricity scuttled up my arm and down my spine making me shiver in a *very* inappropriate, uncomfortable way. "Why are you here?" I blurted as I yanked my hand away. I swallowed. Only one other person affected me like that.

An amused grin revealed a perfect set of teeth. "I see you get right to the point. My parents are in France for business, so instead of staying home alone," he quirked an eyebrow, "well, alone as one can be with a house staff of ten or so, I thought I'd finish out my senior year here with my favorite cousin."

Thankfully he laughed at the horror that passed over my face. Normally I was better at hiding my feelings, but Gin made me feel as if I were standing on one foot in a swift river.

"I hear you're a right nasty piece of work." He rubbed his fingers over his lips.

"Me?" I pointed to my chest.

"Yes, ma'am. According to Gabby, you're trying to steal her man." His jewel toned eyes flickered to the other room.

His accusation sounded like a bad country song. But technically, he wasn't all wrong. Though I wasn't *trying* to steal Layne, I actually stole him. Which kind of did make me a nasty piece of work. If he only knew about all the other stuff I was capable of.

A loud crash came from above. I cringed.

"I believe that's my cue to depart. I'm not one for drama. It was nice to officially meet you Regan." He half saluted. "I'll see you at school sometime. Maybe we can chat more." He strolled nonchalantly from the sitting room as if things weren't crashing from above.

"Yeah, sure," I said. The sound of glass shattering and profanities trailed down the grand staircase.

I poked my head out of the parlor. Layne bounded down the wide steps two at a time. "Come on. We gotta go. She did *not* take that well." Worry creased between his brows.

"You go. I'll be right back."

"No, come on," he pleaded. He held my arm.

Gabby loomed at the top of the stairs gripping a vase in her hand like a baseball player about to throw a wicked curve ball. "You son of a—"

I stopped her before she could finish. Tingles shot from my chest, almost instantaneously warming my fingers all the way to the tips of my toes.

I wish. Stop everything. Stop moving. Stop talking. Stop thinking.

"Go to the car. I'll be right out. You need to trust me," I said, giving him a mental push. Nothing that would make me too sick later. I squeezed his bicep. My hand didn't even reach halfway around it.

He shook his head but said, "Okay."

Gabby stood frozen, her lips clamped down on the word, 'bitch.' I ordered her down the steps, pointed to the fussy room, and made her sit down. "You're going to listen to me. When I'm done, I will *let* you speak."

Her glazed green eyes blinked. Her fake lashes

threw a long shadow on her cheeks.

I allowed her to remember this part of the conversation. Her eyes cleared.

The next few sentences were said without coercion. For a moment, I let her have her free will back. I did not command her. My powers were strong, but I couldn't control what she did when I wasn't near, so she needed to concede willingly to these wishes. "You're going to let Layne go. You're going to tell the peasants you got tired of him. He bored you. If you decide to retaliate, I'll take measures into my own hands. And I promise you that you won't like my tactics."

Last week I asked my mom about the banknote the LaCroix's held against my grandparent's farm. I assumed after these many years, the ranch was paid off. She told that as more wealthy people moved to the area, the property taxes skyrocketed. At first, my grandparents sold off parcels of land to keep up with the growing costs. Eventually, they remortgaged when Gramps didn't want to lose more acreage. That's why the cottage we lived in was empty when we got here. They couldn't afford to pay a foreman anymore. Apparently, Barry had encouraged her to pay their loan off with the rest of what she had from my dad's life insurance. He had said it was dangerous being in debt to those folks and since he was going to help her remodel, she'd be saving a ton of money. Another point for Barry. I was starting to lose count.

I leaned down in front of Gabby's face knowing her family no longer had any control over mine. "I have nothing to lose. The question is: Do you?"

I allowed her to speak, but she seemed mute. She squirmed in the chair but didn't get up. "Cat got your tongue?"

Her eyes glowed greener, brighter with her anger. "You . . ." I stopped her before she got nasty.

"No, no, no." I ticked a finger back and forth. "We're going to be civil. Okay. Try again."

Red appeared under her V-neck shirt on her chest. "What are you doing to me?"

"Whatever do you mean?" I stood up, put my hands on my hips, and blinked my wide eyes innocently. *Or not*. I played dumb.

She crossed her arms. Her boobs squished and plumped. She bit the corner of her cheek and looked at her lap when she said, "You need to leave." She swallowed hard.

"Gladly." I waited for her to make eye contact again. "But remember what I said. If you hurt him, I'll destroy you in ways you cannot even imagine." I showed myself to the exit and walked down the short cobblestone pathway towards Layne. He was pacing in front of his bumper.

When he saw me, he stopped and opened his car door.

"What did you say to her?" Layne said, getting in. Gabby stood in the parlor window. The look on her face was priceless, albeit frightening. Inside that little angry brain, she was planning my demise. So long as she only messed with me and left Layne alone, we'd be fine.

"I told her to tell everyone she broke up with you. That way she didn't have to be humiliated. Over Christmas break, she met a man, and you were just a boy."

"Ouch," he said. "That's kind of harsh."

"Yeah, well, girls like that don't get broken up with.

Ever."

"Gotcha." He squeezed my leg. The outline of his hand burned on my thigh. "Now you're all mine."

Yes, I was. I had promised after all. I was his girlfriend. His protector.

****

We held off going public for a month so Gabby could present a viable front. For the most part, she succeeded. Though when she thought no one was looking, she stared longingly at Layne. If I didn't know her, I would've felt sorry for her.

She showed pictures of her new boyfriend to everyone; she posted his face desperately all over social media. She bought herself a new ring and bragged that he was loaded, unlike her last boyfriend. The loser.

Over the course of the next few weeks, I bumped into Gin often even though we didn't share any classes together. I still couldn't place where I'd seen him before. I rifled through my old yearbooks from Alaska to no avail. I scoured tabloid sites, thinking because he was rich, I might have seen him somewhere. But still, no luck. I cyber-stalked him on Layne's phone since I wasn't active on social media. And while Gin had a presence on all of the popular sites, it wasn't a big one. And it's not like I was planning on sending him a friend request.

I swung by Layne's house on Saturdays to help him with his homework, but we kept getting distracted. The kisses got stronger and longer; the petting got deeper. I said we couldn't go any further until we became official. I wasn't sure I was ready for that step. We'd cross that bridge when we got there. Miss Molly didn't help any.

The first Monday in February, we showed up

holding hands. People shoulder-bumped each other and whispered back and forth. The words *slut, whore,* and *I don't get what he sees in her* floated through the halls. So long as I was with Layne, I was safe. On my own, not so much.

Twice, I ended up flat on my butt. Once, I had gum in my hair, and someone spilled soda *accidentally* down my back. It was a war zone. And I was unarmed . . . but not really.

By Friday, I had to unleash. The golem was done being messed with and if I didn't throw it a bone, things were bound to escalate. As two of the Three Musketcheers approached me, belly-baring attire showing off their muscular abs, I made them stop before they were within arm's reach. All I did was make them stop. Harmless really.

Olivia released a verbal butt whooping. She said everything to my face all the others were saying behind my back. I had to give her credit; she had more *cajones* than most of the student body.

She moved close and whispered, "You'd be smart to break up with Layne before he breaks up with you, you freak."

A knot formed in my throat. I clenched my fists. The golem was anxious to show its teeth.

Olivia stepped away and looked around at her audience. She ended loudly with: "Nobody here likes you, even your dad killed himself to get away from you."

White fury flashed in my peripheral vision. Hatred burned in the pit of my stomach. Acid shot into the back of my throat. She'd gone too far. An electric shock pulsed from my chest outwards.

The lights above flickered and the buzzing got

louder, then silenced completely. The absence of noise imploded in my ears. The pressure whooshed, like heavy breathing, but it made no sound.

Stop!

Everyone in the hallway froze. Some in mid-step toppled over. One person in mid-sneeze. Everyone in the school froze but Jude.

When I messed with people, the dirty deeds kept my anger under control, and the high soothed my emotions, dampened them.

This was different. More. As if my golem suddenly learned how to unlock the glass box without my permission. My anger, my uncontrollable rage was its ultimate fuel. Those emotions fed the darkness, letting it attach directly onto my soul. A parasite that escaped its cage. But truthfully, the golem wasn't the only threat. The arrogance and the all-encompassing knowledge that these humans were under my absolute domination were the true dangers. Compared to me, these people were nothing. Delicate creatures without the ability to fight back. I was a lion. They were only mice. And this cat liked to play with her food. A smile promising fear, pain, and humiliation crawled slowly over my face.

"It's about time you defended yourself." Jude's voice broke through the silence. He strolled over, his hands casually tucked into his pockets, and his torn-up jeans stuffed into a pair of weathered combat boots.

My anger receded, one tiny notch, but I didn't let go. The students still breathed and blinked; all their automatic body functions were intact. They just couldn't move, and I wouldn't let them remember.

"You know it's okay." He laid a hand on my shoulder. A kaleidoscope of silver sparkled in my peripheral vison like fresh falling snow glittering in the midnight sky. He was the shard of light I could hold onto in the vast darkness pulling me down. "She deserves whatever you decide to do."

My anger subsided with every exhale. It was a balloon with a tiny hole, deflating until the internal pressure matched the external force. The darkness obeyed Jude's touch and finally crawled back into its box. My vison focused. But even though I was exhausted, I felt stronger, as if I'd spent a day lifting brain weights.

He stood behind me, placed his other hand on my shoulder and whispered in my ear. His breath rolled over my skin and down my neck, a river of calm caressing my body and drowning my anger. "There's my glitter girl." He kissed the side of my head and murmured into my hair, his lips tickling my scalp. "Now make Olivia pay and, for good measure, Destiny, too, but don't make it too bad, or you'll feel guilty later. 'Kay?"

He leaned back against the wall and crossed his arms, his biceps stretching his short-sleeve shirt, and watched the show.

I marveled at how his simple touch and a few words pulled me away from my anger so easily. He deflated my alter ego, forced my golem inside its cage, and gave me back control.

But now I desperately needed to blow off some steam. The darkness, though contained, was straining against the glass box, bending and warping what should have been a solid surface. I flexed my new muscles. Tingles rolled from my chest to my fingers to the tips of my toes.

I wish. For the rest of the day, when anyone says

your name, you will respond with, "I'm a—" I gave them a number of expletives to choose from. And when you address Gabby you'll say, "Those extra pounds look good on you."

So long as Olivia and Destiny were in my vicinity, probably a two-block radius, it would work.

Then I unfroze the entire high school. It was comical watching the people scramble around on the floor baffled as to why they were laying on the ground. Others continued as if they'd never stopped. Conversations picked up in the same spot where I'd cut them off, a sneeze finished, and footsteps pattered down the hall. A couple students tripped over their unsteady limbs. It was funny because I hadn't stopped time, just them. Little did they know that the mystery minutes—small bundles of time where you can't remember, like driving your car but not knowing how you got home—were actually missing. A look of confusion was plastered on everyone's face when the bell rang and not a single one of them had made it to class on time. Jude messed up my hair as he passed by. Later he texted me. *—Very creative.—* With a devil-horned emoji

By the end of the day, all of the Three Musketcheers had detention for the next week.

Chapter 21

Truth and Lies

Layne stood in front of the living room window, drinking his usual, while I filled the sink with steaming hot water and dish soap. Shimmering, pearlescent little bubbles floated in the air and landed on the red, heart-shaped pillows that matched the couch. Twelve boxes of chocolates sat on the kitchen table alongside three sets of a dozen red roses. Miss Molly had her choice of men. Some of them rich as Midas himself. And some of them probably married. But she'd told me before she settled on any of them, she wanted Layne enrolled in college and well on his way to a career in the NFL. What a dedicated momma.

"So, there are some rumors floating around," Layne said without turning around. The window fogged under his breath.

I flinched and gripped the sudsy glass in my hand tighter. After Friday's events, I wasn't surprised. Someone had done their homework. They found my weakness. My father. Now I just hoped they hadn't found my dirty little secret. I had been assured over and over that my lengthy vacation in the psycho ward wouldn't go public. Records were sealed. I was underage.

"Yeah, like what?" I kept my tone neutral.

"Did your dad kill himself?" He turned around and padded his stockinged feet over to me. He laid his large, strong hands on my shoulders and squeezed. No judgement sat behind his kind blue eyes.

"No," I bit out harshly. I inhaled through my nose, slowly getting a grip on my emotions. I continued calmly, "No, he didn't. And I should know, I was right there. And if you don't believe me, the medical examiner ruled it an accidental death also." I rinsed the glass and set it on the drying rack.

There had been a huge investigation. While my dad had been a decorated war hero, soldiers were known to kill themselves from time to time. At one point, I had to tell a judge what I knew. I swore to tell the whole truth and nothing but the truth.

Then I lied.

It's not like anyone was going to believe me if I told the real story, I would have received a one-way ticket back to the looney bin.

I sat in the hot box in a military courtroom with just the lawyers and the judge, trying to decide if my dad's death was indeed an accident or a suicide. A distinguished, gray-haired judge in his black robe nodded for the attorney to begin. There was no jury since no one was on trial, but nerves made me nauseous nonetheless.

He went through a few niceties, so I could get comfortable, before he asked, "Miss Braaten, what happened immediately preceding your father's death?"

I shifted forward on the edge of my seat. The hard bench cut into the backs of my thighs. "We had an argument."

"About?" The lawyer's blue military uniform,

heavy with medals, was hard for me to look at; it reminded me of my father.

"He told me we were moving again. And I was mad." Perhaps an understatement . . .

"And why were you mad?" The nice man folded his hands together in front of him.

"Because he promised we would stay in Alaska. And he lied." I glared directly at my mom, who was sitting behind the attorney's desk on the hardwood benches that reminded me of church pews. Tear tracks stained her pale face. Her eyes, rimmed with red rings, looked green under the yellow courtroom lights.

"Then what happened?"

I bowed my head and clenched my fists. My breaths came in short, shallow spurts.

"Regan?" he prodded me gently.

This was where the truth and the lies all twisted together. "I told him I hated him," I whispered. Truth. I stared at my lap. The blame on my mom's face was more than I could handle at the moment.

"And?"

"Then he accidentally walked in front of the bus." Lie.

"So, you think it was an accident?"

I lifted my head and gave him a look like, seriously? "Of course, it was an accident." Lie. "I had just said something horrible, unforgivable." Truth. "What happened was my fault." Truth. "He was distracted." Lie. "He was upset." Truth. "He didn't even see the bus." Lie.

"So, you don't believe your father committed suicide?"

"No." Truth.

"Why?"

Because I killed him, you idiots. "Because my father wasn't a coward." Truth.

Testimony on his mental health had already been heard: no PTSD, no depression, and no medications. Perfectly normal. Happy. Stable, even.

Well, normal by most people's accounts. After the accident, I dissected my dad's everyday actions with a fine-tooth comb, like I had my brothers. And some things about him were suspicious. Like how everyone, minus his family, did what he said. How everyone was always calm and collected while he was around. He could deescalate any situation like smothering a flame with a blanket. But was that suspicious? Or was he just good at influencing people? Bringing out their best qualities? I still wondered sometimes. I mean, this curse had to come from somewhere, right?

None of this would have been an issue if they hadn't found that video. Someone had their phone out, filming their girlfriend on their Alaskan vacation, and caught me and my dad in the background. We were unintentional photobombers.

The attorney argued it was shock, not suicide. Both accounts were wrong. . .

Layne bent down and kissed the top of my head and nuzzled his face into my hair. "I am so sorry. I didn't know."

I dried my hands off on the kitchen towel and laid it over the clean dishes to dry.

He wrapped me in his arms from behind; heat seeped from his large frame into my tiny one. "Why didn't you tell me?"

"I haven't told anyone." *Lie.* Except Jude.

"Then how did Olivia and Destiny find out?"

"Seriously, Layne? It doesn't take a rocket scientist." His arms dropped from around me, but he didn't step away.

"I thought you said you had Gabby under control?" A dash of irritation tinged his voice.

"I do." I flipped around and faced him.

"If you did, then how come she's spreading rumors?" He lifted my hands to his chest and rubbed the back of my skin with the pads of his thumbs.

"I told her to leave *you* alone. And so long as she does, I won't retaliate." *At least not much.* "Rumors can't hurt me. But she can hurt you. She can destroy your chance at a football career. I can't let that happen. If it makes her happy to pick on me, so be it." I shrugged like it meant nothing.

"Yeah, well, what if I don't like it?" He started to pace over the hardwood floor. It creaked under his weight. He ran a hand through his bedhead, messing it up even more.

I smiled. "I know you don't like it. But if we fight back, it could get uglier. Eventually, she'll get bored if we don't play her game. She'll forget all about me and move on to her next target." And then I would be waiting.

He shook his head. "I still don't like it."

"So, was that all? You heard the lie that my dad killed himself?"

"Yeah, why?" He looked suspicious. "Is there anything else I should know?"

"No." *Lie.* "Just curious is all."

Chapter 22

She Doesn't Play Fair

When Monday rolled around, it appeared the rumors had actually backfired. No longer did people try to knock my books out of my hands, trip me, spill soda down my back, or shoulder-bump me when there was sufficient room in the hallway for more than two people. Some students even managed small sympathy smiles and brief head nods.

By Thursday, someone other than the stoners invited me to sit with them at lunch. The nerds. I guess they finally figured out I was one of them. I had straight As.

I graciously turned down their offer. It was safer for them to stay away from me. At least for now.

Lately, Layne had been pressuring me to sit with him for lunch. No way was I eating near the G.O.D squad. Or the jocks for that matter. The only one that didn't scowl at me with unmanicured bushy brows was Brad.

He said we could sit at a different table, but I flat-out refused. I told him to eat with his friends. I'd eat in my truck. Some days alone. Some days with Jude. It drove Layne nuts. At first, he said he didn't want me around Jude. I laughed and told him what he wanted and what he got were two different things. He turned all pouty.

Jude's long legs strutted across the parking lot toward my truck. I reached across the seat and unlocked the door. "Guess the cat's out of the bag. You can't expect them to get all the details right, I suppose," he said as he swung into the cab. His cologne, mixed with crisp winter air, had me inhaling deeper.

"Long time no see, stranger," I said. I hadn't heard from him over the weekend.

"Yeah, well, date me. Not him. And then you can see me all the time." His eyes glanced from my face down my body. His gaze warmed me from head to foot.

I threw him a look of *bitch, please*.

He laughed, but the sound wasn't a happy one. "Someday you'll figure it out." He moved my rearview mirror to check out his hair.

"Figure out what?" I snapped. I already had it figured out: date Layne whose kindness would keep me on the straight and narrow. Not Jude, who encouraged me to be . . . well, me.

"Exactly," he said like I should know what he was talking about. He attempted to put the mirror back in its place.

"Do we have to go over this again?" I whined and adjusted it to the correct position.

"Nope, I just wanted to see how you were doing."

I handed him a sandwich.

"Thanks." He tilted his head. "How many sandwiches do you need?" he asked, sneaking a look into my lunch bag.

"I only *need* one, thank you. But Grams packs an extra one for you every day. I made the mistake of telling her all I ever see you eat is a candy bar and a soda. She doesn't want you to go hungry apparently."

"Your grandma likes me." A half-smile rose from his lips.

"Yeah, I know."

"So, what do you do with it when I don't eat it?" He paused with his mouth open over the sandwich.

"I toss it to the pigs when I get home."

"Even if it's ham?" He took a bite.

I smiled evilly. "Especially if it's ham."

Once he finished chewing, he said, "You really are twisted." We both laughed. He mussed up my hair. Tremors shot down my spine to every nerve. As good as it felt, I needed him not to touch me. It messed with my head and confused my heart.

"I would eat with you more often, but I don't want to upset your boyfriend," he said snidely. "More than I already have. He doesn't like me here with you."

"Yeah, well, he'll survive. You're the only friend I have."

His eyes darkened, and he looked miffed. He huffed out his nose. "Yeah, well, that's your choice." He paused for a long few seconds. "The other kids have been warming up, but you keep turning 'em down."

"I know. But that's because being friends with me is dangerous. Gabby *really, really* hates me. And I don't want them punished because of me."

He touched the end of my nose with his finger. "See, you and your wicked wishes aren't near as bad as you think you are. Come on. Let's go. Bell rang."

He scooped my arm up with his elbow as we walked to the school. Layne and his gang stood outside the entrance doors. The charming, good-natured expression vanished the minute he saw us. His eyes darted from our interlocking arms to my face.

"You better put your girlfriend on a leash," one of the jocks said.

"Dude, she's consorting with the enemy," another one clamored.

Jude dropped my elbow and ignored them. "Tell your grandma thanks for lunch. I'll see you this afternoon." He winked and walked into the building alone. My heart pouted.

Layne threw his arm around my shoulder as if he were casting away Jude's scent.

He looked down at me and shook his head as if to say, *how could you embarrass me like that in front of my friends?* But he was too nice to actually say it out loud.

"Come on, you." He didn't let go of me until we stood in front of my locker. "There's an assembly this afternoon for divisionals. I won't be able to sit with you; I'll be back behind the stage." He sniffed. "I'd prefer it if you didn't sit with him. Honestly, it makes me all kinds of jealous." He lifted a shoulder. The truth lay behind his blue eyes. My friendship with Jude hurt his feelings, but what it really hurt was his ego. *Give and take*, I thought as I nodded. I would simply find a way to miss the assembly altogether. One that allowed me to avoid Jude and not hurt his feelings either. I didn't want to go anyway.

Layne backed me up against my locker and lifted my chin with a firm, warm finger. He leaned in and nuzzled behind my ear, inhaling deeply.

"Mm, god, I just want to . . ." he growled into my ear. He kissed my neck. He wrapped his fingers hard into my hair and found my lips. There was nothing gentle about him this time. A wave of desire flooded over me. I pulled him in tighter, completely forgetting where we were.

A rude catcall brought me back to reality. I pushed against Layne's chest. He released me. The smile on his face was one of complete and utter satisfaction. Like he'd won the game. My face turned red. Then my skin paled when I noticed Jude watching from down the hall. Layne kissed me quickly and said, "See you later," before he swaggered away.

I tried to catch Jude's eye, but he was gone.

The short classes flew by. Jude hadn't made it to seventh period. I hoped it didn't have anything to do with me. The final bell rang, and everyone flew out of the art room. Except for me and Mr. Clark.

"Regan, you'd better hurry. It is going to start soon."

"Yeah, I know, but I've been meaning to ask you," I said. If you found a subject Mr. Clark was passionate about, he would talk non-stop for days. Thankfully, he was interested in more than art. "I've been thinking about doing a piece focused around the Friday the Thirteenth superstition. I've been doing some research, and, wow, I didn't know . . ."

And that was all I needed to say before Mr. Clark took thirty minutes to tell me the reason behind Friday the Thirteenth. How the Knights of the Templar created the first banking system and got rich. And King Philip of Spain got jealous. He told the pope they were heretics, and together they had them slaughtered on the legendary day. That's the short version.

When he finally finished, he said, "Regan, goodness, I'm sorry. I get carried away. If you hurry, you can catch the tail end of the assembly."

I strolled slowly down the deserted hall. Discarded

papers were scattered over the checkered linoleum tile. Funny, no noise whatsoever was coming from the gymnasium. I expected chants from the cheerleaders, accompanied by stomping on the wooden bleachers and whoops and hollers from the crowd. I stepped into the open double doors to see the entire student body staring at the large projection screen hanging from the stage ceiling. Their eyes were wide, and their mouths were parted. The smell of sweaty tennis shoes and cleaning solution hung in the air.

Gabby stood in the center of the cheerleaders and the basketball players with a microphone dangling from one hand and the other hand cocked on her hip. She was biting down on her lower lip with a huge grin on her face. Layne, almost a head above everyone else, had a hand gripping the top of his head. He and everyone else were staring at the huge screen in front of them.

My heartbeat stopped. Stopped.

An icy fire rose from my soul and exploded from my body. Its energy flowed from my pores and shot static throughout the air like tiny spider webs weaving their way across the room. Everyone froze. The fluorescent lights shattered. Particles of tiny glass showered down on the crowd. A lone beam of light from the projector sparkled over the falling crystals. The shards sounded like pattering rain falling on the glossy wooden floor.

I watched in horror as my father's death played on the big screen for the entire student body to witness.

In an instant, I was reliving the worst day of my life.

The way I froze and cocked my head toward him was almost alien-like. First, my eyes softened slightly before I digested the news that we were moving. Again. Then they narrowed and became hard as glass. Even from the distance of the camera, they glowed unnaturally, as if they'd been lit up from behind by the blazing fires of hell. My eyes were crazed. Insane. They glowed silver under the camera phone lens. All I was missing was a pair of demon horns. My movements, though tiny, were sharp and stilted. Though you couldn't hear what I said over the traffic and street noise, there was no mistaking my meaning.

My breath fogged heavily in the air, a puff of smoke from the sulfuric pit of hell, giving my words power. "I hate you," hissed from my lips.

My father's face went slack. My intent became my wish. His hand dropped to his side, and his blue eyes glazed over. The muscles in his face relaxed to the point where his mouth drooped open, and any expression vanished. It was almost as if the bones in his face had melted, leaving behind shapeless flesh. Without a shred of emotion—fear, sorrow, or anger— he turned and stepped into the street directly into the path of the speeding bus.

I closed my eyes thinking that this couldn't be really happening, but it didn't muffle out the gut-wrenching thump, screeching brakes, honking horns, and strangers screaming.

"Call 911!" someone shouted.

I opened my eyes, but nothing changed except for the growing crowd at the front of the bus.

A scream welled up deep in my chest and tore violently out of my throat. "Daaaaaddddd!" I dropped my bag and ran.

My feet threatened to slip out from underneath me as I ran over the wet sidewalk. My dull brown rain boots slapped the ground, splashing water and mud on my pants.

I elbowed my way through the rainbow of jackets—neon green, orange, reds, blues, and blacks. I ducked under arms and shoved my way through the wall of bodies.

In the distance, sirens wailed.

A man knelt next to my father and bowed his head. His black-and-white collar peeked out from under his coat. Droplets of water dripped steadily from his thick brown hair onto the frozen figure of my father. He afforded me a quiet glance; his eyes were a startling emerald green behind the curtain of his long-wet bangs. He looked awfully young to be a priest. He held onto my dad's mangled hand, and his lips moved. "Even though I walk through the valley of the shadow of death, I shall fear no evil . . .," he whispered the prayer to the great unknown.

Dark red blood, that looked almost black on the pavement, pooled under my dad's head. Red rivers, diluted by the rain, washed in streaks to the curb and into the gutters.

The sickly-sweet stench of burning rubber and gasoline stung my eyes. Tears and water rolled down my cheeks and dripped off my nose. I wiped the tears, the rain, and the snot with the back of my sleeve, leaving a slimy track.

I threw my body over his and screamed and sobbed. I gulped desperately for oxygen. Glass shards, from the windshield of the car that the bus swerved into while trying to avoid hitting my dad, dug into my knees. A cacophony of noises, human and machine, and camera flashes came from above. The priest continued to whisper prayers. "I will dwell in the house of the Lord forever . . ." His words floated away in the wind.

"I didn't mean it! I'm sorry! Please don't die." But it was too late. I shook his still-warm corpse. The priest, his face still bowed in prayer, set a hand on my back to comfort me. But he removed it quickly upon contact, almost as if he'd been burned. He shot me a sideways glance, not out of fear per se, but out of caution. "This is my fault!" I screamed. "I killed my dad. I killed my dad," I repeated over and over.

An ambulance arrived moments later, and they took one look at my dad and then had the cops grab me. They tried to pull me away from my father, but I fought back fiercely. I twisted; I kicked; I bit. I held onto his body for dear life. My mind was frantic. All I could concentrate on was my dad and how I wouldn't leave him here on the wet black pavement alone.

Red and blue flashing lights flared over the scene. More cops gathered around. They glanced to one another cautiously.

The priest held up a hand for them to stop trying to pull me off my father and said something. They stepped away. He looked at the paramedic who had a syringe out and ready, nodded, and then laid a hand on my neck. He murmured something under his breath. You couldn't hear it on the screen. But I remembered. For a moment, all my sorrow and my rage ran out of me like the bloody water running down the street drains. Then the paramedic stuck the needle into my neck. I fell limp into his arms. He laid me on the gurney and wheeled me into the back of the ambulance as a cop covered my dad's dead body with a tarp. The young priest with emerald green eyes made the sign of the cross over his chest . . .

As I came out of my memory back to reality, I heard

thumps running quickly down the wooden stairs on the far side of the gym.

Then the projector flashed to another scene.

Still photos of me walking out of the metal hospital on the day of my release. My brothers and my mom were in the photos with me. Kennedy and Lincoln were giving me shit. They pointed to the sign, Alaska Psychiatric Institute, and made very inappropriate jokes. There were photos of them messing up my hair and punching me lightly in the arm. But I expected nothing less.

That's how we were with each other. Instead of I love you, it was here, let me make fun of you. Strange, but effective since we weren't the most affectionate family. My mom stood well away from me and stared at the ground in all the pictures.

Then, one by one, my medical records, flashed over the glowing screen.

Altered mental state.

Psychosis unspecified.

Brief psychotic disorder versus acute stress reaction.

Thank God. I'd frozen everyone before they were able to see all of it. I bowed my head and my chest heaved as I inhaled lungsful of air.

Then the nightmare played all over again. The video was on a loop. Everyone had seen it. Possibly multiple times.

My wrath flared again. Cold flames snaked off my skin like a mirage blurring the air. Strong arms wrapped around me from behind. Jude. In my ear, he whispered in a language I'd never heard. Though my brain didn't know what he was saying, my soul seemed to recognize his words, or at least their meaning. Heat from his voice melted my icy rage until my actions were under my control.

"There you are," he soothed. His breath tickled behind my ears.

"They saw all of it, didn't they?"

He squeezed me tighter. That was a yes.

"Who? How?" I asked.

"Gabby, I'm sure. You know her dad is some hoity-toity contractor for the military, right? Security company. Some secret shit nobody knows about."

I nodded. I'd underestimated her.

"He has all kinds of connections." He nuzzled his face into the top of my head.

"But she's out here? Who's in the projection room playing it? And who took those pictures?" I knew about the video, but the photos were new.

"I don't know who took them. We may never know. But if I had to guess who's upstairs, I'd say it's Andy Tullson. He's one of her lackeys. In the boy's locker room, he used to joke that he would take his girlfriend up there and lock and bar the door with a chair so no one could get in. As you can see, Gabby doesn't play fair."

I laughed harshly. "Neither do I," I said. "But I promised myself I wouldn't use my powers for my own gain." I almost whimpered the words. God, how I yearned to destroy her.

"I understand," Jude said, playing with my hair. "But think of it this way: If you humiliate her in front of her subjects, you'll be doing the rest of us a favor. That way she'll never hurt any of us again. Think of it as a benefit for the greater good."

He was right. I could knock her off her pedestal. Take away her crown.

"It's your choice, glitter. Do what you must to protect them." He pointed to the frozen crowd: the jocks on the floor, the nerds in the back row, the stoners in the corner, the hardworking ranch kids, the rich kids who were scared of her, and the poor kids who were even more frightened of her.

I took a deep breath and pulled my energy back, gently reeling in the electrical static still snapping in the air. Rolled it up and forced it back in its box. I wouldn't humiliate Gabby here. I would do it when my emotions were completely under my control. A plan began to form in the deep, dark recesses of my mind. I would destroy her. But not today.

One by one, the crowd came alive. Some were still frozen in shock or horror even though I'd given back control over their bodies. Others wore a hysterical look of confusion on their faces. I had to choke back my laughter. A few of the cheerleaders dramatically collapsed to the ground like fainting Victorian women looking for attention.

Soon a hushed buzz of conversation, mingled with disbelief, ran like wildfire around the room.

The principal grabbed the microphone out of Gabby's hand. She was as stunned as the others and sounded out of breath. "Students, I need all of you to stay calm. There was a power surge, and everything is going to be okay."

A couple of the other teachers opened the back doors, letting some light in the room. Rays of sun flared over the crystals lying on the heavily polished floor. Spots where the light hit looked like a still lake glinting the sun off its reflective surface.

"If any of you are hurt, please, carefully make your

way to the north side of the gym by the stage. Ambulances are on the way."

More staff came back into the room, holding flashlights and helping students from the bleachers. Tiny streaks of blood ran down some of the kids' faces where they'd been cut by flying glass shards.

Panic began to swirl in the air. The principal again tried to be assuring. "Please stay calm. Everything is going to be all right," she said in an authoritative, but soothing tone.

It didn't seem to be working. Some of the girls in the crowd began to cry hysterically, and angry cussing echoed from around the room.

I didn't want to do it, but I had to.

With Jude's hands still on my shoulders, I cast tranquility upon the spooked crowd. *I wish.* They immediately calmed. This I could do. But boy, would I pay for it. Helping this many people was dangerous for me. The last time I calmed people on this kind of scale, it put me in a coma for days. It was early on when I was still in the looney bin. A couple of the patients started fighting, and the orderlies were having trouble containing the mess, so I cast some calming on the crowd. It worked, but I paid for it. Just so long as my hair didn't fall out this time.

Layne brushed off his wide shoulders as he escorted a few of the cheerleaders toward the open doors where I stood. Jude removed his hands but didn't move away

The girls sniffled as they continued past me. Layne stopped abruptly when his eyes found mine. His nostrils flared, and the muscles in his jaw knotted. He took a deep breath.

I started to stutter out an apology. An apology for

not telling him the whole story. At least the part where I'd been in a psych ward. But instead of listening he brushed past me. The disgust on his face tore at my heart. I clutched my chest. A sob bubbled inside.

"Well, well, well," came a soft southern accent from behind. I turned and stared into a set of smiling emerald eyes. His hair was shorter. And he wasn't wearing a priest's collar. But those eyes. "Bless your heart. You are a piece of work after all."

I stepped forward out of Jude's reach. "You!" I meant to say more but the words were lost in the air as a fierce pain struck my heart, and I crashed to the floor.

Chapter 23

When You Are Finished Changing the World

I floated up, up, and away on the back of a fluffy white cloud. Its soft embrace formed to every curve of my body. I didn't know where it began and where I ended. The clean, crisp air— smelling like the earth after a gentle rain shower—washed over my skin. Stars flickered above my head, little diamonds flaring and then softening. The long galaxy sprawled before me. It was vast, infinite, and endless. Muted golds, reds, oranges, yellows, greens, blues, purples, and silvers all glistened in the hazy sky. The colors hovered around stars and planets. My skin, bathed in silver, glowed under the beams of the moon as it grew larger and larger as I floated closer to it. For minutes, or days or years, I hovered under the moon's belly, flying in the heavens. My worries and my life were only a dull pain in the back of my head. It was as if someone kept poking me in the same spot, trying to wake me up.

Riding inside the current of air, a soft voice nudged my subconscious. "Come back to me, glitter. Don't leave me here alone," it whispered as it passed by.

I peeked over the edge of my cloud. A small silver thread, no thicker than a spider's web, kept me from soaring higher into the glorious galaxy above.

Faces flashed before me, disrupting my peaceful existence. First, a dark-haired, bronze-skinned beauty, whose serious eyes held a heavy amount of pain, hovered in front of me. Too soon the image faded and was replaced by a blonde-haired Viking god with a gentle face and a heart of gold. Next came a woman with tears streaking down her ethereal face. Then, finally, she faded to the one person I recognized. My father. I reached out and touched him. His skin was firm and warm under my fingers. Hot tears burned my eyes, stinging the back of my nose and a lump knotted in my throat.

"My girl doesn't back down. She never gives up," my father said, his voice strong and proud. "Not my baby girl. Never my baby girl. Go home, kiddo. Those people need you. I'll be here when you've finished changing the world." He kissed my forehead and disappeared. I lifted my hand and reached for him, but he was gone. Only the dark-haired, dark-eyed beauty remained. He held on to that cord as if my life depended on it.

Every once in a while, through my blissful high, I could hear as he begged and pleaded for me not to go, until a spark of blinding white light flashed through my head and left me with a name: Jude.

"Uh," I moaned. With every breath of air my head split, ripped open at the seams. The familiar smell of medicine mixed with chemical cleaner and urine hung ripe in the air.

"Oh, God, Regan, you're awake. Thank God."

The heavy weight of Jude's head rested on my stomach. Parking lot lights outside the window shone through the open curtains and glowed softly on his thick hair.

"Uh," I said, "I'm in the hospital, aren't I?" My lips

were thick. I cringed at every tick of the clock. Every beep of the monitor was a hammer to my skull. My brain was raw; it felt as if the gray matter had been exposed to the elements.

"Yup," he said. His voice was muffled in my blanket.

"Again," I whispered the statement.

He lifted his head and laughed quietly. The sound rumbled but didn't hurt. "The regular one this time. You know, the one where normal people go?"

"You're hilarious," I croaked out of my dry throat. "How long have I been here?"

He stood up slowly as if he'd been in that position for too long. He held my face in his cool hands and caressed my cheek. "Two days. This is the first time you've woken up. I should probably go tell someone, even if I get in trouble."

"Wow, it feels like it's been longer."

He let go of my face and squeezed my hand. "Tell me about it." His voice was gruff with pent-up emotion. He pulled away.

"No, please, don't go." I refused to let go of his hand.

"Okay, easy. I'll stay here as long as ya need me." He handed me a drink of water with his free hand and managed to hold the straw steady as I took a deep swig, clearing the cotton feeling from my mouth.

"What time is it? And where is my family?" I expected my mom to be here or at least my grandparents.

"I don't know. Somewhere around midnight? I'm not supposed to be here, but I snuck in anyway. Have for the last two nights. And your family has been here every day, but they don't let anyone in after visiting hours."

"Then how did you get in?"

"I'm sneaky." He smiled. The monitor lights reflected blue on his white teeth.

"Anyone else come in?"

"Molly."

"No Layne?"

He took a deep breath before he answered. "Not that I'm aware of. But I could be wrong. I show up right before visitor hours are over."

My chin trembled. I'd ruined everything. I should've told him I was crazy.

"Hey, don't cry. Please." He brushed my cheek with the back of his hand.

I nodded. Every shake of my head was a knife in my skull. I scooted over and patted the spot beside me.

He sighed and crawled up next to me on top of the covers. "Go to sleep. I'll wake you before I leave. I promise."

I flipped on my side, and he spooned his long, hard body next to mine. A heady buzz painted along my spine, then stroked its soft brush over the curves of my flesh. Every move of his hand on my hip made it difficult to breathe steady. Our heartbeats mingled until they became one, drumming to the same tempo. The rhythm hypnotized me, relaxed me, and lulled me to sleep. The last moment before I drifted off, I thought I heard him murmur into my hair: "Love, you're killin' me."

I woke up again sometime in the morning. Jude was already gone, but he had woken me before he left, kissed me on the head, and said he would be back after school.

I pressed the call button hanging from the side of my bed.

Nurses and a doctor came running, their shoes

slapping on the worn floor.

Shortly after, my mom, grandparents, and Barry arrived in a veritable flurry of joy and panic, and questions.

"Oh, thank God! How are you feeling? Why did you do that to us? Don't ever do that again. We love you." And so on.

They pretty much drove me crazy. *Oh, wait, aren't I already crazy?* Ha. Ha.

I told the doctors I was ready to leave. They said no. I argued that I felt fine. Even my headache was mostly gone. Now there was only a dull ache where the stabbing used to be. They said they needed to run more tests.

"Mom, I tell you: I am fine." They'd already run a million tests. As usual, all of them came back normal. This was part of the reason my mom never believed I was sick. I wasn't sure my ailment was physical. But I couldn't make this stuff up; I wasn't that talented of an actor.

"Honey, I don't know. They're the doctors. If they say you need to stay, then I think you should." She looked very uncertain.

I turned my head to my grandpa and lifted my eyebrows like, *well, help me here.*

"Sara, darling, I think if Regan says she's okay, we have to take her word for it." Gramps folded his fingers together and picked at the cuticles on his thumb with his other thumb.

"Dad, I don't know."

"This girl is the toughest kid I know. An old soul, that one, probably the oldest I've ever seen. I say they do as many tests as they need to today, and if all turn up normal, then she comes home."

The doctor started to protest.

Gramps held up a firm hand. "And we can bring her back tomorrow if need be."

Finally, by mid-morning, everyone (meaning the doctors) agreed.

I sighed. Tonight, I would sleep in my own bed.

I texted Jude and told him they were going to release me sometime after five. If he wanted to see me, he could come to the house. Mom was making my favorite: chicken pot pie and fresh, homemade ice cream for dessert.

Little typing bubbles appeared in my phone, disappeared, and then appeared again. Double thumbs-up.

One of the nurses helped me shower. I was happy to have an endless supply of scorching hot water.

I came out bright pink and threw on a pair of black sweats and a gray T-shirt my mom brought in earlier. She and Barry would be here soon to pick me up. I didn't want to admit it, but the dude was kind of growing on me.

I shimmied onto the unmade bed and flipped through the TV channels until National Geographic popped up.

"Hey," a meek voice came from the opened door. Layne leaned on the doorframe, almost dwarfing the entrance. A bunch of roses were gripped tightly under his white knuckles.

My chest squeezed. "Hey," I said back. I shrugged my shoulders. "I'm surprised to see you."

Miss Molly had been here before her lunch shift at work started. She told me Layne hadn't been here at all. "I'm so mad at him," she said, balling her fists. "And ashamed. I thought I raised him better."

"He's angry. He has a right to be. I should've told him. I should've told you. I was scared, is all."

"I know. I don't blame you. That's a heavy burden to carry around. But I want you to know, it doesn't change the way I feel about you. You know that, right? No matter what happens, if you and Layne get married and have babies or you end your relationship today, you are *my girl*. I need you in my life." She motioned aggressively to her chest. "From now until the bitter end. You got it." She pointed a finger at me. She'd worked herself into a frenzy.

I grabbed her hand out of the air and squeezed it hard. "I do."

"Good." She had kissed my cheek before she had left for work.

Now, two hours later, Layne stood inside the doorway shifting uncomfortably. "Can I come in?" he said hesitantly.

I patted the spot on the bed next to me.

He set the roses on the rolling cart and sat down, his weight causing the side of the bed to sag. "I owe you an apology," he said formally. He wasn't his usual buoyant self.

"What?" I shook my head. "It's me that owes you an apology. I was the one who lied."

"Yes, about that . . . Why didn't you tell me?" He reached out to push my hair away but stopped midway and ran his fingers through his own hair in frustration.

I huffed loudly. "Isn't the answer obvious? Because of this. Because I was afraid you wouldn't like me anymore."

"That isn't the reason I bailed. So what if you had

trouble after your dad died? Seriously, after what you went through, who wouldn't? Why would you think I wouldn't understand?"

I started to answer. He held a finger up to my lips. It was cool next to my skin.

"What I'm mad about is that you didn't tell me. You didn't trust me. Did Jude know? Will you lie to me again?" He cocked his head, this time waiting for me to answer.

"He knows everything." Far more than I would ever admit to anyone else.

"See, that's why I'm mad. You trust him. You spend your lunches with him, not me. He's the only other person in the school you talk to." He looked down at the floor. "I thought I was your boyfriend."

"You are. Or were. I'll understand if we're over."

"Is that what you want?" He looked up. Lines furrowed the skin between his eyes.

I didn't answer. I was so confused. I didn't know what I wanted.

He grabbed my hand and put it up to his chest. "Because it's not what I want. Not even close. When I'm around you, I want to be a better person. A stronger person. I feel as if I'm invincible with you standing by my side. I can't explain it, but it's like, well, I don't have the words. But God, it's like . . . nothing I've ever felt before. Please, please forgive me. When I carried you to the ambulance, I thought you were going to die. And then I was mad at you all over again for scaring me." His voice cracked, and tears pooled in his eyes, making them swim in aqua-colored water. I understood part of what he said intimately. I also wanted to be a better version of myself when I was around him.

“Then when you didn’t wake up right away . . .” He was trying to appear relaxed, but the tight tendons and the pulse racing in his neck said otherwise. “I will understand if you can’t forgive me. I don’t know if I can forgive myself.” He looked down at his lap, and the tears spilled over. He wiped them away before they got far.

I turned his handsome, tortured face to me, his blond five o’clock shadow rough on my fingertips, and bit my bottom lip. “How about we call it even? I lied, and you stood me up. Slate clean.”

“Really?” Hope flooded back into his eyes. If he was willing to work out our problems, so was I. With one truth at a time.

“I should probably tell you Jude is coming over for dinner tonight.” He clenched his teeth but nodded. His nostrils flared as he inhaled deeply.

“You can come too if you want. Invite your mom. She said she was working a short shift tonight.”

His face softened, and he nodded quickly.

“But you have to promise to be nice. I can’t handle the two of you trying to mark your territory.”

“What?” His eyes flew open.

“You know what I mean.”

He nodded sheepishly. He leaned in and kissed me deeply before he left. My bare toes curled. I had made the right decision. He needed me, and I needed him.

I texted Jude. Told him to invite Jacy also.

Then I told my mom about her dinner party when they arrived to pick me up. She was all kinds of excited. I really wasn’t. But I couldn’t not invite Layne when I’d already invited Jude. Especially after everything he said about spending more time with Jude than I did with him.

Surprisingly, the night went well. Both boys were

on their best behavior, and everyone left soon after dinner. I think they could tell I was tired.

Twenty minutes later, after they were all gone, someone knocked softly on our door. I answered it in my penguin pajamas. Layne.

"I . . . I just wanted another hug."

I smiled from ear to ear.

"Come in, Layne," my mom invited from the couch. "Why don't you go tuck Regan in?" She and Barry were watching a movie.

"Really?" he said.

Sara nodded.

He scooted in behind me in bed and wrapped his strong arms around me. The second boy in one twenty-four-hour period held me while I fell asleep.

Chapter 24

Crazy is a Communicable Disease

I skipped school Tuesday as I promised my mom. I would go back on Wednesday. We argued about it again before I left. She didn't want me to go back to that school. Ever.

"You don't have to go," she huffed, crossing her arms. Mismatched socks poked from underneath her long pink bathrobe. Her sticking up for me was kind of cute.

"Of course, I do," I said patiently. We'd already had this disagreement. As my dad always said, 'Disagreement is not disrespect.' Now I knew what he was talking about. "It's kind of illegal not to. Besides I need to get back. I don't want anyone pulling ahead of me." I put my stocking cap on.

"What those kids did to you was awful. Unforgivable. I talked to the school, and they said with your credits and grades, you could finish your classes from home. They were willing to let you take online courses and independent studies for the rest of the year. It's not like you *need* them. You're the smartest person I know. Eventually, you would've given your father a run for his money. He always said you were the one who took after him." It was nice to hear her talk about him without breaking down in tears.

"Momma," I said firmly. "I will not show weakness. Those kids do not scare me." My dad's words rang in my head. His girl didn't back down. Didn't give up. Ever.

She laid a hand on my coat, refusing to let go. "Well, they should. Barry filled me in on what kind of kids go to that establishment. I was shocked. That was never the case when I was there."

"Times change, Momma." I kissed her cheek. "Remember, 'The opposite of courage in our society is not cowardice, it is conformity.'"

She finally choked back tears. Yeah, my dad said that one a lot. I stepped forward, standing eye to eye with her.

"I am my father's daughter. Now let me go do what needs to be done." I pried her tiny fingers from my jacket.

She nodded. "I always thought it was hard when he left for deployment. This . . . This is worse. How do I let you go up there alone?" She pursed her lips, tilted her head back, and blinked rapidly to keep the tears from spilling over.

"Oh, Momma, I'm a wolf in sheep's clothing." I tipped two fingers to my forehead in a mock salute. "Everything's going to be okay." I was the alpha.

I hopped into my truck and drove to school listening to the soundtrack from a famous musical about an opera house. Even though it wasn't really an opera, I loved the music. It was angsty and darkly romantic all at the same time. And it was exactly what I needed.

A pair of headlights on bright blinded me in my rear-view mirror. I tipped the mirror up to avoid the irritating glare wondering who was following me and why. I chalked it up to paranoia. I did tend to suffer from the condition if I didn't use my gift often enough. Today I planned on remedying the problem.

By the time I got to the school, I walked—okay, I strutted—through the front doors with my head held high. Layne wanted to pick me up, but I told him no. Matter of fact, I didn't want to see him until lunch. These people needed to know they couldn't break me.

I would eat with him today wherever he chose.

Inside my locker was a plastic bag filled with a mixture of peanuts, almonds, and walnuts. The word *nut job* was scrawled across the front in black marker. I chuckled as I popped a handful in my mouth. *How thoughtful.*

Someone passing behind me said, "Crackhead."

If they only knew.

Someone else answered with, "This one's off her meds."

Okay, so that one made me snort.

"Oh, seriously? You're going to have to do better than that to hurt my feelings," I yelled over my shoulder. Then I wished for them to trip over their own feet.

I wish.

That was all it took. It was almost too easy. And it felt good. Relieved some of the pressure.

Most students avoided me. Looked away as I got near. Pretended I didn't exist. As if crazy were a communicable disease. *No such luck.* I poked the girl in front of me with a finger; she screamed and ran away. I laughed, cackled really. I wanted to yell *boo* at everyone in the hall.

After the bell rang for our first class, I found the person I'd been looking for. Obsessing over. Scouring the internet for information.

Gin. It's like he was waiting for me to find him. He was outside sitting on the edge of a cement picnic table.

"You were there." I stabbed my finger into his chest.

Amusement sparkled in those brilliant eyes. "It took you long enough."

I gritted my teeth. "Why didn't you say anything?"

"Well, darlin'," he drawled and touched his chest pushing my finger politely aside. "What kind of gentleman would I be to dredge up that kind of past."

"You were the one who gave the information to Gabby." I wasn't asking a question, I was verifying the answer.

Surprise widened his eyes. "Actually, I didn't. The little wench gets credit for that discovery all on her own."

"Why were you in Anchorage? Why were you there?" I yelled. My hands flayed beside my head. My golem was starting to get agitated. I closed my eyes and focused on my breathing.

"Funny coincidence is all. I was preforming at the Anchorage Opera. I was one of the three child-spirits. And a priest. That's why I was dressed like that when you saw me. I'd forgotten to take off the priests' collar is all. Here look." He tapped his phone.

On the screen was a picture of him with his name below. Christian Landsing.

"That's not your name." But it was him in the photo.

"It's my mother's maiden name. My grandmother was a professional opera singer. So, what if I use my family name for recognition. It's not a crime."

Well, that would explain why my internet search came up short.

"I don't believe in coincidences." I crossed my arms.

"I don't know what to tell you."

"And weren't you supposed to be in school?"

"My tutor was with me. Tonight, when you do your internet search—don't shake your head like you're not going to—you'll see. I've been traveling like this since I was a freshman.

He's right. I would do a search. "Then for God's sake, why did you pretend you were a priest?" I managed to keep my voice from cracking.

"Before you arrived, someone in the crowd vehemently insisted I help. Instead of arguing, I did what they asked. I'm a good Catholic boy and there was no way my praying could hurt a dying. . ."

He stopped when his eyes met mine. I clenched my teeth to ward off the stinging tears.

A hint of remorse clouded his expression. "I'm sorry. I didn't mean to say that. Just know, I had no ill intentions."

"How in the world did you end up here?" I muttered. I wasn't really expecting him to answer.

"I told you my parents—"

I interrupted, "Yeah, yeah, yeah." I waved my hand about. "They're away on business. Sure. Whatever."

I stormed away. I didn't believe him. So, I skipped class and went to the library. And everything he said was true. But I still didn't believe him.

****

After fourth period, Layne waited for me at my locker. I'd promised to go to lunch with him. He picked me up and kissed me before he escorted me to the cafeteria. The chaos and noise ceased upon our arrival. Some students glanced nervously over to Gabby's table; others stared down at their lunches, like pizza and milk were the hottest commodity around. A few snickers and giggles broke through the tense air.

We chose our food; the lunch lady gave me a tired smile. We walked across the scuffed turquoise-and-white floor and took a seat at an empty table. I dusted the crumbs off the surface before we sat down.

"I won't make you sit with my friends yet." He smiled tightly.

I poked at the greasy pizza and instead drank my chocolate milk.

After a few minutes, most of the student body forgot we were there and went back to normal. His friends, the wide-shouldered angry mob, stared and glared. They didn't like me before, and now that I was a certifiable psycho, I was even less worthy. If we continued to eat here, I might lose weight. It was hard to eat when half of the room pitied you and the other half hated you. It was an excellent appetite suppressant. And honestly, I couldn't afford to lose more weight. The stress of the last ten months had taken its toll.

"See, not so bad?" Layne said as we dropped off our trays.

I snorted. "The atmosphere or the food?" Because I thought both sucked.

He shrugged.

"Tomorrow I'll have Grams pack us a lunch. We can eat it in here or in my truck." A twinge of guilt twisted in my heart. That was Jude's and my tradition, but if Layne and I were going to work, I needed to focus on being his girlfriend.

"Deal," he said before he darted off to class. He seemed almost relieved to leave my side. Maybe I was being too sensitive. But if he were, I couldn't blame him really.

I cornered Jude in the back of the art room. "Hey, how's it going?" I scooted next to him and took a peek at his latest painting. Nothing so far but a rough outline on the canvas.

"Good," he snapped. He didn't look up from his work; his pencil dangled between his beautiful lips.

"What is wrong?"

He pulled the pencil out of his mouth. "Look, I gotta be honest with you."

"Okay, sure." I scrunched my brows. My heart started beating faster. My palms became clammy.

"I can't do this anymore." He stepped closer to me. Energy flared between us. My invisible tentacles of electricity reached out for him. He stared down, first into my eyes, and then his gaze traveled to my lips and then down the length of my body. I could feel him, as if his eyes were a flame burning a path over my skin.

"Do what?" I held my breath. The hairs on my neck and arms tingled with static.

"This whole you and me thing."

"You mean our friendship?"

A darkness flashed over his face: pain, longing, and anger. Then he smiled, but it wasn't a look of happiness. "Yeah, that." He stepped back.

My eyes widened and shallow breaths heaved my chest like I couldn't catch enough oxygen without him near.

"Look, you and I can be friends. But I have to do it from afar. If there's anything you ever need, please don't hesitate to ask. But other than that, I need to stay away from you." He crossed his arms over his wide chest. His skin contrasted with his white T-shirt.

"Why?" I winced as I heard the desperation in my voice.

"Don't you get it?" He looked at me like I was stupid. "I . . . I . . ." He tossed his pencil down on the easel and threw his hands up. "You know what? If you don't understand by now, there's no need for me to explain." He grabbed his hair and pulled hard, and then he messed it up. "You . . . You pick him every time. No matter what I do. What's so wrong with me?" Confusion creased his forehead before his face morphed back to its normal hard edges. He shook his head and a cynical laugh escaped between his lips. "You know what? Never mind. Please don't answer that." He stormed out. I heard him tell Mr. Clark he needed to go.

I wasn't stupid. I knew what the problem was. I wanted my cake, and I wanted to eat it too.

Layne was who I needed. But Jude was who I wanted.

And I had already made a choice, no matter the pain it caused me.

On Thursday and Friday, Jude treated me the same as the rest of the student body did. Like I ceased to exist. Except he took it to a whole other level. Complete avoidance seemed to be his M.O. He showed up to the classes we had together, handed his work in, and then immediately left. The teachers didn't bat an eyelash.

I could tell my pariah status was taking its toll on Layne also. His friends still hung around him, but only as long as I wasn't near. By Friday, we sat in my truck for lunch.

"You know, Layne, if you want out, I'll understand." In the background, rap music played on his phone. His choice, not mine. He didn't like my opera music. I handed him two sandwiches, an orange, and some baby carrots.

I had told Grams that Layne needed something healthy. Like a vegetable from time to time. I figured carrots were a safe starting point. I might have been mistaken by the way he was staring at them like they might bite. He pushed them aside in favor of the sandwiches.

"What?" he said.

"Dating me is a chore. God, even I can see that."

He shoved a sandwich in his mouth and finished chewing before he said, "No it's not." He peeled the orange, its citrus fragrance cleaning the air. Then he ate it in two bites. "I . . . really like you. Don't take this wrong, but you're like a drug. I can't get you out of my head. No matter what I try. Football doesn't even work. Every time I close my eyes, you're there."

I ran my fingers over my swooping bangs. I'd contemplated growing it out, but I kind of liked its spunkiness.

"You make me feel . . ." He shrugged his shoulders, leaned over, and kissed me. He tasted like fresh, ripe juice. His hands traveled from my face, down my neck, to the top of my breast. I trembled. He smiled. He unzipped my jacket and wove his hand behind my back. With one arm, he pulled me over the seat closer to him. I crawled up and straddled his lap. His stubble scratched my face and lips. I gripped the back of his hair and kissed him harder. He rested his hands low on my hips and dug his strong fingers into my backside.

The bell rang.

Layne growled and rested his forehead against mine. "You're coming to senior night tonight, right?"

"Yeah, I'm meeting your mom at your house. We're going together." I slid back to the driver's side and hopped out of my truck.

He pocketed the other sandwich and even the carrots before he blew me a kiss.

I had big plans for senior night. Or should I say Gabby had big plans? Just thinking about it made the golem shudder and slither to the edges of the glass box.

By art class, I had the logistics figured out. Jude was in the back room, avoiding me.

"Mr. Clark, can I go to the library to do some research for my Friday the Thirteenth project?"

"Absolutely. No worries. See you on Monday. Have a great weekend."

Oh, I will.

I found Gabby and her goons down a deserted hallway, working on posters for tonight's big game. Anger swirled in my gut at the sight of her curled blonde hair. The golem woke from its nap with a deep sigh.

Andy Tullson took all the blame for releasing the video footage of my dad's death leaving Gabby's hands squeaky clean. He said a manila envelope arrived in the mail and offed him a thousand dollars to play it at the pep rally. Everyone knew it was a lie. But it was safer to let Gabby slide. She had the ability to destroy the faculty's life as well. Andy received a week's suspension. That was it. It made me so angry that Gabby got away with it again that I wanted to. . . I flexed my fists by my side and took a few deep breaths to center myself. It was imperative for the task at hand.

I stopped in front of the cheerleaders, most of them sitting or kneeling on the floor, decorating posters with stupid sayings on them like, "Go, Team, Go!" painted in acrylic. Cans of paint—with long, dark brushes resting inside—dotted the checkered hallway floor like colorful chess pieces. Though I would be shocked if any of the Three Musketcheers knew how to play.

Most of the squad were down on their knees while they madly drew away. But not Gabby. She was, as always, directing the show.

"Gabby," I said.

Her head flew around at the speed of sound. I almost worried she was going to have whiplash.

"What are you doing here?" She propped her hands on her hips, straightened her back, and puffed her chest out, trying to make herself larger.

"We need to talk." All of her followers stopped what they were doing and stared. Their eyes darted nervously back and forth between us. Destiny blew a stubborn curl out of her face. Olivia started to get up off the floor.

Stay. I ordered her. She dropped back down.

Gabby huffed a laugh. "I've no need to talk to you."

"You're going to want to hear what I have to say." I smiled maliciously. "Or if you would rather—I can just tell you with everyone listening." I rose the pitch of my voice toward the end of the sentence. I needed her to believe that's exactly what I wanted. For everyone to hear.

"Fine." She stormed into the nearest empty classroom. The door slammed against the wall with a violent thump. A yellow number two pencil rolled off the desk and fell on the floor.

I made a blanket statement to the other girls. "Don't let anyone come in."

"What do you want?" Gabby folded her arms across her chest. She stood in the front of the room as if she was in charge.

I got right to the point. "Were you the one who made the little slideshow last week?"

A satisfied smile bloomed on her face. She raised her eyebrows like, *yeah, what if I did?*

But I needed to know for sure. She needed to admit all the evil things she'd done. And though I could control people, I couldn't make them tell the truth.

"It was pretty impressive. You hit me right where it hurt." I flicked the end of my nose with the side of my finger.

She deliberately blinked her long black eyelashes at me. "Are you trying to make me feel sorry for you?" She tapped her spotless white tennis shoe on the floor. The overhead fan blew the loose hairs around her face.

"Not at all. But seriously, how did you do it? It's not like you're smart enough to get the information on your own." I sat down on top of a desk in the front row.

Her green eyes narrowed. I may have been pushing her anger button slightly. Fueling the fire. Pumping her ego. She *wanted* someone to know.

"Oh, I don't think you're giving me enough credit. I'm plenty smart. Just not book smart. I use my other gifts." She swayed her body and looked down at her own perfect physique.

"Oh, did you get your daddy to find it for you?" I said it like I would say *poor baby*. "And seriously, what kind of relationship do you and daddy have?" I said scandalously as if their relationship might be incestuous. *Push. Push. Push.* I tapped at the hate sitting barely contained under the surface of her skin.

Horror, anger, and disgust tensed her whole body, starting with her face.

"Besides, couldn't he get in a load of trouble? That's a crime. Like a *big one*," I emphasized with my hands as a measurement, spreading them about two feet apart from each other. It wasn't really surprising that nobody got in trouble except for Andy. Once he 'admitted' to the crime, there was no need to investigate further. Besides, were billionaires and their megalithic companies ever held accountable? For anything?

"My dad didn't help me. One of his minions did. Besides, you can't prove anything. And nobody in this town is stupid enough to try. Right now, it's my word against yours." She gave me the quick once over like she'd already won this battle. Little did she know, it hadn't begun.

I was surprised. I figured she'd throw Gin under the bus. Maybe he didn't tell her.

"And how about Andy Tullson? Did you make him play the film? And did he take the blame willingly?"

"Maybe a little of both," she said.

"And Brenda? Why?"

"Because she was a whore." She cocked her head like it was no big deal.

"Jude?" I asked. Though I already knew she was guilty.

She laughed silently, knowing full well he was the only one I was really concerned about. "I couldn't find enough dirt on him or his family. Surprising, really, considering his dad is a pervert." She shrugged her shoulders. "So, I got creative. Besides, he got what he deserved."

Yes! Score! I had what I needed. Confirmation. I wanted to jump up and down. Fist pump the air. But I had to stay calm. "Well, it's pretty hard to destroy my life. You see, I don't care what other people think. But God," I slowed my voice way down, "I'm going to enjoy destroying yours."

"Nobody will believe you. You're crazy." She smiled nicely. Her white teeth were perfect. She tilted her head and shrugged a shoulder. It was cute.

"You don't understand. They don't have to believe me."

I pulled a notebook out of my backpack and handed it to her along with a pen. I opened my little glass box and the golem pirouetted inside its prison. Tendrils of darkness and webs of deception flowed over my nerves.

"What's this for?"

"You're going to confess everything you've done to destroy people's lives." I needed her to forget the next part.

"Ah, no I'm not." She shook her head.

"Oh, but you are." The tingles warmed my chest to my fingers to the tips of my toes.

I wish.

Her face drooped and became slack. The bones under her skin appeared to liquefy. Much like melting wax.

After I'd made her write her own confession, I had her sign the bottom with her flowy signature followed by a heart. I couldn't force her to tell the truth, even on paper, but I could tell the truth for her. I could make people talk, but only what I wanted them to say, which wasn't necessarily the truth. That's why a verbal confirmation of all the awful things she'd done to people was necessary to my plan.

After she finished her confession, she walked out the door and down the hall. I had her holler over her shoulder to her confused squad, "Keep working. I'll be back."

I stood over the posters and thought perhaps some of these girls could benefit from an art class. Most of their work was juvenile to say the least. I gave Gabby a good head start, then I followed.

She veered into the newsroom right as I turned the corner. I caught up and stood quietly outside the door in case the conversation needed my help. My job was trickier when there was more than one person. And only one under my control. If need be, I would step in and make the editor do what I wanted. I leaned up against the wall and listened.

"Caleb, I need you to put this in the paper now." Her voice was sweet but slightly robotic.

"Ah, it's too late. I'm just about done. You okay? You kind of look, uh, sick?"

"Oh, that's sweet of you to worry about me." I had her put a hand on his shoulder. "I have a terrible headache is all. But I really need this to be in this week's paper. It comes out Monday, right? So, it can't be too late, can it? I'll owe you a big favor." I made her flutter those long fake lashes and smile, then bite her bottom lip.

Come on, I was trying here. Flirtation was not my strong suit.

"Okay, Gabby. Anything for you," he stuttered. I don't know if it was because he was nervous or scared.

"Oh, Caleb, you don't know what this means to me."

A minute of silence ensued. "Gabby, are you sure? I read it. I don't think this is a good idea." He sounded worried.

I hardly prompted her. Nowadays my powers were so strong there was no need for me to concentrate too hard for little things like this. I simply forced the conversation in her head.

"I know, but that's why my head hurts. I've been struggling with this all day. Actually, for a while now. But it's time I did the right thing. I have to do this. Don't you understand? This is the only way I can live with myself."

"Well, okay, if you're sure." He still sounded reluctant. I pushed him to do what she asked. No more questions.

"I'm sure. But please don't mention it to anyone. This needs to be our secret," she said. I could almost taste the sweet sugar in the air. I made her kiss his cheek.

"No problem, Gabby. I'll take care of it," Caleb assured her through his nervous-but-pleased voice.

Then I had her walk back to her art project in the hall. If her friends asked what she was doing or where she'd been, she was going to tell them it was none of their business. Besides, she wouldn't remember anyway. *Mystery minutes.*

Chapter 25

Mic Drop

I parked in front of Miss Molly's house with one wheel on the curb. She hurried out, purse in one hand, coat in the other.

She jumped into the cab of my truck. "Okay! Ready." She turned to me with a big smile. Loose curls framed her face. A little black dress, a nude shade of lipstick, bronzer, and mascara completed her ensemble.

Her eyes widened. "Wow! You look, hmmm, great. Stunning really," she said before the overhead doom lights of my truck faded out. "What prompted this?"

I shrugged before pulling my truck away from the curb. But I knew. I was tired of blending in. From now on, I planned on embracing my alter ego. A warrior. A vigilante. I wore knee-high leather boots over shiny leggings and a draped top with a cowl neckline. My coat, with its military collar and tight-fitting silhouette that flared out below my waist, finished the look. I lined my eyes with black eyeliner and threw on three coats of mascara. Pink lips and a little blush. My mom helped.

As we walked into the gym, parents and students threw me startled glances. I didn't know whether it was because of my attire or if they thought mentally unstable people should stay home—not come out after dark. As if only vampires were allowed out after the sun went down.

"Let's sit in the front," she said as she pulled me forcefully to the bleachers.

"Really, no, let's sit in the middle." I planted my feet firmly on the gym floor. She tugged, but shy of picking me up, I wasn't moving.

"I want to be able to see Layne, and besides, they make all the parents go out on the floor with them."

"See Layne? The guy's six foot five. We'll be able to see him better from up there. You can sit by the stairs. That way you can get out easier."

"Okay," she huffed.

Whew, I didn't want to sit near the floor.

At halftime they introduced the seniors. Miss Molly stood with Layne's hand in hers. Even she looked vertically challenged standing next to him. Layne's life plan took longer than the rest. People cheered long and loud. I was relieved. My filth hadn't stained him as bad as I'd thought. Most people didn't want to make an enemy out of the only person they knew that would become famous.

After all the senior athletes had been introduced, the cheerleaders scrambled to the floor, shaking their pompoms and other assets.

Earlier, I'd followed Gabby to the concession stand that smelled of hot dogs and chili, where she bought a big bottle of water and a liter of Mountain Dew. I made sure she drank them both. And instructed her not to use the restroom.

She did a strange skipping dance before they began their routine. They clapped and jumped and shouted to a catchy little tune. They performed flips and splits, their black skirts and white, sleeveless, midriff-baring shirts displaying plenty of muscled skin.

One by one, they formed a pyramid. Gabby was the star on the top of the tree. Excitement blanketed my skin. I flexed my evil little brain muscles. The golem practically twirled its imaginary mustache in anticipation.

Gabby's eyes twitched as I slowly took away her ability to control her physical body. But I left her awareness intact. I wanted her to remember.

Even though I was about to humiliate her and destroy her life, she didn't have the tenacity or strength to fight back much. A twinge of guilt tickled my conscience until I reminded myself of what she'd done to Jude. To me. And to so many other students. She deserved a taste of her own medicine. A strong surge of tingles flowed from my chest to my fingers to the tips of my toes.

I wish. Pee. Let it go. You're in the vast open ocean. Let loose. No one will ever know.

Her eyelids lowered in relief. A steady drip of urine fell from the middle of her panties. The rest, the majority, ran down the sides of her legs, soaking a bright acidic yellow liquid into her ankle socks until they could hold no more. It took the two girls below, holding Gabby's feet, a few seconds to realize that it was warm urine streaming over their arms and absorbing into the armpit area of their uniforms. Olivia, directly below, shook her head when she felt the drops in her hair. Unfortunately— or fortunately— she tilted her head forward to shake out whatever it was only to have pee run down her face into her mouth. I gagged a little. But I didn't even feel bad about it. Two birds. One stone.

Olivia screamed. At first, the pyramid swayed to the

left and paused before one of the cheerleaders dropped Gabby's foot. Then it toppled.

An old rock song pounded in my head as a heap of bodies, screaming and swearing, hit the floor. My brothers, being four years older than me, introduced me to all kinds of inappropriate music at a young age. I started laughing, holding onto my gut. The sharp sound echoed around the brick building. I couldn't help myself. I was high as a kite.

Startled inhales of shock ran through the crowd when they finally processed what was happening.

Cheerleaders jumped up, horrified and stunned. Strands of wet pee-hair stuck to their faces and stained their white uniforms. Some of them tried shaking off their hands, as if that were going to work. Destiny fell to her knees and vomited; her back arched as the waves of nausea commenced. So much for her tough-guy act. One girl stood frozen, blinking as if her brain hadn't caught up to what really had happened. When it did, she started crying.

Gabby rose slowly, took center stage, and squatted to finish what she'd started. The principal and coaches ran to stop her, but not before some people captured the whole act on their phones.

The crowd didn't move. But that wasn't me. They were mesmerized by the shit show playing out on the floor. Most of them forgot to breathe.

Gabby's mother, a prettier version of her daughter in her wool coat and flawless dye job, sat stiff in the front row next to Gin. When she got it together, she stood up and hiked her purse high on her arm. Instead of going to help her kid, like a good mother would, she walked out of the gym. Her expensive high heel shoes clacked angrily as she hurried out.

I snorted. I covered my nose and laughed in my hand but it did nothing to muffle the sound. Gin turned those startling eyes on me. But in place of anger, which would be a normal reaction to someone laughing hysterically at your family, he grinned. A slow lazy smile of satisfaction. Maybe he hated Gabby too.

My phone dinged twice.

Jude.

—Wow, you really r crazy . . . your evil knows no depths!— Winky face and a kiss emoji

—By the way u r hot tonight. I'm a fan of the all black. It's like we match.—

I looked around, but I couldn't find him. My work here was done.

"Oh, my God! What just happened?" Miss Molly asked me. Her eyes were wild with shock.

I smiled my drunken smile and shrugged my shoulders. I was afraid my words might be slurred if I spoke.

"You okay?" Concern wrinkled between her eyes.

I nodded slowly, exaggeratedly. My head felt dizzy and unattached to my body.

"Hey," I heard Jude's voice from beside her.

I looked up at him with a goofy smile. I straightened my arm with my hand in a closed fist and pretended a mic drop.

He shook his head and cocked a brow above those broody dark eyes. My heart revved. Jude spoke to Miss Molly. "She doesn't look too good. I'm gonna take her to get some water. Maybe a little fresh air? Don't you think?"

"Yeah, I think that's a good idea. Should I come

with?" She was torn between wanting to help me and staying behind in case Layne needed her.

"Nah, I got this." Jude practically lifted me from the wooden bench and helped me down the stairs. The only person who seemed to notice us leave was Gin. Others were busy whispering and watching the janitors clean up the floor so the game could continue. It was divisionals after all, and the show must go on. Probably minus some cheerleaders. I started laughing again. I was *so* funny.

Jude walked me outside to the back of the school and propped me up against the side of the building. The cold, crisp air soothed my sweating skin. I wanted to ride this wave of euphoria forever, free of other people's opinions of me, including my own. It was dangerous, addictive and easy to come by.

Every time I used my gift with clarity and minimal emotions, like I'd done just now, I was the eye of the storm. I was in control and my body scorched from the inside out. The high that coursed through my blood nullified my self-deprecating thoughts. It made me feel powerful, indestructible, and invincible. I loved it. I craved it. God, I wanted to feel like this all the time.

When beyond angry, I was the storm and all the chaos to go with it. I lost control and the golem took over, my powers glowed with an icy blue flame hotter than fire—like when something is so incredibly cold that when you first touch it, you think it burns. I missed out on the high and went straight to overloading the power outlet and shorting out. I hated it. I dreaded it.

"Well, that should take care of her." He ran his fingers over his thick, dark hair. The light from above cooled it to a deep blue black.

I smiled again. It was all I could manage. The drug

running through my body left me limp and carefree. I started to slide down the wall. Jude caught me. His strong hands snaked under my armpits before I fell to the ground. He heaved me back up, flattening his palms on the wall to keep me from slipping.

I inhaled deeply, slowly, thoroughly enjoying my high. A slight hint of sawdust wafted above the scent of his cologne. I stared at the swell of his lips wanting to taste him. I had to taste him. I tilted my chin up, reached for the back of his head, and pulled him in. Fire. Ice. Hot. Cold. I couldn't tell. His chest rubbed up against mine. My body tightened; my nipples hardened, and a shock pulsed through me so violently that I moaned into his mouth. I was a bad girl.

He turned his face away. "No!" he growled. "We're not doing this again." He pushed himself as far away from me as he could without letting go. "The next time we kiss, I'm going to be the only one you are kissing. Until then, you and I are just friends. Remember?"

He was breathing heavily and trying to avoid my eyes. "That thing that happens when we touch." He flicked underneath my chin with his index finger. Angry sparks zapped my skin. "That. That doesn't happen in real life." He slapped the wall above my head. Tiny particles of brick dust fell into my hair. He leaned down and whispered into my ear, "Someday you're going to want me." His breath ran hot over my neck, and warmth spread all the way to my feet. "Worse than you want your high." And he was already right. My high was fabulous, freeing, and liberating. But his kiss was as alluring as using my power. I physically ached for him. Every cell in my body begged for him. But I'd made a promise to Layne. My sweet Layne. The one who made me want to be a better person. I was failing miserably right now.

"Sorry. I make bad decisions when I'm in this state. You're such a good friend not to take advantage of me." I bit my bottom lip.

His teeth clenched so tightly that I was afraid they might break. He slapped the wall above my head again. Hard. And used some very colorful language. Some of which I really wanted to take him up on.

"Come on, I gotta get you back. I don't know why I do this to myself . . ."

By the time he set me down next to Miss Molly, I was feeling better. Just buzzed. Layne threw me a dirty look from the middle of the floor. I wondered what it would be like to kiss him when in the throes of my high. I licked my lips and stared suggestively at him, my eyes wandering from his beautiful blond hair and blue eyes, to his thick biceps, and down his long golden legs. Then I waved, fluttering my fingers. His eyes popped open wider, and he grinned before he concentrated back on the game.

I needed to try it sometime to see if it came anywhere near what it was with Jude. Maybe he wasn't the key. Maybe I'd feel the same way with Layne.

Chapter 26

Confessions of a Rich Girl

Gabby didn't show up for school Monday. I was disappointed but not surprised. I was sorry she wasn't going to be here for her finale. She was, after all, the star of the show.

Shortly after lunch, the school newspaper was dropped off to all the classrooms. I hadn't even realized it until I heard a fellow football player apologize to Jude in the hallway.

"Hey, man. I'm so sorry. I didn't know. No hard feelings, okay?" he said as he patted Jude on the back.

"Yeah, sure, no problem," Jude said dryly, irritation pulling at his lip.

"You did this, didn't you?" Jude scooted in behind me. The heat from his large build engulfed me like a warm blanket over my skin.

"Huh?"

He slipped the newspaper over my shoulder. The article was right there on the front page. They scanned and copied her handwritten letter. I would have worded it more eloquently, but I needed it to be believable.

"Let's just say I highly encouraged it. Now you no longer need your scarlet letter." I patted his chest. I used any excuse to touch him. *Pathetic,* I know.

Confessions of a rich girl

-I wanted to be the captain of the cheerleading squad, and Brenda Marx was in my way. I sent her parents her medical files from the doctors' clinic.

-The accusations I made against Jude Mason are lies. I was angry because he broke up with me. Not once did he force himself upon me. I was trying to ruin his life. And it worked.

-Showing the footage of Regan Braaten's father's death, along with her stay in a mental hospital, was my idea. Andy Tullson played the video for the whole school to see because I threatened him.

-If you haven't figured it out by now, I have a man on the inside of my dad's corporation. He provides me with the information I need to blackmail almost anyone.

-To all the people I have extorted or hurt in any other way, I apologize. I cannot live with the guilt any longer. I hope you all can forgive me.

Gabriella LaCroix

He bumped into me and caught me before his weight knocked me over. "Oops, sorry. I always forget how tiny you are."

My head snapped sideways to throw him a dirty look.

"Oh, don't worry. You pack quite the punch." He winked. "Thanks, by the way. Not that I'll be friends with any of these losers. They lost their chance the minute they believed her—when there was no proof!"

"Well, you always have me." I squeezed his arm. His bicep was rock hard under my grip. Even then, a jolt of electricity traveled through me. I shivered and let my hand drop.

"Yeah and look how that's working out?" he said

sarcastically.

"Uh, I'd say pretty good."

"Could be better," he muttered before he turned into his next class and left me walking alone.

While people were willing to ask forgiveness from Jude, they weren't willing to overlook my perceived mental instabilities. *If they only knew how right they were*. He had started kindergarten with at least half of the students. Me, I didn't have that kind of longevity.

By Tuesday early, early morning, the bubble burst. Layne called me well before the roosters crowed. My sleepy-eyed mom brought me the phone. I'd left it on the kitchen table.

"Here, it's Layne. He sounds frantic." She shuffled her floppy slippers over the wood floor and handed it to me. She switched on my bedside table light. Its normally soft glow was blinding. I shielded my eyes.

"Hello," I slurred into the phone.

"Oh, God, Regan, Gabby tried to kill herself. That letter in the paper was her suicide note."

My mind reeled to catch up. "No, it wasn't," I said, rubbing my eyes. I tapped my phone to check the time, it was shortly after five in the morning.

"Of course, it was. Didn't you read it?" He was agitated.

No, really, it wasn't—I actually wrote it. But now, looking back upon *her* written words, I could see how it could be taken that way.

Nausea threatened the back of my throat. I swallowed. This was my fault. I'd gone too far.

"Is she okay?" I croaked out.

"I think so. Olivia called me. Her mom works at the hospital. Said Gabby was brought in by ambulance. She overdosed *and* slit her wrists. Should I go up there?"

"Wh-wh—" I stuttered. "What?" I finished angrily. My first thought was: *He didn't come see me in the hospital when I almost died. But his first instinct was to go see her.*

"I thought I should at least go see if she is okay."

The golem, not quite awake, slithered like cold syrup towards the edges of its prison and nudged at the glass. "Are you for real?" I said quietly. My rage was slowly steaming. I needed to get off the phone and cool down before I did something else to regret. I didn't need another fiasco on my conscience. I could only deal with one screw-up at a time.

"Uh—uh—" he stammered.

"You know what? Do whatever you need to. Goodbye," I growled.

"Wait," he screamed frantically into the phone. I held it away from my ear.

I huffed. He must have heard me. I curled my knees to my chest and rocked back and forth.

"I didn't want to do the same thing to her that I did to you. I feel so bad about it. Still."

I tried focusing on my breathing, but white lights pulsed, slowly closing in. I had to get off the phone.

"You need to do whatever you think is right." I hung up and turned off my phone.

"Is everything okay, honey? What's wrong?" My mom stood in my doorway. The yellow haze from the dated living room lights made her glow like an angel.

I held up a finger, clenched my teeth, and shook my head. A kaleidoscope of silver curved in a half-moon shape along the corners of my vision.

She inhaled sharply and covered her mouth with her

hand. "Oh. Oh, no. I've seen that look before. You need to take a cold shower. It always helped your father. Go." She moved away from my door and pointed down the hall.

I tossed back my covers and stomped out of bed. As I passed by, she ordered. "Cold. As cold as you can stand it."

I made it to the toilet only seconds before I vomited. Yellow bile and last night's supper gushed into the bowl. I kneeled down and panted heavily as the rest of my stomach emptied. Tendrils of spit dangled from my mouth. I used a wad of toilet paper to wipe them away.

I waited for a few minutes to make sure I was done before turning on the cold water. I didn't bother with the hot. I pulled the striped shower curtain aside and stepped in. A gasp escaped between my lips as the icy spray hit my fevered skin. I could almost feel the steam rise. Unwanted tears, scalding hot, scorched a path down my face and dripped off my chin. I slid to the floor with a thud and let the water pound a rhythm on my back.

Giant sobs racked my body. I shivered so violently that it was hard to think. Which was probably the whole point. My brain needed to reboot. Focus before I did something worse. But honestly, what could be worse? I had made a girl try to kill herself. I did something so awful, so devastating, she wanted to die. That was never my goal. I only wanted to give her a taste of her own medicine. Knock her off her high and mighty horse. Make her understand what it was like to be humiliated, shunned, and judged. I wanted to take away her throne so she couldn't bully anyone else. Now I was the biggest bully of them all.

The pelting water stopped abruptly from overhead.

Mom wrapped a fresh-scented towel over my back.

"Come on, honey. We don't want you getting hypothermia. You just needed to cool off."

She helped me up and dried me off like I was a child. My teeth chattered violently, and my body quaked. She held up a T-shirt. I slipped my arms in, and she pulled it over my head. She shimmied my underwear up my still-shivering legs, then made me step in to my pajama bottoms.

"There's someone in the living room waiting for you, so when you are ready, come on out." She softly shut the bathroom door behind her. I managed to brush my teeth and comb my hair, even with my shaking arms. It was much easier to see the mirror when it wasn't steamed up from one of my scalding hot showers. But I didn't want to repeat the icy one any time soon. I threw on the sweatshirt she left me and slid my frozen feet into my slippers.

In all honesty, I expected Jude. I wanted it to be Jude. He always seemed to be there when I needed him. Instead, sitting on the couch, with a cup of cocoa in his hand, was Layne. His hair was messy, but he was dressed, sort of. He wore jeans, a T-shirt, and slippers. He'd forgotten to put on shoes.

A little anger flared inside. I took a deep breath and smothered the flame. It was easier now that I was awake, coherent, and freezing.

"Hey," he said when he noticed me standing behind him.

I tipped my head, but I didn't move.

"Can we talk?"

Without me killing you? I don't know. My track record kind of sucks so far.

"Are you going to go see her?" I stared at the floor.

"How can you be so coldhearted?" He sounded truly surprised.

"Me?" I stomped my foot hard on the wood floor. "I'm the one that's coldhearted? Because I don't feel sorry for a girl who repeatedly destroys people's lives?" I did feel guilty for pushing her that far, but I couldn't wrap my mind around it yet. The ugly little voice in my head kept saying, *did she do it because she really wanted to die? Or did she do it to gain sympathy? Or to keep from getting in trouble now that her true character had been revealed?* I tried shutting it out, but it wouldn't go away.

"She confessed and said she was sorry."

In reality, she hadn't, but Layne didn't know that.

"Oh, and that makes everything okay?" I exaggeratedly threw my arms in the air. Then dropped them back to my sides. I needed to stay calm, but he wasn't helping.

"No, but she's trying."

Actually, she wasn't, I wanted to scream at him.

"Why are you so angry?" He seemed honestly perplexed.

Was he for real? "Hmmm, where should I start?" I laughed lightly, sarcastically. I padded over to the couch opposite of him and sat down on the edge. My mom hovered in her bedroom, her shadow dark against the dawn's rising light.

"That's what I am here for. So we can fix this before it is broken beyond repair," he said it so softly, so reasonably that my body, prepped for a fight, relaxed. It took me a moment to switch gears. Be an adult. I settled back onto the couch and covered my legs with a worn patchwork quilt. Nothing in our house matched.

"I'm angry because when I was in the hospital, my boyfriend refused to come see me because I lied. Because I didn't want to confess my darkest fear. The guilt that plagues me daily. I'm the reason my dad is dead." I fiddled with a frayed corner of the blanket, rolling the material between my fingers. I couldn't look up at him.

The clock on the wall ticked loudly as I waited for him to response with an 'I'm sorry' or 'it's not your fault'.

When I didn't get it, I finally braved a look into his blue eyes and whispered, "And, yes, because of that, I lied about being in the mental ward. I didn't want you to think I was a freak."

Again, I waited for the appropriate response. An 'I understand why you lied' or a simple 'you're not a freak' would suffice. Getting neither, my nostrils flared.

My voice started low and rose in pitch and speed as my anger grew. "Then when your ex-girlfriend is in the hospital because her sins finally catch up with her, you want to go running to her side like a friggin' knight in shining armor." I pointed my finger at him, stabbing it in the air. So much for acting like an adult.

He tapped his pottery mug; his lips thinned into a white line.

"Where were you when I needed you?" I threw my blanket off of me and crossed my arms. My goosebumps refused to go away. I wanted to stay covered up, but I thought maybe he was safer if I were cold.

He lowered his head, then looked at me. "I thought we agreed that was water under the bridge?"

"It was until I figured out that she's more important

than me." I was back on the edge of the couch.

"That isn't true, Regan. That's why I'm here. And not there." He set his cup on the coffee table and leaned forward with his elbows on his legs. "Though I thought you would be more understanding. Gabby tried to kill herself. Her friends have abandoned her; her father is furious. He could get into a lot of trouble."

I couldn't take much more. "I understand perfectly. You have made yourself loud and clear." I stood up and pointed to the door.

"What do you mean? Stop. You're confusing me. Please, Regan," he begged. His face was twisted with pain. He really didn't get it.

I sighed and tilted my head to the ceiling and scrubbed my hands through my still-damp hair. "Let me spell it out. Imagine a big white screen above your head and on it is the worst thing you have ever done. *The. Worst. Thing.* And it's on display for the whole school to see." I pressed my finger to my lips in thought. "Let's pretend Miss Molly is walking with you. She tells you she is getting back together with your dad. You get really, really angry, and you tell her you hate her. Wished in your head that she would die. Then because she is so upset, she accidentally steps in front of a speeding bus. Bam!" I yelled and smacked my hands together.

He jumped and spilled cocoa down the side of his glass onto the floor. I threw my towel at his head. He snatched it out of the air.

"And all of that, your worst moment in life, is now available for everybody's viewing pleasure. Then, suddenly, a stabbing pain rips through your already mangled heart and shatters it again. Now you go to the hospital. Nobody knows if you are going to live or die."

He started to interrupt. I cut him off.

I continued faster and faster and louder and louder. "Now imagine that I didn't come and see you because I was angry. Because you lied. Because you didn't want me to know your *second* worst secret. That because of your guilt, you were thrown into the psych ward. The mad house. The looney bin!" Angry tears pooled in the corners of my eyes.

"That's not—"

"No! I get to finish!" He looked contrite.

"Now, say Jude decides to kill himself because everyone hates him. They all believe the rumors about him. And I fly down there the minute he needs me."

He threw his hands up. "That's exactly what you would do!" He seemed vindicated.

I slowed down. "You're right. I would. I'd be down there in a heartbeat." I stared at his smug face long and hard. Tears spilled over and ran in hot rivulets down my icy skin. "But I would've been there for you, too," I said softly. "I would've understood why you lied even if I weren't happy about it. I would've been by your bedside until you woke up. I'm not sure they could have made me leave. *That* is the difference between us. And you call me coldhearted."

"But you told Jude," he said, verging on the edge of a pout.

"Yeah, because I knew he, of all people, would understand what it was like to be a freak, a pariah. All because of your ex-girlfriend."

He sat there breathing hard. He didn't look so smug now. "I told you how sorry I am. I made a huge mistake."

I swiped the tears from my face with the back of my sleeve. "Yeah, well, sometimes sorry ain't enough.

Actions speak louder than words."

"But don't you see? That's what I'm trying to do here. I wasn't there for you. I made a huge mistake. I don't want to have the same regrets." He stood up and took a hesitant step toward me. He towered over me, his head only inches from the ceiling.

"Surprisingly, I do see your point." I *was* trying to be reasonable.

"Thank you." His tense shoulders sagged.

I crossed my arms. "But sometimes you have to choose sides."

He cocked his head and narrowed his eyes. "You won't. I've asked you not to spend so much time with Jude. But you do it anyway."

"That's because he's the only friend I have."

"You have me." He seemed almost angry. He took another step toward me.

I stood my ground. "Do I? Because right now it doesn't feel like it."

"Don't say that." Panic flashed over his face, and he reached out and pulled me to him. "I'm yours. Don't give up on me."

I nodded into his chest.

He held me back so he could see my face. Read my reaction. "So, when I leave here, if I go see Gabby, are you going to be mad?"

I was going to be so much more than mad. Furious. Broken. Devastated. Betrayed. "Do what you must."

"But are you going to be mad?" He lifted my chin, then cupped my cold cheek.

"Yup."

"But you're not going to break up with me?" The corner of his lip rose.

"Nope." I would not issue an ultimatum. Because I was afraid I might lose.

As I watched him drive away, my heart actually hurt. I rubbed my sternum.

"You okay?" Mom asked from behind me. She handed me a cup of coffee with extra cream.

I shrugged. She sat down on the couch and patted the spot next to her.

"I know you probably don't want my advice, but I'm going to give it to you anyway. Layne is a nice young man. And devastatingly handsome." We both smiled. She tucked her feet under her. "I can see now, what your father said is true. That you're going to need someone in life to keep you grounded."

"I don't need a man in my life," I growled between clenched teeth. The mere thought made me cringe.

"No. I'm proud to say, unlike myself, you are perfectly capable of doing life on your own. But you are going to need someone to hold you to this earth."

My eyes snapped open. My fear and curiosity were piqued.

"Your dad always said that's what I did for him. I kept him centered and grounded. I kept him from burning out. At first, I was angry. I was the type of girl men dreamed of." Her cockiness was cute and well warranted. Men still tripped over their feet and stumbled over their words when she was around. "They would walk over hot coals just to hear my voice. And your dad had the nerve to say I kept him *grounded*," she said with a fair amount of disdain, disgust, and contempt all packed in one single word. "Well, he could go, well, you know . . . himself."

My mom didn't like to cuss so she simply skipped the bad words—allowed others to fill in the colorful blanks.

"I was so angry that I tried breaking up with him, but I couldn't." Her arrogance faded, and the depth of sadness that weighed heavy in her eyes made my throat knot up. "It's like he was the other half of my soul." Her voice, so strong only seconds ago, now sounded small and far away. The coffee cup in her hand trembled. "I know, I know," she held up one dainty hand, "how stupid this sounds. I can't explain it. He made me want to be a better person, and he always said I made him a better man. Your father had a gift."

I snorted coffee out my nose. "Sorry." I dabbed it with a tissue and avoided looking directly at her. Here was the perfect time for me to confess. But try as I might, I couldn't find the words. I could only deal with one emotional problem at a time when the golem was busy testing the security of its prison.

"He was like the animal whisperer, except with people. He always laughed that he couldn't control me. Said I was his kryptonite. But sometimes, after he had a hard day at work, he would just want me to hold him. Said I was his tether to this earth. He said I was the only person in the world who could keep him calm, contained, and grounded. He said to watch out for you. You, too, might need a tether someday. I always thought it would be me. But I was wrong."

"Then who is it?" I asked. But I already knew.

"When you find it, you'll know." She kissed my head before she left.

My poor mom. I'd never taken a moment to put myself in her shoes. She said he was the other half of her soul. And he'd been ripped away. And now she had a gaping hole in her heart. I laid my face in my hands and cried for the love she had lost the day I killed my father. I began to understand her pain. Why she turned to alcohol to drown her sorrows. I used my high to vanquish my guilt. I sat there on my high horse and judged her but never once looked in the mirror.

By God, it wasn't even eight a.m., and this day was shit.

Chapter 27

Feed the Dark Wolf

When my mom headed over to my grandparents' house for breakfast, I made an executive decision to skip school. I didn't think it was safe for me to attend. My emotions were raw and jagged, leaving me open to the golem's creative suggestions. I left a note on the table saying I needed some space. Some time alone to think about how to tell my mom what I was capable of—all the horrible things I had done. Today just being my latest infraction.

I stopped at work to get my paycheck and gassed up my truck as I waited for the bank to open at ten. Once it was deposited, I drove. With no destination in mind, the lonely highway kept me company for at least an hour as I attempted to outpace my thoughts and my memories. And the jerk driving a black SUV tailing me.

I contemplated brake checking him but didn't want to deal with the consequences if he wasn't paying attention and he rear-ended me. Instead, like a responsible driver, I turned on my blinker and pulled off into one of the empty trailhead parking lots. I gathered my things: cold-weather gear, snacks, and water. I stretched my boot spikes over my shoes and put on my gloves. I didn't plan on going far, but I always liked to be prepared, especially out here. Living in Alaska taught me well.

I tossed my backpack onto my shoulders, locked my truck, and randomly chose a trail. Okay, not so random. I took the one that had been traveled the most. Which wasn't saying a lot since not many people hiked here in the winter.

The crisp, cold air in the slight breeze stung my cheeks. I pulled my scarf tighter over my chin. Most of the snow had blown from the branches to the forest floor. The trees, although covered with green pine needles, still somehow managed to look skeletal against the stark white background. My feet crunched over the frozen ground; the sound was loud and somehow comforting in my ears.

About five miles in, I made it to the overlook, a slight cliff about twenty feet above the lake. My shirt clung to my sweating skin. I found a spot under a tree, out of the wind, and leaned against the trunk. Animal tracks zigzagged over the thick blanket of snow covering the frozen lake. It was a wildlife highway. Crazy birds, the ones who didn't fly south, chirped from above. They sounded so spring-like. But the beginning of March was not spring here. The world was still deep in the slumber of winter. The sun, having made its way over the mountain from behind me, glistened over the vast expanse of the lake and on the surrounding peaks.

My deep breath puffed into the cold air, and my mind had a chance to wander. Today at school, the whispers, the shock, the sadness, and the excitement were buzzing in the air. I didn't need to be there to know this. The teachers had already been pulled aside and instructed on how to deal with this tragedy. The one I had caused. The second one in less than a year. I'd hurt Gabby so badly she felt the need to kill herself. Now that Layne wasn't here making me angry, I could take a second to gather my feelings. I *had* meant to demean her, humiliate her, and make her feel like the lowest creature on earth. The same thing she had done to so many people before. But I'd gone too far. I rationalized that I didn't mean to, but then I concluded that it didn't matter. Another sin to atone for. My shoulders slumped.

And what my mom said about my dad. That I was so much like him. That he needed a tether to the earth—someone to keep him from burning out. Despite my stubborn streak of independence, I needed those things too. Was there something she wasn't telling me? Something they'd kept from me. It's not like after I'd discovered my gift I hadn't wondered where it had come from or if it was simply a fluke in my genetics. Kennedy was unusually perceptive, I used to call him psychic, but my mom insisted I stop the nonsense. She'd get really angry with me. And Lincoln was athletically gifted. But he never seemed interested in pursuing his talents. I once asked him why and he got all pissy. Told me to go ask our parents. And now looking back, had I missed something? Or maybe…I'd hit the nail on the head.

I sat there stewing in my thoughts for a long while, when crunching snow made me pause. It wasn't unusual for locals to hike, but this trail was also used by animals. Most of them were not dangerous. But mountain lions were. Thankfully, bears were still sleeping. More than likely, if a cougar was hunting me, I wouldn't know it until it was too late.

"Regan." A black-hooded figure bent over and peered at me sitting under my tree. Jude.

"How did you find me?" I pretended to be irritated, but, really, I was happy to see him. My heart reached up for him, held out tiny little hands, and begged to be picked up. I smothered its desires with my self-loathing.

"Your mom called." He squatted down in front of me.

"Still doesn't add up to how you knew where I was. Do I have a frigging tracking device on me somewhere?" I threw my arms in the air, then patted down my coat.

"I could find you anywhere." He pulled off his hood and studied my pink-cheeked face.

I narrowed my eyes.

"What?" He threw me a quizzical look and lifted a shoulder. "I told you, I grew up partly on the Res. My grandfather's a well-known tracker. He's been teaching me since I was a kid." He turned his head to the right, then to the left, scanning the forest. "You know it's dangerous out here. What if you got lost?"

"Seriously? There's a trail." I semi-pointed with mittens on my hand. "I think I can manage. And if any dangerous *people* come along, well, I'm the most dangerous one of all. Obviously. Look at my track record. So, really, I got this," I snapped.

The muscles in his jaw tightened under his skin. "Yeah, sure you do." He let his acerbity sink in before he continued. "Did you know there have been reports of a large cat in the area lately? And last week, a ranch near here lost one of its cattle to a pack of wolves?"

Blood drained from my face. I'd forgotten about wolves.

"Correct me if I am wrong, but I believe animals are beyond your control?" He pushed his hands together into a prayer position and tapped them against his lips.

I glared, but he held my angry gaze until I looked away. He was right.

"Oh, are you out here feeling sorry for yourself?" he mocked.

My head snapped back. My mouth hung open. Of course, I was.

"Are you that stupid?" Jude asked. Confusion and anger tinged the question. "You're blaming yourself for her actions. So you humiliated Gabby in front of the entire school. The same thing she has done to countless people, myself included. She falsely accused me of rape." Obvious shame flashed through his anger, even though he was innocent. "Left a big black stain on my name. There's no innocent until proven guilty in this country. Don't fool yourself. And to top it off, I still hear some of them in the hallways whispering as I walk by: savage, half-breed, stalker, rapist." The last word he said so softly I almost missed it. "'Oh, his family is from the reservation'—like that has anything to do with it. Not once have I tried to OD, slit my wrists, or put a gun to my head."

He knelt down from his squatting position and grabbed the sides of my head in his large warm hands. Even through his thick gloves and my rainbow hat, a buzz hummed in my ears. He stared me down hard. He didn't blink. He cornered the market on the stare glare. I couldn't compete.

"That was her choice. Not yours. Do you hear me?" He shook my head up and down slightly. "Don't you get it? All you did was stand up for those who can't protect themselves. You think you are dark, cursed, evil—but you're not. You can't see the forest for the trees. Open your fucking eyes! You, too, made a choice. To help people the only way you can."

He tore off his gloves and pinched the bridge of his nose. "And God knows, you could be a monster if you chose to."

I started to say something, but he held a finger to my mouth and shook his head. He took a deep breath, his agitation fading, and rested his bare hands on my knees.

"My grandpa told me of an old Indian legend—I can't remember which tribe off the top of my head, but it says we are all born with two wolves battling inside of us. One light, one dark. One good, one evil. The one that wins is the one you feed. But you're different. Your choice isn't as simple. You choose to feed the dark wolf in order to save the light wolf. Don't you see?" He dropped his forehead to mine. A soothing heat spread down my face and over my shoulders. He understood things I refused to see.

His breath tickled the skin of my neck under where I had loosened my scarf. My heart stuttered, and my stomach twisted. An effervescent tickle spread over my face to my lips. They almost vibrated with want. But that wouldn't be fair, so I bit down painfully on my bottom lip to stop the unnerving feeling pulsing through them.

He inhaled sharply and turned his head to the side. He didn't say any more but maneuvered back in behind me and leaned against the tree. He pulled me tight against him. I hugged my knees to my chest, and he wrapped his arms and legs around me. I'd never felt safer. Out here, in the middle of nowhere, with Jude's body holding me, there was no place on earth I'd rather be. We sat in silence for a while, watching the sun measure time. An eagle soared overhead, and crows gurgled and cawed to one another in the treetops. Jude's arms never loosened.

"Layne called me this morning to tell me about Gabby."

His body tightened and froze. Then he relaxed. "Mm-hmm."

"He wanted to know if he should go to the hospital and see if she were okay."

Jude didn't say anything; his breathing was deep and even against my back.

"Let's just say I didn't take it well."

I felt a chuckle rumble through his chest. "I can imagine."

"It hurt," I whispered, staring out at the lake. On the far side, a five-point buck walked out onto the frozen surface. He paused and looked around, his nose twitching and his ears swiveling and searching for danger. Having assessed the situation safe, he rambled across. His dainty legs and black hooves were stable on the slippery snow.

"I bet it did." His arms squeezed me tighter. He nuzzled his head into my neck. I curled my fingers into a fist inside of my mittens. I was doing everything in my power not to turn around and kiss him.

"My mom called you to come find me. Why?"

"Because Sara likes me. And she hurts for you. And she knows I'd do anything for you. She knows I was at the hospital with you every night."

"She does? How?" I tried to look at him, but he held me tight and wouldn't let me move.

"I think one of the nurses suspected and probably told her. Asked her if it were okay. She worries about you, you know."

"She does?"

“Seriously, I don’t think you give your mom enough credit.”

“I think you’re right.” I was just discovering her hidden depths. Though perhaps they weren’t that hidden, I’d just been too selfish to ever see them. I was learning, but mostly I was learning that I had a lot to learn. And damned if it didn’t hurt.

“She says you’re so much like your dad.”

“How?”

“She said he had an uncanny gift of persuasion. Could get people to agree with him, even if they didn’t want to. Though we know your gift goes well beyond that.”

I crawled out of his grasp and knelt before him. I searched his dark eyes. The afternoon sun had crept under the boughs of the tree and glowed on his bronze skin. I wanted to touch his smooth cheek, run my finger over the deep bow in his top lip, slip off his hat, and run my fingers through his thick hair. I refrained and swallowed. Afraid he might know the answer. “Do you know what I am?” My voice cracked.

He reached out and stroked my cheek with the back of his hand, “No, I’m sorry. I don’t. But I do believe that you’re not the only one out there. I mean, every society has their legends.” He gripped my chin between his fingers and thumb. “But I do know who you are, even if you don’t. It hurts me to watch you try and change . . . conform to who he needs you to be. Don’t you get it? For me, you’ll never have to change. The light or the dark.”

I leaned forward, unable to resist the pull between us, but he turned away. Refused my kiss. My heart twisted, and a sob almost escaped from my chest. The fear that I had lost him was overwhelming. But how could I lose what wasn't mine? I knew now that he was the one I needed. Not Layne. But fear stopped me. What if he no longer wanted me? Why would he? I turned him down more than once. I opened my mouth to tell him I'd made a mistake, beg his forgiveness, but before I could, he said tensely, "We need to go." He nodded his chin toward the lake.

Beyond the tree line, past the edge of the far side of the lake, stood a lone black wolf. And where there was one, there'd be others. It stalked out onto the lake, its shoulders rolling under his black fur. He sniffed the tracks in the snow, then raised his nose in the air. My eyes widened in fear.

"It's okay. Wolves don't usually bother people. As soon as we start moving, he'll leave." He patted the side of his jacket. "And if not, I have us covered."

"What? A phone? Do you even get service?"

He laughed. "Yeah, that too, but I carry my pistol with me out here. You never know when you'll need it."

"You're not old enough."

He threw me a look like, *seriously?* "Come on." He helped me up off the ground.

We hiked back down the trail to the parking lot. I wanted to tell him how I felt, but I couldn't concentrate on the path and talk at the same time. That's what I told myself.

"Where's your car?" My truck was the only vehicle in the lot.

"I had my mom drop me off." He walked over to the passenger side door and waited.

I hopped in and pulled up the lock. "What if you couldn't find me?"

"I told you. I could find you anywhere. Anywhere,"

he said softly, one side of his lip curling like it was a fact and an apology all at the same time.

Chapter 28

Scariest Tale of them All

I gave the truck a few minutes to warm up before we left. “What do you want to do? I really don’t feel like going home.”

His smile traveled all the way to his eyes. “Ya wanna meet my grandparents? I told my grandma I’d stop by later this afternoon.” He glanced at the time on his phone. “We better hurry.”

I grinned like a fool. “Yeah, I’d like that, but the reservation is quite a way from here.”

“I know, but they don’t live there anymore. At least, not in the winter anyway. My dad adores my grandparents and, before my mom and he split, my dad bought them a small place right out of town so they could see us more. Grandpa grumbles about it, but Grandma loves it.”

“So, what happened after your parents split? Do they still keep in contact with your dad?” I headed toward town, following Jude’s hand signals.

“Yeah, they do. With my mother’s blessing actually. Course, now that he’s not in town so much, they don’t see each other as often.”

“And what do they think about your father’s behavior?”

"Mom says it doesn't matter. Their marriage and divorce were about them. Not anyone else. She insists we all get along for the whole family's sake. Works pretty well."

He pointed to the right onto a dirt road, then the left into a long driveway. "Right there."

I pulled up next to an old pick-up with rusted fenders and a tiny newer car in front of a small log house. Red trim and a red tin roof matched the outdoor chairs sitting under the covered front porch. They had a beautiful view of the surrounding mountains. A few scattered abodes, gray smoke rising from the chimneys, dotted the sloping hillside.

A couple of Appaloosa horses stood outside the small barn behind the house. Fat and happy, they were content to stare at us while they chewed their mouthfuls of hay.

Jude didn't even knock. He held the door open for me and walked in behind me. It smelled like fresh bread and coffee with a slight hint of tobacco, as if someone smoked, but not inside.

A short, round woman with a silver-streaked bun on the back of her head and deep wrinkles surrounding her dark eyes welcomed me by name into the house. Jude's Scottish terrier danced around my feet, begging for his due. I bent down and gave him a good butt-scratching. Another dog, a hound, stood silently, wagging a long whip of a tail.

"This is my grandma, Rose, and my grandpa, Tom." Jude bent way down and gave her a big squeeze. Then he handed his grandpa a small package wrapped neatly in crinkly paper and tied with a string.

Rose took my cold hands in hers. Even I looked

down at her. "It's so nice to finally meet you. Jude talks non-stop . . ." she said.

Jude cut her off with a forceful, "Grandma!"

I caught the sly grin on Tom's face as he opened the door to the outside. He shut it quietly behind him.

She covered her mouth with a callused, cracked hand to hide her amusement. A single gold band circled her ring finger. "Regan, it's nice to meet you," she said.

She shuffled around the quaint kitchen and put a kettle of water on the stove, intent on making us some homemade apple cider. Mismatched potholders hung from under the cabinets, and a colorful dishtowel was laid neatly on top of the hand-washed dishes in the drying rack. The stainless-steel dishwasher looked brand new, as if it had never been used. Dozens of pictures, put on with random magnets, graced the front of the white refrigerator.

She opened the cupboard and pulled out two pottery mugs—one glazed in blue, one in orange—and poured us some cider. Hot steam swirled in the air.

"Jude, darling, do you think you could give me a hand? I have some shelves in the laundry room that I can't seem to install myself, and I don't want to ask Grandpa because of his shoulder and all. And if he knows they aren't done, he'll insist on doing it himself."

"Sure thing, Grandma." Jude turned to look at me as he followed Rose down the dim hallway. "You can come with me or go sit on the porch with my grandpa if you want."

I waved at him and flittered my fingers knowing I'd be in the way. I checked out the photos on the fridge. Pictures of Jacy and Jude littered the surface. Fat baby Jude to hot high school Jude and every awkward moment in between. A family picture of him, Jacy, and his dad looked straight out of a magazine photo shoot. I could see the resemblance to both his parents. No wonder he was so good-looking. His dad was tall and strikingly handsome with dark hair and light eyes. He had his dad's jawline and eye shape but got his cheekbones, lips, and coloring from his mother. Lucky boy.

I threw on my coat and hat and wandered onto the porch. I was curious about the man Jude always spoke so highly of.

"Regan," Tom said in a weathered voice, "have a seat. I suppose Rose has Jude putting up the shelves in the laundry." He had a full head of silver hair that was pulled back into a ponytail at the base of his neck. It contrasted with his dark, creviced skin. He looked as if he'd lived most of his life under the relentless sun and in the frigid cold. I was sure every line held a story.

I laughed and sat down. I set my cup on the slatted iron table and stared at the mountains in the distance, waiting for my drink to cool off. The early evening sun hovered over jagged peaks casting the valley in an orange hazy light.

"I hear high praise from my boy." Tom pulled a small silver box from his pocket and opened it. He set out his supplies; cigarette papers, a filter and the fresh tobacco that was in the package Jude brought him. Quickly, he rolled it and tapped it on the table.

"Yes, sir. Same here."

He lit it with a flip-top lighter and took a deep puff before blowing the smoke away. "I hear you have quite the talent."

My shoulders stiffened. My breathing stopped. I froze. I wasn't sure if I was angry or relieved. Both, really. Mad because he'd promised to keep my secret. Relieved because if anyone could tell me what I was, my best shot was probably sitting across the table.

"Oh, child, relax," he said, flicking his cigarette ash into the tray on the table.

"But he promised not to tell anyone . . ." I whispered, hurt. My hands started to shake. What if he didn't believe me? Worse, what if he told another adult, and they wanted to put me back in the looney bin? I tensed my muscles, ready to flee at a moment's notice. Even though running wouldn't have done any good. I felt inside my pocket to make sure my keys were there.

"Well, I'm not just anyone." A half-smile quirked the corner of his lip. Reminded me of someone else I knew.

I cocked my head. "And you believe him?" I said suspiciously. What adult would really accept that tale?

"Yes." He nodded.

"Without proof?" I tried to keep the challenge out of my voice.

"There are many things in this world that I can't see." He studied me, his eyes a soft coppery brown, much lighter than Jude's. Deep crows' feet etched his skin. I wanted to close off whatever he was seeing. Slam it shut. Because whatever was inside of me couldn't be good. "Doesn't mean they don't exist," he finished.

He did have a point. I simmered down a notch. Neither my intuition nor golem were reacting. Just my flight-or-fight mechanism. The same reaction normal people had. Made me wonder if my powers would even work on Tom. I had too much respect for him to try.

And my secret was out. I picked up my chair, turned it toward him, and put my elbows on the table. "So, do you know what I am?" I sounded desperate.

He mashed out his cigarette "There are many names for people like you. Though I don't believe you need a label. I think each of you are unique in your own way. Take Jude for instance. He can see people's auras. Says yours is as black as the moonless night."

My eyes dropped, and I let out a sad breath. He had told his grandpa everything. The good. The bad. The ugly. For some reason, I didn't want him to think poorly of me.

"But within, it shines with bright stars from the heavens. Different isn't always bad, Regan. Just different." He tapped the steel table with his finger. He waited until I looked up. His eyes said, *Capisce?*

A wave of relief washed over me.

"Has Jude told you about his other gift?" He sat back and crossed his arms.

My eyes shot open. No.

"His tracking abilities?"

"Oh." I relaxed. "Yes. He said he learned those from you."

"The art of tracking perhaps, but his gift goes far beyond that. He can reach out with his mind and follow. Animals and people. It's like a lasso. He can throw it out and catch whatever he is searching for. Then he can go right to it. In most instances, as soon as he finds his target, he is able to release the connection. Sever the tie. And no harm comes to either party."

Well, now I know how he was able to find me all the time.

"But with you, I think perhaps he has made this tie permanent."

Confusion and fear prickled my brain. My heartbeat

pulsed in my neck. "What? What do you mean?"

He rubbed his hand over his mouth. "I think you should ask him."

"I don't get it. Ask him what?"

He smiled at me but didn't answer my question. He rose slowly from the table and took a second to regain balance before he said, "Let's go inside and see if they are finished."

My head was spinning. I hadn't moved past my question. What was he talking about? Some kind of permanent tie . . . *Well, just untie it then.*

I stood up and grabbed my cup. Tom patted me on the back, then squeezed between my neck and shoulder. It was a *hang-in-there, kid* sort of squeeze. The door squeaked when he opened it. I cringed.

Jude and Rose stood in the kitchen, talking and laughing. Their volume, probably normal, seemed loud and abrasive. "Hey, ya learn anything new? Grandpa is full of stories."

I tried to smile, but my cheeks tremored.

"You okay?" Jude stepped out from behind the counter and took a step toward me. He glared at Tom. "Aww, you didn't tell her one of the scary stories, did you?" His voice changed from humorous to concerned. "You did, didn't you?"

Chapter 29

Rubber Band

I thanked Rose for the cider, told both of them it was nice to meet them, and then insisted I had to get home. What I really needed to do was get Jude alone.

The pavement was smooth compared to the washboard dirt road as I pulled out on the highway and flipped on the headlights. The hum of my tires was the only sound.

Finally, Jude broke the silence. "What's wrong?"

"How do you know something is wrong?" I hissed, not taking my eyes off the dark road. Dotted yellow lines sped by.

"Because you're quiet, and ya just bit my head off." His eyes bore into the side of my face. He wasn't one to back down easily.

"Why don't *you* tell me what's wrong?" My tone was menacing.

"And how exactly do you propose I do that? I can't read your mind."

I turned my head. "Can't you?"

He froze, stopped breathing, and squinted his eyes. "What did my grandpa tell you?"

I stared back down the road, keeping my expression neutral, while anger simmered beneath. At least I couldn't hurt him.

"What did he tell you?" Jude demanded. He grabbed my arm. His touch sent shivers down my spine. I shrugged his hand off of me. I did not want his shivers right now.

"How about what did *you* tell him?" I smashed my teeth together.

He released a deep breath. "Pull over so we can talk."

"Nope, I'm fine."

"Look, what I am about to say is gonna piss you off, and I'd rather not be in a moving vehicle with you when you're mad. So, either pull over or this conversation will have to wait." He folded his arms and stretched his legs out under the dash.

I flipped on my blinker and stopped at a scenic overlook beside the river. I put the truck in park and shut it off. The half-moon sparkled on the flowing water and outlined the trees in its milky glow. Heavy, gray clouds leisurely moved along, obscuring some of the light. The rushing current was white noise in the background.

Jude unbuckled his seat belt and turned sideways. "Yes, I told my grandpa about you. I know I promised I wouldn't tell anyone. But you have to believe me, I thought maybe he would know something."

I took off my hat and patted my hair down. "That's where you came up with the idea of the Trickster, or Loki, isn't it?"

"Yeah."

I unhooked my seat belt and faced him. The moonlight from above shone on one side of his face and shadowed the other. It cut under his high cheekbone and glimmered on his lips, muting their crimson color.

"That's not why I am upset."

"It's not? Then what?" He tilted his head away from me, more toward the light, but his eyes didn't stray from mine. His voice was guarded.

"You tell me," I whispered.

The muscles in his jaw tensed and his eyes hardened, black pools refusing to let in any light. "How can I tell you what I don't know?" he shouted and tossed up his hands.

"Start by telling me how you can find me so easily." I stayed calm. It was better that way.

His face paled—out with the bronze skin, in with the silver. I waited.

"Because I'm a good tracker," he said with a tinge of scorn. Or touchiness.

He had told me all of this before. I dug deeper. "And?"

"And what?" he barked. Now who was biting whose head off?

"Tell me. Tell me now." I tapped my leg hard with a pointed finger. The wind picked up and blew through the trees. The skeletal branches swayed with the force. The shadows crawled over the rutted pavement, their bony fingers curling and reaching.

"What? That I can find people and animals? That my abilities are more developed than some? That I can link my mind to their aura and follow the trail. Are you happy now?" This was the most irritated I'd ever seen him. Most of the time, his emotions were well under lock and key.

"Why didn't you tell me?"

"I did. It doesn't matter how I get the job done. Just that I get it done. Same as you. I know what you can do.

It doesn't matter how you do it. Seriously, I can't believe you're so angry about it."

I sat quietly with my hands gripped on the cold steering wheel. "Your grandpa said he thinks you permanently bound yourself to me. What does that mean?"

"Are you kidding me? He had no right." Jude lifted the door handle. A gust of wind caught the corner and flung it all the way open. He jumped out and slammed it behind him. He paced over the rough pavement. He tore off his hat and ran his fingers aggressively through his hair.

I followed. I stepped in front of him, stopping him in his tracks. I pointed to his chest, but didn't touch him. I didn't want to feel all warm and tingly right now. I was mad. "And you had no right to tell him my secret. It seems to me we're even."

"What did he tell you?" He crossed his arms, brushing my finger out of the way.

My bangs flapped all around me, slapping me in the face. I tried pushing them out of the way. I didn't answer. I didn't want him to know that I knew nothing, really. Nada. Zilch. Zero. Tom hadn't told me anything except to ask Jude.

"You're not going to tell me, are you?" He glared. If I didn't know him, I might have been frightened. Even so, goosebumps rose along my forearms. "Fine," he growled. His nostrils flared as he inhaled and slowly let it go. His anger deflated along with his breath. "It's like I am a hound dog but instead of following someone's scent, I pick up an energy trail. I find their color and follow. I can do it with people and animals. Everyone has their own shade. Animals are much brighter, purer —

easier—because they don't travel in cars or planes. The farther away someone gets, the more difficult the trail. I don't use it often on people because I don't want law enforcement asking too many questions. I'm sure it would seem suspicious."

"Tom said you linked to me permanently."

"How does he even know?" He scrubbed his face and turned in circles. I waited for him to stop.

"Remember, it doesn't matter *how* he knows, only *that* he knows." I threw his words back at him. I didn't tell him his grandpa didn't know for sure. He only suspected. Because I had no doubt in my mind, Jude would deny it if he had a choice.

"So, did you?"

He looked like a trapped animal trying to find a way out. His eyes darted from one side to the other. He leaned down in front of me. The fear on his face almost freed him. I almost told him whatever it was, it didn't matter. But it did. I needed to know what he'd done. "Yes. But you have to understand, if I didn't, you would be dead. Gone. When you passed out at the school, you dimmed. All your shimmer fell to the ground and didn't replenish itself. By the time we got to the hospital, your black had faded to a soft gray, then paled even more. You went from being a storm cloud to a cumulous cloud, all puffy and white like a cotton ball. Then you started to drift away."

His chin quivered. I lifted a finger and traced his bottom lip. It was soft and warm and perfect. I snatched it back like I'd been burned. I needed him to finish.

"I linked my energy to yours like I do everything I track, but you kept slipping away. The rope was like silk, soft and fine, and I couldn't hold on without making our connection permanent. And even then, there were moments I thought I would lose you." He reached out and grabbed my shoulders, like if he didn't hold on, I would again float away.

I tried to hide the pain on my face. I bit down hard on the inside of my cheek. "Don't you get it? That's what I deserve. I deserve to die. You should've let me go."

He shook me. My head wobbled. "Don't say that! What do you think your grandparents would do? And your mom? She just lost her husband; she wouldn't survive losing you too."

"And I'm the reason he's gone!" I twisted out of his grip and walked away toward the river. I screamed, "I killed him!" I yelled it to the trees, to the moon, to the river, and to the darkness. To anything listening.

Over the swishing of the water, I didn't hear him follow me. He grabbed me from behind and wrapped me in a steel embrace. I struggled but couldn't break his grip. He whispered in my ear over the sound of the rushing river and gusting wind, "I understand the burden you bear is heavy. One most people wouldn't survive. But you're not most people. Your dad knew this already. Someday you're going to have to forgive yourself."

"I can't." Tears scalded my face.

He swiveled me toward him but didn't let go. "Yes, you can." He hugged me tight. Any fight I had drained out of me. Floated away on the wind. Jude lifted me up, set me in the passenger side of my own truck, and plucked my keys from my pocket. He had to move the seat back before he could even crawl in. He started the truck but just sat there.

"So, what does this permanent connection mean?" I stared out the window, tracing a tic-tac-toe pattern on the fogged window.

"Can we just leave it here?" he begged.

I spun around. "No."

"Please," he pleaded.

I shook my head.

"Fine. It means I know where you're at—all the time. I have a basic link to how you are feeling—all the time."

"Does it work both ways?" I didn't like the idea of anyone having a link to my feelings. It was bad enough I knew what I was feeling.

He shrugged. "I think so. It's not like I've done this before. But I believe in time, when you have sorted out your own issues," he raised his eyebrows, "then you'll be able to at least have a barometer on my feelings."

Good because this one-sided bit was crap. "But what does this mean for you? And me?"

He shook his head and tipped his face toward the sky. I snapped a mental picture. He looked like a bronze statue carved from moonlight. The light disappeared in the chiseled valleys under his cheekbones and reflected silver off the soft curves of his cheeks and lips.

"It's like you're one end of a rubber band, and I'm the other end. The farther you go, the more I feel it. The pull toward you gets, not stronger per se, but more uncomfortable."

"And can you break this? Just cut the rubber band in half?" Hope bloomed.

He glanced down and pinched his top lip between his fingers and thumb. "I think so, but like a rubber band, there will be a snap back, and I'm not sure of the repercussions."

"How do you know all of this if you haven't done it

before?"

He twitched his upper body, shoulders, neck, and chin. "I don't know. It's just a feeling. And not one I'm willing to test."

"What if I am?" I challenged.

He pressed his lips together. "Well, then I guess we can try it."

"And what will happen?"

"I told you, I'm not sure," he growled and gripped the steering wheel.

"What do you *think* will happen?"

"I think one or both of us will die," he said every word very clearly, keeping control of his tone.

"How could you do this?" I buried my face in my hands. I wanted to scream.

"How could I not! Don't you get it? I—I—" He took a deep breath. "I couldn't let you die."

"Yes, you could have. That shouldn't have been your choice." I scooted up on my knees and got in his face.

He turned his head away toward the truck window, his breath fogging up the glass. "Whatever. It's too late now. Unless you want to cut the cord? See what happens." His voice was far away.

If I knew it would have been me that died, I might've said yes. But, as mad as I was at Jude, I could never willingly hurt him. "So that's it. You and I are bound." I flopped back in the seat like a rag doll.

"Yes," he huffed like he hated the idea as much as I did. "But it doesn't need to be more than that. We can both live normal—well, as normal as possible—lives. You can do whatever you want. Live however and wherever you want. The cord will stretch however far you need it to. Can we go now? I need to get home. My phone keeps buzzing in my pocket."

He needed to get away from me. I didn't blame him; I needed to get away from me, too.

I stared out the window as he drove my truck to his house. I didn't say another word. Even when he said goodbye, I ignored him.

Chapter 30

Try Harder

At first, I was so angry that he bound himself to me. And without my permission. I ground my teeth, the noise loud and aggravating in my ears.

I stepped on the gas. My speedometer was well past the speed limit. How could he do this? I'd been backed into a corner, and the person that trapped me was the only one who couldn't be controlled. He should have let me die. I pounded on the wheel and half-yelled, half-growled. It would've been better for everyone.

And that's when the real problem hit me. My foot slipped off the gas pedal, and a hysterical sob caught in the back of my throat. Hot, angry, unwanted tears spilled from my eyes.

All this time, I'd been feeling sorry for myself when I should've been feeling sorry for Jude. In order to save my life, he threw me a rope and was now permanently attached to me. Me. The witch of wicked wishes. Since I'd gotten to this sleepy little town, Jude had been following me around keeping me out of trouble the best that he could. Simmering down my anger before I could cause the ultimate damage. And now he was going to have to do that for the rest of his life. He was worried about me living a normal life, but normal wasn't an option. And the minute he'd tied himself to me, his semi-normal life was off the table. A scream rattled out of my mouth—a terrible, painful wail ripping at the back of my throat. God, I ruined everything around me. And everyone.

My rage grew slowly, like a volcano building pressure. Steam escaped every crack in my well-fortified armor. But this time my anger was directed at me.

I flew down our bumpy dirt road. Rocks shot from my rear tires, and the backend of my pickup fishtailed, but I didn't slow down until I got home. Slamming on the brakes, I skidded to a stop in front of my house; dust whirled around my headlights and up into the patio lights.

My feet pounded up the porch, and I threw open the front door so hard it bounced off the side of the house and smacked me in the back. I stumbled in and stood in the doorway with wild eyes.

"Regan!" my mom yelled, panic in her voice. She set her glass down on the coffee table next to her dinner. The beautiful burgundy color of the wine reflected on the white paper napkin. "Are you okay?" She got up and started heading toward me. Barry scooted to the edge of the couch, ready to help her if need be. "Is Jude okay?" She covered her mouth with a dainty hand. The horror on her face contrasted with her bubblegum pink fingernails.

"No!" I screamed. My fists balled into the air. "Nobody is okay! I'm not okay. Jude's not okay. You," I pointed violently to her, "are not okay! All because of me." I pounded my chest like a gorilla.

Barry stood up and placed his hands on her shoulders. He was studying my outburst with the clarity of an officer. Keeping calm but assessing the situation to see when and where true danger was about to strike. Too late. But I wasn't here to hurt anyone other than myself. "But mostly Dad's not okay because I killed him. And it's about time you believed me. I killed him. I wished for him to die. I wished he would walk in front of that bus and die. I . . ." I tapped my chest fiercely with my finger. Pain rippled into my hand. "I made him walk in front of that bus." I needed her to hate me as much as I hated myself.

I expected her to deny it to try and make me feel better. But with Barry here, I was prepared to demonstrate.

Her shoulders slumped, and her eyes filled with tears. She patted Barry's hand and said, "I know, baby. I know." She squeezed his hand tight, then she let it go and took a step toward me.

I puffed up my little body as big as I could. "No, I mean it. I killed him."

She replied with utmost faith. "I know," she said softly but firmly.

My angry eyebrows relaxed into uncertainty. "What? What do you mean, you know?" My head reeled backward, and I cocked my ear to her. I must have misunderstood.

"Exactly what I said. I know you were the one who made him walk in front of the bus." She took a tiny step forward as if she would scare me away if she came too close. "But you have to believe me when I tell you, I didn't know that you knew. I didn't realize until earlier this morning you'd figured it out. That you are like your father. I thought—or I wanted to think—you believed you killed him because you told him you hated him. Not because you actually made him walk in front of that bus."

My knees began to shake and then my whole body. I slumped to the floor. She rushed over, knelt next to me, and wrapped her tiny body around mine. "We need to talk," she whispered in my ear. She rocked me back and forth. The smell of her sweet perfume was familiar and comforting in my nose.

I nodded. I stared at the yellow wood floor, the wide cracks between the planks filled with years of dirt and mud.

"Would you like me to send Barry home?"

I tried shrugging beneath the pressure of her arms. "I don't care."

They both helped me off the floor and practically carried me to the couch. She took off my coat and hat, slipped off my boots, and covered me with a blanket. This morning she'd dressed me. This evening she'd undressed me. She stood in front of me, and Barry sat on the other couch.

"I killed Dad. It's my fault he's dead," I mumbled. My earlier fight was all washed away. Now all I had was an empty pit of despair in my heart. The absence of anger left a void that I filled with guilt. I didn't know which was worse.

"No, baby girl," she said and bent over so she could meet my eyes. I cringed at the endearment. That's what dad always called me. "It's not your fault he's gone." She couldn't bring herself to say dead. "It's your dad's fault and my fault. Not yours. God," she grabbed the top of her head, "there's so much I need to tell you." She pinched the bridge of her nose.

The weight of a thousand guilts that burdened my

soul fluttered a tiny bit.

"Both your dad and I knew this was a possibility. But after puberty came and went, we thought you were in the clear. That's when their powers manifested. Your father's and your brothers'."

"What?" I knew there was something weird about them. "Why didn't somebody tell me?"

She bent down and looked me in the eyes. Really looked me in the eyes for the first time in a long time. "Focus. I'm going to get there, okay?"

I nodded. A thousand questions were racing through my mind, but it was important to follow what she was saying. She sat down next to me, her knees touching mine. She placed a cold hand on my chin and pulled me toward her. Though her touch was chilly, her hand gave me great comfort. As if, for the first time, I wasn't alone with my burden. My sin. That maybe there was someone that could help me carry the weight. Shift some of the load. Not take it, I would never completely let it go, but perhaps carry a corner, at least for a little while.

"I've had my suspicions about your powers. Enough to move us out of Alaska. And enough to confide in Barry a while ago." She glanced up at the ceiling, her eyelashes fluttering as if she were holding back tears. "But I wasn't strong enough to watch the video until today. After seeing your eyes flash this morning just like your father's used to, I knew I had to. I called Barry and asked him to watch it with me so I didn't have to do it alone. When I finally saw it," she inhaled a stuttered breath, "God, Regan, I'm so sorry. I should have watched it a long time ago. It was just so hard . . ." A trail of tears ran down her cheeks and dripped off her chin. "Your father and I wanted a normal life for you so badly that we refused to see what was right under our noses. You have a gift too. So, while you may think you killed your father, in reality, you didn't. Our denial did. You are not to blame."

I started to panic, she had to understand. "But I am! I made him do it. I took control of him and made him walk in front of that bus."

"Okay, okay. Yes, you did. I understand—you have the ability to control others," she said quickly and patted my leg like she was trying to soothe a flighty horse. But it wasn't her actions that calmed me. It was her words. Her confirmation of the blame. She continued, "But don't you see? If your father and I would've seen the signs sooner, he could've taught you to control it. So it didn't control you. Therefore, this is *our* fault. I refuse to allow you to take any more of the blame. Not one second from this moment on. Do you understand me?" Her words were firm and unyielding. She wiped the tears from her chin.

"Why didn't you tell me? After it was all over? Why didn't you tell me?" So many emotions flooded through me. Relief. Anger. Sadness. Regret.

"Because I knew that if you knew what really happened, what you were capable of, you would blame yourself. And I was right. Look at you! Why didn't I see this earlier?" She wrung her hands in frustration. I could see Barry wanted to come over and comfort her. Concern and worry were written on his face. He perched on the end of the couch. His hands were folded, but the stiffness in his shoulders gave him away. I threw him a shred of a smile. He really cared about her.

"You've been blaming yourself this entire time. Damn it! The harder I try to shield you, the bigger the mess I make. And then I did the worst thing of all. I checked out. I let my grief, my pain, and my guilt consume me. I left you alone in the cold. I realize I don't deserve your forgiveness. But I am truly sorry." She closed her eyes. Large tears fell like raindrops down her face. Red streaks stained her skin. It was the only time my mother wasn't beautiful. But I was beginning to learn her beauty wasn't just skin deep. She understood my torment. She knew from experience.

She wrapped me in a fierce hug, and together we sobbed like babies. Our chests heaved, trying to catch our stuttering breath. Together we released our pain and our suffering and began to forgive ourselves and each other.

Once we'd wiped away our tears, she told me everything.

After the accident, we moved here to avoid suspicion. It was the only place she knew of that we could run to without the government thinking we were running. While my dad may have started out in the military as a pilot, someone eventually figured out he had a gift. His was more like mass crowd control. He could temper peoples' feelings. He could calm them, anger them, and sway them into his way of thinking. Which was however the military *told* him how to think. They controlled his every move. He traveled the world going to important *meetings*. His *conferences.* In reality, he was stacking the deck for the federal government.

Apparently, the Feds had been keeping tabs on me and my brothers for years. And my parents had been doing everything in their power to keep my brothers' abilities off the radar. Funny thing was they joined the military to avoid detection. Because so long as they were together, they had powers. If they were separated by a fair amount of distance, they were almost normal. It was like their powers depended on each other to work. It must have been the twin thing.

Lincoln was super human fast, or, as he said it, everyone else was painfully slow. I remember thinking he thought we were all *slow*, as in stupid. Mom and Dad used to snap at him and tell him to knock it off. Linc had a cocky side. Liked to brag. He was an incredible athlete—surprise, surprise. Now I knew why my parents didn't allow him to compete in sports. There was no way Linc would have been able to control his arrogance at that age. Since we were being watched, someone was bound to figure out he had powers.

Kennedy had the gift of foresight. Caught multiple glimpses of the near future. That's how he always knew what he was getting for Christmas. Together, Lincoln and Kennedy were a dangerous team; apart, they were as normal as everyone else.

Their gifts had shown up during puberty. Same as my father's. But for me, I apparently needed a *very* strong emotion to release my gift. And nobody had ever made me mad enough or sad enough until my dad. So, while my gift may have shown up around thirteen or so, nobody knew I had it. They thought I was free and clear.

"How did I not see any of this? How did I not know about their powers?" I wrapped my fingers in my hair and squeezed.

"Well, if you think about it, you grew up with them. Why would you think they were abnormal? Your father was very good at controlling his gifts, and your brothers, well, they were good most of the time," she said like she didn't really believe the last part.

"Then how come Kennedy didn't see this coming?" I motioned towards myself.

"When this all happened, he was apart from his brother. Otherwise he would've been able to warn us."

I buried my head in my hands.

Now Mom's greatest worry in life was protecting me. All by herself. Keeping me out of the hands of the government. Because my gift was the most dangerous of all. People were my marionette dolls. I could make them do whatever I wanted them to. I could kill people, and no one would be the wiser. I was the ultimate assassin.

Barry shifted slightly but didn't seem that uncomfortable. My mom's gaze bounced from me to him. Barry nodded.

"So, we might have another problem," Mom said, squishing her lips to the side.

My mouth dropped open. *Seriously?* I wasn't sure I could handle another problem.

"Around October or so, a couple of strangers showed up in town asking questions about our family—more specifically, you. Barry's been keeping tabs on them. We're trying to find out who they are. So far, we haven't found out much."

I looked to Barry, and he nodded.

My phone started buzzing inside my pocket. I ignored it.

"Wait," I said. "What do those strangers look like?" I wondered if I'd seen them around. Occasionally I had the feeling someone was following me, but I'd chalked it up to my paranoia when I didn't have the opportunity to use my powers enough.

"Military. Feds perhaps. High and tight haircuts. They started out in black suits but they must have realized they stuck out in this tiny town like a sore thumb."

My eyes narrowed. "Does one of them have really big dimples?"

Barry thought for a moment. "Yeah, I believe so. Why?"

"Because they've been in the restaurant a lot. I didn't give them a second thought. I just assumed they were new here." I'd met them the first time in their matching suits Halloween night. I thought they were dressed up as Feds. Apparently, they weren't. *Give me a break, it was Halloween.*

"I wonder if they're employed by the same people who interrogated me at the military base right before we left Anchorage? Ya, remember? When I said they spent an hour questioning me without you present and you insisted I was the one who went missing?"

My mom's eyes darted back and forth. "You're right. I remember but I still don't remember it the way you do. Do you think they have powers too? Oh God. What if they all do?" Her voice rose.

My phone buzzed furiously in my pocket. Message after message. Call after call. I glanced at the screen. All from Jude.

Soon the landline started ringing, then Mom's phone played some silly pop music. She glanced at her screen. And lifted it for me to see. Jude.

"He knows, doesn't he?" she asked, but it wasn't really a question—more an affirmation.

"He knows about me," I said.

"He's the one that keeps you grounded, isn't he? He's the one that does for you what I did for your father."

I clenched my teeth and nodded. I didn't tell her

about everything he did for me. I wasn't ready to admit it aloud.

"I think you should call him and tell him everything's okay before he shows up at the door. Unless that's what you're hoping for?" A knowing smile lifted the corner of her lips. Her eyes sparkled neon blue against their bloodshot background. Her eyelashes clumped together in spikes. For the first time in my life, I thought, *I like her*. I always loved her, but right now, I actually liked her.

I realized this whole time it was never her; it was always me. Spoiled, angry, rotten me.

I glared at her. Why did she have to be right?

I texted Jude. *–I'm fine. Just talking with my mom.—*

—R u sure because I feel like I am on a fucking roller coaster ride here.—

I typed back, my finger stabbing the words into the phone. *–Yes. Fine. Will talk later.—*

Mom hadn't wanted me to go back to school after Gabby played the video of my dad's death, because she was afraid I might hurt someone else . . . or myself. End up back in the hospital. Or worse—dead. The initial incident with my father piqued her suspicions, but she buried her head in the sand like an ostrich. After the fiasco at the school, well, my mom figured it out.

She said she thought of a million different ways to tell me about my powers, but none seemed right. Now it didn't matter. I came clean. Told her everything I'd done. And that I was to blame for Gabby's attempted suicide.

She agreed with Jude. I may have humiliated Gabby, but everyone makes their own choices. And I was to *never, never* do something like that again. Though, as I told her the story, she had a hard time keeping a smile off her face. Even Barry's lips twitched.

For now, we needed to keep up appearances. We all needed to pretend the Feds following me were of no importance. And definitely no using my powers while they were around. And be on guard in case they had secret abilities of their own. I needed to finish my senior year and not draw any more unwanted attention to myself. That's what I'd tried to do in the first place. I'd have to try harder now.

Chapter 31

Damsel in Distress

I skipped school on Wednesday and Thursday. I sat in my bed all day and caught up on my homework. Jude and Layne texted and called me. I said that I was fine and wanted to be left alone. Both capitulated.

Friday morning, I was ready to face the world. Gabby had the same idea. Test the waters on Friday, then take a weekend break.

She pulled into the parking lot, not in her usual queen bee spot. One of the Musketcheers had confiscated that prime real estate. She stepped out of her red European SUV and adjusted the tie on her white wool coat and tossed the violet leather purse over her shoulder. Her long blonde hair caught under the strap. She pulled it loose, inhaled deeply, threw her chin in the air, and headed to the school. Her high-heeled wedges were unsteady on the graveled parking lot.

Layne jogged up from behind, said something, and then fell in line next to her, holding out his strong arm for support. Her face bloomed into a smile. She ran her fingers through her glorious mane and tossed it over her shoulder. She curled an arm around his black-and-red letterman jacket. The rigid stance of her body relaxed a fraction. Mine tensed. I told him I'd be here this morning. We hadn't talked since Wednesday, but I was pretty sure we were still dating. He had begged me not to break up with him. I was so confused . . .

I slid from my truck seat to the ground, determined to make it through one day without killing anyone. As I looked ahead to the happy couple, I thought perhaps I'd set my goals too high.

I smacked my lips together, refreshing my gloss, and tampered down the ire tingling along my nerves. *Breathe. Breathe.* I needed to take a yoga class or something. I kicked a few rocks out of my way as I meandered into the school with my head held high. No worries here. It's not as if my boyfriend had just walked his ex into school or anything.

Just as I entered the building Gin fell in step next to me. He tucked his hands into the pockets of his down jacket. "Seems like your little shenanigans might have backfired?"

My breath hitched in my throat. No. There was no way he could know. "What are you talking about?" I snapped.

His chin darted towards Layne and Gabby ahead of us.

I huffed. "I had nothing to do with that."

He chuckled, dark and humorless. "Right." He winked at me before he veered off down a different hallway.

I shook my head. *No*, I convinced myself. There was no possible way he could know. Though the pile of coincidences was getting rather large. He was there the night my father died, conveniently dressed in a priest's getup. Then right before the ambulance took me away he whispered something in my ear and I collapsed. *And* he just happens to be Gabby's cousin and he moves here because his parents are in Europe. Add in the way he looked at me the night I humiliated Gabby in front of the entire gymnasium. And now? Saying *my* little shenanigans might have backfired? My heartbeat picked up its pace until the pressure pounded in my ears. *How? How could he know?* I slammed my locker shut. I thought about running after him and forcing him to tell me what he knew. But I wasn't sure my powers would work on him. There was something about him that was off. Just like me. I headed to class to give myself some time to think. I'd deal with Gin later.

Jude picked the seat in front of me in homeroom, telling the kid who usually sat there to get lost. His cologne wafted under my nose. It was my favorite scent.

Gabby sat in her assigned spot. Her spine was stick-straight, but no one talked to her. She wore a long-sleeved pink sweatshirt with thumb holes to cover her wrists. I glared at the back of her head. An uncomfortable tension hung in the air. Students' eyes darted around the room, unsaid messages passing in secret glances. Mrs. Glasgow handled it well.

She simply said in her endearing accent, "Welcome back, Gabriella. We're happy to have you here." Then she proceeded with the morning report. Mrs. Glasgow had grown on me in the last few months. Gabby looked around and smiled, but it was as tense as the line of her shoulders. She was trying not to show any weakness. Because we all know what happens to the weak. They are sacrificed at the altar—necks stretched over stone, throats slit and bled dry.

Jude twisted around and searched my eyes before he said, "Friends, right?"

I confirmed with a single nod. His lip twitched, but it wasn't really a smile. More like a consolation.

I dropped my purse off in my locker and picked up the books required for my next three classes. "Hey," Layne said, leaning in above my head.

I wanted to kick him in the shin. "Hi," I said with no inflection. He'd walked *her* into school and had forgotten all about me.

"What's wrong now?" He was instantly irritated.

You're a dick. That's what's wrong. But I refrained and put on my big-girl pants. Or at least tried. I put my fist to my forehead, then ran my fingers through my grown-out bangs. "Nothing. I'm fine. Did you want to have lunch together today? I haven't seen you in a few days."

He hesitated.

I curled my tongue around my teeth and tried to stifle my attitude. I flared my fingers out, my blue knit sweater falling up my arm. "Or not. Looks like you have other plans."

"Well, I kind of told Gabby I'd sit next to her today. It is her first day back, and I don't want anyone harassing her. You can eat with us."

I actually started laughing so hard people stopped and stared. I bent over and held my stomach. It hurt from laughing. Dirt, rock pebbles, and salt de-icer puddled in the low spots of the hallway. Once I caught my breath, I stood up and started to walk away. Layne put a hand on my shoulder and said, "Wait." No shivers. No pleasure whatsoever came from his touch.

I wish. Let go, I ordered. And he did.

The fluorescent lights overhead only flickered for a second. His blue eyes glazed over, and I walked away.

I ate in my truck. Alone. I peeled an orange, its oil perfuming my truck in citrus. I tossed the rinds on my floorboards and popped the sweet flesh in my mouth. Jude's words came back to haunt me. *"Don't you see? You are trying to change who you are . . . conforming to who he needs you to be. For me, you will never have to change. The light or the dark."*

He was right. It slapped me in the face like a rude awakening. I held an imaginary mirror in front of my soul and stared deep down into my core. And I didn't like what was looking back at me. I was becoming my mother. Though we had come to respect one another, I didn't want to be a warped, dark, distorted image of her. She was truly a good person. Kind. Generous. Caring. I, too, had these traits, though they were twisted with my other not-so-pleasant attributes. But my mom molded her personality to fit the man that she loved.

I was trying to change for Layne's sake. To be the person he *needed* me to be. The damsel in distress. It was his kryptonite. I'd been so blind.

I saw myself through Layne's eyes.

The new girl who had lost her father in a tragic accident. Whose brothers had abandoned her. A mother who buried her sorrows in a bottle of vodka. Then, only seven months later, she found solace in the arms of a stranger. The girl everyone in school picked on or ignored. In he rode, a knight in shining armor to save the day. And, for a while, he had.

But I couldn't live this lie any longer. In the shadows, there stood a man who might still love me for who I really was. In his words, a wolf who fed the dark to save the light. *That's* who I wanted to be. And, according to Jude, that's who I already was.

Ain't irony a bitch. The one person I couldn't control was the one I needed. Yes, *needed.* He was the anchor that held me to earth. The logic that grounded me. He was the one I loved. Kicking and screaming all the way. Even when I made the wrong choice, I knew who the right one was. Now I needed to rectify the problem. Even if Jude didn't want me anymore, it didn't matter. I couldn't continue this charade with Layne any longer.

I left before school was over. I had to break up with Layne. But first I had to tell his mom. She was my only girlfriend—and though she was Layne's mom, she was more like a sister to me. She'd had Layne when she was only fifteen.

I parked behind the restaurant, next to the overflowing dumpster, making the inside of my truck smell like rotten meat and rancid fish. I willed the tears to cease, refusing to let them drip over the edge.

Miss Molly was in the back refilling the ketchup bottles.

"Hey, you got time to take a break?" I asked.

Her blue eyes, so much like Layne's, narrowed. "Yeah, sure thing. It's not busy right now anyway. Connie, cover me if anyone comes in? Thanks." She grabbed us each a soda and sat down in the back-corner booth.

"What's up? You look all kinds of stressed. Layne says you haven't been to school in a couple days. He's been worried."

I had all kinds of nasty comebacks for his alleged worry. But I was trying to be the adult here . . .

"You told me once that no matter what happened between Layne and me, you would still be my friend. Do you really mean it?" Overhead a sad country song whined on the radio.

"Oh, God! You're going to break up with him, aren't you? Don't do it right now. Please." She pressed her thumbs upside down on the space between her eyes. "Gabby has her claws prepped and ready."

I knew that. But I couldn't let it stop me. If I continued my relationship with Layne, I would be leading him on, and that wasn't fair to either of us.

She balled her fingers into fists and pressed them against her lips. "I think she tried to kill herself just to get his attention. It's the same thing she did last time. Played the victim after she said Jude raped her. And Layne fell for it hook, line, and sinker. I love my baby, but he isn't very smart when it comes to girls." The worry in her eyes was overwhelming. "That's why I was so happy when the two of you got together. Because you're the best. You'll always take care of him—even when he thinks he's the one taking care of things."

She was far more perceptive than I'd given her credit for. I sat there with my hands gripped around my cold drink and let her vent. This was going to be way more difficult than I'd planned.

"If you break up with him now, he's going back to her."

"I know." He was already halfway there. I about lost my cool when an old country song came on the radio talking about another woman stealing her man. Country music was going to be the death of me. The desire to throw my glass at the speakers was strong. No wonder I preferred music where I couldn't understand the words.

"Then why would you do this? He loves you."

I shook my head. "He doesn't. What he loves is the idea of me. The damsel in distress. And we both know that isn't who I am." She started to interrupt. I held up a hand.

"I do love Layne. He's one of the kindest human beings I've ever known. And I'll watch over him and protect him from anyone that threatens to harm him. Especially Gabby," I said, lowering my voice menacingly. "I haven't let you down. She's hurt many people. But not him. Never him." I held up a firm finger. "But I can't tell him who to date. Or who to love."

"Why do you have to be so smart?" she moaned.

"Today I don't feel smart. Only sad…" I mumbled. She reached out and grabbed my hands to comfort me, even though I was the one giving her bad news. It was such a mom move. And I loved her even more for it. "So, are we going to be okay?" I asked. "Because, honestly, I love Layne, but I love you more. And what hurts you, hurts me. So, by proxy, I'm hurting myself here."

She stood up and twitched her hands in a come-here motion. "We'll always be good. If you could just be gentle about it, I'd appreciate it."

She bent down and hugged me. I whispered into her ear, "Don't worry. I'm going to let him break up with me. And then we're going to be friends. Because I need him in my life."

"No, sweetie, he needs you. As naïve as he is, he's going to need both of us."

I dragged myself out to my truck. This emotional crap was draining. My truck smelled exactly how I felt. Rotten.

I tapped *Hottest Guy in School* on my phone. Jude's handsome face appeared on the screen.

"Hey," he said.

"Can we meet somewhere?"

“Yeah.” His voice was hopeful. “Where? I can leave right now if you want me to.”

“I’ll pick you up in ten.”

When I pulled up in front of the school, he was already standing on the sidewalk, waiting for me, hands pushed into the pockets of his black jacket. He cocked his head at my miserable face. He mouthed and motioned, “Move over.”

I shifted into neutral, stepped on the parking brake, and slid to the passenger side. He hopped behind the wheel, his knees practically hitting his chin, and grumbled something humorously derogative about my height as he put the seat back. I didn’t even ask where we were going. I was surprised when he turned on his street and we pulled up in front of his house.

“I need to let the dog out. My mom’s gone for the weekend.” He turned off the ignition and left the keys in the truck.

My heart pounded weirdly in my chest. He threw me a questioning look and raised a dark, sexy eyebrow.

This wasn’t a good idea.

His house was eerily quiet besides the buzz of the fridge and the hum of the heater. “You can have a seat if you want,” he said almost formally. He switched his weight from one foot to the other.

I sat down on the plush leather loveseat overlooking the mountains and the town. A bunch of green plants lined the windowsills. Some reached for the sun; others tumbled their vines to the floor. He switched on the gas fireplace through the remote in his hand.

Strange, I could have sworn it was a wood-burning fireplace.

“It’s one of those fancy gas or wood-burning

fireplaces." He set the clicker on the coffee table.

My eyes snapped open. He said he could pick up on my feelings. He said nothing about reading my mind. And now that I knew my brothers and dad had gifts, and Gin was still under suspicion, as were the Agents, I wasn't above questioning Jude.

"I can't read your mind," he said, which made me warier. "Sometimes what you're thinking is written on your beautiful face."

I couldn't help myself. I smiled. He called me beautiful.

"Yes, I think you're the most beautiful girl I've ever seen." I shifted from smiling to scowling. "And again . . . not reading your mind." He waved his hand in front of my face. "Everything I need to know I can see right here." He tapped the end of my nose with a finger.

I clenched my teeth, refusing to allow any emotion to trek over my skin. He laughed, then let the dog out. He was gone only a few minutes. He came back in smelling like fresh, crisp, cold outdoor air—pine trees, snow, and wood smoke from the neighboring houses.

He sat down next to me, the couch sagging under his weight. I held my hands to prevent them from grabbing his.

I had a lot to say first. "I owe you a million apologies."

He started to shake his head, "No, you don't."

"Yes, I do. Now, sit there and listen." I pointed an authoritative finger at him.

He arranged his face into a false seriousness.

"You were right," I sulked. "Gloat for a minute before I continue. Because that was hard for me to say."

"Oh, I have no doubt." Humor ran abundant in his

almost-black eyes.

"I was trying to change for Layne's sake. To be the person he needed me to be."

His grin shifted at the mention of Layne's name to a tight-lipped frown.

"To him, I was the damsel in distress, Layne's one true weakness. And all this time, I convinced myself . . . you were mine. My weakness. Because I thought I needed you."

I felt Jude pull his energy back from me. This conversation wasn't going as he'd planned it. Cocky little turd. I wanted to reach out and touch his pouty lips. Run my finger along the smooth pink skin.

"And needing someone, in my book, is the biggest weakness of all. But I was wrong. I don't need you." He stopped breathing and stopped moving altogether. The hurt in his eyes made me hurry. "I am messing this all up! Ahh," I growled. "What I am trying to say is: I don't need you. But I want you." He still didn't move. The pain in his eyes narrowed to anger.

I felt like I was opening my mouth, inserting my foot, and then shoving it farther down my throat. "You aren't getting it. What I am trying to tell you is—I love you." His eyes snapped open. Now I'd gotten his attention. "You're the one I love. Even when I didn't want it to be you. Because in the end, I do need you, but only because I want you. You are not my weakness. You are my strength." I felt as if I'd exposed my very soul—opened my heart and left it unprotected.

His chin trembled. I kneeled on the floor in front of him.

"You are the force that holds me to the earth. The magnet beneath my feet. The calm that contains my chaos. Without you, I'm only half of who I can be. Can you ever forgive me?" I clawed my fingers into his jeans.

His hands were so fast I didn't even see them coming. He snaked an arm around me and pulled me to him. His lips met mine with such force it knocked the air out of me. I struggled to breathe, but I refused to pull away. His fingers on one hand dug into my hair; the other held tight to my hip. The pulse in my neck thumped to the racing of my heart. Fire, lined with electricity, exploded as his hand worked its way under my shirt. The skin-on-skin contact was hotter than my most euphoric high. Callus-tipped fingers, rough and demanding, pulled me closer. My breasts flattened against his hard chest. His lips traveled down my neck, hot kisses searing their mark into my sensitive skin. My breath shook in my chest. Both of his hands were skimming along my waist, slowly lifting my shirt. He paused and looked into my eyes, silently asking if I wanted him to stop, before he pulled it completely over my head. He stared at me for so long, his eyes dark and hungry, I thought he might have changed his mind.

I didn't give him a choice. I grabbed the hem of his T-shirt and lifted it off. The fire's light flickered over his wide shoulders and etched stomach. The amber glow warmed his skin even further. I ran my fingers slowly over his rippled muscles. He shivered under my touch. His reaction to me sent the blood pulsing between my legs. I inhaled sharply. He stood up and held out a hand with our t-shirts thrown over his shoulder. I set my tiny pale fingers over his. He intertwined them with mine and led me to his room.

He flipped on the bedside table lamp and lifted me up onto his bed. My whole body trembled.

"Look, before we go any further," he said while he ran his hot fingers over my neck and down my arm, "I need to be completely honest with you."

I wasn't actually listening. The pounding in my ears was all I could hear. And the light feathery touch of his fingers was all I could focus on. A need that I couldn't scratch without him.

"Hey," he lifted my chin, "are you listening to me?"

I shook my head and stared at his hard stomach and the V-shaped muscles leading down below his low-slung jeans.

He snapped his fingers in front of my face. It was like his whole body hypnotized me.

I startled and a red glow stained my cheeks.

He ran his fingers over my scalp, caressing my hair. I wanted to close my eyes and float away on the sensation. "If we do this, I don't think our bond can ever be broken. I feel in my heart that this will seal it forever. And forever is a very long time." He pressed his forehead to mine. His breath tickled my neck and chest, caressing my aching, longing skin. "While I am sure that you're the one, the only one, you recently made this decision, and I think you should take some time to figure out if this—us—is what you really want."

I pushed him back and stared into his smoky eyes. I rested my palm on the square of his jaw. "I figured it out a long time ago. I just wasn't willing to accept what I didn't want to hear. I have a cut-off-my-nose-to-spite-my-face kind of problem."

"Well, admitting the problem is the first step to recovery, I hear." He grinned. I slipped the pad of my thumb over the swell of his bottom lip. His eyelids drooped heavily, and his mouth parted.

I bit the inside of my cheek to keep myself on task, but it was so hard when what I wanted was waiting and willing. I retracted my fingers from his face and crossed my arms over my chest. If I was going to get through this, my hands needed to be kept to themselves. "But before we do this, I have to break up with Layne. And I have to do it without hurting him. I do love him. But I'm not in love with him. There was never any room in my heart from the moment we met." Jude swallowed tightly. "And then when you kissed me in the barn. That was forever for me."

The smile that painted his face was the most beautiful thing I'd ever seen. It took shape slowly, spreading wide until the sharp hollows under his high cheekbones disappeared, filled with dimples and straight white teeth. Long gone was the cynicism and sarcasm that accompanied his every gesture.

"Wait for me? I don't know how long this will take. Days? Weeks?" I wanted to make Layne break up with me on his own accord.

"Forever," he finished for me. His eyes slowly roamed over my body until they shut tightly. He picked up my shirt and slipped it back over my head. Disappointment wound inside my stomach and clenched in my heart.

He scooted me over on the bed and spooned his hard body around mine. With his size, he completely engulfed me. He threw an arm and a leg over the top of me and held me close.

All I could think of was what I actually wanted to be doing in this bed. And snuggling wasn't at the top of the list.

He groaned into my ear. "I'm not a strong enough

man for this." He rolled over on his back and clasped his hands behind his head. I ran the tips of my fingers over the inside of his bicep. His skin was silky and warm.

He inhaled abruptly; his nostrils flared, and he clenched his teeth. His jaw knotted under his already sharp cheekbones. He clamped down on my hand, stopping it with his. "Nope," he said, "Not strong enough. It's bad enough having you lie here next to me. But when I know you're thinking the same thing I'm thinking, and that only a tiny nudge would make you stray from your plan . . . Yeah, I'm not strong enough for this."

He propped himself up on an elbow. He raised a dark eyebrow and scanned my face dangerously. "So, either we do this," he growled. My body tightened at the thought. "Or I'm sorry, but you have to go. I don't trust myself even in the same room with you right now. Your thoughts and your feelings are too loud . . . too clear . . . Ya have to help me here," he begged.

I squeezed my eyes shut. What I wanted and what I should do were two different things. "I'll go." I refused to look at him because I was afraid it wouldn't take much to change my mind.

"I was hoping you would pick the other option," he said under his breath.

I hit him lightly with a closed fist on his solid chest. "Not helping."

He mimicked my tone, "Not trying to." He grabbed my fist and kissed it. A shudder ran up my arm. I needed to go home and take another cold shower.

Chapter 32

The Escape Plan

I scooted my chair up to the round kitchen table covered with a blue-and-white gingham print cloth. A fresh bouquet of bright yellow daffodils sat on the counter. Grams cooked a piping-hot feast while Gramps, Jude, and I did chores. Together we made a pretty good team, and we managed to complete our tasks in record time. I piled my plate with French toast, added a large pat of butter, and drowned it in real maple syrup. I took a quick swig of coffee, the mug warm on my cold lips. I avoided looking at Jude, just the thought of Friday made my cheeks grow hot. The things I wanted to do with him were not appropriate thoughts during breakfast with the family.

Grams wiped her hands on her apron, then sat down between Barry and Gramps. Her gray cat jumped onto her lap and curled up. Almost everyone that knew about my gift sat around the table. Mom had decided it was best to let my grandparents in on our secret. I didn't agree with her; I was afraid that one day having any knowledge might put them in danger. Enough people were in danger simply knowing me. But I didn't win the argument. They ganged up on me. My powers didn't work well on Mom.

I sat in silence, shoving the food in my face. At first,

my grandparents looked disturbed by the information Mom was feeding them. Their expressions soon changed to fear, as if she'd lost her mind. I choked back a laugh. God, that look was familiar. Seemed like these days it was the only one I got from most people. Gossip traveled fast. The whole town knew about the crazy girl attending school with their precious children. Eventually, I asked my manager at the restaurant for a sabbatical. She agreed for the time being. She said eventually everyone would forget, and she could have one of her best servers back out on the floor for the summer. It was nice to know not everyone thought I was certifiable.

Even after Mom informed them of all the things I'd done, including making Barry back into the tractor, they still didn't believe her. She threw me a *little help here* look.

I groaned. I'd hoped it wouldn't come to this. I didn't want to make either of my grandparents do anything bad, so in the end, I was going to pay for this.

Maybe I could do something mischievous that would result in something good.

I concentrated.

I wish.

Gramps, I wish you would get up and do the dishes for a change. Give Grams a nice break.

It didn't go over well. He resisted. I started laughing. Let the battle of wills begin.

I liked it when people resisted. I felt like they had grit. Character. In the end, I won. I always won.

I released more dark smoke from my little glass box. Pleasure numbed any guilt I might have felt for using my powers on my own grandpa.

I made him rise from the old oak chair and grab

Grams's plate first. Her blue eyes shot wide open, and she jerked her head from me back to my mom. I winked. His fingers turned white, matching the dish he held in his hand. Then I made him rinse it before he came back for the rest. The hard clench to his jaw informed me that he did not approve of my strategy. I was going to pay for this later, all right. But not by getting sick.

He bent over, loaded the dishwasher, added some soap, and pressed on. Then I let go of control.

I wanted to make sure he would remember how to do the dishes—for future reference.

In an act of defiance, he slammed the vase full of flowers back onto the middle of the table. "Good Lord." He pushed his chair back and stretched out his long legs. He scrubbed his hands over his thinning gray hair. "I think I need a drink." He pointed to me, letting me know it was all my fault.

Grams hopped up and pulled some homemade Irish cream from the fridge and poured a large splash into his coffee. Then added some to the rest of ours.

To make my point clear—I had her add an extra dose to mine. Whether she wanted to or not. Her eyes widened and I smiled and blinked my lashes playfully.

Yum.

She slowly stirred her coffee as she digested what had just happened. "There are stories from the old country," Grams mused. She rubbed her temples as if trying to ward off a headache. Her accent was stronger than usual. "But it's not like I believed them. They were just fables, myths, and legends."

"Yeah, well…fact? Fiction? What's the difference?" I guzzled my tasty drink and held it out for more. Mom shook her head and then finished the story.

And she told them of the "escape plan."

According to Barry, the Feds, or whatever they were, were still a mystery. Every avenue of information he tracked led to a dead end. At the time, I thought they were in costume because they were at the restaurant on Halloween. *No judgement, it was a valid assumption.* After that, they came into the restaurant dressed as civilians. How was I supposed to know they worked for a secret government entity? They were obviously there to keep an eye on me. And up until that point, I'd been good. No slips of power. It was probably the day I'd busted all the overhead lights in the gymnasium that tipped them off. And the fact that so many students were missing time. They all remembered the video, just not the ten mystery minutes following my temper tantrum. Since then, the agents had been hovering.

We devised an exit plan. If the government—or whomever these people were—got too close, I was to run to the reservation with Jude. His grandparents still had a place there and it was on sovereign territory. The federal government only had jurisdiction if we'd committed a crime or if the local tribal police asked for their help, which was *very* unlikely.

I didn't like the idea. I didn't want anyone getting into trouble on my account. They didn't care one iota about what I wanted.

Jude already had his things packed under the canopy of his truck. Mom made me pack a bag of clothes, and she filled his truck with food supplies. Then Barry gave me a backpack full of burner phones. If we had to run, any devices we had were to be left here phones, computers, and tablets. *No exceptions*. I'd watched enough crime TV to know a personal cell phone will get you caught every time.

I wondered why he was doing all of this for us, then I realized he was doing it for my mom. At least if I had to disappear, she would have someone to take care of her. Someone who loved her enough that he was willing to sacrifice his career just to be with her. I hoped it never came down to that. I was quite fond of him. And honestly, I think my dad would've liked him too.

"Sara," Grams said, looking worried and not convinced at the same time. "Do you really think it's going to come to this? She's just one girl." She fiddled with the flowers on the table, picking off the dead leaves. She piled them in front of her.

"Momma, you didn't see how they treated Craig. They controlled his every move. Followed him. Tapped our phones. Invaded every aspect of our lives. Harassed my boys."

I hadn't known it had gone that far. If they would have only told me, maybe I could have helped.

"And he was nowhere near as powerful as Regan. That *girl* can control an entire room. She can make most anyone do anything. Use your imagination if the government got ahold of her. She would never even have to pull a trigger or push a button. She can *make* you do anything she wants you to. And, if I am right, the more she uses her gift, the stronger she becomes."

God, I sounded like a monster. My breakfast threatened to come back up. I swallowed the big wad of phlegm in my throat.

She was right, though. Using my powers was almost too easy. I mostly had my golem on a leash.

Jude nodded in agreement. She'd already told them he was the yin to my yang, so to speak.

“Well, baby, then stop using your gift. Then maybe it would go away.” Grams patted the back of my hand with her cold, papery fingers.

“I wish,” the phrase coming out of my mouth in this context made me sad, “I wish it were that easy. If I don’t use my gift, I go crazy. Literally. And I mean the cuckoo kind of way.” I rolled my finger around the outside of my ear. The universal sign for crazy. “And when I do good things or defend myself without ill intent, that’s when I get sick. Really sick.”

Reality dawned on her face, brightened her eyes, and deepened her forehead wrinkles. That’s why I’d almost died that day. I’d frozen the school and shattered the lights so they couldn’t see more of my humiliation. I didn’t do it to hurt them—I did it to save myself the humiliation. It didn’t matter if it was on purpose or not. Then I used my energy to calm the whole room. That had been the bump that pushed me over the edge.

Chapter 33

Kryptonite

For the next two weeks, I tried to stay off the radar. I created just enough mischief to satisfy the golem sitting below the surface. It scratched at my brain, making me jumpy and paranoid. More than usual. I could feel eyes watching me, an invisible gaze making the hairs on my arms stand at attention. I checked my rearview mirror constantly for black SUVs with tinted windows following me. They freaked me out the most. I watched too much TV where all the FBI agents drove them. Of course, a lot of rich people here drove them too.

From afar, I kept a watchful eye on Gin. We never revisited our earlier conversation. I thought it was best to pretend it never happened. I didn't want to appear guilty by bringing it up again, giving weight to his accusations.

Layne and I walked on eggshells. I pushed his buttons, trying to make him leave me. If I actually made him break up with me, it wouldn't work. I could make him do it, but he wouldn't mean it.

These days he was right where he wanted to be. He had his cake and was eating it too. And I was sick and tired of pretending.

He split his time neatly between Gabby and me. Monday, Wednesday, and Friday were her days, and mine were Tuesday, Thursday, and Saturday. I wanted to end things immediately, but I'd promised Miss Molly I'd do it gently. It wasn't happening, and it needed to be over. He really didn't see a problem with sharing his time. He said they were friends. Just like Jude and I were friends. I had no rebuttal. I felt guilty about kissing Jude when still dating Layne.

On our lunch day, we'd sit in his car, but otherwise, he sat with Gabby in the cafeteria. His football friends welcomed her back with open arms like she was their little darling that they needed to protect and shelter. Her Musketcheers were a different story. They were snide and mean. They pointed, whispered, and laughed behind her back and sometimes to her face. She pretended not to hear or see them.

Layne and some of his friends told Olivia and Destiny to be nice, but everyone was a little afraid of them. They'd picked up where Gabby had left off. Though, they weren't quite as successful. Olivia led by force. Destiny with cruelty. Gabby had always led from her high horse with flattery, compliments, and unspoken promises. And with the added bonus of classified material, well, she was more like a politician than a mobster. That's what she used Olivia and Destiny for. Her hired thugs, even though they couldn't see it, were missing the key component for success. Their fearless leader. Without her insider information, they were nothing more than your run-of-the-mill bullies.

I couldn't help but admire Gabby's manipulation skills. Sometimes they almost rivaled mine.

I caught a glimpse of the scar going across only one wrist. My suspicions were confirmed. She'd never meant to kill herself. Not really. She did it to gain sympathy and get out of trouble. As far as I could tell, it worked. The school hadn't suspended her for any of her crimes. There were whispers amongst the students that the principal and school board were afraid if she were punished, she might try again.

Even though today was Friday, Gabby's day, I'd insisted Layne have lunch with me. I couldn't go make it through the weekend worrying about *us* anymore.

"Hey, can I see your phone?" I asked Layne as we sat in his car. He'd been unusually protective of it lately. Sometimes he shielded the screen with his wide shoulders, pretending it was his mom texting him. I knew better. Now if I could just use it to my advantage. I wanted things to end amicably between us, but our romantic relationship needed to end. If I had to flee in the night, I didn't want Layne left out in the cold. Because once I was gone, Barry told me I was to contact no one. If I did, they could be in danger.

While Layne's childish behavior might have irritated me, I loved him and never wanted anything bad to happen to him or Miss Molly because of me. If the government started asking them questions, they needed to think I was just a normal teenage girl who dated the quarterback of the football team and worked with his mom.

"Uh, why?" he asked.

I held my hand out for his phone. "Because mine's dead, and I need to text my mom," I said innocently.

"Uh, mine's almost dead too." He started to put it in his coat pocket.

"Give me your phone." I looked into his flaming blue eyes and highly encouraged his cooperation. Oh, he didn't want to do it. Must be something worth hiding. I snapped my fingers and held out my hand.

His hand shook, but he did what I'd told him.

I typed in his password and went to his texts with Gabby.

Little stabs of manipulation were dotted throughout the conversation.

—*I saw Jude with her again today. So sorry. She just doesn't know what she has.* — Frowny face

—*Sometimes she's so mean to you. I don't know how you put up with it. You are a much better person than I am.* — Kissy lips

—*I wish she would stop rolling her eyes when you talk about football. Doesn't she know how important it is to you?* — Football and red hearts

—*She had lunch with Jude today. You know, you don't need to eat with me. I'll be okay.* — Winky face and more hearts

Then she started with the emotional pull.

—*Thank you for being my friend when no one else will. You are the strongest man I have ever known. I don't deserve you in my life.*— Prayer hands

He replied with the predictable: —*Don't be silly, of course you do. Besides you can't get rid of me that easily.*— Smiley face

—*I am so lonely. Everyone hates me. And they should. I deserve it, you know.*— Teardrop. But really it is a raindrop emoji

—*I don't hate you and everyone else will come around. Just give them time.*— Cool sunglasses emoji dude

Then began the selfies. A snapshot of her waking up in the morning with a simple text of —*Good Morning*—

A picture of her in glasses studying. A picture of her

in her fancy car listening to music. Something about their song playing on the radio . . .

Then she narrowed in for the kill.

—I know you don't want to hear this but I miss you. I miss us. — Red broken heart. Kissy lips

And the text Layne didn't want me to see.

—I miss you too.— Red broken heart. Kissy lips.

Though the text wasn't that bad, it gave me an excuse to break up with him. Not the best justification, but right now I would take the evidence presented. Miss Molly was right. The minute I broke up with him, he'd run right back to her. Sometimes people had to make their own mistakes. I should know; I'd made more than my fair share. And when I made a mistake, I aimed for the stars.

I puffed a deep sigh out from my cheeks and gave Layne back his phone.

"Yeah, I thought so." I pressed my lips into a sad smile.

"No, Regan, it's not what you think." He laid a large hand on my arm.

"Seriously, Layne? It is. Come on, man. We've been over for a while. Just admit it."

Pain rippled over his handsome face. "I don't want us to be over. If you make me choose between the two of you, I pick you. I'll always pick you."

At least my ego would stay intact.

"Well, that's the beauty of it. I'm not going to make you choose."

Relief flashed in his eyes. I wanted to run my finger over his face to memorize the cut of his jaw, the arch of his eyebrows, and the gentle line of his lips. This would be the last time I would be able to touch him like this. I refrained, not wanting to make it more difficult for either of us.

"All I want is for us to stay friends."

"Wait. What do you mean? Friends?" He cocked his head slightly and put a hand on the roof of his car, holding himself in place.

"Layne, you're the nicest guy I've ever known, and the last thing I want to do is hurt you. But you and I, we can't do this anymore."

I filled the space in his car with calm energy. I was getting better at the subtleties of my gift. If I only used a tiny amount, I didn't get too sick.

"I love you. But as a friend. Nothing more. And now that I have proof," I pointed at his phone, "that your heart's torn between me and Gabby, it's easier for me to let you go."

"Please, Regan, this isn't what I want." He sat very still.

"Then, Layne, what do you want? But be honest. I promise I won't get mad."

His massive shoulders fell, and he ran his fingers over his blond hair. "I don't know what I want. I feel like I'm being pulled in two directions at once. And you have been so understanding. I want you, but on the other hand, she needs me. She has no one else. And I feel so bad for her."

The damsel in distress. His kryptonite.

"I don't know what to do," he said.

"I do." I reached out and placed both of his hands in mine. He squeezed tight like he didn't want to let go.

"We stay friends, always. And since we're being honest with each other, I've been feeling the same way. Pulled in two different directions. It's a horrible place to be."

He nodded.

"But, Layne, I'm not in love with you. And really, when you give it some time, you're going to realize you aren't in love with me either. The best-case scenario for this is that we stay friends. Whatever you decide. I'm leaving the ball in your court. But know this, I will always be here for you. If anyone ever messes with you, I'll destroy them." I reached up, touched his face, and ran my fingers over his jaw. The stiff hairs scraped my skin. "I can be your friend. Now you just have to decide if you're willing to be mine."

"I would rather have you in my life than not in my life. Though," he paused and glanced at his lap, "if we could perhaps avoid each other for a while, I'd appreciate it. And I do have a question for you. Is there something going on between you and Jude?"

I answered as honestly as I could, trying my best not to hurt him any more than I had. "It's the same thing that's going on between you and Gabby."

Though I felt guilty about my momentary indiscretion, there was no reason to hurt him worse than needed. He pressed his lips together in a hard line and nodded. I wanted to tell him to be careful of her, but I didn't think he would welcome my advice.

If Layne chose Gabby, so be it. As Jude pointed out, we all make our own choices. But first, she and I were going to have a talk. A come-to-Jesus meeting.

Chapter 34

Lesser of Two Evils

After school, I cornered Gabby in her fancy red SUV before she had the chance to race out of the parking lot for home. She didn't hang around school much these days. I slid into the black leather seat. It smelled like cotton candy and gum. Soft pop music played on the fancy speakers. A puffy, red, fur ball hung from her rearview mirror.

Her nostrils flared, and a fire burned behind her grass-green eyes. Her hands clawed the steering wheel, white knuckles glowing under her tanned skin. She wanted me out of her car but was too scared or too smart to say anything.

"You and I," I wiggled my finger between the two of us, "are going to have a chat."

She reached for the door handle. "Oh, come on, Gabby," I said as nicely as I could manage, then sharpened my tone, "we can either do this the easy way or the hard way. I promise I'm not here to hurt you."

She dropped her hand to her lap but refused to look at me. A curtain of blonde hair fell alongside her face. Its texture seemed smooth and silky.

"I don't like you. And I don't think there's a scenario in this world that could change my mind. But that's not the point. I do believe in the last month you have learned a few things about yourself."

I, too, had learned some things about myself. Good. Bad. Ugly.

"And about all those people around you that *used* to be your friends. Correct me if I'm wrong." I held my hands up.

Her head snapped around.

"Yeah, yeah, I know you hate me, too. I can see it in your eyes. But, alas, there's nothing you can do to hurt me." I exaggeratedly pointed to me, then to her. "Because I can destroy you."

Her teeth clenched. Her jaw knotted tightly, to the point that I thought she might break her pretty veneers.

"But remember this: There's nothing I crave more. Try me." Fear replaced her anger. Her lower lip trembled, and tears welled in her large green eyes. It was quite becoming on her face. I could see why Layne's inner knight in shining armor couldn't help himself.

"Anyway," I said, steering the one-sided conversation away from my innermost desires. "I can tell Layne still has feelings for you."

A visible tide of emotions ran the gambit over her face. Fear to confusion and back to fear. The queen of faking her emotions to get what she wanted was having trouble masking the real ones.

"We aren't meant to be together," I said.

Another wave of confusion and then fear washed over her face. She balled her hands up in her lap and twisted them around.

I held up a finger. "I do love him. Always will. He's seriously the greatest guy I've ever known. But the truth is: he's way too good for me. And he's way too good for you too."

Her eyes dulled. She recognized what I said was true. With a shaking hand, she tucked the curtain of hair behind her ear.

"So, here we are. This is the point I've been meaning to make. From here forward, with me, you have a clean slate. All grievances washed away. I figure you have three choices. You can run and hide like you've been doing. Which is embarrassing. You are Gabriella LaCroix, head cheerleader, queen of this establishment. Two, go back to your old ways. Rule this school with your iron fist of fear. Punish those who trespass upon you. Hurt them and humiliate them so all others will pay you false worship." I paused to let that choice sink in. She had been on the other side of humiliation; she knew what it felt like to be bullied, laughed at, and picked on.

"Or you can choose door three. Personally, it's not my first choice for you. But I'm not here to make your decisions." I had to force the words out. They wanted to stay inside. Though I didn't want Layne, I didn't want her to have him either. Partially because she wasn't good enough for him, and partially because I hated her and didn't want to see her win. I coughed, and I pulled out the words that were stuck in my throat. "Become the woman Layne deserves." Her eyes snapped open, searching my face for deception. "Someone worthy of him."

"You're fucking crazy!" slipped off her tongue before she could catch it. She froze all on her own accord, no help from me. Her face was a mask of terror; it gave a whole new meaning to 'scared stiff.'

A smile exploded on my face. I covered it with my hand, but I couldn't hide the joy in my eyes. "Oh, my

God! I know, right?" Gabby's eyes got even wider. Her eyelashes extensions brushed her eyebrows.

"I *am* fucking crazy! It is such a relief when people realize that about me. It's like a weight lifted from my shoulders."

Her eyes darted back and forth between mine, but at least she started breathing again.

"So, again, you have some choices. Stay a coward. Reclaim your throne. Or become a princess of football. The question is: What do you want more? The kingdom," I held up one hand palm facing the car roof, "or the prince?" I held up my other hand as if weighing her options. "Or neither?" I shrugged.

"But before you make your final decision, remember this: Even though our slate is clean, no matter your choice, I'll be watching. Layne and I will always be friends. And I'll do anything—*anything*," I emphasized, "to see he has a happy, successful life. I'm like his guardian angel, only a fallen one." I winked and got out of her car.

I tapped the roof, then gave her my final piece of advice. "And the best way to get your revenge on me is to become the person I couldn't. Believe me, you have a far better chance than I ever did."

I shut the door softly and left her fate in her hands. Her choice.

I walked to my truck, hoping with all of my heart that I was the lesser of two evils. But I wouldn't bet money on it.

Chapter 35

Friggin' Illiterate

Jude opened the passenger side door of my truck, letting in more cold air, and slid in.

"Hey," I said. "I thought we talked about this. I just broke up with Layne. It probably isn't a great time to be seen together. I don't want to hurt him anymore than I already have." I was emotionally exhausted but seeing him made all of the earlier effort worth it.

"Yeah, I know. It's like a weight has been lifted from your shoulders since lunch time. And then, like twenty minutes ago, something made you feel all cocky and badass." He flicked my chin with his finger. "But that's not what I'm here for."

He handed me his phone. Barry had texted. —*Can you go check on your grandparents? There was a report of a prowler in the neighborhood.*—

That was our code to run.

My stomach flipped, twisted, and then shot up to my throat. I tried swallowing, but my mouth was too dry. Adrenaline kicked in, and my heart began to race. Sweat beaded behind my ears, and my palms got all cold and clammy.

I nodded and slipped my phone into the glove box behind Jude's. I was going to miss the music on it. And the pictures.

He started his truck, and we gave it a few minutes to warm up before we switched vehicles. I hiked my backpack onto my shoulder and climbed up into the cab of his pickup. He slowly pulled away from the school parking lot, tires crunching over the loose gravel on the pavement. A feeling of melancholy sank in my chest, rising and falling with each breath, and I wondered if I would ever see Layne or Miss Molly again.

No matter, they were safer without me.

Jude felt around the seat and my leg until he found my hand. “Everything’s gonna be okay.” He squeezed with reassurance.

I pulled away. “How can you say that? We don’t even know what’s going on. And now we have no way of knowing.” I leaned forward, balancing my elbows on my knees, and pressed my face into my palms. They smelled like stinky hand soap.

“That isn’t true. When Barry gets a chance, he’ll contact us on one of the burners.”

I stared out the window, down the narrow highway, and created scenarios that went from bad to worse in my head. As the hour wore on, jagged, snow-covered mountains and trees turned into a narrow, red-rock canyon. The road followed the winding river, its fast waters cutting a path through the rusty walls. As dusk descended on the day, the gorge opened into a rolling valley. Long pink clouds, rimmed in gold, floated in the dimming blue sky over the flat buttes and distant peaks. It was pretty in its own way, but I preferred the mountains. Here, amongst the great wide open, I felt exposed. Naked.

“Stop,” Jude said. “There’s no use worrying.” While

driving, he twisted the top off of a bottle of water and handed it to me.

"Easy for you to say. You're not the cause of all of this." I took a deep swallow; the cool liquid eased my tightened throat.

A sly smile curved on his lips, and he glanced over with an appreciative look. "Well, at least you're worth it."

I rolled my eyes. Was I? I sure didn't feel like it. I tossed around the idea of turning myself over to whomever was looking for me. If it meant keeping my family and Jude safe, that's what I would do.

Flashing red and blue lights ahead tore me away from my thoughts, turning my doom and gloom into panic. Two highway patrol cars blocked the two-lane road onto the reservation. Two officers wearing khaki pants, olive-green jackets, and bucket hats stood outside of their black patrol cars.

"I thought you said the government couldn't come on the reservation?"

"They can't. Besides, these are highway patrol officers, and they aren't on the Res yet. Looks like they're doing a random alcohol stop." He glanced my way. "It's Friday. Happens all the time. Relax and let me do the talking."

I didn't like the coincidence. A film of sweat sheened my forehead.

The taller of the two troopers walked over to Jude's truck with a flashlight in hand. He was an older man with round, gold-rimmed glasses, but he appeared fit.

I gripped my water bottle tight and tried to appear bored.

Officer Kent, his name tag said, tapped the flashlight

on the glass. A whiff of aftershave drifted in as Jude rolled down his window. I wasn't sure how the cop could smell alcohol over the overwhelming power of his cologne.

He flashed the light over our faces. I squinted under the brightness. He then checked out our feet. "Driver's license, insurance, and registration."

"It's in the dash," Jude said. The cop nodded. I dug out the copies of the needed documents.

"And you kids are doing what?" He left the question open-ended.

"Bringing back a grocery run to my grandparents' house." Jude pulled his license out of a beat-up leather wallet and handed it to the cop. He shone the light on the paperwork and license, then handed them back.

The officer's nose flared, and his jaw rolled under the clenching of his teeth. "You're Tom and Rose's grandson," he said. But the way he said it was like an accusation.

"Yes, sir," Jude replied politely.

"The one that had a run-in with the law a few years ago?"

Jude pressed his lips together and exhaled slowly out his nose. "Yes, sir."

The cop shone the light in my face. I squinted my eyes. "Do your parents know you're here, young lady?" he asked. It took me a second to realize he was addressing me.

"Uh . . ." I stammered my tongue feeling thick inside my mouth. "My mom does and so does Officer Baylock, her boyfriend. And, since you didn't get the memo, Jude was never charged with anything because Gabby was lying." I probably should have kept my mouth shut, but sometimes things just needed to be said.

His eyes narrowed and he paused for an uncomfortable minute like he was contemplating harassing us. “Mind if I flash my light in?” He tilted his head toward the canopy.

“Not at all,” Jude said.

I stopped breathing. I turned sideways and watched as the cop walked around the truck, shining his light over our stash. I wouldn’t interfere unless he wanted to actually open the back and look through the bags with the burner phones. A powerful beam of light traveled over our black duffle bags, then over the groceries and supplies. Jude hadn’t been lying. He had made a run to a warehouse store in Pocatello, Idaho, the week before. Stacked in the bed of the truck was toilet paper, paper towels, laundry detergent, bleach, coffee, flour, sugar, and all the rest of the items that didn’t go bad by buying them in bulk.

Thankfully he didn’t seem to think it was necessary to inspect further.

He patted the window frame of the truck and said, “You kids have a good night. Drive safe.”

My cheeks puffed out in relief. “That scared the crap out of me.”

“Yeah, I could tell, but why? I told you what it was.”

“Sorry, I’m a little jumpy.” I stared out of the passenger window. We drove slowly though a tiny town with one dilapidated gas station, a few watering holes and a church with peeling white paint.

A mile or so out of town, he turned onto a graveled road with big potholes and washed-out culverts. We passed a few rusted mailboxes mounted on rotting wood posts before we pulled up in front of a ranch-style house.

The dusty headlights shone yellowish on the vinyl siding and reflected on the darkened windows.

"Uh, where is everyone?" I hugged my backpack to my chest.

Jude opened the car door, the overhead light glowing down on his confused face. "What do you mean?"

"It looks deserted."

He got out and faced me. "No one's home. My grandparents are at their other house. They winter there. I told you that already."

A shudder ran through my chest, leaving me shaking.

He froze, not a muscle twitched. "You're scared of me," Jude whispered.

"No, I'm not." I blew him off.

"Yes, you are. I can feel it." He clutched his heart. "I can't believe it," he said, sounding angry. "After all this time, you still give weight to Gabby's accusations." He gripped his hair in a fist and slammed his door.

"Seriously, I just defended you back there. And, as for having a 'direct line to my feelings,' you're friggin' illiterate," I yelled and slid out of the truck also slamming the door behind me. I stomped to the house and turned the door handle, but it was locked.

Jude came up behind me, anger radiating off him. He stuck a key in the lock, reached above my head, and pushed it open. He switched on the inside and outside lights and threw his bag on the tan and white linoleum floor before he stormed out.

I stood inside a neat, but small, kitchen with white cabinets and a butcher-block counter. A toaster, a coffee pot, and a microwave all sat on the clean surface.

Flowered curtains draped over the planter box window above an old, original farmhouse sink stained with rust. A green-cushioned couch and a brown recliner huddled around an old box TV with rabbit ears. A basket of colorful yarn sat under the coffee table along with a stack of hardback books.

Jude shoved past me with a bundle of wood stacked in his hands and headed over to a giant woodstove in the living room. He dropped the load into an iron container beside the fireplace and scooted past without looking at me.

I slipped off my shoes but left on my coat. It was just above cold in here. My stocking feet padded over the brown carpet, and I knelt down on the brick tile surrounding the stove. I crushed and twisted some old newspaper into a pile over the burnt ashes and then made a pyramid of kindling before lighting the pyre.

"What are you doing?" Jude snapped. "I can do that."

"So can I." I backed out of his way with my hands in the air, giving up. My dad always told me to pick my battles . . . I thought maybe this was a wise time to heed his advice. At least until Jude decided to be reasonable. I slid my shoes back on and headed out to his truck. I filled my arms with groceries and dumped them on the counter, then went back for another load.

He stood up. "What are you doing?" Behind him, flames roared from the open door on the woodstove. They popped and sparked and whooshed in the oxygen-rich air.

"What does it look like?" I said sarcastically. "Bringing stuff inside."

"I can get it." He glared down at me.

"What's your problem?" I tapped him in the chest with the flat of my hand. So much for listening to my father's advice.

"My problem is that you're scared to be alone with me!"

"There are more ways than one to be scared and obviously you can't tell the subtle differences." I shook my head waiting for him to understand without me having to explain. He didn't say anything. "Damn, you're thick sometimes. But you're right, I am scared to be alone with you!" I yelled to conceal my embarrassment.

A split second of pain radiated across his face before he was able to hide it behind his mask of anger. He stepped back and glared. The chandelier hanging above the kitchen table mirrored tiny gold flecks in his dark eyes.

"I am not afraid *of* you. But I'm afraid to be alone with you. Don't you get it?" I swallowed the huge lump in my throat.

"Why don't you explain it then?" He folded his arms. I refused look at his wide chest and roped biceps for fear I would show him instead of telling him. This was going to be uncomfortable enough as it was.

I stared at the black scuff marks on the floor and pressed my lips together. I couldn't do it. I shook my head.

"Please, please, tell me why. Otherwise, I'm just gonna think the worst."

I knew what it was like to think the worst about a situation. To weave a story into something it wasn't. "Because with no one here, who's going to stop me?"

He took a step forward, his black stockinged foot

stark against the white floor. "Stop you from what?"

I reached up and ran a finger along his bare arm. His skin was firm and smooth under my touch.

"See? I can feel you. You're scared. Like I'm going to hurt you. I would never . . ." I stopped him with my hand over his mouth.

I chanced a glance at his face. "I know. But what if we do this." I traced the swell of his lip, then moved along his strong jaw. His breath halted in his chest. "What if you don't want a forever with me?"

The other day, when I told him I loved him, he didn't say it back. I was scared he didn't love me. He only loved what I was capable of becoming.

First shock, then great laughter built from his belly and spilled out. Hot tears of mortification and anger instantly pooled at the corners of my eyes. I fumbled backward, my mouth open in horror at what I'd just admitted to. What I was afraid of was rejection from the one person who had the ability to hurt me.

His hand snaked out, grabbed me by the arm, and yanked me to him. His grip was almost painful under the material of my jacket.

"You gotta be kidding me, right? You're the one who doesn't get it. I already signed on for forever. I'm just waiting for you to get on board." He stepped in so close his chest brushed mine. I had to look way up to see him.

"What if I . . . what if I don't, I mean, I haven't ever . . ." My tongue was tied in my mouth.

He pushed me back slightly to get a better view of my face and cocked his head, relief and victory playing on his face. "You haven't ever . . . Even after three months of dating the golden boy?"

Blood rushed up my chest and to my cheeks. An uncomfortable heat spread over my face. I shook my head.

He grabbed the sides of my head with his warm hands. "I'm surprised. Every time he touched you . . . I could feel you. Your reaction to him. It took all my strength not to . . ." He looked down and squeezed his eyes shut for a second before he continued. "Now I can delete those images in my head. The ones that made me want to throw him out a third-story window. Not high enough to kill him, but maim him, yeah. Not that it would make me feel any differently about you. But at least *now* I know what you're scared of." He rubbed the pads of his callused thumbs over my cheeks. "But you weren't scared the other day . . ."

"That's because I didn't have time to think about it! It was kind of spur of the moment."

"Don't be scared. We'll only go as far as you are comfortable with."

"That's the problem . . ." I bit the side of my bottom lip.

His eyes dropped to stare at my mouth. "If for one second you want to stop, you have to tell me." He tapped my lip with a finger. "Because between my feelings and your fear, I can't tell whether we should do this or I should run away. So, if you want to stop, you have to voice it out loud. Okay?"

I nodded. I was too nervous or excited or I don't know . . . But I needed him to say it. I needed to hear those three words.

He reached out and unzipped my coat, slid it off my shoulders, and let it drop to the floor, a puddle of blue beneath my feet. He grabbed the hood ties of my sweatshirt and pulled me closer.

"You have no idea how beautiful you are. Your face." He cupped my cheek in his hand. "Your body." He slid his hand to my neck. His touch was like a drug, soaking into my veins and spreading to the farthest regions of my being. "Your skin. It's so pale and clear sometimes. I feel like I should be able to see right through it down to your beating heart."

He leaned down and whispered into my ear. "But what I love most about you, is your spirit." His palm flattened over the swell of my chest. I stopped breathing. My heart pounded rapidly under his hand, its rhythm deafening all other noise. "I love you, Regan Braaten. Every tiny, frustrating, infuriating, beautiful inch of you."

Happiness swelled inside. He loved me.

With his other hand, he tucked my fallen bangs behind my ear, paused for a second, wrapped his fingers behind my head, and brought his lips to mine. What started out gentle and hesitant soon turned to impatience, desperation, and hunger. He threw an arm around me and lifted me, one handed, against the kitchen door. I wrapped my legs around his waist and buried my fingers in his thick, dark hair. His tongue danced in my mouth. He tasted of cool water and cinnamon sticks. The window frame in the door dug into my back. He bit my bottom lip and pulled away slowly. He rested his head on the door, his breathing heavy in his chest.

"What?" I said, afraid he'd already changed his mind.

"You . . . You wanna go upstairs with me?" he whispered in my ear.

"Yes." I remembered about having to speak it out

loud.

"You sure?"

"I'm not changing my mind."

"Okay, but you remember what I said?"

I nodded.

"If we do this, the bond will become stronger. Permanent. Unbreakable. I will not be able to let you go. Ever. It's bad enough already. Any man that looks at you sideways, I want to knock 'em out. It's been hard. Having to watch you with him. Knowing that if I hurt him, you would never forgive me. I don't know if the feeling is going to get better or worse after. I'm hoping it gets easier. But I have a feeling I'm wrong." He banged his head on the door. The glass jingled in the frame.

"Why didn't you tell me it was this intense?"

"Because I didn't want you to make your decision based on my needs. I wanted you to want me without any strings attached. That's why I was so mad when my grandpa said something to you. I didn't want you to feel like you had to be with me. That there was no choice in the matter for you."

"There's always a choice."

"You'd think so, right? But if we do this, it's a forever thing. There's no going back. It will be more binding than marriage. There is no such thing as divorce. Are you sure you're ready for that?"

I swallowed tightly. I wanted him more than I'd ever wanted anything in my life. But forever was a very long time. If the relationship didn't work between the two of us, it didn't matter. We would be bonded for life. Why did my life have to be so difficult?

He smiled sadly. "It's okay. I understand. Believe me, I understand." He kissed my forehead and set me down.

I yanked off my sweatshirt and hung it next to the door. I no longer needed it—I was burning up.

He threw his black bag up on his shoulder and carried my backpack in his other hand. He led me up a narrow set of stairs to what used to be an attic. The ceiling followed the roofline, leaving only a small area in the middle where Jude didn't have to duck to keep from hitting his head. He pulled a string, and a single blub flashed on from above. Jude's paintings hung on the pale blue walls. A pile of cardboard boxes was stacked on top of the white dresser, obscuring the mirror.

"Whose room?" I stepped in, the wide pine-board floors creaking under my feet. I was trying to sound casual while struggling with my emotions. I was excited. I was terrified. I was standing on the edge of a precipice, ready to take the leap, but momentarily petrified.

"It's a guestroom, so pretty much mine. So, you can sleep here and I'll take the couch downstairs." He dropped our bags on the woven area rug.

A double bed with a white down comforter and two fluffy pillows sat directly under a large window. He tossed the fluffy pillows to the end of the bed and reversed the sheets.

"I like to sleep this way so I can see outside." He flipped on the bedside table lamp, then turned off the overhead light. Outside the window, big, powdery flakes fell slowly and heavily to the ground.

Heavy waves of tension roiled in my stomach. Jude transferred his weight from one foot to the other and tucked his hands deep into his pockets. Even under the fabric of his shirt, the lines of his hard muscles showed through. I clenched my fists and pursed my lips.

A wistful smile formed on one side of his lips.

I jumped off the edge of the cliff, an action I'd probably come to regret. I flipped off the light and pulled my shirt off before I could chicken out. I dropped it on the floor and stared at him.

He let out a deep breath. Confusion rippled behind his eyes. "Are you sure? Forever is a long time."

A smile curled the corner of my lip and I nodded.

With one hand he grabbed his shirt by the collar and ripped over his head. The moonlight reflecting off the white snow shimmered into the room. Shadows rippled over the valleys and peaks of his hard-muscled stomach. He stared back, his eyes following the silver glow on my skin. His eyes caressed the line of my neck, the curve of my breasts, and down the flat plane of my belly. He stepped in front of me and pulled my head back gently by my hair. He traced hot kisses over the path his eyes had already ventured. My skin blazed. Deft fingers popped open the button of my pants, unzipped them, and pulled them slowly down my legs. I stepped out and tossed them to the side with my foot. I reached for the button fly of his jeans. He backed away and shook his head. "Nope."

My delirious head didn't have the capacity to argue. He lifted me up onto the bed, knelt down, and pulled off my socks.

He started at the tops of my feet and slowly kissed his way upward. One at a time, he inched closer and closer to the pounding between my legs. His breath skimmed hot over my sensitive skin. I gripped the comforter tight in my balled-up fists. He dragged a finger over the thin purple material of my panties. My breathing stopped as a kaleidoscope of colors flashed in my peripheral vision. He stood and continued up my stomach to the crook of my neck, where his kisses turned to soft nips. I inhaled sharply, then remembered to breathe. His fingers slid over my back and easily unclasped my bra from behind. The straps fell from my shoulders, the only thing holding it up were my arms. He waited for me to let go. I relaxed, and he hooked the middle and pulled it away. His jaw knotted under the pressure of his gritted teeth.

He grabbed my hand and pulled me off the bed. "I thought so," he whispered under his breath. He ran his hand down the side of my breast. "Looks like somebody carved you from marble. Every perfect square inch of you. Then sprinkled you in silver dust."

He scooped me up in his arms, pulled back the covers, and laid me down on the bed.

Chapter 36

Southern Twang

I awoke disoriented until images of the night before flooded my brain. Tingles warmed my skin, and my cheeks flushed hot and tight. I wasn't embarrassed, more like surprised. I knew what we had was good and beautiful, but in my wildest dreams, I'd never expected it to be like that. There had been moments where I didn't know where he began and I ended. Flashes of fire and ice amongst our tangled sweaty bodies. A hunger had risen from the depths of my soul I didn't know was there. It was more than a want; it was a desperate need, and he was the only cure. After the first time, I understood what he meant—knowing how I felt. It wasn't like I could pick up on his thoughts. It was more like a recognition of emotions that were not mine. It added fuel to our fire. I had known what he wanted. And how he wanted it without him ever saying a word. And in turn, he had known the same.

Watery morning light filled the room. I shifted under the sheets; the soft cotton rubbed uncomfortably over my raw, sensitive skin. I propped up on an elbow and watched the rise and fall of his chest. He appeared younger when he was asleep, like the eighteen-year-old he was. The square line of his jaw was softer; his mouth was more relaxed. I ran a gentle finger over the swell of his bottom lip. It twisted into a sleepy smile.

"Morning," he mumbled. He opened his dark eyes and turned his face to me. Sunlight warmed his brown eyes and skin. "We good?" He tried putting on a brave, cocky face, but under the façade, he was worried.

"We're far more than good," I said, addressing more than one issue. "I'm not sure we could get better."

A smile of relief bloomed on his face. "Challenge accepted."

I leaned back on my pillow, covered my eyes with my hands, and laughed. Though I wanted to, my body needed some time to recover. I rolled out of bed and padded to the bathroom to take a shower.

"Hey," he said before I closed the door.

He was sitting on the edge of the bed naked. Parts of me instantly constricted.

"I love you," he said.

"I love you, too." I shut the door gently behind me. I did love him. Too much, perhaps.

A white pedestal sink, toilet, and a corner shower unit all sat on tiny black and white tiles, more missing than not. The hot water instantly steamed up the mirror in the tiny bathroom.

The shower door opened and startled me. He didn't ask; he just climbed in. There wasn't much room, but I didn't care.

After the water ran cold, we got out and dressed. As I was slipping into a pair of soft leggings, a fierce knock came from the downstairs. The pounding tremored under my feet.

I jumped. Jude froze mid-shoe.

"You stay here." He grabbed me by the shoulders.

With his eyes, he made a plea and a command. "Let me see who it is before you come down. Okay?"

From the attic you couldn't see the front door or the driveway.

"It might be one of the neighbors wondering who's in my grandparents' house. I don't want anyone to see you."

I nodded.

He ran down the stairs, hollering, "Just a minute!" as the pounding continued.

I slipped on a hoodie and tip-toed down the creaky staircase.

"Is Regan here?" I recognized the Southern twang. Gin was the last person I expected to show up here.

"Nope," Jude growled. Inside I felt his fear. It prickled at my senses to run. But first of all, there was no place to go, and second, it was just Christian, not a secret government agent—he was a high school student. I brushed Jude's overreaction away.

"Then why is her sweatshirt hanging here?"

I cringed. I'd left my Alaska Salty Dog Saloon sweatshirt on the coat rack by the door. Rookie mistake.

I poked my head around the corner. "What are you doing here?"

Jude glared. I smiled. I was curious.

"Looking for you." He wrapped his arms around his waist as if he were cold. Sunlight haloed his brown hair and shaded his face. Though his eyes were as bright as a faceted emerald.

"Why?"

"Can we sit down? It's kind of a long story. And it's freezing out here." He shivered.

"No," Jude said without consulting me. I elbowed

him. I didn't need anyone coming to my defense and it irritated me.

"Of course," I invited. Gin stepped quickly over the threshold and shut the door behind him.

Jude grabbed my shoulder. "Regan, if you don't mind, can I talk to you privately?" I shrugged out of his grasp. He was really beginning to push my buttons. Maybe last night wasn't such a good idea. Dread pooled in my stomach. If this was how it was going to be, I wanted none of it.

Jude pressed his lips together. "Please, Regan. Trust me."

I huffed. "Fine. Gin, have a seat if you want." I pounded my feet up the stairs. When I was certain we were out of hearing range, I whispered violently, "What?"

"There's something not right about him. His aura is off."

I mentally kicked myself. Jude wasn't trying to control me, he was arming me with information.

"What do you mean?" I whispered calmly this time.

"His aura shakes like an earthquake."

"And how come you didn't notice this earlier?" He'd been going to school with us for a couple months now.

"I didn't pay any attention to him. It's not like we have any classes together. Besides, at first glance, it's just green. The vibrations are subtle."

"Maybe he's just cold," I said. I hadn't told Jude about my suspicions of Gin. I was starting to wonder if that was a mistake.

He rolled his eyes. "That's not how it works, Regan. I just want you to be careful. I'm telling you, his aura is unusual. Like yours."

"Well, that doesn't mean he's bad," I said slightly defensively.

Jude threw me a deadpan look. Because it didn't mean he was good either.

Gin stood next to the woodstove with his hands all but touching the surface. I started a pot of coffee, for clarity and Gin's shivering.

"So, Gin, why are you here?" I asked after the coffee finished brewing. I narrowed my eyes and poured him a cup as he sat down at the kitchen table.

His hands curled around the warm surface and he took a sip. "Because it seems my colleagues frightened you."

"Your colleagues?"

"Yes, I believe you've mistaken them for federal agents."

I almost spit out my coffee. I had to swallow hard to keep from choking.

"They showed up at your house yesterday looking for you and your mom said you were gone. She refused to say more."

"Wait. Slow down. Go back to your colleagues. Aren't you in high school?" I knew he'd been lying to me.

"No, I'm afraid not. That's what I'm trying telling you, if you'd just let me finish."

"By all means." I held up my hand. I wiped at my runny nose with a napkin.

"First, my name is Christian LaCroix and Gabby is actually my cousin. But I'm not in high school. I was sent here by my employer to keep tabs on you. Observe and report." He held up a finger to silence me.

"And what better way to do it than attend high school? As you are probably aware, the government has been keeping tabs on your family for years. That's why our agents where there in the first place. They were almost convinced you were powerless until you slipped." He tapped the side of his mug with a finger.

I froze. Jude sat forward, the muscles in his jaw tightened.

"First Craig walking in front of a bus?" he questioned. "There was no way he did that on his own accord. I knew him well enough to know suicide wasn't a possibility. But my boss didn't take my word for it."

I bristled at my dad's name.

"But that little fiasco in the gymnasium. Yeah, that along with your dad's 'accident'," he used air quotes, "made my boss curious. And after I've had time to observe your skill, I'm confident you are your father's daughter."

"You were there," I whispered.

"I was."

"Why were you really there? And why were you wearing a priest's collar?" Every word shot off my tongue. There was no way he was singing for the opera.

"Calm down. I'm getting there. I was undercover, in disguise, and simultaneously performing at the opera, and that's all I'm allowed to disclose on that matter. As for your father, we worked together from time to time. I was supposed to meet with him while you were in your therapy session." His eyes hardened. "But that didn't happen."

Shame colored my cheeks.

"Hey, it's really not your fault. Your dad should have seen this coming."

I stood up. My chair tumbled to the ground. My breathing was heavy and rapid. Dark smoke whirled inside the glass box. I could feel the golems excitement building within, jumping and diving like a frolicking seal. “It wasn’t his fault!” I shouted.

Surprisingly Christian stayed completely calm and dismissed my anger away with a hand. “Yeah, well, it wasn’t yours either. You need training. You need to learn how to control your powers before they control you.”

Jude leaned back in his chair and clasped his hands behind his neck, a picture-perfect display of lackadaisicalness. But I knew differently. He was ready to spring out of his chair at any given second.

I crossed my arms. “Who says I have powers?”

“Oh, come on, don’t play coy. I don’t have the patience for it. Nor do I have the time,” he reprimanded. “While this farce has been a nice break, I’m ready to get back to work.”

I stared at him. Though I was calmer now, the golem still slithered along the edges of its prison.

“How old are you?” Jude growled.

With his elbow resting on the table, he pointed at Jude. “Irrelevant. But if you must know, twenty-two. Back to my point, we all know you have a gift Regan,” Gin glanced at Jude. “Am I right?”

Jude didn’t deny it, though he didn’t confirm it either.

“Okay. Let me make an educated guess. You have the power to control people.”

I worked very hard to mask my surprise.

“Anything else?” He paused for a moment. “Not that you would need anything else. I mean seriously, I saw what you did to Gabby.” The corner of his lip curled.

"I'm not saying she didn't deserve it. That girl is a bully. But that's all she'll ever be. Now you on the other hand, you have the potential to be. . . magnificent," he said the final word bordering on worship. "With the right training? You could be unstoppable." His eyes practically glowed.

I wasn't sure there was any point in denying my abilities further. I'd messed up. I'd messed up royally.

"You knew my dad?"

"Yup, I believe he was planning on working for us after he got out of the military."

"Was it your people who took the photos of me and my family when I got released from the Alaska Psychiatric Institute?"

I was curious if he was going to lie. Though I didn't have any concrete proof, I now knew his company had the motive, the means and they were obviously in Anchorage at the time. As far as circumstantial evidence went, it was fairly solid.

"Yes, ma'am. Willa Zehn and John Smith."

My eyes dipped to the floor. I knew it. These people had been hounding my family for a while now. I picked up my chair and sat down. I propped my elbows and clasped my hands together. "So, Gin, what's the point of this ambush."

"Ambush? I'm here to offer you a job. That's what my co-workers were supposed to be doing yesterday but obviously, they failed. So here I am, doing their work," he said as if this was beneath his pay grade.

I almost laughed. He couldn't be serious. Could he? All of this, just to offer me a job. I started to feel embarrassed by all of the panic we'd created by assuming the worst-case scenario.

Jude kicked my leg under the table.

I shot him a dirty look then turned my attention to Gin. "If you've known about me for that long, why wait until now to offer me a job?"

"First, obviously, my co-workers spooked you and I didn't want to lose you if you ran. Second, just think of me like an athletic scout. I wanted to assess your powers before I agreed to train you. I don't come out of the field for just anyone." Gin took a sip of his coffee. "I'll personally be in charge of your training."

I looked him up and down. "Why you?"

He chuckled. "Because I'm the only one equipped to handle you."

"Are there others like me?" I played dumb. He hadn't mentioned anything about my brothers having powers and I didn't want to give them any reason to believe differently. And there was also Jude to think of.

"Of course. You didn't think you were the only one, did you?" Gin said.

I swept my long bangs out of my face. "Well, sort of. I mean besides me and my dad."

"There are a few of us," he hinted cryptically.

I cocked an eyebrow. "So, you have powers too?"

He smiled.

"What can you do?" I prodded.

He blinked slowly and smiled. "That's for me to know and you to find out, darlin'."

Chapter 37

GSS

After Gin left, Jude tromped down the rickety stairs, carrying our duffle bags. He said nothing. He simply kissed the top of my hair and loaded the truck. We stopped for gas before we headed back home.

Barry had called and said he thought it was safe to come home. The people following me were from some hoity-toity security firm and they were waiting to talk to me. Though he said not to let our guard down. He didn't trust them. Before Gin left, he'd asked that we not tell his co-workers he'd been to see us. He didn't want to step on any toes. But he did want to warn me about what was going on so I didn't hurt someone unintentionally.

I chuckled. I had a feeling his co-workers were harmless compared to him. I didn't know what kind of powers he possessed—yet—but if he was capable of handling me, they must be significant.

Jude parked behind a black SUV in my grandparents' driveway. Long strands of yellow grass, poking between the patches of melted snow, quivered in the chilly breeze. The smell of spring floated in the air. It was a big lie. Wyoming liked to promise spring, then snow two feet just to be spiteful.

He squeezed my hand. "Are you ready for this?"

I nodded. I was curious. Maybe I would get more answers from Gin's co-workers.

On our way home, we'd had a long conversation. We agreed to never divulge Kennedy's and Lincoln's powers. And I was never to reveal Jude's. If, or when, he wanted to share his gifts, it was his decision. We talked about the possibilities. We talked about the future. Underneath his confidence, I could feel his hesitation, his apprehension.

A billowing cloud of gray smoke rose from the brick chimney stack. Soft light shone through the slats of the window blinds. Our dearly departed Christmas tree laid askew off the edge of the porch waiting patiently to be drug to one of the many slash piles on the ranch. Currently, there was still too much snow on the ground. Stubborn remnants of tinsel flashed in the sunlight practically blinding me.

Jude held the front door open as I walked inside. The scent of wood smoke and freshly baked chocolate cookies wafted in the room. Mom, Barry, and two familiar gentlemen were at our kitchen table with a cup of coffee in front of them.

They both stood up and came around the table. They wore identical suits: black pants and jacket with a white shirt and a black tie.

"Wearing your Halloween costumes again, I see," I said.

"Regan." The guy with small close-set eyes held out his hand. That and his prominent forehead made him look a bit like a Neanderthal. I looked to Jude before I shook it.

Jude hesitated, then nodded once. He told me if their auras were off, he wouldn't let me past the threshold.

I gripped his hand hard.

"I'm Paul Metz, and this is Andrew Templeton."

Andrew flashed a smile revealing his deep dimples.

"If we could have a seat? We'd like to speak with you," Paul said.

I didn't tell Mom and Barry what was going on. I wanted their surprise to be authentic. There was no reason to betray Gin's trust at this point.

The two men sat down next to each other across from Mom and Barry. That left one end of the table for Jude and one for me.

"We work for Global Security Systems. We have branches all over the world. We deal with all kinds of security issues. Domestic and international. And we are here to offer you a job." Paul folded his neatly manicured hands together and set them on the table.

I lifted the corner of my lip in a questioning snarl. I peeked at my mom. Her face gave away nothing. Hmmm, another thing I could learn from her.

I plucked a still-warm cookie off the plate. "Why would you want to offer me a job? And doing what?"

"Well, as you are aware," Paul's eyes darted to my mom, "we've been monitoring your family for some time now. We work closely with the federal government, and your gifts have recently come to our attention."

My shoulders stiffened, and I stopped breathing. I thought my acting skill were on point.

"With your abilities and our connections, it's our belief that together we can accomplish great things for the US."

"And what abilities do you *think* I have?" I acted bored. I afforded myself a quick glance at Jude while the two gentlemen were focused on me. Jude was focused on

Andrew.

Jude propped an elbow on the table and rested his hand against his mouth. He pinched his top lip between the side of his thumb and index finger. He looked calm. But he wasn't. His heart was pounding but he wasn't ready to react. He was weighing his options. For now, he was content to observe.

Paul continued, "To be honest, we are not one hundred percent sure, but we hope you have the same gift as your father. Are we correct?" A small smile of hope creased the crows' feet around his eyes.

I shrugged my shoulders.

"Anyway, we're here to offer you a job. We wanted our names on the list early."

"What do you mean?" I said with my mouth full of cookie. Mom's lips pinched at my rudeness.

"We will not be the only organization offering you employment. Others also know about your gift. They'll not be far behind. Our employer has requested that soon after graduation, we schedule a meeting. We'll fly you and a guest first class. Then you can tour our facilities and see what we have to offer."

I finished chewing the cookie that had turned to chalk in my mouth and swallowed. "I need some time to think about it." Despite my nonchalant attitude, underneath I was terrified. How many people knew about me? And what did that mean for my future? To hide my trepidation, I got up and went to the cupboard and pulled out a glass. I filled it to the rim with ice cubes, then poured milk over the top. They crackled in the glass as they settled under the warmer liquid. I inhaled a shaky breath before I flopped like a ragdoll back in the chair. I really wanted them to think I was a normal, disrespectful teenage girl.

"Absolutely. All the time you need. But I believe you will find our company reputable and our offer generous."

"And what is your offer?" I snatched another cookie, even though I wasn't going to eat it. My stomach churned. I thought the milk might help, but the minute I took a drink, it soured. I didn't like that multiple organizations knew about me.

Andrew smiled. "We don't know what the offer is."

I laughed through my nose. "Then how do you know it's generous?" I discarded the cookie on the bare wood surface and dusted off my hands before I folded them together and rested them on the table.

"Because we wouldn't be here if it weren't." Paul stood up and handed me a business card. Andrew stood and pushed in his chair and silently waited for Paul to finish. Jude's eyes squinted, then he cocked his head as if he were trying to look at Andrew from a different angle. He'd looked at me that way once, early on.

"When you've made your decision, whatever it may be, please call me at this number." The matted card in my hand had *GSS,* typed in bold, centered on the paper over the gray shadow of an eagle. Underneath was an email address and his phone number. I stuck it to the fridge with a magnet.

Paul thanked my mom and Barry, said it was nice to meet all of us, and then left.

We watched them drive down the dirt road. Rising dust muted the bright red of their taillights. "So?" I asked whoever was willing to answer.

"I don't know," Barry said, shaking his head. "I don't like that so many people have you on their radar."

My mom's eyes glassed over and tears pooled, but she managed to contain them. She sniffed and blinked rapidly before she said, "Well, we're going to have to figure this out." I knew, in that moment, even though I couldn't read her mind, she desperately missed my father. They were supposed to handle this—me—together.

She squeezed Barry's hand. A lump formed in my throat. He would never replace my dad, but I was truly happy he was in our lives. She was going to need him. And as much as I didn't want to admit it, he'd been a huge help already.

I walked my glass over to the sink and poured it down the drain before I rinsed it out. I sponged the table clean and reached for the plate of cookies so I could cover them with plastic wrap.

Jude sat back down. My mom followed suit. Barry covered her legs with a blanket before he pulled up the chair next to her.

I put the cookies on the counter. I sure hoped I was in the mood later to actually enjoy them.

"There's something off with the younger guy," Barry said.

"You're right," Jude said. "I think now's the time I let you guys in on a little secret."

On the trip home, Jude and I had discussed telling my mom and Barry about his abilities. I told him not to. I didn't want anyone to know we were bound. Not because of embarrassment, but because I needed some time to come to terms with it myself before I dealt with anybody else's feelings on the issue. He said in order to protect me, he felt telling them was necessary. I informed him I didn't need his protection. He simply thinned his lips and stared, unblinking, until I admitted I did need him. But not for my safety, I insisted it was only for the safety of others. He didn't argue.

Without warning, my stomach twisted in fear. Every nerve ending in my body fired at once. It took me a second to realize those feelings weren't mine. Jude was scared, but I was the only one in the room who could tell. He laid the palms of his hands on the tabletop. He held them there for a few seconds, then raised them off the surface. He repeated the gesture until I finally caught on. Jude was sitting in the same spot as Andrew had.

"What secret?" Barry said, looking very confused by Jude's odd behavior.

"Jude and I are getting married!" I blurted out, jumping away from the table.

Surprise, then confusion, followed by terror settled in Jude's dark eyes. *So, he's okay with forever, but not marriage*, I thought sourly. *Dick.*

"What?" my mother snapped. She stood up. The blue-and-green afghan fell from her lap.

Barry looked from Jude back to me with disapproval in his eyes. Jude said Barry had "the talk" with him before he picked me up to take me to his grandparents' house. Beyond that, he refused to tell me what had been said.

I held up my hand for them to stop. Then I pointed rapidly down to the surface of the table.

Mom and Barry looked very confused. I held up my index finger and scrambled to the junk drawer for a pencil and a piece of scrap paper. The whole way I kept up with my charade. "Yeah, we decided after school was out. Maybe this summer. Keep it simple, ya know. Just family. I thought Mom and I could fly to Seattle to get a dress."

Barry's eyes narrowed at Jude. I was glad at that moment Barry wasn't carrying his sidearm. Jude splayed his hands and shook his head.

I scribbled fast.

Not getting married.

Need a distraction.

Bug under table. Right, Jude?

He exhaled, and his shoulders slumped. I wasn't sure if the relief was from the not-getting-married part or that I figured out there was a bug under the table.

I held it out for everyone to see. I rambled on, "But now with this whole job offer, maybe we'll have to rethink our plans."

The air solidified as they read. Realization, then fear replaced the confusion behind their eyes. A heaviness settled in my chest.

Barry knelt on the floor, looked under the table, and nodded.

"Let's go over to Gramma's house so we can discuss this," Mom said in her disapproving mom voice. "I'm hungry, and I don't feel like cooking. Besides, she has better luck talking sense into the two of you."

We all slipped on our shoes, pulled on coats, and left the house.

Barry led us to the tack room in the barn. Hay, old leather, and the scent of manure hung in the dry, dusty air. Barry and Mom sat on the gray wooden bench; Jude and I took the straw bale.

"Here's the deal," Barry said. "We can't get rid of the bug. So, we're going to use it to our advantage. Plant what we want them to know and leave out all the rest."

Everything my parents feared was coming true. All

the effort they put in to hiding our family gifts, I destroyed.

I wish. I wish it wasn't me. But no amount of wishing could fix me.

Barry quirked a dark eyebrow at Jude. "I believe you were about to say something before Regan informed us of your pending nuptials. Which, from the note we read, I'm assuming are a farce?" He double-checked.

"Of course. We're not getting married," Jude said as if it were the stupidest thing he'd ever heard. His emotions, now connected to mine, didn't contradict his words.

My breath hitched in my throat. It's not as if I wanted to get married, but I didn't want him to hate the idea that much.

Jude wrapped his arm around my shoulder and pulled me close. He knew he'd hurt my feelings.

"Not yet anyway," he tried to smooth thing over. I wasn't convinced. "But, yeah, I was about to tell you that Regan isn't the only one who has a gift."

Both my mom and Barry wore identical expressions of shock.

Jude told them he could read auras and track people by their auras. Thankfully, he left out the part about us being bound. I guess he didn't want to deal with their disapproval. I couldn't blame him. If they didn't like the idea of us getting married, they wouldn't like *this* any better.

"What color is Barry's aura?" my mom asked. She loved anything spiritual and unusual.

"He's the color of the greenest grass. Pure and bright. That man, he's a good man," Jude said.

Barry's normally serious face tinged pink.

"I know." My mom looked at him with adoring eyes. She leaned forward. "And mine?" she whispered like she wanted to know but didn't.

"A dusty pink with moments of cotton candy. Yours shifts with the way you're feeling." She nodded with her lips pressed down in contemplation.

"Regan's?"

"Well, hers is different. It's black as midnight sky but glitters with bright stars." He petted my hair. Warmth spread down my body like a hot blanket fresh from the dryer wrapped around my bare skin.

"And that brings me back to my earlier point. The young guy. His aura was a steel blue. Not pure. Not bright. But that wasn't what concerned me. Most people's auras aren't bright, but it doesn't mean they're bad . . . more like they carry baggage." He shrugged his shoulders. "I've only seen one or two that were undoubtedly evil. They were dark and soupy. The outline not crisp. More like a swamp and its muddy edges. This guy, Andrew's, it slithered, but not all the time. Just during certain moments. Kind of like when you see something out of the corner of your eye, but when you look, nothing's there. I don't know what to make of it. I just know his outline wasn't crisp, and that worries me."

I was beginning to see a connection with the strange auras. I had powers, Gin had powers and I was willing to bet Andrew did also. "This whole situation worries me," I mumbled. "I can't believe they know everything about me."

"They don't," Barry said. "If they knew, they wouldn't have placed a bug under the table. They're fishing. Holding out the bait, praying you bite. We need to assume our vehicles are bugged and tracked."

"But they do know about me," I said. Then I told them about Gin's visit. And though he wasn't sure about the nature of my gift, he'd guessed it spot on.

Worry pinched my mother's beautiful face.

"Hmmm," Barry contemplated. "That's too bad. But there's nothing that can be done. I do think our best option, for now, is to pretend Jude doesn't have any gifts at all. You're the ace in the hole. Let's keep it that way. No one outside of this circle can know."

"Both my grandparents know about me." He paused. "And about Regan."

Mom's eyes bulged.

"Sorry, I was trying to figure out what Regan is, and my grandpa is a wealth of knowledge. And not the kind you can find in a book."

"Well, when you get time, tell them the situation," Barry said. "We're going to have to assume everyone's houses are being monitored. No communication about this on any electronic devices. Use your phones as you normally would. We have to keep up appearances. But *do not* do any research on your computers unless I instruct you to. They're going to expect all of us to look up GSS. That would be normal. But we only discuss this situation in person," Barry said.

Tears slipped down my mom's face.

"Momma, I'm so sorry." I knelt on the dirt floor in front of her with my hands on her legs.

"No, baby. I'm sorry." She wiped at her eyes and pressed her tiny, cold hands on my cheeks.

"But don't cry, okay? Cause you look terrible when you do," I said.

An unexpected laugh exploded from her chest. Her hand flew to her mouth to cover her outburst. "I suppose

I do."

"We're going to get through this," I said. The whole time I was thinking of what I could do to make sure my family didn't pay for my sins.

"We are," Barry said. "Together." He stared at me, then tipped his head once. He had pretty eyes. A combination of green and brown. He opened them wider, waiting for my response.

"Yes, together," I vowed. It made me think that perhaps he didn't just care about my mom. Maybe he cared about me, too. The back of my nose tingled uncomfortably with the burn of impending tears. I blinked them away.

When we got back in the house, Barry double-checked the bug under the table.

And I wondered, *How did I go from Wyoming's biggest bully to America's most wanted?*

But for now, I wasn't going to worry about it. I had people. I didn't have to bear this burden alone.

I planned on taking a step back and relaxing into a normal rhythm. As normal as you can get living under surveillance. Finish high school. Get to know my mom as an adult, not as a child. Get to know Jude as his girlfriend, not as a friend. Heck, I wanted to get to know Barry better now that I'd come to accept his place in my mom's life.

So, for the rest of the school year, I would do just that. Get to know the people I loved. The rest, all of that craziness, I'd worry about later.

A word about the author…

Alex Gordon is a bit of a wanderer, having lived in Washington, Montana, Germany, Alaska, and Tennessee where she currently resides with her husband and two rescued German shepherds. When not writing, you can probably find her hiking, or if she's lucky—fishing, though she's not opposed to camping out on the couch with dessert and bingeing murder mysteries.

Thank you for purchasing
this publication of The Wild Rose Press, Inc.

For questions or more information
contact us at
info@thewildrosepress.com.

The Wild Rose Press, Inc.
www.thewildrosepress.com

www.ingramcontent.com/pod-product-compliance
Lightning Source LLC
Chambersburg PA
CBHW072305020726
47501CB00002B/395
* 9 7 8 1 5 0 9 2 4 9 4 6 6 *